THE
SILENT
SERVICE
LOS ANGELES CLASS

D0042130

H. JAY RIKER

author of *SEALs, The Warrior Breed*

MORE EXPLOSIVE UNDERSEA ACTION
IN THE HEAT OF THE COLD WAR

THE
**SILENT
SERVICE**
GRAYBACK CLASS

H. JAY RIKER

author of SEALs, The Warrior Breed

EAN

ISBN 0-380-80467-0

9 780380 804672

50699

THE FIRE BELOW

The year is 1987. Ronald Reagan is in the White House. A secret arms deal for hostages has just been exposed. The Middle East is fiery hot. The seas of the Russian Pacific are ice cold—and teeming with some of the most sophisticated weaponry humankind has ever devised.

U.S. Navy SEALs are brilliantly proving their courage and extraordinary skill in a daring raid on Lebanon, a plan devised by Commander Frank Gordon. In acknowledgment of his first-rate strategic skills, Gordon is assigned to head up a bold undertaking into dangerous enemy waters. Placed in command of the Los Angeles Class submarine *Pittsburgh*—a realization of his life's greatest ambition—Gordon, along with his crew and a hand-picked team of SEALs will venture into the deadly, Russian-patrolled seas off the Kamchatka Peninsula. For intel has sent reports of an awesome new Soviet sub that no one in the West has ever seen before. And it's Gordon's mission to go up against the phantom boat—even at the risk of a shooting war.

The SEALs are to go where the *Pittsburgh* cannot. But the game is more perilous than anyone has imagined. For the enemy has its own reasons for luring U.S. forces onto Russian turf. And there is a highly placed spy in the American ranks who may, even now, be leading a boat full of brave men to their doom.

Other Silent Service *Titles by*
H. Jay Riker
from Avon Books

G RAYBACK C LASS

THE
SILENT
SERVICE
LOS ANGELES CLASS

H. JAY RIKER

AVON BOOKS
An Imprint of HarperCollins*Publishers*

This is a work of fiction. Names, characters, places, and incidents are products of the author's imagination or are used fictitiously and are not to be construed as real. Any resemblance to actual events, locales, organizations, or persons, living or dead, is entirely coincidental.

AVON BOOKS
An Imprint of HarperCollins*Publishers*
10 East 53rd Street
New York, New York 10022-5299

Copyright © 2001 by Bill Fawcett & Associates
ISBN: 0-380-80467-0
www.avonbooks.com

First Avon Books paperback printing: February 2001

Avon Trademark Reg. U.S. Pat. Off. and in Other Countries, Marca Registrada, Hecho en U.S.A.
HarperCollins® is a trademark of HarperCollins Publishers Inc.

Printed in the U.S.A.

10 9 8 7 6 5 4 3 2 1

*To the memory of J. Andrew Keith,
author, comrade-at-arms, brother, friend*

PROLOGUE

Thursday, 25 June 1987

Sea of Okhotsk
Between Kamchatka and the Soviet Far East
0435 hours local time

Descending. . . .

Two hundred miles above the horsetail wisps of cirrus cloud decorating the rich cobalt of the approaching Siberian dawn, an American KH-12 reconnaissance satellite sailed southeast into the sudden, golden glare of the rising sun as it exploded above the purple-hazed curve of the Earth's horizon. Crossing the coast between the tiny fishing villages of Ul'ya and Mys Enken, the robot spy raced to greet the distant sunrise above dark waters still lost in night.

The satellite had originally been scheduled for a routine photo recon pass over the great port of Vladivostok, a thousand miles to the southwest, but hours earlier, a specially coded transmission with the electronic authorization of the National Reconnaissance Office itself had directed the satellite to use some of its dwindling stores of onboard fuel to shift its orbit farther north, in order to let it peer down on

1

the drama unfolding in the predawn darkness below.

East, dawn touched the snow-locked peaks of the Sredin-nyy Khrebet, the mountain spine of Poluostrov Kamchatka, a dazzling embrace of gold and ice silver. South, the long and ragged finger of Sakhalin pointed at Hokkaido, north-ernmost of Japan's home islands, just visible as a dark blur on the horizon. Ahead, southeast, like pearls on a string, the long-contested Kuril'skiy Ostrova, the Kuril islands, stretched across 650 miles of sea, from Mys Lopatka at Kamchatka's extreme southern tip all the way to the slender Nemuro Strait along Hokkaido's northeast coast.

Digital infrared cameras that could pierce even overcast skies peered down, searching the night-clad seas west of the Kurils. The resolving power of those electronic eyes on the KH-12—"KH" stood, appropriately enough, for "key-hole"—was highly classified, but was well under half a me-ter at orbital ranges. They could not, as was popularly supposed, read the newspaper headlines over the shoulder of a man in a Moscow street, but they had no trouble at all picking out the principle players in a rapidly unfolding drama on the surface far below. . . .

Descending farther. Beneath the chill near-emptiness of low orbit, beneath the sun-gilt twists of the cirrus clouds and deep within the thin envelope of air far beneath the satellite's keel, four aircraft, hounds to the surface-bound hunters be-low. Two *Chaika* ASW flying boats—they were known as "Mails" in the West—and a pair of IL-38 "May" subhunters were dropping patterns of sonobuoys, blunt white canisters drifting into the sea beneath small parachutes. As each splashed home, it began sending out piercing chirps of sound, seeking, seeking, seeking through the black waters beneath . . . and transmitting the results to the listening air-craft above.

Descending farther still. Beneath the probing aircraft, a dozen surface vessels converged on the same patch of sound-blasted ocean. Warships, lean and knife-prowed all, they ranged in size from the tiny Pauk class corvettes *Kom-*

somolets Moldavy and *Kirovskiy Komsomolets* to the 173-meter Kara class ASW cruiser *Ochakov*. Summoned by the baying aircraft, they approached from every point of the compass, feeling their way with their own sonar tapings, listening for their invisible prey.

And descending still farther . . . three . . . four . . . five hundred meters down, at depths where even at high noon the light of day never penetrated, the prey twisted silently through the black and the frigid cold. Long—almost 110 meters from rounded prow to cruciform tail—and as sleek as any sea creature evolved for speed and silence within its watery universe, the submarine encased a sliver of light and warmth and air, temporary home to twelve officers and 120 men assigned to her.

She was the USS *Pittsburgh*, SSN 720, a 688 Los Angeles class nuclear attack submarine. Normally the hunter, designed as a killer, the *Pittsburgh* now was the hunted as the air and surface-naval forces above closed on her position. Shrill pings from sonobuoys and the blindly probing sonars of the surface ships chirped and jittered weirdly as they caressed the sub's hull, and every man aboard knew that the echoes, despite *Pittsburgh*'s anechoic hull coating, were pinpointing the fleeing sub's position to her hunters.

With deepening dread, they listened now for the inevitable high-pitched whine of the approaching antisubmarine torpedoes. . . .

Thursday, 25 June 1987

Spook Hut, USS _Parche_
South of Magadan on the Sea of Okhotsk
0445 hours local time

Commander James Edward Travers pressed the headset against his ear, listening to the warble of coded transmissions plucked from the cold, wet air somewhere above the spaghetti of pipes and wiring bundles that decorated the Spook Hut's overhead. An adjustment on one of the verniers . . . there!

Red lights flickered across the array on the receiver mounted on the bulkhead in front of him, an extremely sophisticated and expensive broad-bandwidth scanner that one sailor had irreverently referred to as his "big-ass CB." Citizens band it certainly was not; each flash of a red LED pinpointed a different transmission on a Soviet military frequency. He made another slight adjustment on the console, as the big tape heads on the cabinet at his back rolled.

"Neechivah ni slishna!" a voice said with explosive clarity and strength. _"Gavaritee medlina, Yedenitsa P'yat-dvah-adeen!"_

4

"*Shtob! Shtob!*" a second voice came back, distant but shrill, almost hysterical. "*Zdess' P'yat-dvah-adeen! Amerikanskyy podvahdnya lahtka . . .*"

The burst of Russian, sent in the clear, was startling. The Soviets were usually meticulous in their use of coded and scrambled transmissions. Travers listened with intent fascination, translating the exchange as the tapes rolled.

"Unit Five-two-one, this is Headquarters," the near voice said, interrupting. "You are in violation of regulations. Cease transmission at once."

"*Fuck* the regulations!" the shrill voice replied. "The American submarine is getting away! He is maneuvering now for the Proliv Yekateriny. We need antisubmarine air to cut him off!"

Travers smiled. Whoever Unit Five-two-one was, he had a thing or two to learn about tact. Or, possibly, he was well connected enough that he didn't need to worry about tact . . . or the penalties for transgressing the regulations regarding unsecured radio transmissions.

Still, it was exactly this type of unguarded moment that ELINT specialists lived for, a brief and narrow window into the forest of scrambled signals and fiendishly convoluted encryptions.

"Additional forces are on the way, Unit Five-two-one. Cease transmission on this channel. Switch to scrambled mode at one-five-nine-nine."

"*Bastards!* I know reinforcements are coming. Deploy them to the Proliv Yekateriny if you want to slam the gate on this pig!"

The hairs at the back of Travers's neck prickled with excitement. He'd definitely picked up a part of the search net cast for *Parche*'s fellow provocateur in this exercise, the LA-class boat *Pittsburgh*, some thousand miles almost due south of the *Parche*'s current lurking point. He made a note on a piece of paper on the console before him and continued listening.

But this window, at least, had just closed. He heard no

more outbursts of unguarded plain Russian. The warbles and chirps of coded, burst transmissions, however, continued to fill the air above.

He turned in his swivel chair to the Radioman First Class crowded into the cramped confines of the Spook Hut at his side. "Keep on 'em, Joe," he said. "I've gotta get this to the skipper."

"Aye, aye, sir," RM/1 Joseph McNally replied. He, too, wore a radio headset as he monitored the Soviet transmissions. "Maybe bring me some coffee, huh?"

"You got it." He shook his head as he squeezed out of the Spook Hut . . . which was in fact the Sturgeon class boat's torpedo room, redecorated for the occasion as an intelligence ESM listening suite. As with the Navy's submarine service, the SEALs, and a handful of other elite groups that prized professionalism above the formal hierarchies of rank and privilege, Naval Intelligence operatives—at least in the field—tended to accept casual fraternization between officers and enlisted men more than was possible within the regular naval service. You would never find a full commander fetching coffee for an enlisted man in the *real* Navy.

Ducking out of the cozy confines of the Spook Hut, he made his way aft along the main corridor, trotted up a companionway ladder, then entered the larger but still claustrophobic enclosure of the *Parche*'s bridge and combat center, red-lit, now, to preserve the night sight of men whose duty schedules took scant notice of whether it was light or dark in the world above. Commander Richard Perrigrino, *Parche*'s captain, stood at one of the two gleaming, silver tree trunks in the compartment's center, the housing for one of the boat's periscopes. With eye pressed against the rubber-cushioned ocular, his arm draped over one of the turning arms, he looked every inch the rugged U-boat skipper he sometimes pretended to be. Skip Jones, the boat's Exec, stood beside him.

"Whatcha got, Commander?" Jones asked, looking up from the clipboard and pen he held in his hands. "What brings you out of your cave and into the red light of day?"

"Something the captain might be interested in," Travers replied.

"Hang on just a sec, Commander," Perrigrino said. "Got a hot one here. Smile for the birdie. . . ." He touched a button on the side of the periscope housing, snapping a rapid-fire series of high-resolution photographs through the scope's lens. "Mark, Sierra Six-one, bearing three-three-four. Log it."

"Sierra Six-one, bearing three-three-four, aye, Captain," Jones said, noting the information on his clipboard.

Captain Perrigrino pulled back from the scope and grinned at Travers. "Hey! You want to see something damned cool?"

"Certainly, Captain." It wasn't every day that anyone other than the tight little coterie of senior submarine officers got to have a peek through the boat's periscope. He walked across the combat center to the periscope housing, leaned forward, and pressed his eyes up to the objective eyepiece.

The low-light image-intensifier system was on, flooding his eyes with a green-yellow glow. It took him a moment to begin to pick out shapes and meaning from the jumble he was seeing.

The water, for the most part, was a black swell low in the field of view. Against an equally black sky, mountains reared in shades of deep green and streaks of black, while closer blazed the whites and yellows of city lights, sparkling on the water.

Nearer still, he saw movement. . . .

It took Travers long seconds to understand what it was . . . a long, low hull barely above the swell, supporting a rectangular sail above, all painted in yellow-green. Human shapes, tiny with distance, could be discerned in the vessel's weather bridge, high atop and forward on the conning tower. A submarine, definitely . . . but it didn't look like any Russian boat he'd ever seen. That long, low, and right-angled sail looked like the silhouette of an Oscar or a Papa, both cruise-missile subs . . . but the sliver of tail fin he could see above water was all wrong . . . as was the shape of the part of the hull he could see. He glanced at the range and bearing figures visible on the scope display. At a guess, the sub he was watching was three to four hundred feet in length . . . way too small for a monster Oscar, which measured a good 501 feet and some inches, and displaced 13,600 tons when submerged.

Besides, the Soviets only had one Papa class boat, a prototype test bed built at Gor'kiy in the late sixties to test cruise-missile concepts and later transferred to the Northern Fleet.

"What the hell is it?" he asked the captain. "If it's their one Papa, they're a hell of a long way off course."

"Ehhhh," Perrigrino said, making a sound like a game-show buzzer. "Wrong answer."

"Fair guess, though, Skipper," Jones said. "They look a bit alike."

"Fair but still a clean miss," Perrigrino said. He enjoyed needling the Naval Intelligence operative and liked to rub in the fact that there was an enormous gulf between books and think tanks and the inescapable realities of real-world experience. "So . . . would the gentleman from Maryland care to try for Double Jeopardy, where the cash prizes get really serious?"

Travers took another look. Those sleek lines on the hull . . . It had to be an attack boat, a hunter-killer, rather than a fat-pig SSGN or a Russian boomer. The most advanced H-K boats in the Soviet naval arsenal were the Alfa, which looked like a sleek cigar with a teardrop-shaped sail, low, mean, fast, and deadly; and the brand-new Akula, which looked like a big Alfa with a streamlined pod fixed atop the tail to house a towed array sonar.

"An attack boat," he said quietly. "But not one I know." He pulled back and looked Perrigrino in the eye. "Has to be a Mike."

Perrigrino's eyes widened, his bushy eyebrows climbing

high. "Nice guess, Commander," he said, with just the slightest emphasis on the second word.

"But . . . that's not possible. They only have one Mike, and she was launched from Severodvinsk three years ago. She's still with the Northern Fleet."

"Well, either their lone Mike got a transfer," Perrigrino said, "or they have a second one." He picked up a microphone. "Sonar, Conn."

"Sonar, aye," a voice replied over the bridge speaker.

"You got a make on Sierra Six-one yet?"

"It's a Mike," the sonar watch replied. "But not the one in our library, the one recorded off Murmansk a couple of years ago. We're designating this one Mike Two."

"A new boat," Jones said. "This'll perk up the boys back at the Squirrel Cage."

Travers watched the Mike as it cruised slowly out of the Tauyskaya Guba, scattering the reflections of the lights of the port city of Magadan. It was moving quickly—he estimated fifteen knots or better—and a small flotilla of harbor craft and patrol boats escorting it clear of the port approaches were struggling to keep up. The figures on the weather bridge, he noticed, were gone, and in another moment, the lean, rounded hull began to slip beneath the rippling, light-smeared water.

"They're submerging," he said.

Perrigrino tapped his shoulder, cutting in. Travers stepped back as the *Parche*'s captain took another look . . . and another round of photographs. "Going . . . going . . . and gone," Perrigrino said.

"Are they going after the *Pittsburgh*, you think?" Travers asked.

"Down scope," Perrigrino said. He stepped back, looked at Travers, and shrugged. "Only if our boys are *real* slow. Even at forty knots, that's a full day's cruise."

"I just overheard something broadcast in the clear. One of our Russian friends on the site was calling for more help, saying the American sub was making a break for the . . ." He stopped and glanced at the note in his hand. "The Proliv Yekateriny."

"Katherine's Straits, huh? Let's have a look."

He led the way to the chart table behind the periscope walk. Several charts lay open, and he thumbed through half a dozen before finding the one he wanted. "There," Perrigrino said. "Between Iturup to the north and Kunashir to the south. Both contested. The Soviets grabbed 'em from Japan in 1945 and never gave 'em back. Good, deep-water channel between them."

"How far away are they?"

"Guessing from their last recorded position . . . I'd say fifty miles. A couple of hours, if they can give their playmates the slip."

"So that Mike shouldn't be a problem," Travers said. "They'll be long gone by the time it gets there."

"That's the general idea," Perrigrino said. "And while the Russians are off chasing the 'Burgh boat halfway back to Yokasuka, we'll have our chance to get the hell out of Dodge."

Travers picked up one of the other charts and studied it, a general large-scale navigational chart of the entire Sea of Okhotsk.

A *Soviet* sea. . . .

Not that the United States recognized the unspoken but vigorously defended claim. Almost completely enclosed by the Siberian mainland, the Kamchatka Peninsula, Sakhalin Island, and the pearl-string necklace of the Kurils, the only bit of land touching the sea *not* belonging to the Russians was a two-hundred-mile stretch of Hokkaido, Japan's northernmost island.

There were only two ways in or out of the Sea of Okhotsk. One was through La Perouse Strait, between the southern tip of Sakhalin and Hokkaido, near the port of Wakkanai, and that fed into the shallow and land-encompassed Sea of Japan. The other was through the Kurils, that chain of some thirty small, volcanic islands forming an imperfect wall between the Sea of Okhotsk and the open waters of the Pacific. They comprised yet another of the geographical curses laid against Mother Russia, a choke point through which Soviet warships had to pass if they wished to transit to the open sea.

As for the Sea of Okhotsk, the Soviets had been battling for years to have it accepted as an internal sea, belonging to them and from which all foreign vessels might be excluded. The United States, as ever determined to enforce freedom of the seas, insisted that the Sea of Okhotsk should be considered international waters, and free to all.

The international situation was further complicated by Japan's claim to the four southernmost islands of the chain. In 1875, Japan had traded the southern half of Sakhalin to the Russians in exchange for the Kurils. In September of 1945, however, at the very end of World War II, Soviet army and naval elements had landed on the Japanese islands. Japan had been trying to effect their return ever since, and still referred to the captive islands as "the Northern Territories."

Lieutenant Commander Roger "Skip" Jones joined Travers beside the chart table. "So, Commander," the XO said. "You think Silent Dolphins is worth it?"

"I guess that depends on what you think is important," Travers replied. "I hate to think of the boys on the *Pittsburgh* being deliberately put in danger."

The XO shrugged. "That's the Navy's mission. To go in harm's way, and all that." He grinned, the expression emphasizing his boyish looks. He couldn't have been more than thirty. "Besides, as far as we're concerned, these are international waters, right? We kicked Kadhafi's ass in the Gulf of Sidra, we'll do the same to Gorbachev here!"

"The two situations aren't the same," Travers said quietly. "Kadhafi isn't sitting on a few thousand megatons, ready to launch at a moment's notice!"

"Aw, c'mon! You don't think the Russkis would hit the red button over something like this, do you?"

It was Travers's turn to shrug. "All I know is that we don't know what they would do. That *is* the real reason we're here, after all!"

"The man has a point," Captain Perrigrino said, coming up from behind. "Washington doesn't give squat whether Liberian-registered freighters can freely transit the Okhotsk. But they'd love to get a look at the bastards sinking one!"

"The *Pittsburgh* is hardly a freighter, Captain. Moscow could see her presence as a threat."

"But not one worth more than a few rattled sabers, son. Chase and his boys'll come out of this okay. You'll see."

"I hope you're right, sir."

"We do know how to play this game," Jones added.

A game. Was that all it was to the men at the cutting edge? Travers glanced at the other officers and enlisted men, quietly, even stolidly at their duty stations around the circumference of the *Parche*'s command center. Some looked nervous, some bored. Most simply wore masks of professionalism, watching their consoles and boards with studied focus and concentration. How many of them were even aware of what was going on in this, Operation Silent Dolphins. How many knew the stakes?

What, Travers wondered, did they think of this "game?"

The cover story of enforcing international rights to free passage on the high seas had been invoked more than once before. A year earlier, in 1986, the United States Navy had enforced its interpretation of maritime geography by sailing into the Gulf of Sidra in the Mediterranean, of which Libya claimed sovereign ownership. The incident had resulted in missiles fired, some Libyan MiGs downed, and a couple of Libyan missile boats sunk. It had also almost certainly led to a Libyan-backed terrorist bombing of a disco in Germany frequented by American soldiers . . . which in turn had led to the U.S. air strikes against Libya in April of 1986.

The U.S. had never tried enforcing a similar interpretation over the Sea of Okhotsk; as Travers had pointed out, the Soviet Union was not Libya, and, in any case, the waters off the Siberian east coast were not as heavily traveled by international shipping as the waters of the central Med. The entire Sea of Okhotsk, all 610,000 square miles of it, iced over from October to May, was virtually empty save for military traffic, a handful of Russian fishing boats, and the occasional missile test.

Still, the U.S. Navy had a keen interest in access to the Sea of Okhotsk, legal or not. Operation Silent Dolphins was a case in point.

American activities in and around the Sea of Okhotsk went back three decades at least. One of the greatest espionage coups of the Cold War, a covert op known as Ivy Bells, had been carried out by elements of the American submarine force. Over the course of nine years, from 1972 through 1980, American submarines with special towed-array instrument platforms had sought out undersea telephone cables stretching across the Okhotsk seabed to the Kamchatka Peninsula, connecting the major Soviet naval bases at Vladivostok, Sovetskaya, and Magadan with the major Pacific port on Kamchatka, Petropavlovsk. Time after time, divers from the *Halibut*, the *Parche*, and other Special Ops boats, had attached electronic taps on the cables, allowing American intelligence bureaus to monitor everything from fleet movements to romantic phone calls to distant loved ones; telephone traffic across the Okhotsk had not been scrambled or encrypted because, it was thought, the submarine cables were completely secure. American submarines had serviced the taps at least once a month for years, picking up the long-duration tapes when they were full and replacing them.

Only in the last few years had the Soviets discovered this open back door to their Far Eastern operations and slammed it shut . . . and that thanks not to their Pacific Fleet and coastal defense forces, but to an American, Ronald Pelton, an employee at the National Security Agency who'd sold out his country for the munificent sum of roughly $15,000. The KGB was not known for its generous pay scales.

So the glory days of Ivy Bells were over, but American

operations in the region continued, almost as though a tradition had been established, one that could not be abandoned without a certain loss of face and prestige.

The theory behind Operation Silent Dolphins was deceptively simple. Two Sturgeon class submarines, including the *Parche*, had crept stealthily past the Kurils and into the Soviets' backyard, parking themselves outside the port city of Magadan and within the shallow waters of the Sakhalinskiy Zaliv, on the northern approaches to the port of Nikolayevsk. Another Sturgeon, the *Batfish*, was outside of Petropavlovsk, on the Kamchatka Pacific coast, and a fourth was in the Sea of Japan in the Zaliv Petra Velikogo, south of the great port of Vladivostok and within easy listening range of the nearby secondary ports at Nakhodka and Vostochnyy. All four Sturgeons were experienced at sneak-and-peek inshore ops, and were equipped with high-tech ESM gear for monitoring Soviet radio and radar transmissions. Following their operational orders to the letter, they took up their assigned positions and waited. At a prearranged moment—0330 hours that morning—all had risen to periscope depth and extended the slender radio masts studded with ECM listening gear.

And at the same time, a fifth American submarine, the Los Angeles class boat *Pittsburgh*, had surfaced ten miles off the east coast of Sakhalin, opposite the port of Yuzhno Sakhalinsk.

The Soviet reaction had been predictable, and instantaneous. The *Pittsburgh* was well outside the three-mile limit declared by the United States, but well *inside* the twelve-mile limit claimed by Moscow . . . not to mention being a good two hundred miles within a body of water claimed in its entirety by the Soviet Union.

Pinpointed almost at once by half a dozen radar transmitters, from Novikovo in southern Sakhalin to an Ilyushin-38 May operating out of Petropavlovsk, the *Pittsburgh* had instigated a leisurely turn back out to sea, then submerged once more with an almost royal arrogance.

With four electronic surveillance submarines listening, a full alert had been sounded throughout the Soviet Far East, from Vladivostok in the south to tiny, remote Anadyr, far to the north on the Bering Sea. ASW aircraft had lifted into the dark, partly overcast skies. Ships had gotten under way. SAM batteries had been manned. Radar had swept skies and sea alike.

And the four spy subs had recorded every movement, every radio call, every radar bandwidth from their watery blinds in the icy black waters off the Soviet homeland.

It was an old game, a game as old as the Cold War itself, a matching of wits and nerve, of technology and crew training in secret and out-of-the-way arenas around the world. It was also a war, and a deadly one. The battles, the heroes, the stakes were never published, never revealed to the civilian community . . . but the casualty lists were real. If the Russians managed to corner the *Pittsburgh*, they would find a way to bring her to the surface. By their way of thinking, they were defending their sovereign territorial waters; they were as skittish about U.S. subs lurking in the Sea of Okhotsk as their American counterparts would be about Russian boats cruising up the Chesapeake to eavesdrop on electronic chitchat coming out of the Pentagon or Fort Meade.

"How much more time are you going to need?" Perrigrino asked, breaking Travers's reverie.

Travers looked at his watch. Operational orders called for listening to Soviet signals and recording them for at least three hours . . . but dawn in these waters was at 0451 hours . . . several minutes ago, now. He knew Perrigrino was less than enthusiastic about trying to slip away from the approaches to a heavily traveled military port under the light of day. These waters were shallow, this close inshore, and a submerged submarine could be picked out sometimes by its shadow, from the air.

"We either move out now, so we can be in deep water by the time it's fully light," he said, "or we stay put until after dark. Your call, Captain. We have a lot of good stuff already . . . including the sighting of that Mike."

"Yeah, but another twelve hours would give us a lot more, right?"

"Certainly." Travers nodded. Perrigrino had the rep of an aggressive sub skipper, one who wasn't afraid to get in close and tight when it counted.

Perrigrino pulled up another chart and studied it for a moment. This one was a close-up look at the Bay of Tauyskaya and the approaches to Magadan. An island, Ostrov Zav'-yalova, marked the southern boundary to the bay.

The captain pointed, indicating the waters just north of the slender island. "We've got us a great hide here," he said. "There's enough junk in these waters to cover us even if they start active pinging. I think we're best off staying put. If anything, it'll give us a longer run in darkness to make it out of this hole, down Kamchatka's west coast and out through the Kuril'skiy Straits. XO?"

"I concur, Captain."

"Okay," Travers said. "We'll keep our ears on."

He was still troubled, however, as he made his way down the ladder, turned left, and headed forward toward the torpedo room. While U.S. subs had performed a variety of espionage operations in the Sea of Okhotsk, everything from cable tapping to monitoring the splashdowns of Soviet missile tests, this was the first time they'd tried deliberately *provoking* a Soviet military response. The idea, Travers had heard, had come in the wake of the Soviet downing of a civilian airliner, the ill-fated Korean Air Lines Flight 007, in 1983. U.S. and Japanese intelligence assets, including an American ELINT aircraft over the Pacific, had picked up a wealth of data on Soviet military responses as the Boeing 747, with 269 people on board, had been pursued by a MiG and shot down by close-range missile fire.

Those civilians had been among the casualties of this sometimes not-so-cold war. Soviet actions that night had fully demonstrated their willingness to defend their territory with lethal force.

How, he wondered, would they react to the unprovoked intrusion by an American attack submarine?

Joe McNally grumbled about the fact that he'd forgotten the coffee.

Thursday, 25 June 1987

USS _Pittsburgh_
Sea of Okhotsk
0525 hours local time

Commander Mike Chase leaned in what he trusted was a casual manner against one of the stanchions next to _Pittsburgh_'s periscope walk and looked up at the heavily painted maze of pipes, fittings, and cable bundles running among the fluorescent lighting fixtures of the combat center's overhead. The pings were coming faster now, shrill, hard punches of sound that rang through the boat's hull and internal spaces like the tolling of enormous, high-pitched bells.

This, he reflected, with just a trace of bitterness, _is one hell of a way to end up my final cruise aboard this boat._

"Of course it's just a guess," the boat's XO said quietly, "but I think they just might have us where they want us." LCDR Frederick Yates Latham, as always, was unhurried and unperturbed, an expert at the subtle understatement and the faintly sardonic quip. Just once, Chase thought, he'd like to know what the young Executive Officer was really thinking. As always, though, those pale, ice-blue eyes and recruit-ing-poster features gave nothing away.

"Diving Officer," Chase said. "What's the depth below keel?"

Lieutenant Francis J. Carver looked at a gauge on his board. "One-nine-six feet beneath the keel, Captain," he said. "We're coming up on the hundred-fathom line."

"Very well. Tell me when we hit the line."

"Report crossing the hundred-fathom line, aye, sir."

Carver was new aboard the *Pittsburgh*, young and green, but he seemed to have all his shit in one seabag, as the say-ing went. He'd come aboard back at Mare Island just before the *Pittsburgh* had gotten under way, replacing the boat's previous D.O., John Quimby. After almost three years of sea duty, much of that spent aboard the *Pittsburgh*, Quimby had finally swung a billet in a postgrad course at Monterey, headed for a master's in aeronautical engineering.

Quimby was going to be missed, damn it. The '*Burgh* was about to move into some shallow and treacherous waters, and chances were they were going to have to do some fancy depth changes, hard, fast and accurate. Chase would have liked a more experienced man behind the planesman.

Still, Carver seemed to know his stuff, and he deserved a chance. It wasn't his fault that his first tour aboard the *Pitts-burgh* was taking him into a hot Kuril passage.

"These are the waters Flight 007 went down in, aren't they?" Latham asked.

"Not quite, XO," Chase replied. "Northern Sea of Japan. They managed to overfly Kamchatka and Sakhalin before the Russians finally got fighters up." Another piercing ping echoed through sea and hull. "I'd say they're a bit more on the ball up there, now, wouldn't you?"

PING. . . .

"Captain?" Carver said. "Crossing the hundred-fathom line."

"Very well."

PING. . . .

The one-hundred-fathom line—six hundred feet—was the arbitrary topographical boundary marking the edge of the continental shelf. The shallows surrounding Kunashir, southernmost of the Kurils, humped up above the much deeper water to the west, averaging a depth at the top of about thirty to forty fathoms. But just beyond that flat-topped ridge, if they stayed on this heading, was a deeper channel . . . and a safe escape to the open Pacific beyond.

But a hundred fathoms wasn't much to work with . . . less than twice the *Pittsburgh*'s 340-foot length. At thirty fathoms, the sub would be practically pinned in a shallow film of water half as deep as the boat was long. Submarines by nature were three-dimensional creatures, capable of taking advantage of maneuvers up and down, as well as ahead and back, port and starboard. Periscope depth for an LA-class boat was 52 feet; in water 180 feet deep, she wouldn't have much room to maneuver.

But the Russians would know the channels between the islands well, and would have them blocked by now, or worse, mined. Chase was taking a gamble, but a calculated one, trying to slip over the ridge and into the deep channel beyond halfway along the undersea valley's sinuous length.

If they could make it that far . . . another five miles . . .

"Conn, Sonar," a voice announced from the 1MC overhead speaker. "New sonar contact, designated Sierra Two-five, bearing zero-zero-six. Twin screws, estimate twenty knots, making fifteen turns per knot. I think it's another Krivak I, Captain."

"Very well." He looked at Latham. "That makes four Krivaks up there. They're eager."

"KGB Maritime Border Guard," Latham replied. "They're not usually this far out."

"Probably a blocking force stationed in the Kurils." He picked up a microphone and keyed it. "Sonar, Conn. Keep on 'em, Rodriguez. And keep a sharp ear out for any air traffic."

"Aye, aye, Captain."

Chase smiled. SM/2 Enrique Rodriguez, at least, was an

old hand on the *'Burgh*, and one of the best sonar men he'd served with. Rodriguez was one of those sonar magicians, men who could listen to the wash and rumble of sound in the ocean around them and extract information that seemed like the product of nothing less than witchcraft.

The Krivak I was an old sub hunter, her equipment long out-of-date. Likely, the Soviets were employing her as a driver, to chase the *'Burgh* toward the real hunters astern, or else to serve as a barrier force to keep her penned.

"Conn, Sonar."

"Conn. Go ahead."

"New contact, designated Sierra Two-six, bearing three-five-zero. This one sounds like an aircraft, probably big and low over the water."

"Let me hear. Put it on the horn."

He heard it then over the speaker, a low, droning rumble, muffled by water and distance.

"Sounds like a big four-engine turboprop, Captain," Rodriguez added. "Not a clatter, like a helicopter."

"Thanks, Rodriguez. I want—"

"Conn! Sonar! Splashes close aboard, port and starboard! Sounds like sonobuoys! They're going active!"

A barrage of pings hit the *Pittsburgh*, each one a finger reaching down to touch the vessel and pinpoint its location to the surface hunters. The aircraft overhead must be an ASW plane, a May or a Mail, and the fact that they'd laid a pattern of sonobuoys suggested they were pretty sure exactly where the *Pittsburgh* was.

"Helm, come right to zero-nine-five," Chase said. "Make depth five hundred feet."

"Helm, right to zero-nine-five," Lieutenant Daly, who had the helm watch, echoed.

"Coming right to zero-nine-five," an enlisted man repeated. He was seated at the right-hand set of what looked like the control yoke and instrumentation for a commercial aircraft. The deliberate redundancy of orders repeated, then repeated again, was an essential part of submarine operational procedure, a way to check and double-check that the captain's orders had been correctly heard and correctly acted upon.

"Fifteen degrees down bow planes," Latham said. "Make depth five-zero-zero feet, aye."

"Fifteen degrees down bow planes. Make depth five-zero-zero feet, aye, sir," the planesman, on the left-hand yoke, repeated.

Chase grabbed the periscope walk stanchion as the deck tilted beneath his feet. They were already at 115 feet. For the next few seconds, Latham chanted off the depth figures from his readout. "Passing two-zero-zero feet, sir. Two-one-zero. Two-two-zero . . . two-five-zero . . ." And the *Pittsburgh* continued her long, silent descent into blackness.

"Sonar, Conn," Chase said into the mike. "Any sign of a layer we can hide under?"

"Conn, Sonar. Negative, sir. Not in these waters, not this early in the season."

Temperature inversions, a layer of warmer, less salty water beneath a colder, heavier layer, created a kind of barrier to sonar. The curtain wasn't opaque, necessarily, but a submarine had at least a fighting chance of shaking her echo-hungry pursuers by slipping beneath an inversion layer that channeled most of the searchers' sonar away from the target.

Unfortunately, the Sea of Okhotsk was cold, especially now, with its seasonal ice cap only recently melted. The upper layers were somewhat warmer than the lower, but the temperature was fairly constant top to bottom, the waters well mixed. There would be no help there.

"Sonar, Conn. What's the status on Sierra One-nine?"

"Conn, Sonar. Sierra One-nine bearing now zero-zero-two, Skipper. Heading one-eight-three, making turns for twenty knots. I estimate his range at nine thousand yards, sir."

That might work. Contact Sierra One-nine had arrived on the scene almost an hour ago. Rodriguez had identified her as a Kresta II class ASW cruiser, probably the *Admiral Yumashev*.

A Kresta II was big—521 feet in length and pulling an un-loaded displacement of 6200 tons. She was also noisy, with her twin steam turbines and high-pitch screws. She was a dangerous adversary, with a powerful, medium-frequency sonar forward, and mounting RBU-1000, RBU-6000, and two quad launchers for the rocket-delivered torpedo NATO had designated as SS-N-14 Silex for attacking submerged targets.

But there might be a way of using her bulk and her noisy power plant. The Kresta was almost bow-on, bearing down on the *Pittsburgh* like an oncoming express freight.

"Leveling off at five-zero-zero feet," the planesman said.

"Captain, we are at five hundred feet," Latham announced.

"Very well. Helm, come left to three-five-eight degrees. Make turns for eight knots." That put them precisely on a re-ciprocal course with the Kresta; the two were approaching one another now bow-on, with a combined velocity of thirty knots.

"Helm left to three-five-eight, aye, sir. Making turns for two-zero knots." The litany of orders given, repeated, and re-repeated was like a kind of intricately and meticulously cho-reographed ballet. There was a sense of affirmation, of rightness, of certainty that had its effect on every man in the combat center.

And on none more than Mike Chase. Hearing the orders called back to him allowed him to close his eyes and visual-ize the tactical situation developing around them, allowed him to enter a mental zone where the *Pittsburgh* was an ex-tension of his body, of where he *was* the *Pittsburgh*, carrying out her dance on a dark and three-dimensional stage.

"Diving Officer, make depth one-five-zero feet."

"Depth to one-one-zero, aye, sir. Planesman, up forward planes ten degrees. Make our depth one-one-zero feet."

"Up forward planes one-zero feet, aye, sir. Make depth one-five-zero, aye, sir."

The deck tilted up as the planesman brought back his

yoke. For long seconds, the command center was silent save for the recitation of depth figures. "Passing three-five-zero feet. Three-two-zero feet. Now passing three-zero-zero feet, sir. . . ."

"Sonar, Conn. Rodriguez, tell me the moment you detect any aspect change on Sierra One-niner."

"Will do, Captain. He's still coming straight for us. No active sonar. He's following us on the sonobuoys."

"Watch him. He's your priority target right now."

"Aye aye, sir."

At last, the *Pittsburgh* leveled off, still traveling directly toward the Kresta, bow-on. As the range narrowed to less than a thousand yards, the men in the combat center could actually hear the oncoming Soviet warship, an urgent, pounding thrash muffled by the sea, but quite distinct, and growing louder moment by moment. Faces throughout the compartment looked up toward the overhead; Chase was cutting this one pretty close, given that the *Pittsburgh* measured just over fifty feet from keel to the top of her sail, not counting her periscopes, and that a Kresta II typically drew about twenty feet of water. Chase was "dusting off the keel" of the warship above, allowing something like forty feet clearance.

A dangerous ploy. And also his best chance for eluding the enemy's sonar net.

The Kresta's screws churned directly overhead now. The helmsman and the planesman kept their eyes rigidly on the readouts above their yokes, but every other man in the combat center looked up, as though waiting for the deadly crunch of a steel-on-steel impact.

"Mr. Daly, come right sixty degrees . . . now!"

There was only the briefest of hesitations as Daly looked back at his board. "Come right sixty degrees, to bearing zero-five-eight, aye, sir!"

As the Kresta rumbled overhead and aft, chugging like a slow-moving locomotive, the *Pittsburgh* swung to the right. They could all feel the vibration of the cruiser's passing, as her twin screws thrashed through the water. "On new heading, zero-five-eight, sir," Daly announced.

"Hard left rudder. Bring us back around to a heading of two-three-eight. Planesman, watch our depth. I don't want us popping up and broaching."

"Hard left, to two-three-eight, aye, sir. . . ."

"Son of a bitch!" an enlisted man, Torpedoman's Mate Second Class Benson, his station at the combat center plot board, exclaimed. "He's pulling a Wilkinson!"

"Belay that chatter, Benson," Master Chief Warren, the Chief of the Boat, snapped from his post at the ballast controls.

Chase said nothing. He didn't mind Benson's outburst, but he would not interfere in the COB's disciplining of one of the men . . . not in front of the crew, at any rate. Maybe later. . . .

If there is a later, he thought. As the sound of the passing ASW cruiser dwindled, the *Pittsburgh* continued her turn to port, ending up on a reciprocal heading from the previous course. She was now behind the Kresta, and following her, hidden from Russian listeners in the froth of white noise churned by the cruiser's screws.

Even the pings of active sonars, from other ships and from the line of sonobuoys dropped by ASW aircraft, faded as they dogged the Kresta's wake. For a moment, at least, *Pittsburgh* had just rendered herself invisible.

"Sonar, Conn," Chase said into his microphone. "Let me know the instant you get *any* aspect change on Sierra One-niner . . . or any change in his revs."

"Will do, Captain. Right now, he's just charging straight ahead, blasting away with sonar. Don't think he knows we just disappeared into his baffles."

"Good." Russian sonar operators—their people were all officers, as opposed to the American Navy which used highly trained enlisted sonar men—were not as well trained as their American counterparts, and originality and imagination were not encouraged in any part of the Soviet military.

It was one thing to listen to a target and know it was dead ahead . . . but something different, and more difficult, to determine which way it was going. Kresta's sonar operators had known the *Pittsburgh* was in front of them and that they were closing, but they could not have been sure whether the American sub was running away from them, or charging them head-on. Chances were, they hadn't been expecting *Pittsburgh*'s sudden Wilkinson turn right under their fantail, and since other ships in the area hadn't picked up the American boat coming out from behind the Kresta, the Americans must still be ahead, possibly trying to hide in the bottom clutter of the rapidly shoaling water. The depth, now, was down to less than three hundred feet.

Moments crawled past. The Kresta slowed, and *Pittsburgh* slowed with her. With her engines turning over slowly, the white noise from her wake was lessened, but the American sub continued to lurk in the Kresta's blind spot, pulling in a bit closer, until her sail was somewhere just abaft of the Russian warship's turning screws.

After a time, the Kresta swung due north, *Pittsburgh* continuing to follow her. "Nuts to butts," the COB said quietly, apparently forgetting his earlier injunction to silence as he intoned an old and crude litany from boot camp, addressed to recruits required to line up close behind one another. "Make the guy in front of you smile." Sierra One-niner began sprinting again, and *Pittsburgh* stuck with her. Their contact with the American sub lost, the other sonar contacts began scattering over a wider and wider area, casting sonobuoy and active sonar nets farther and farther abroad as they searched for the missing target.

And as the Kresta moved north at twenty-five knots, she and her unseen shadow came abreast of Proliv Yekateriny, north of Kunashir Island. "All stop," Chase ordered. "Let her drift. Down planes five degrees. Level off at one hundred eighty feet."

"All stop, aye, sir. Down planes five degrees. Level off at one-eight-zero feet, aye."

Drifting silently, now, the 6,927-ton boat continued moving forward on sheer inertia, but the Kresta, still pinging ahead, swiftly outpaced the slowing *Pittsburgh*, racing for the northern horizon. *Pittsburgh* fell out of the Soviet warship's baffles, but her departure went unnoticed as she drifted gently toward 180 feet, slowing to a near stop, her neutral buoyancy holding her suspended between surface and seabed.

"All ahead one-third," Chase said. "Make revolutions for seven knots. Helm, come to course zero-nine-five. What's our depth below keel?"

"Depth below keel now eight hundred twelve feet, Captain."

"Diving officer, take us down to seven hundred feet."

The orders echoed back at him in confirmation and the steel deck tilted sharply as the *Pittsburgh* dove for deeper, safer water. The passages between the Kurils were narrow, but tended to be quite deep. Chase had ordered them to make the transit at a crawl, however. Those passages were almost certainly strung with the Soviet equivalent of a SOSUS net, sensitive underwater microphones designed to pick up the sounds made by a passing submarine. By remaining quiet, however, and keeping her speed well below ten knots, *Pittsburgh* was nearly as silent as it was possible to be . . . a "hole in the water," as her crew liked to describe her.

In another two hours, tense minutes, but without incident, the *Pittsburgh* entered open water once more, the broad, wide emptiness of the North Pacific. With Rodriguez's assurances that there were no enemy vessels close by, Chase ordered the *Pittsburgh* back to within a few feet of the surface once more, so that she could extend her radio mast in order to pick up orders . . . and to broadcast a mission complete.

"Well, XO, we skinned the cat again," he said, after ordering the '*Burgh* ahead full, with her prow set toward distant Hawaii, her next scheduled port of call.

"Yup," Latham said, nodding. "With all those sonar contacts banging away up there, it sounded like the whole Red Banner Pacific Fleet was after us. I hope it was worth it."

"If the other boat skippers did their jobs, it was," Chase replied. "It'll help to know just how good their reaction time is."

"Sometimes, I think the Beltway bean counters don't really care one way or another for the information we bring back," Latham said, folding his arms. He looked uncharacteristically troubled.

"Oh?"

"It's got to be some kind of a game for them. See how far they can push the other guy, see how hard they can stomp on his toes before he blinks . . . or throws a punch."

"Could be," Chase replied. "Could be. But God help us all if you're right."

Crew's Mess, USS *Pittsburgh*
North Pacific Ocean
0918 hours local time

Breakfast had been served already, but coffee, juice, and various snack foods were always available in the *Pittsburgh*'s galley. Every man aboard agreed that the chow served in the Silent Service was the best in the Navy . . . a tradition that went back as far as World War II.

"So, whaddaya think of the Old Man's performance, Big C?" TM2 Roger Benson said, grinning as he topped off a cup of bug juice at the mess dispenser. "Was that slick or what?"

"Not bad," BM1 Charles Scobey said. He'd opted for coffee. "Not fucking bad at all. He gets points on originality, at least."

"Not bad? Hey, he was fucking incredible! Doubling back and dusting off that cruiser's belly, then pulling a Wilkinson like that, cool as you please, and then following the son of a bitch right up to the mouth of the channel. Man, I ain't seen nothing like it!"

"Ahh," Big C replied with a negligent wave of his hand. "Saw the same thing on Swifty Larson's boat, back in '80. And that was in the Barents Sea, too, with Russkie boomers and attack boats crowded elbow to elbow, and half the Northern Red Banner Fleet lookin' on. It was in an old Sturgeon class, not one of these fancy Lala-Land boats that do everything for you 'cept take a piss when you need it."

"Ha! You think that was bad?" TMC Bart Allison said, taking an empty seat at one of the mess-deck tables. "Back when I was a very raw newbie on board the old *Seawolf* . . . now that was *primitive*. Nothing ever worked right on that boat. Yeah, I remember the time when the reactor scrammed, left us shut down and drifting under the Bering ice. The skipper was threatening to rig oars, but the chief nuke puke figured out how to use the COB's breath to recharge the reactor."

"You're full of shit, Chief," Big C said.

"Nah. Just finished using the crapper in the goat locker, thanks."

"Damn, I *thought* I smelled something putrid wafting aft," Big C said.

"Must be a conspiracy, Scobey," Benson said. "Better tell the captain."

They all laughed. "Big C" had acquired his handle not by his size—he was short even for a submariner, and almost painfully thin—nor by his first name. Big C was a conspiracy theorist, big-time, and could always be counted on to regale his listeners with stories of deep, secret, and mysterious conspiracies, everything from both Kennedy assassinations and Chappaquiddick, and how they all *obviously* tied in together, to cattle mutilations and black helicopters out West. The other 'Burghers teased him unmercifully about his paranoid thinking.

Which was fine by Scobey. He liked being the center of attention.

"Anyway, in my expert opinion," Benson went on, "our skipper is the best damned sub driver in the fleet. Listening to him in the CC today, it was like watching a master craftsman at work, y'know? Cool as the Pole Abyssal, givin' orders like it was some kind of damned training simulator. It's gonna be a real shame to lose him."

"Is this really his last cruise?" EM3 John Boyce asked, joining them at the table with a cup of coffee and a couple of doughnuts on a plate.

"That's the word," Chief Allison said. "He'll be off to some nice, cushy job in the Pentagon for a few years, I suspect. Or maybe captain of a sub base."

"Y'know, the Brits have the right idea," Big C said. "When their sub captains get too senior to drive boats, they move 'em up to skipper an ASW surface ship. Set a fox to catch a fox, right?"

"Nah, wouldn't work for the skipper," Allison said, shaking his massive head. "He's a true submariner, and that means that as far as he's concerned, there's only two types of ships, you know . . . submarines . . ."

". . . and *targets*," Benson and Scobey chorused, completing the line. It was an old joke, a favorite of submariners.

"Fuckin' A. I can't see the skipper backsliding so far as to start driving targets. Uh-uh. Not his style."

"Well, we don't have to worry about a new skipper yet," Scobey said. "We're headed for *Pearl*! . . ." and with that he stood up, ground his hips in a lewdly suggestive hula, and moved his hands to outline a woman's curves. "Man, there ain't *no* liberty like Honolulu, man! The girls there are so . . . are so . . ."

"Know exactly what you mean, Big C," Allison said, laughing. "No words for it."

"But you're a married man, Chief!" Boyce said.

"Doesn't stop me from appreciatin' the finer points of biology, son." The others laughed.

"So, did you guys hear the scuttlebutt about our next mission?" Scobey asked.

"There can't be no scuttlebutt about no next mission," Allison said, "on account of the orders ain't even been transmitted yet."

"Well, maybe. But I heard it from a buddy of mine in personnel back at Mare Island. They're planning on starting up something like Ivy Bells again. You know, slipping into Oshkosh, tapping a telephone cable, and—"

"Belay that," Allison growled. "I think the name of that op is still classified."

"Sure, but the op is over, right? The Russians found out and pulled the plug."

"That may be, but we're not supposed to talk about some things, even among ourselves."

Scobey shrugged. "Sure sounds like a conspiracy of silence to me."

They laughed.

Benson wondered, though, if Scobey really did have an inside track to the straight dope. Oshkosh—the enlisted submariner's slang name for the Sea of Okhotsk—was damned hot and getting hotter, if the Soviet fleet's performance there that morning was any indication.

And he was beginning to wonder if all the sneaking and peeking was worth the lives of *Pittsburgh*'s twelve officers and 120 men. It was something he'd never admitted to anyone . . . even himself, but after that morning, he was forced to see it.

Roger Benson was afraid. The captain had pulled their fat out of the fire that time, but he was leaving the ship as soon as they got back, to be replaced by an unknown.

He was wondering if he was going to be able to stay in the Silent Service himself, and the thought left him feeling both afraid and ashamed.

Friday, 26 June 1987

**Office of Naval Special Operations Command
D-Ring, the Pentagon
Alexandria, Virginia
1900 hours, EST (Greenwich –5)**

"Working late, I see."

Commander Frank Gordon looked up from his desk, startled. Admirals did not pay friendly visits to junior officers in their Pentagon offices, especially long after closing time. The Pentagon was always alive—there were always people working late, or on the night watches—but the place still generally felt more like a civilian office than a military base, and most of the personnel, including nearly all of the civilians employed there, came in at seven or eight and went home by five.

"Admiral Goldman!" He started to rise. "I didn't hear you come in, sir."

"Sit, sit," the older man said, gesturing with his hand. "No formalities. It's after hours."

He nodded toward the coffeemaker on a table against one wall. "Can I get you some coffee, Admiral?"

"No, thanks. I heard you were working late. What's up?"

"Putting together my notes for a dog-and-pony show to-morrow. Another briefing for some budget wonks and bean counters from the GAO on programs that we can't tell them about because they're not cleared for it."

"You know, Frank, Rebecca hasn't been seeing a lot of you, lately. She's been complaining about being a Fort Fumble Widow."

Gordon's jaws clamped down hard. He was careful with his words. "I know, Admiral. And I'm truly sorry." He spread his hands, taking in the computer and the pile of papers on his desk. "But I just haven't been able to get clear."

"I know, son. And I'm not blaming you. But it's been damned tough on Rebecca."

"And on me, sir." He hesitated. "I . . . I really do love her, you know."

There. He'd said it.

Admiral Benjamin Goldman was the father of his wife, Rebecca. His relationship with the admiral had started off badly . . . just about as bad as was possible. He'd met Becca at a service dance and he'd been smitten hard. Well, so had she, though the word around the base had been that he'd deliberately put the moves on and swept her off her feet. The only trouble was, she'd been engaged at the time, and a sudden change of mind and the resultant late-night elopement had not sat well with the conservative elder Goldman. He'd not spoken to his daughter for several years after that, and the word was that Frank Gordon was on the old man's shit list . . . that he was never going to rate a decent command.

That was all old news now, thank God. He'd received command of the *Bluefin*, an aging diesel boat fitted out to carry commandos, and he'd acquitted himself well in a highly secret covert op in the White Sea two years before. After the success of Operation Arctic Fox, he'd received the promise of another submarine command, after his required rotation ashore.

That promise, frankly, had been pretty much all that had

kept him going these last twenty months. Sometimes, he thought that his posting to the Pentagon—as a staff assistant in the Office of Naval Special Operations Command—was going to drive him stark, raving bug nuts, a pure Section Eight.

"I know you do," Goldman said, in response to Gordon's blunt statement. "And I regret the years lost. Petty. Stupid, really. But that's all behind us, right?"

"Absolutely, sir," Gordon said, but even yet, he felt a small, deep-buried and sullen bit of suspicion. Benjamin Goldman never did anything without purpose. Why was he bringing all of this up now?

"So . . . you got a moment?"

"Of course, sir."

"Come with me."

Puzzled, Gordon rose from his desk, towering over the small, wiry Goldman. Where was the man taking him?

"I expect you're anxious to get out of the Puzzle Palace," Goldman told him, using yet another of the countless names Pentagon employees used for the huge structure. Most simply called it "the Building," but those in a more critical mood referred to it as "the Fudge Factory," "Fort Fumble," "the Squirrel Cage," or—Gordon's favorite by far—"the Five-Sided Wailing Wall." "The Puzzle Palace" was a pet name contested by the occupants of the National Security Agency's huge facility at Fort Meade, Maryland. Both claimed title to the name with a jocular, my-place-is-worse-to-work-in-than-your-place proprietorship.

"Yes, *sir*," Gordon replied, with neither hesitation nor fear of ruffling Goldman's feathers. The admiral knew how he felt about his Pentagon assignment. For almost two years, he'd been marking time . . . doing an important job, yes, but driving a damned desk instead of a submarine, which to his way of thinking was among the more inhuman of mental tortures.

"Hmm. Does that mean," Goldman said, "that you think you'd be doing a better job, a more important job, somewhere else?"

The question caught Gordon by surprise. They'd been walking clockwise down the gleaming main corridor of D-Ring, but now Goldman swung them left into Corridor 4, heading deeper into the Pentagon's heart. Where the hell was the admiral taking him?

"No, sir," he replied carefully. He knew Goldman expected straight answers, but Gordon was feeling now like he was treading through a minefield. "But I do know that my best work isn't done behind a desk."

"Sea duty means long stretches away from home."

"Yes, sir. And Rebecca knew that when she married me."

For a moment, he wondered if he'd gone too far. Goldman's leathery face was impassive, but could easily be masking anger. They reached one of the red-framed security elevators, which Goldman summoned with a magnetic-strip ID card. The doors opened a moment later, and they stepped inside. Goldman used his card again to access a subbasement level that Gordon hadn't even known existed.

There were plenty of rumors about deep-underground chambers beneath the Pentagon, and some of them were even true. Gordon knew that a nuclear-safe war room existed down there, and fairly reliable rumor had it that there was at least one small nuclear plant as well . . . a fact that would not sit well with many of the civilian residents of Washington and its Virginia-side ring city had they known. The word was that secure communications and command facilities had been tunneled out of the bedrock beginning back in the fifties or early sixties, when it was taken for granted that the Building was ground zero for at least a couple of Soviet ICBMs.

"I want my daughter to be happy," Goldman said, as the elevator began descending rapidly. "But you also understand, I know, that I can't let my feelings as a father interfere with my duties as COMSUBSPECLANT."

"Of course not, Admiral." Now Gordon was *really* puzzled, and curious.

The elevator slowed, stopped, and opened up. They

stepped into a narrow corridor with concrete-block walls and naked fluorescent tubes on the ceilings. As a top-secret underground facility, it bore little resemblance to Hollywood's concept of such mythic places. "Just where is it we're going, Admiral?"

They stopped at a checkpoint manned by two stolid-faced Marines, one prominently armed with an M-16. Goldman gave the other his ID card. "He's with me," Goldman said. "Temporary clearance, Blue-Five."

"I need you both to sign in here, sir," the Marine said.

"We call it the Bunker," the admiral replied as Goldman scrawled his name, rank, the date, and the time into a log, then handed the pen to Gordon. "Part of the Washington scene the tourists never see."

They went on past the checkpoint, taking several turns along the way and eventually climbing aboard an electric car, like a golf cart, which took them through a maze of subterranean tunnels. By that time, Gordon's sense of direction was thoroughly scrambled. There were places where water dripped from the ceiling and puddled on the bare, concrete floor, and he wondered if they were somewhere under the Potomac by then. Interesting thought. There were rumors of similar buildings and tunnels beneath the White House, and even of an ultrasecret underground highway going all the way from the White House subbasement out to the National Naval Medical Center in suburban Bethesda. Did this warren of labyrinthine tunnels connect somehow?

"Do you remember a report you wrote nine months ago?" Goldman asked as they parked the golf cart and passed another security checkpoint. " 'Use of Intelligence/Strike Assets in Certain Middle East Field Operations,' I think you called it."

"Yes, sir. That was one I did for your office. Using SEAL Teams for deep-ashore intel gathering and hostage-rescue ops in Lebanon. I never heard anything else, and assumed it was shitcanned."

"It wasn't. It was going the rounds of various desks in

Special Ops, at Langley, even at the White House, but nothing much was happening. At least, not until Terry Waite vanished."

Terry Waite. Gordon knew the name well, of course, since much of his work in the last year had concerned the hostages held by Hezbollah in Lebanon. A no-win situation if ever there'd been one.

Ever since 1982, the Iranian-backed, pro-Palestinian extremists that called themselves Hezbollah, the Party of God, had been collecting hostages in Lebanon. The well-remembered ploy by Iran in holding fifty-two American embassy personnel for 444 days while a horrified world watched must have been considered a success in terrorist circles, because they'd made a career of kidnapping foreigners, especially Americans. Some had been held for five years, now, and the American public—and Congress—was growing increasingly angry and frustrated. In an apparent replay of the Vietnam tragedy a generation before, the American giant was being held impotent by a tiny and dedicated group of terrorist-revolutionaries.

Hezbollah claimed to be taking hostages to protest the treatment of fellow Shi'ite fundamentalists in Lebanon, and to win the release of Shi'ite terrorists now in prison in Israel. There were few options in dealing with them. Israel flatly refused to bargain with terrorists under any conditions . . . as did most in the American military. The hostages were held in scattered and well-concealed locations, and even discovering where they were was a major problem for the U.S. intelligence agencies tasked with finding them. An all-out, overt military strike was likely to result in the death of at least some of the hostages, in friendly-fire incidents, or when they were executed by a vengeful Shi'ite militia. The only alternative seemed to be to wait and hope for a break . . . while year after year slipped by, with American citizens imprisoned for no crime other than being Americans.

Terry Waite had offered an unexpected hope. An envoy

from the Church of England, he'd presented himself to the Muslim fundamentalists as a neutral negotiator hoping to end the standoff that threatened the delicate balance of conflicting powers throughout the Middle East, a standoff that was unfairly painting all Shi'ites worldwide as terrorist, hostage-taking madmen. Over the course of several months, he'd won freedom for three hostages. Twenty-three remained imprisoned, however . . . eight Americans, one Indian, two Saudis, and eleven Europeans.

Then, in January of this year, Terry Waite himself had vanished . . . another hostage for Hezbollah demands.

"What's so important about Waite?" Gordon wanted to know. "Just the fact that he was so high-profile?"

"There's more to it than that. Here we are."

Goldman ushered him into a door flanked by Marine sentries, through a carpeted anteroom, and past another set of doors. Inside was a combat command center setup much like that aboard an Aegis cruiser, a technology-cluttered room filled with computer displays, TV monitors, communications consoles, and dozens of men, civilians and military, speaking in low-voiced tones.

Several men looked up from the display monitor they were studying. One, a young man with a long face, in shirtsleeves, frowned. "Who's this? What's he doing here?"

"Commander Gordon," Goldman said. "He's the gentleman who first conceived this op. I thought he should be here."

"Welcome to the Bunker, Commander," the young man said. His ramrod posture, his crisp manner made it clear he was military, even though he was casually attired in civvies.

"Thank you, sir."

"This is Marine Lieutenant Colonel North," Goldman said. "Former National Security Council aide. He's also had something to do with this scenario tonight."

"Colonel North?" Gordon said, shaking the man's hand.

"Yes, *that* Colonel North." He sounded tired.

The previous November, a Lebanese newspaper had printed a story declaring that the Reagan administration had sold high-tech missiles to Iran in a bizarre-sounding ploy to free the hostages held by pro-Iranian Shi'ite guerrillas in Lebanon. Weeks later, Attorney General Edwin Meese had dropped a bigger bomb: American officials had taken the money from the missile sales and diverted it—illegally, as it turned out, under the terms of the 1984 Boland Amendment—to the anti-Sandanista contras of Nicaragua. If President Reagan was directly involved, he could easily be impeached.

Meese had added, however, that the entire operation had been run by one man working on his own in the White House basement, a "loose cannon," as Meese put it, named Oliver North. . . .

North had been fired. His boss, National Security Advisor John Poindexter, had resigned, but ongoing investigations by Congress and a special prosecutor were turning up new pieces of the story daily, including involvement by the NSC, the CIA, and members of the president's cabinet, including Vice President Bush, a former CIA director. It looked like North was going to be subpoenaed to testify before Congress soon.

The fact that North still had security clearance for this place, that he was here in the Pentagon at all, spoke volumes.

The Marine must have read the thoughts behind Gordon's eyes. "Operation Free Sanction has been in the works since last year," he said. "I wasn't going to jump ship *now*! Not with so much at stake. . . ."

"Free Sanction?"

"Your plan, Commander," a Navy captain, whose name was Rafferty, said. He pointed at the big-screen display. "It's going down as we speak."

Gordon looked at the screen. His mouth gaped. There, in green light of varying shades, was an aerial view of rugged terrain, and a massive building or fortification of some kind. He could see people there, too, dozens of them inside the big structure . . . many of them visible *through* the walls and roofs of interior buildings.

And in the bottom left corner of the screen, fourteen men, heavily armed, were just moving into view.

"Ah, Starbase, Alfa," a voice said from a wall speaker. It sounded like the man was whispering, but the volume, kicked high, turned the whisper to a near shout. "In position, Waypoint Three. Objective in sight."

"Roger that, Alfa," an Army major with a communications headset said, cupping his needle mike. "You are go for execute."

"Starbase, Alfa, copy."

"My God," Gordon said, awed. "This is really happening? Right now?"

"It's happening," North said. "Welcome to the Bekaa Valley, Commander. You might not have known it, but you . . . and *they* are about to make history tonight!"

SEAL Special Strike Force
Alfa Platoon, SEAL Team Two
Al Biqa, Lebanon
0215 hours local time (Greenwich + 2)

"My God," Lieutenant (j.g.) Kenneth Randall said, peering through the night-sight binoculars at the mammoth construction squatting on the hillside a hundred meters ahead. "It's a frigging fortress."

He'd known what it would look like, thanks to the training runs, but seeing it here, for real . . . it brooded over the Bekaa Valley like a squat, ancient gray monster.

"It was, once," Lieutenant Gerald Gallagher whispered beside him. "The Ottoman Turks built the place a hundred fifty years ago. It's seen better days, though."

"Yeah," MM1 Rich Bowman said from nearby. "Nothing like an Israeli air strike to turn a classy neighborhood into a dump."

Randall scanned the structure a moment more, taking in

the chips, gouges, and craters in those massive stone walls. A sentry stood on the wall, cupping his hands as he lit a cigarette. A stiff wind was blowing in from the Med, twenty-five miles away, beyond the saw-toothed bulk of the Lebanon Mountains to the west. Somewhere in the distance, another sentry called out a challenge, and the grinding and rattle of an ancient truck rose from the dirt road winding up the hill to Al Kufayr. The scene was calm . . . but charged with hidden tension, a bomb with a fast-burning fuze.

He handed the binoculars back to Gallagher, and pulled his night-vision goggles down over his paint-blackened face. The goggles restricted his view somewhat, cutting off his peripheral vision, but they enabled him to see the pitch-black of a moonless, overcast night painted in vivid shades of yellow and green.

The three Navy SEALs lay on a ridgetop south of the compound. At their backs, the rest of Alfa Platoon, eleven more men in black combat dress, black face paint, and black wool watch caps crouched or lay in a wide perimeter, facing out in all directions.

Gallagher studied the walls a moment longer through the binoculars. "Okay. Everything looks just as advertised. I don't see a reason for an abort now."

"I concur, Wheel," Randall said.

"Yeah, let's take the sons of bitches down," Bowman added.

"Okay, as we rehearsed it, then. Plan Dagger. We secure the walls and main gate together. First Squad grabs the approaches and the main building, and sets overwatch on the road. Second Squad goes in and finds the packages. Let's do it!"

This is it, Randall thought, heart hammering beneath Kevlar vest and equipment-laden combat harness as he made his way back to the center of the perimeter, and signaled Squad Two to join him. *This is what it's all been about.* . . .

They'd been practicing this op for six weeks, ever since

word had come down from G2 that four of the Mideast
hostages were being held in a couple of small rooms inside
the war-torn Ottoman fort deep in the Bekaa Valley of southeastern Lebanon. They'd studied satellite and recon aircraft
photos of the objective, including high-penetration IR shots
that peered down right through the wood and straw or clay
shingle roofs of some of the structures. They'd practiced
with a mock-up of the fort on a sand table behind the SEAL
Two barracks at Norfolk. Then they'd practiced in killing
house mock-ups, first at Norfolk, and later at the big Special
Operations Command compound at Fort Bragg. They'd
practiced a dozen different possible scenarios and deployments; the one they were using now, Dagger, was one of
three honed to perfection; the other two were in place as
backups, should the unexpected turn up. The great and terrible Murphy was always very much a part of these operations, a god of war to be feared, respected, and placated with
backup plans and assets held in reserve.

Unfortunately, Alfa Platoon had damned little riding in reserve.

Randall led the six men in his squad down the north face
of the ridge, keeping to the black night-shadow of boulder
and hillside. BMC Donald Hughes, QM1 Charles Goddard,
GM1 Lawrence Kyzinski, GM2 Barry Neubauer, ET3
James McKenna, and MN3 Sidney James followed at ten-
meter intervals, keeping well spread apart, moving silently
into the gully south of the objective.

Kyzinski had point, moving ahead of the group with silent
steps across the rocky ground. He stopped suddenly, hand
held high. His fingers moved in the code SEALs used under
silent op conditions—*two men . . . armed . . . that way . . .
twenty meters*.

Randall had already slung his primary weapon and drawn
his pistol, an H&K USSOCOM-issue .45, muzzle-heavy
with its blunt sound suppressor screwed onto the barrel. As
he moved up to take position next to Kyzinski, he could
make out the yellow-white-green shapes of two Palestinian

sentries just ahead. "Starbase," he whispered into his needle mike. "Alfa Two. We've got two tangos. Taking them down."

"Roger that, Alfa Two," a voice crackled in his ear. "You are weapons free. Take 'em out."

Randall grimaced. He didn't like this op-to-HQ immediacy, didn't like the feeling that a bunch of stars and suits and prima donnas back in the Pentagon were literally looking down over his shoulder.

He exchanged hand signals with Kyzinski; he would take the one on the left, Kyzinski the one on the right. They crept forward, as silent as death.

A sudden flare of white light dazzled Randall's night optics. One of the Palestinians had just struck a match, and was cupping it to light the other's cigarette. Side by side, Randall and Kyzinski approached swiftly now, crouched low. At ten meters, Randall dropped to one knee, took careful aim, and squeezed the trigger twice, a double tap, the soft hisses of his shots mixed with Kyzynski's quick one-two. One sentry coughed and groaned; the other looked startled and opened his mouth to scream, but only blood, black in the night-vision goggles, came forth. Both men collapsed in a huddle, bodies tangled with one another in a macabre embrace.

Kyzinski made sure both were dead with his Mark I dive knife; a covert op deep in enemy territory was no place for chivalry. Ahead, the ground rose steeply beneath the brooding walls, green-lit, of the fortress. "Alfa Two, two tangos down," Randall reported. South gully clear."

"Copy that, Alfa Two," Starbase said. The speaker had an annoying nasal twang to his voice. "We have IR traces on one sentry on the south wall and another in the southeast tower. You're clear to move in to Objective Nevada."

"Copy."

Idiots, he thought, as he started working his way up the slope. This was step-by-step micromanagement at its worst and, so far as Randall was concerned, a recipe for certain disaster.

The Bunker
Pentagon Sub-Level 3
Alexandria, Virginia
1925 hours, EST (Greenwich −5)

"Where are these pictures coming from?" Gordon wanted to know. "I've never seen anything like this."

At the touch of a few keys on a keyboard, the technicians at the big display console could zoom in on any part of the scene being shot from overhead, with a close-up tight enough to pick out details of the SEAL Team's weapons, or the insectlike masks of their LI goggles. A touch of another key actually identified individual men by name and rank, or tagged others of the ghostly green figures as "Unknown, presumed hostile."

The camera view drifted slightly as he watched, but would occasionally recenter itself on the fortress from a slightly different angle, as though it were circling the compound counterclockwise. He didn't know of any spy satellites that could do that; most spysats passed overhead rather quickly, with, at best, five or ten minutes above the horizon. This camera seemed to be loitering somewhere in the sky overhead.

"Believe me," Goldman whispered, in response to his question, "you *don't* want to know."

But Gordon had already decided that the camera platform must be a high-stealth recon aircraft of some kind, rather than a satellite in orbit. The name "Aurora" flashed through his thoughts. There'd been lots of rumors lately of a whole new generation of reconnaissance aircraft coming on-line to replace the now-ancient technology of the U-2 and the remarkable Mach-3+ SR-71 Blackbird. Dubbed "Aurora" from a classified document mistakenly released to Congress and public scrutiny, the new aircraft were rumored to be so stealthy they were all but invisible, powered by a whole new type of propulsion plant that sounded more like magic than technology, and so black-project secret that their very existence would likely be denied for decades to come. Whatever they were called, it probably wasn't Aurora any longer.

No, Goldman was right. He didn't want to know about things like that.

He watched as one group of seven SEALs scrambled up the south wall of the fortress, a low and bomb-damaged barrier only about ten feet high, while another group of five slipped around the west side to approach the front gate in the north. Another Hezbollah sentry, standing on the south wall, was taken down, this time by someone wielding a knife from behind. Gordon winced as the blade slashed; blood, glowing hot yellow under IR imagery, stained the front of the Hezbollah guerrilla's uniform. The SEAL lowered the corpse to the stone surface of the parapet walk.

Frank Gordon was a trained and experienced military officer, used to the idea of sudden death on the battlefield. But his direct exposure had been from the combat command center of a submarine, where the enemy was represented as a sonar target designated Sierra and a number. He'd never seen a man killed before . . . certainly not taken from behind with the sweep of one arm, and instantly killed with a quick thrust-and-slice of a razor-edged combat knife. It was . . . disconcerting.

"This is the Bekaa Valley?" Gordon asked, trying to keep his thoughts from morbidly fastening on the sprawled corpse on the screen. "That's a hell of a long way inland. How'd you insert them. HALO?"

"No," North said. "Too risky. We took advantage of the fact that our Israeli friends have complete air superiority over southern Lebanon. A word to our counterparts with Israeli Military Intelligence, and they let us fly three Sea Kings off the *Nimitz*, bringing them in nape-of-the-earth right along the Lebanon-Israel border."

"The ragheads think the choppers are Israeli," an Army colonel said, "*if* they see them at all."

"The teams were put down in open country north of Marj'Uyun three hours ago," North explained, "at an LZ secured by a Ranger pathfinder team that infiltrated yesterday. They made their way on foot from there, about seven miles over some pretty rough terrain. Those SEAL guys are damned impressive."

"Almost as good as Marines, eh, Ollie?" Captain Rafferty said. They chuckled.

"E and E?" Gordon asked.

"Primary extraction point is right down the hill from Al Kufayr," North told him. "They call in the choppers when they have the package and the LZ is secure. Secondary LZ in case of trouble is two miles south, near Hasbayya. And they can always infiltrate through into Israel, and make contact with our people there."

"So . . . I assume the 'package' is a hostage."

"At least two hostages, maybe more," the Army colonel said. "Good, solid intel on this one."

"Good, solid intel" was always the big problem in this sort of op. In this case, it almost had to be from HUMINT—human intelligence—assets on the ground at the objective; a satellite or high-tech spy plane couldn't ID hostages in a basement prison cell.

Something bothered Gordon, though. "What about reprisals? There are twenty-four hostages, now. If you rescue two, won't the others suffer for it?"

"These are *important* hostages, Commander," Rafferty replied. "We get them out, we'll be able to bring pressure to bear on the Hezbollah terrorists who grabbed them. They won't dare hurt the others, for fear of a bad world press, and because we'll demonstrate our ability to hit them where it hurts, no matter where they hide."

Which left Gordon more bothered than before. *Important* hostages? What the hell were the criteria for determining which captives were important, which ones were not? As for bringing pressure to bear on their captors, that sounded like sheer wishful thinking. Hezbollah was just as likely to shoot a few of the prisoners still in their keeping, just to warn the United States not to try these sorts of cowboy tactics again.

Gordon was beginning to get a bad, bad feeling about the whole situation.

Saturday, 27 June 1987

SEAL Special Strike Force
Alfa Platoon, SEAL Team Two
Al Biqa, Lebanon
0232 hours local time (Greenwich +2)

Randall was getting a distinctly bad feeling about this situation. He'd been on field ops often enough in his SEAL career to learn to trust instinct, that eerie sixth sense combat vets developed which told them when things were going down smooth, and when the op was turning into a cluster fuck. The rest of Second Squad had boosted one another up the ten-foot stone wall, and after taking out the sentry on the parapet, they'd slipped down into the enclosed courtyard beyond.

At the southeast corner of the compound, a ramshackle tower of tree trunks and planks rose twenty feet above the top of the wall. A Hezbollah gunman stood there, staring with a most unmilitary lack of interest off toward the east, cradling his AK-47. He'd taken no notice of the SEALs slipping over the wall almost literally under his nose, but it was time to guarantee that he remain oblivious to the stealthy infiltration. "Longarm, Alfa Two," Randall called, switching channels. "Gunman in the south tower. Time to reach out and touch someone."

"Copy, Alfa Two," GM2 Hernendez said. "On the way."

Hernendez and ET3 Lederer, the two remaining members of First Squad, were posted atop a hillside nearly a mile to the south. Hernendez was the platoon sniper, armed with a Barrett .50 and a light-intensifier scope that let him look into a target's eyes at two thousand yards. At that range, they never heard the shot when it was fired, save for the short, sharp crack of the bullet's sonic boom. It sounded like a falling rock or a bottle breaking against stone, not like a gunshot at all. The tower sentry's chest simply exploded suddenly in a spray of black, and the man's body slumped out of sight.

A Hezbollah guerrilla emerged from a warehouse, looking about as though searching for the source of the unusual sound. "Youssef!" he called. "Youssef, *en*—!" Neubauer took aim with his .45 and softly double-tapped the man down.

The SEALs rushed forward, cutting down three more men along the way. Four checked inside the warehouse while the other three stood guard outside. "Warehouse clear!" Kyzinski called, emerging a moment later. "Two more tangos down. Moving!"

"Alfa Two, Alfa One," Gallagher's voice said. "Front gate secure. Three down."

"Alfa, Starbase," another voice, the annoying one, said. "Walls and courtyard are clear. Alfa Two proceed to Objective Texas."

"Copy. Two moving."

A number of buildings and structures were scattered about the fortress courtyard, from the warehouse to canvas tents. Objective Texas was a large, two-story building growing out of the western wall, its roof stripped away by a recent air strike. The assumption was that the local Hezbollah militia had their headquarters here . . . and that there would be a basement or secure rooms inside where captives might be safely held.

"Alfa Two, Starbase. We have what looks like four guards in the big room behind the front door of Objective Texas. Suggest you check there for the cellar entrance."

"Copy, Starbase."

A swarthy, bearded man in crisp fatigues and a black beret stepped out of the front door and onto the building's front veranda, his eyes widening as he saw four black-garbed figures rushing toward him across the dimly lit courtyard. "*Allah!*" he cried . . . and then the word caught in his throat as a volley of sound-suppressed .45 rounds ripped into his body.

Randall holstered his pistol and slid his primary weapon off his shoulder. Holding the H&K SD5 high on his shoulder, he advanced up the steps and past the body of the fallen officer, keeping the heavy sound-suppressor muzzle aimed at the screen door.

A part of his mind noted that the dead man wore a more formal uniform than most of the Hezbollah guerrillas, and the silver badge on his beret. Syrian army, almost certainly . . . and that was *not* good.

Uniform details would not be visible to the airborne IR cameras transmitting the scene to Starbase. Randall wasn't going to tell them, not now. All the SEALs needed was an abort order from nervous Pentagon REMFs.

Don Hughes—"Runcible"—pulled the door open and Sid James and Goddard rolled through, SD5s held high, tight, and ready. Randall heard the fast-triggered semiauto bursts from their weapons as he followed, entering the big, stone-walled entryway as three more Syrians, soldiers in fatigues and berets like the officers outside, were still falling. Two flanked a massive wooden door at the far side of the room, collapsing in bloodied, choking heaps. Weapons ready, Randall and Kyzinski moved forward. . . .

The Bunker
Pentagon Sub-Level 3
Alexandria, Virginia
1933 hours, EST (Greenwich –5)

"Are you sure we're just dealing with Hezbollah here?" Gordon asked, watching as the green-lit figures of the SEALs spilled through the main door to the big house. "The Syrians have been keeping a pretty strong presence throughout the Bekaa Valley lately."

"The nearest Syrian encampment is ten miles up the road, toward Rashayya," Goldman said. "There might be Syrian observers or liaisons at the objective, sure, but our intelligence sources on the ground say no. The guerrillas have been working on their own."

"The Syrians don't want to be linked to Hezbollah, remember," Colonel North said. "They were brought in to control the guerrillas in the first place."

"Yeah," Goldman said. "That's their story, and they're sticking with it."

Civil war had been raging in Lebanon for ten years. By now, dozens of factions were going at one another, though the main struggle was between the Christian right-wing militia and the Shi'ite fundamentalist guerrillas of the Party of God.

Within the Bekaa Valley of southeastern Lebanon, though, it was the Syrians who were most powerful, at least on the ground. They'd been invited in, at least in a theoretical sense, by the Christian government in Beirut, though everyone accepted that the Syrians had all but ordered the Lebanese parliament to send the request in the first place. Obviously, the Syrians were concerned about a major war on their southwestern border; historically, Lebanon had always been within their political sphere of influence.

A major concern among Western intelligence agencies, though, was whether the Syrians were suppressing the Hezbollah factions in the territory under their control . . . or cooperating with them. Certainly, the Syrians hadn't been able to help with finding the hostages held by the fundamentalist militias. The question was whether they were even trying.

"The Hezbollans are Shi'ite, remember," the colonel said. "The Syrians are Sunni, and the government is secular. The militia would never cooperate with them."

Gordon had his own thoughts about that, but kept them to himself. People were people, not machines and not ciphers, and the most fanatic of Shi'ite fundamentalists could be pragmatic when the situation called for it.

"Uh-oh," a technician at a nearby console said. "Colonel? Zoom back to check the north road."

The moving green figures on the screen dwindled to dots as the view expanded to take in not only the rectilinear shape of the fortress, but the rugged hills and the narrow, S-curve of a dirt road leading to the front gate. A line of vehicles, engine blocks glowing white-hot under infrared, was coming up that road. Gordon could make out the distinctive shape of a Russian-made BDRM, leading two pickup trucks, a flatbed piled high with troops, and a pair of canvas-covered deuce-and-a-halfs.

"Alfa, Alfa, this is Starbase," the technician said. "You have company on the way, north road. ETA . . . five minutes."

"Copy." The reply was flat, without emotion. Things were starting to go to hell now with startling speed.

"Estimate sixty troops and one piece of wheeled armor. Looks like a BDRM-60."

"Starbase, Alfa. You people are just full of good—"

The voice was cut off by a sudden, ripping blast of sound, as unsilenced machine guns opened up. . . .

SEAL Special Strike Force
Alfa Platoon, SEAL Team Two
Objective Texas
Al Biqa, Lebanon
0233 hours local time (Greenwich + 2)

Randall heard the sudden burst of automatic gunfire from somewhere outside.

"Alfa Two, Starbase!" the voice called over the tactical channel. "Alfa One is compromised! Abort the mission! I say again, abort the mission!"

"Like fuck," Randall said. He slammed back to the wall next to the basement door. "Kizzy!" He shouted, pulling a flashbang from a combat-vest pouch. "Locked door! Let's have your Masterkey!"

Micromanagement. It was the bane of military operations, especially within the highly technical, highly specialized world of covert operations.

In World War II, a general would send his battalions in, following a plan outlined through meticulously written battle orders, but the maxim that no plan survived contact with the enemy still held true. As the battle gelled, as friendly forces blundered into those of the enemy, plans might be adjusted, with contingency plans called into play or reserves shifted to meet an unexpected enemy deployment, but battlefield communications were still in their infancy. All frontline communications depended on primitive radio equipment with a range of only a few miles and subject to enemy jamming or atmospheric interference, or on telephone lines vulnerable to enemy patrols or random artillery hits.

The older SEALs, the retired members of the Teams, especially, still talked about Vietnam, when SEALs operated with almost complete independence . . . and how when they ran into official red tape, they'd pulled an UNODIR.

When they'd decided they needed to pull a particularly risky op—gather some vital intelligence in a VC-infested area, say—and there was a real possibility that some REMF farther up the chain of command would say no, some of the SEALs had taken to writing up their plans headed up by the words UNLESS OTHERWISE DIRECTED . . . "UNODIR." The plan would then be sent to HQ, but too late for a refusal to come back down the chain. Some SEALs would have gone out, pulled off the op, and returned before their more cautious superiors could even draft a reply.

That sort of shoot-from-the-hip operating just didn't fly these days. Communications had improved dramatically in the decade and a half since Vietnam. The SEALs not only had headset radio communications with everyone in the field unit, they had a satcom link to assets offshore that could launch air strikes, call in a battleship salvo, or send in rescue helicopters. And on some ops, the sensitive and high-risk missions like this one, a special channel had been set up to allow Washington not only to eavesdrop, but to kibitz.

The debacle at Desert One, during the attempt to rescue American hostages held in Tehran, was still discussed by field operators, sometimes in hushed tones. That had been the night when General Charlie Beckwith, commanding the rescue force code-named Eagle's Claw, had pretended that he was having radio trouble so that he could make his own decision based on what he was experiencing at the site. On the other end of that "malfunctioning" communications link had been members of the Joint Chiefs of Staff and the commander in chief himself, President Carter.

In a sense, General Beckwith's actions had been a replay of Nelson's, at the Battle of Copenhagen almost two centuries before. When Sir Hyde Parker, Nelson's commanding officer at Copenhagen, had used signal flags to order him to break off in the middle of the fight, he'd held his telescope to his blind eye and calmly stated that he saw no signal. . . .

Sometimes, the guy on the ground at the knife's point was the only one who could call it, and he didn't need second-guessing by swivel-chair REMFs.

Kyzinski hurried up to the locked door. His primary weapon was an M-4 carbine—smaller cousin of the M-16—with a highly modified Remington 860 shotgun mounted underneath the carbine's barrel ahead of the curved, banana-clip magazine. He pointed the weapon at the door's lock and squeezed the trigger. The shotgun blast rang off the stone walls; the sixteen-ounce slug smashed through lock and doorknob, splintering the wood beneath. The door flew open and Randall tossed the flashbang through. Both SEALs turned away as the basement beyond flared and dazzled, for an instant brighter than the sun, and a chain of seven deafening explosions thundered from below.

Randall was first down the stone steps. A Hezbollah guerrilla groped blindly on hands and knees. The SEAL put two rounds through his skull, then scanned the rest of the basement. It was filled with crates, barrels, and piles of canvas, but two more solid-looking doors sat side by side in the west wall.

Kyzinski racked the slide on his Masterkey shotgun and took out the lock on the door to the left. Randall banged through the door into the tiny room beyond. . . .

Empty. Horrifyingly, disappointingly, infuriatingly empty.

A single straight-backed chair lay on its side in the middle of the bare stone floor. In one corner was a doubled-over mattress, large rents leaking white ticking, and a glazed stoneware jar, a honeypot, possibly, rested in one corner. A naked bulb dangled from the high ceiling. The bare, windowless room reeked of urine, sweat, and vomit.

He could *feel* the room's last occupants, but there was no one there now.

Another shotgun blast echoed from next door. An instant later, Kyzinski joined him. "Dry hole, sir. *Someone* was being held here, and not too long ago, either. . . ."

"So I see." Kneeling by the wall, he reached out and lightly touched some crude scratch marks on the stone. Someone had used a small chunk of rock, or an eating utensil, possibly, to scratch a terse handful of numerals and letters.

"Let's get the hell out of here, Kizzy. There's no one home. No one we want to meet, anyway."

"Aye aye, sir!"

They pounded back up the stairs, then out the front door, ducking low as they emerged into the night.

Gunfire stuttered and cracked, as muzzle flashes stabbed from the darkness. "Alfa Two, Alfa One!" Gallagher called over the tactical channel. "We've got tangos coming from the west buildings!"

"Alfa Leader, this is Alfa Two," Randall called over the command channel, now that his Motorola was out of the stone-bound basement. "Dry hole. The packages are not here, repeat, not here."

"Copy, Alfa Two," Gallagher replied. "Rendezvous at Objective Kentucky."

Kentucky was the front gate, but that was going to be a problem. More and more guerrillas were emerging from cover, laying down a steady, vicious fire that swept the open courtyard. A green-lit figure moved behind a pile of wooden crates twelve meters away, trying to get a good position under cover from which to open fire. Randall flicked the selector on his H&K to full auto and hosed the crates, sending splinters and fragments hurtling as near-silent 9mm rounds sliced through them. AK-47 rifles, still wrapped in plastic and Cosmoline, spilled onto the ground, as the lurking Hezbollah gunman toppled out from behind his less-than-adequate shelter and lay shrieking on the ground.

Randall tapped a mercy round into the man's head as he ran past.

"Alfa, Starbase," the command channel voice called. "You've got shooters on the wall, shooters on the wall to the west!"

"Tell us something we *don't* know," Kyzinski replied.

"Damn it, Starbase, talk to us when we're not busy," Gallagher added. An explosion lit up the darkness.

Randall zigzagged across the courtyard toward the front gate, dropping to cover behind a stack of oil drums as bullets snapped and sang above his head. Rising, he aimed at a muzzle flash on the west wall and sent a burst winging toward it. "Come on, Ski!" he called over the tactical channel.

"Cover fire!" Kyzinski called back. "Moving!"

Kyzinski dashed across the courtyard as Randall put down a covering fire, driving two tango gunmen in the west to the ground. On the south wall, a Hezbollah tango suddenly stood on tiptoe, then toppled over, cut down by an unheard bullet. Hernendez and Lederer were still on guard, picking off tangos when they could get a clear shot.

At the front gate, at his back, he heard the loud, shrill whoosh of a LAW being fired, followed an instant later by a loud explosion. Glancing back, he saw the fireball, dazzling against the night, momentarily overwhelming his night-sight optics. The tango convoy with the BDRM-60 must have reached the top of the hill; QM2 Van Dorn had just taken it out with his Light Antitank Weapon, a single-shot, shoulder-launched weapon effective against all but the heaviest armor.

He turned back as Kyzinski dropped to cover behind the oil drums. "Getting a mite hot out tonight," Ski observed, dropping a dry magazine and snapping home a fresh one.

"Just a bit." Randall loosed a string of three-round bursts at muzzle flashes and green shadows. Some of the tangos were using red tracer ball ammunition, which helped pinpoint their positions.

It also confirmed how damned many there were of them. Where were all these people coming from? Still firing, he began backing toward the fortress's main gate. Kyzinski and Hughes covered him.

"Starbase, Alfa leader," Gallagher's voice called. "It's a trap! There are no packages, repeat, no packages for pickup, and we are encountering heavy force!"

"Alfa, Starbase. Copy. Abort the mission. Proceed to primary extraction point for pickup and evacuation."

Randall reached Gallagher's position, sheltered behind a

pile of rubble and sandbags. The gate was wide-open, the BDRM and a canvas-covered truck burning wildly in the night outside.

"Ah, that's negative on primary LZ, Starbase." Gallagher was shouting now, as a heavy machine gun opened up somewhere out there in the night. "We have Sierra Alfas crawling all over it! We are falling back to secondary LZ for extraction. I say again, we are proceeding to LZ Sacramento for pick-up. Over!"

"Copy that, Alfa Leader. Disengage and evade to LZ Sacramento for extraction."

The primary LZ, designated LZ Green Bay and designed to facilitate pickup with rescued hostages in tow, was only a few hundred yards north of the fort, on a level area partway down the hill, but Randall could see what Gallagher had been talking about. The whole north side of the hill was alive with muzzle flashes and moving figures.

Sierra Alfas. That was the phonetic code name for Syrian Army troops. They were going to just *love* that back in Washington.

"We need air cover here," Gallagher went on, consulting a small, plastic map pulled from his pocket. "Coordinates one-seven-three-five-five by two-zero-zero-seven-one-niner!"

"Roger that, Alfa. We'll pass it up the line."

Pass it up the line. Meaning that the Pentagon REMFs would be chewing over the SEALs' request for an air strike.

An explosion detonated just outside the gate . . . probably a rocket-propelled grenade.

"We're not getting out that way," Gallagher said, "and we'd better not sit on our asses waiting for the folks back home to bail us out."

"Over the wall?" Randall asked.

"That's a roger. Same way we came in." Gallagher touched his microphone. "Alfa Team, Alfa Leader! We're going over the south wall! First Squad provide cover. Second Squad, go! Rendezvous at LZ Sacramento! Let's do it!"

"Let's go, Alfa Two," Randall added. "South wall. Watch your fire, Longarm, we're coming over the top."

"Copy, Alfa Two," Hernendez replied. "We're watching for you."

SEAL extraction tactics had been worked out through years of experience, and constant training, and they began putting those lessons into practice now.

The Bunker
Pentagon Sub-Level 3
Alexandria, Virginia
1937 hours, EST (Greenwich −5)

"A dry hole!" Captain Rafferty exclaimed. "How the hell did that happen?"

"Bad intel," North suggested. "Wouldn't be the first time."

"We didn't pull all of this together for another Son Tay, damn it!" an Army general exclaimed.

Son Tay was the prison camp north of Hanoi raided by Army Special Forces in 1972 in order to free American POWs being held there. The raid was a brilliant and unqualified success. The only problem was that the prisoners weren't there; they'd been moved not long before, possibly because someone in Saigon had talked.

"Well you don't need to blame Intelligence," a man in a dark, civilian suit said, sounding angry. "We had good solid intel on this one. One-A! The best there is!"

"Yeah," another suit said. "Maybe it's the conception and planning this time."

"Did you hear that guy, Dean?" the general said. "Sierra Alfas. That's Syrian regular Army, goddammit! They weren't supposed to be within ten kilometers of the objective! What the hell went wrong?"

"Gentlemen," Admiral Goldman said, "I think we can de-fer the traditional postop recriminations until after we get our people out of there."

"What about their air cover request, sir?" Captain Rafferty wanted to know. "They're standing by with a full alfa strike on the *Nimitz*, hot and ready to go!" An "alfa strike" was the general term for a full carrier-borne attack against any shore target.

"That really isn't advisable at this juncture," the first civilian said. "If we needed to protect our helicopters coming out, yes . . . but we can't afford to have this come out now, and an air strike would guarantee that it *would* come out."

The general chuckled, a grim and humorless sound. "It's a little late to worry about ass covering now, isn't it, Dean?"

"It's not ass covering. We have to think of the hostages. A failed rescue attempt is bad enough. If we bomb them, they're just liable to take it out on our people."

And wouldn't they have done the same if we'd been successful? Gordon wondered. *Does this make any sense at all?*

But he said nothing. Right now, the men in that Pentagon basement room were more concerned about fixing blame, salvaging careers, and controlling damage than they were about the SEALs now fighting for their lives in southern Lebanon.

"We've got to do something about those SEALs, though," North said, his boyish face creased with worry. "Damage control later. We've got to get them out *now*!"

Rafferty shrugged. "We're doing all that can be done, Colonel. We'll dispatch choppers off the *Nimitz* to pick them up at the secondary extraction site. But it's going to be up to them to get there."

"That might be a bit easier if you give them the air strike they called for," Gordon said, breaking his silence.

"Eh?" the captain asked, turning to look at him. "What's that?"

"Send in that air strike, sir. That'll keep the bad guys off their backs long enough for them to get to where they need to go."

"I don't believe we asked for your opinion, Commander," the general said.

"He's right," Goldman said. "Damn it, you can't abandon those people."

"The political risks are unacceptable."

"So how did you get the SEALs in?" Gordon asked Goldman, whispering.

"We took advantage of the unstable politics in the region, actually. The Israelis hold undisputed control of the airspace over southern Lebanon, from their border all the way to Beirut, sixty miles up the coast. Their troops held a southern strip of Lebanon as well, a security zone designed to keep Palestinian terrorists from shelling Israeli towns and kibbutzim from across the border. We made an under-the-table deal with Israeli intelligence to fly three Sea Kings into the Bekaa Valley at hedge-clipping height. The locals will assume the helos are Israeli."

"Cute. And they get the blame for the firefight and any breakage?"

"Exactly. That sort of skirmishing goes on all the time in there."

"But an air strike off the *Nimitz* would give the game away. Shit."

"As you say, Commander. Shit."

Gordon watched the fight on the big display, as running green figures moved among white flashes in an eerie silence punctuated by bursts of radio transmissions.

"*Alfa Team, Alfa Leader! We're going over the south wall! First Squad provide cover. Second Squad, go! Rendezvous at LZ Sacramento! Let's do it!*"

"*Let's go, Alfa Two. South wall. Watch your fire, Long-arm, we're coming over the top.*"

"*Copy, Alfa Two. We're watching for you.*"

How long, Gordon wondered, before the Syrians sent in reinforcements and the game really got hot?

Saturday, 27 June 1987

**SEAL Special Strike Force
Alfa Platoon, SEAL Team Two
Al Biqa, Lebanon
0240 hours local time (Greenwich + 2)**

"Time to get the hell out of Dodge," Randall said as he reached the southern rampart and crouched beside the head-shattered body of a Hezbollah militiaman, weapon at the ready.

"I could live with that, sir," GM2 Neubauer told him. Together, they dropped over the southern wall of the fortress and onto the rocky ground outside as red-and-yellow tracers flashed across the night, and the sky lit up with explosions, and the rest of Second Squad followed close behind. Randall and Neubauer dropped to the ground twenty meters from the loom of the fortress wall, aiming their weapons at it as the rest of Second Squad filed south between them, crouched low and moving fast.

QM1 Goddard and ET3 McKenna paired off and took up an overwatch position twenty meters farther south.

"Set!" McKenna called over the tactical channel. "Go!"

"Moving," Randall replied, and he and Neubauer rose from the ground and made a low-stooped run to the south, passing Goddard's and McKenna's positions just as McKenna loosed a pair of quick, sharp, three-round bursts at bad guys coming over the wall. Someone screamed in the night, the sound much larger than the thuttering hiss of McKenna's sound-suppressed MP5SD.

With a close-knit and practiced coordination reminiscent of a meticulously choreographed dance, the SEALs leapfrogged back into the valley south of the fortress, then worked their way down the valley, always careful that at each moment, at least two of them were covering the withdrawal of the others. Once, a pair of Hezbollah gunmen tried rushing the group, shouting in Arabic as they bounced down the valley wall. Goddard and McKenna were on guard at the time, catching the men with a pair of hissing, three-round bursts that tripped both attackers and sent them tumbling heels-over-head all the way to the valley floor.

Clear of hostile pursuit, they reached Point Tucson, their first E&E waypoint, a tangle of boulders where the valley opened onto a broad, sloping plain. They dropped into a defensive perimeter, holding their position until First Squad could join them. Minutes dragged past, an agony of waiting, while gunfire continued to bang and thunder from the direction of the fortress.

Abruptly, the voice of Chief Matthew Anderson came over the tactical channel. "Man down, we have a man down!"

"Alfa, Starbase. Please clarify," the nasal voice said.

"Alfa Two, Alfa One," Anderson said, ignoring the call from Starbase. "The Wheel is down, I say again, the Wheel is down!"

"The Wheel" was SEAL slang for the head honcho, the man in charge. Lieutenant Gallagher had been hit.

"Alfa One, this is Two," Randall said after a moment, when no further information was forthcoming. "One, this is Two. Do you copy? Over."

Still there was no answer, and he had to repeat the call.

"Two, One!" Anderson's voice came back, a bit shrill with excitement, or something worse. "We've got a problem."

In clipped, tight tones, Anderson described the situation. The five men of First Squad had cleared the fortress moments after Second, but a sudden rush of Syrian troops and Hezbollah militia had cut them off, forcing them to move northeast up the valley, instead of southwest. They'd reached a road, where more Syrians had cut them off, blocking their planned escape over the south ridge and back toward Waypoint Tucson. Gallagher had been hit by machine-gun fire from the back of a small truck as they'd tried to move south across the road.

"We have two men down, now," Anderson continued. "Spiney took a round in the side. We're pinned in a culvert and can't move. Ammo critical. Over!"

Randall chewed that one over for a moment. He was responsible for Second Squad, for getting them clear of the AO and safely to LZ Bravo for the rendezvous with Seahawk One and an emergency dust-off.

Essentially he had three choices. He could lead Second Squad to Bravo and pray to hell First Squad made it clear, possibly with intervention from Starbase and the Navy assets offshore. Or he could send a couple of men to help, while leading the rest to Bravo.

Or he could go back and help First Squad himself, possibly with one volunteer . . . scratch that, *definitely* with one volunteer, so they could watch each other's backs.

His first responsibility was to the men of Second Squad, the men under his command. But they were clear of the Area of Operations, now, and it didn't look like the bad guys had their scent. Not yet, anyway.

A quick call over the tactical channel verified that Lederer and Hernendez were already clear of the combat area and were well on their way to LZ Bravo. That left five men in First Squad trapped by the road, two of them wounded.

"I need someone to come with me to give First a hand," he

told the others. Six hands went up, green in the glow of his night optics.

"McKenna," he said. ET3 James McKenna spoke excellent Arabic, better than Randall's own. "Chief?"

"Sir," Chief Hughes said.

"Get 'em all to Bravo. You've got the maps and the glow sticks." Chemical light sticks would guide the Navy choppers in for the dust-off.

"Aye aye, sir," Chief Hughes replied. "What about you?"

"We'll join you if we can . . . but don't hold up the show for us. If the choppers come in, you mount up and get the hell out. There's more than one way out of this damned country." He was thinking of slipping south—just a few miles—across the border. They'd have to be damned careful about drawing fire; Israeli sentries were notoriously trigger-happy. Still, the day a team of Navy SEALs couldn't invisibly slip across just about any border in the world was the day to pack it in for Navy Special Warfare.

"One, Two," he called on tactical. "Hang tight. Help is on the way."

"Roger that, Two. We'll be here."

"Alfa Two, this is Starbase," he heard in his headset. "Two, Starbase. Please advise of your intentions, over."

He ignored the voice. "Let's move out, Chief."

"Aye aye, sir!"

Keeping low, Randall and McKenna slipped off into the night.

The Bunker
Pentagon Sub-Level 3
Alexandria, Virginia
1958 hours, EST (Greenwich –5)

"Damn it!" General Childess, one of the senior Army officers, said. "What the hell are they doing?"

"Splitting up, looks like," Rafferty replied. He sounded excited, as though he were watching an especially thrilling ball game. "Two men going north to help First Squad, the rest hightailing it for LZ Bravo."

"That's suicide. Call them back!"

You're the one who decided not to send in the air cover, asshole, Gordon thought with a viciously savored righteousness.

"I don't think that's practical," Colonel North said. "We have to let our people on the ground decide how best to handle this."

"Not when *we* have the technology," Childess said. "Not when we know what's best." Somehow, though, he didn't sound entirely convinced.

"The first rule of the SEALs, sir," Gordon said quietly. He'd known SEALs, had worked with them aboard the *Bluefin*.

"What the hell are you talking about?"

"The SEALs never leave their own behind. Not alive. Not dead. I think your 2IC just made the best choice out of a handful of bad ones. He's going back to help the guys who're pinned down."

"They don't have that option. They need to stick with the plan, dammit!"

"You going to go down there and tell them that?" Captain Rafferty asked.

Then he grinned at Gordon and winked.

SEAL Special Strike Force
Alfa Platoon, SEAL Team Two
Al Biqa, Lebanon
0322 hours local time (Greenwich + 2)

Randall could see them now, a group of eight Hezbollah militiamen in and around a rust-bodied pickup truck with a

Russian-made PKM, a 7.62mm heavy machine gun pintel-mounted above the cab. The two in the truck were aiming the heavy weapon off toward the north, squeezing off long, rattling blasts of thunder, spraying the night with bright red tracers.

He and McKenna had made their way up the South Ridge, then hurried northeast, staying just below the ridge crest as they moved to avoid showing giveaway silhouettes against the sky. A five-minute jog over loose gravel and a steep, crumbling slope brought them to a spot above and behind the enemy gunners.

The Hezbollah truck was well positioned, able to sweep the culvert on the far side of the road and force the SEALs concealed there to keep under cover. Other men, including Syrian Army troops, were moving in the darkness farther north, and to the south as well, spilling into the valley behind the fortress and closing on the ambush site with appalling speed. It didn't take a Napoleon, Randall decided, to see that if something didn't happen in the next couple of minutes, it just wasn't going to happen. Waiting for air cover from the *Nimitz* was clearly a hopeless cause. He had to do something *now*.

"Alfa One, Alfa Two," he called over the tactical channel. "We see your problem. Wait one."

"Two, One. Glad you could make the party."

"Roger that." He took a deep breath. "Let's take 'em," he told McKenna. Snapping a fresh magazine into his H&K, he brought the weapon to his shoulder and took aim at the two men in the truck, their backs to him as they worked the PKM.

He triggered a pair of three-round bursts, knocking the machine-gunners down and silencing the heavy weapon. McKenna fired at the same instant, taking out one of the militiamen standing next to the truck.

The fusillade was so sudden, so death-silent that the other militiamen didn't realize at first that anything was wrong. One called to the men in the back of the truck, then pitched back onto the ground as Randall shifted targets and took him down. The others looked confused, some calling out, some simply standing with their weapons at their sides as they searched the darkness for the source of the gallingly accurate fire. Two more went down, then two more. The last militiaman broke and ran, desperately trying to flee the killing zone, but covering only a few yards before McKenna cut his legs out from under him and sent him rolling in the dust.

Randall leaped from cover and raced across open ground toward the truck. The driver was still in the cab, groping for a pistol when Randall put a single 9mm round through his skull, yanked open the door, and dragged him out onto the ground. "Truck's clear!" he called over the tac channel. "First Squad! Get up here!"

Unsuppressed fire barked in the night, but without clear targets or focus. McKenna loosed a burst at a nearby muzzle flash, then ran toward the truck as the flash was cut off with a sharp, short scream. Several strangely shaped, hulking figures emerged from the shadows of the culvert ditch across the broad, dirt road. HM1 Payton came first, supporting a limping, sagging Spinelli. MM1 Bowman followed, with Lieutenant Gallagher over his broad shoulders in a fireman's carry. Chief Anderson brought up the rear, covering the squad's six.

They lowered Spinelli onto the truck's flatbed. Blood, jet-black in the greens of Randall's LI goggles, soaked his right side. Someone had removed his combat harness and vest and cut his blouse open in order to pack the wound with a sterile dressing, but the dressing itself was already nearly soaked through.

Gerald Gallagher was dead, a neat, round hole just above his left eye, and most of the back of his skull completely gone.

But there was no time to mourn fallen comrades. That would come later, if, *when* the team made it back to the world. What was important now was to put as much distance between the hornet-mad local troops coming up the valley from the southwest . . . and the cold, grim knowledge that SEALs never left behind their own.

Not even their dead.

The bodies of the Hezbollah gunmen in the back of the truck were unceremoniously dumped overboard. Bowman, McKenna, and Payton began stripping headgear, jackets, weapons, and ammo from the dead militiamen and dragging the bodies away to a spill of massive boulders, where they would remain undiscovered for a time. With the hills crawling with hostiles, there was no way in hell the six SEALs were going to make the rendezvous with Seahawk One at the LZ.

But Randall was pretty sure they could make it out another way.

The Bunker
Pentagon Sub-Level 3
Alexandria, Virginia
2034 hours, EST (Greenwich –5)

"We've lost them," the technician said. "Eagle Eye reports they're widening the search."

"Eagle Eye," Gordon thought, must be the you-don't-want-to-know intelligence asset circling high above the Lebanese frontier. The images on the big display showed only disappointingly empty stretches of rock-strewn dirt and scrub brush.

"Switch back to Second Squad," General Childess ordered.

"Yes, sir."

Tactical imaging for the dust-off at LZ Bravo had been handed off to another reconnaissance asset—probably a KH-12 satellite, Gordon thought, since the picture had less resolution than the images from the recon aircraft, and was drifting across the target zone fairly quickly.

That was the trouble with low-orbit spysats. A satellite could be parked at geosynch so that it remained above a particular spot on the Earth's surface as it circled the globe once each twenty-four hours, matching the planet's rotation, but the geosynchronous point was over 22,000 miles out, good for weather and communications satellites, but not up-close-and-personal reconnaissance imaging. Spy satellites were usually placed in lower, eccentric orbits, their apogees placed above the spot that needed coverage to allow a longer targeting window, but still limited by their own orbital movement to relatively brief observation periods.

The view of LZ One was already growing hard to interpret as the satellite neared the horizon, but Gordon could see a flat stretch of terrain marked by the bright glow of chemical light sticks, and the dimmer glows of human bodies crouched under cover nearby. A brief radio exchange confirmed that five SEALs from Alfa Platoon's Second Squad had made it to the LZ, along with two men—the sniper and his spotter—from First Squad.

There was no sign of the two Second Squad men, or the five from First Squad trapped south of the fortress.

"Seahawk is inbound," the technician said. "ETA ten minutes."

"First Squad isn't going to make it," North said. *"Damn!"*

"We knew they wouldn't," Childess said. "That j.g. is asking for a military court, haring off that way."

"I don't see it that way, General," the captain said. "He made the best call he could in a tough situation."

"SEALs don't leave their own behind," Goldman said. "Not ever."

"They're leaving," Childess said, indicating the soft-glowing figures on the screen.

"Let's see how it plays out, General," Goldman replied.

"Alfa Two, this is Alfa One," sounded from the overhead speaker, harsh with static. *"Situation resolved. We're moving."*

"Roger that," another voice replied. *"Want us to hold the LZ down for you?"*

"Negative, negative, Alfa Two. Follow the plan. We're taking another way out."

"Copy, Alfa One. See you back aboard."

"Roger that, Two. And good luck! Alfa One out!"

"What other way?" Childess demanded. "What are they doing?"

"Not compromising their plans by broadcasting them," North replied, "even on a scrambled channel. We'll just have to wait them out."

Minutes dragged past. To Gordon, the small basement room was becoming close and stifling, ripe with the smell of sweat and aftershave. The tension was palpable, a thickness in the hot air.

"We're going to lose the satellite feed pretty soon," the technician said, glancing up at a large, LED time readout.

"Ah, but here comes the cavalry," North said, pointing. Three helicopters, their images ghostly, but their engine exhausts white-hot in the spy satellite's IR-imaging lens, were approaching at treetop altitude from the left. They could hear the clipped conversation over the tactical radio net.

"Free Sanction, Free Sanction, this is Seahawk One. I see four lights, two green, two blue, over."

"Seahawk, Free Sanction. Confirmed, two green lights, two blue lights. Come on in. Over!"

"Copy, Free Sanction. Coming in now."

"Hawk One, this is Hawk Three," another voice interrupted. *"I'm taking ground fire, repeat, taking ground fire, three o'clock!"*

In the Pentagon bunker, they could hear the distant hammer of automatic weapons fire, could see the muzzle flashes on the television monitor. The details were too fuzzy to tell whether the attackers were Hezbollah or Syrian.

"Starbase, Hawk One! The LZ is hot, repeat, LZ is hot!"

"Shit, shit, shit," Childess said, a monotone litany.

"It happens, sir," the colonel added.

"Hawk Three, this is Hawk Two. I've got the hostiles. Watch my LOF."

One of the helicopters suddenly spat a dazzling, stabbing spear thrust of light, accompanied by the shrill whine of a high-speed multibarreled autocannon. The M134 minigun, mounted in Seahawk Two's main door, flooded the target with high-velocity rounds as the other two helicopters settled toward the ground. The SEALs were already moving from cover and sprinting toward the waiting helos.

"Starbase, Seahawk. We have five packages, all secure. We're out of here."

"Copy that, Seahawk," the technician said. "RTB."

On the screen, the two grounded helos lifted off and swung clear of the LZ. The third hovered a moment, continuing to lay down a devastating spray of high-velocity minigun rounds, before it, too, swung away and accelerated clear. Seconds later, the televised image broke into a flickering ripple of pixellations, then went black.

"Satellite just went below the horizon, sir," the technician said. "Next window will be for Sierra Echo Four in twenty-seven minutes."

"We need to get an image on Alfa One," Childess said. "Raise 'em on the horn. Let's see if we can talk them out of there."

"That could be a problem, General," the technician said.

"Why?"

"We've lost their signal."

"Well . . . get it back!"

"Sir, the ground team is equipped with tactical radio gear, but they don't have any long-range equipment. The only reason we can listen in and kibitz when necessary is we have Eagle Eye in the area to pick up their transmissions."

"So?"

"We don't know exactly where they are now, but we know they're moving. That's pretty rugged terrain back there, and their transmissions, if they're making any, are being blocked by the mountains."

"So how do we reestablish contact?"

"We wait, sir, and listen. And hope to hell we're close enough to pick them up when they come out from under cover."

"Suggestion, General?" Goldman said.

"What." It was a demand, not a question.

"Let them work it out themselves. They'll find a way to yell if they need us."

Childess scowled, but, after a moment's hesitation, nodded. "We can't help if we can't see them. But, damn it, the waiting is hell."

And the waiting *was* bad. Gordon found a chair and sat down after his boss had done the same. He was only now beginning to realize the enormity of what had happened, of what *he* had brought to pass.

At the moment, he was remembering a suggestion he'd made in his original report, that the ground team wouldn't need to pack ground-to-space communications equipment if an aircraft such as a Navy Hawkeye or Air Force AWACS was orbiting in the area, say, over Israel, or just off the coast. The possibility that part of the team might become cut off from the main body and fall out of communications with headquarters simply hadn't occurred to him . . . and apparently it hadn't occurred to anyone else.

Those men were cut off deep in hostile territory, and the responsibility, at least in part, was his.

Ten minutes later, the helicopters reported going feet wet—passing the beach five miles south of Tyre and flying west out over the Med. Twenty-five minutes after that, they reported their approach to the USS *Nimitz*, steaming slowly south with her battle group thirty miles off the coast.

But there was no further word from Alfa Platoon's First Squad, left behind in the Bekaa Valley.

He looked at his watch. Rebecca was going to be furious, but there was no way he could leave now. Not yet. Not until he knew the people *he* had put out there were safe.

SEAL Special Strike Force
Alfa Platoon, SEAL Team Two
Near Habbush, Lebanon
0528 hours local time (Greenwich + 2)

It was just a half hour before sunrise, and the sky was already bright with the twilight, clear and crystal blue. Trailing a plume of dust, the truck descended the gray-brown bareness of the Jabal Lubnan, the Lebanon Mountains, approaching the coast on the winding road. To the west, the Mediterranean stretched to the horizon, mirror-smooth and ultramarine black, the "wine-dark sea" of Homer.

For the past two hours, they'd been racing along the mountain-twisted roads of southern Lebanon, moving south down the Bekaa Valley with the snowcapped bulk of Mt. Hermon, traditional site of Christ's transfiguration, looming huge against the stars on their left. They'd removed their LI gear, harnesses, and vests and used gasoline-soaked rags to wipe most of the camo blacking from their faces before donning the fragmentary uniforms and mismatched headgear they'd taken from the dead militiamen. Armed now with AK-47 assault rifles, they looked the part of a band of Hezbollah militia, patrolling the roads north of the Israeli frontier. They couldn't permit too close an examination, of course, not with face blacking playing the role of the ubiquitous Hezbollah mustaches and beards, but they looked convincing enough from a distance, and in the dark.

They'd hoped to cross into Israel at Metulla, but a large and heavily armed force had challenged them at Marj'Uyun. After a brief, sharp firefight at a roadblock, they'd been forced to swing right, heading west, then north along the spine of the Lebanon Mountains. Twice more they were challenged at roadblocks. The first time they managed to bluff their way through by waving their rifles above their heads and shouting *Allah akbar . . .* God is great. The second time they were stopped with gunshots, and smashed their way through by loosing their last LAW into the side of a Syrian BDRM. The Syrian Army, it seemed, was harder to bluff than the enthusiastic bands of half-trained militia roving like gangs across the dusty Lebanese landscape.

The Israelis were hard to bluff, too. Alerted, perhaps, by the gunfire, the artillery rounds had rumbled in from the south like incoming freight trains, detonating among the hills with earthquake thunders. That had been when Randall had decided that they would have to make for the sea.

Every SEAL is taught to think of the water as an asset, as a friend. Few enemies would pursue a man into the water, especially if that man's training rendered him deadly in the alien world of the sea. During BUD/S, the basic training all SEAL trainees underwent before winning their coveted Budweiser SEAL badges, they survived a series of ordeals casually referred to as "drownproofing," which included maneuvers in a deep swimming pool, with hands and feet tied.

The water was something to be used, an ally, a weapon, even.

And out there beyond that dark, western horizon lay an American aircraft carrier battle group, the *Nimitz* and eight or ten lesser vessels in support.

But first they would have to reach the sea, still ten miles away . . . and it was swiftly growing light. They would need to find a place to stay out of sight until after nightfall.

And there was the matter of communications. Starbase had been able to eavesdrop on Free Sanction's tactical radio broadcasts through the agency of the unseen reconnaissance aircraft circling above the Bekaa Valley. They didn't have a satellite uplink or dish antenna, and so their communications right now were limited to the line-of-sight range of their Motorolas. They all carried emergency homing beacons, of course, but the Syrians could home in on those as easily as could American rescue forces. Until an American aircraft flew overhead, they were totally and completely on their own.

Randall found he rather preferred it that way.

Saturday, 27 June 1987

Gordon Residence
Alexandria, Virginia
0510 hours, EST (Greenwich −5)

Frank Gordon pulled his Skylark to a stop in the driveway of his Lincolnia Park home, on the suburban outskirts of Alexandria just south of I-395. Though it was past sunup, the sky was still dark, mantled in a low ceiling of heavy, gray clouds promising rain. Early as it was, traffic sounds were picking up on the nearby highway, and the flashing headlights of early commuter traffic glimpsed through the trees were growing more numerous. Rush hour on a Saturday morning wasn't nearly so bad as during the week, but enough military and defense corporation employees worked on the weekend to make him glad he'd made it home before the traffic really picked up.

Letting himself in the front door quietly, he tiptoed into the front hall.

"Good morning."

Becca's voice was cold, and a trifle hard. She was curled

up on the big, overstuffed chair in the living room at the end of the hall, wearing her blue nightgown, and with her legs tucked under a blanket.

"I'm sorry, Becca," he said. "Something came up."

She yawned as she uncurled from the chair. Rebecca Gordon was lovely, a bit pudgy since she'd turned forty, but still attractive and possessing a beauty that had more to do with grace and presence than weight. "It's funny," she said. "I thought the Pentagon was pretty damned high-tech. There's this new invention out, called the telephone."

"I'll have Appropriations look into that," he replied, trying to turn it into a jest.

"Damn it, Frank. We were supposed to have dinner with the Pattersons. Remember?"

He closed his eyes. He'd completely forgotten about that, even before Goldman had entered his office. "No," he said. "I forgot. Were they upset?"

She shrugged. "It's kind of becoming a habit, you know? So, something came up that you couldn't call home?"

He thought about that. The truth was he hadn't even thought about calling, not after he'd been taken into the underground combat center. "No. I couldn't. I was with your dad all night."

She arched one perfect eyebrow at that. Mentioning her father was virtually a code phrase between them, meaning he'd been engaged in business that he simply wasn't allowed to discuss. Not with *anyone*, even her.

"And you didn't check your messages."

"No, damn it!" he snapped. "I didn't! What we were dealing with . . . well . . . I wasn't at my desk, and I couldn't get away. That's all!"

He saw her eyes darken and felt the rise of her anger, but she nodded after a moment. "Fine. I'm going back to bed."

"You didn't need to stay up for me."

"Of course not! My husband could be lying dead in an alley somewhere. He never calls, and I never know when or *if* he's coming home! I should just go to bed and wait for the police to call me! Of course I can sleep when I don't know if I'm going to be awakened by him coming in at dawn, or by a phone call from the hospital!" Whirling, she stormed down the hallway toward the stairs.

"Becca, please . . ."

"You know where the blankets and pillows are. You can sleep down here! *If* you ever sleep, of course!" She was crying now. "Sometimes I don't know whether I married a man or a computer!"

"O . . . kay," he said softly after she was gone. He heard the bedroom door slam upstairs. "Looks like I fucked up again, big-time."

He was too damned tired to be angry in response. The exchange they'd just played out was fast becoming the rule rather than the exception. Late hours at the Pentagon, missed dinners and social events, forgotten opportunities to call . . .

Rebecca put a high priority on social formalities and propriety. He understood why that was important to her. She'd gone through seven kinds of hell from her father when she'd broken off an engagement to elope with a certain young submarine officer. She'd been accused of impropriety and worse, he knew. She'd been fighting clinical depression for years, now, and was taking Valium to combat it. Lately, it had been as though she was trying somehow to demonstrate she was socially competent, going through the proper whirl of dinner parties and social engagements, as if to prove to the world that she could do the social thing with the best of them.

Dinner parties, while a grim necessity for any naval officer, were simply not on Gordon's priority list . . . not in the top twenty, at any rate. For the past year, especially, he'd been bearing down on his career to the virtual exclusion of everything else, taking on more and more responsibilities at ONSOC, working longer hours, and generally obsessing over the future course of his naval career. That career had very nearly become beached. He'd been working hard to catch up . . . and to prove, especially to Goldman, that he had what it took to skipper a nuke boat of his own.

He was only recently beginning to understand that excluding everything but career in his life was also excluding his family. He rarely saw Ellen and Margaret, his two girls, anymore. And Rebecca . . . were her moods and down periods worse, lately? "Excitable depression," her doctor had called her condition. The Valium, he'd warned, only suppressed the moods, and couldn't in any way be considered a cure.

So far as Gordon was concerned, everyone got a little down from time to time. If Becca would just get *over* it, pick up and get on with her life, everything would be fine. *Fine*.

He looked at his watch. Almost 5:30 . . . and though he was tired, he didn't feel like he could sleep at all. For a moment, he hesitated, wondering whether or not he should go upstairs and try to talk to Becca.

Another part of his mind translated 0530 hours EST to 1230 hours in Lebanon. Where were the SEALs left on the ground after the evacuation at LZ Bravo? How were they planning on reestablishing contact and getting picked up?

He decided to go back to the office and wait the situation through . . . both situations, in Lebanon and at home. He rubbed his eyes, then giggled at a sudden, wry gallows-humor thought. Which was the more desperate situation right now? The Bekaa Valley? Or Becca's Valium?

Maybe, he decided, he was more tired than he knew. No matter. He could catch a nap on the sofa in his office later, and maybe get caught up on the Quarterly Reports that were due next week

Quietly, and with a last guilty glance up the stairs, he let himself out the front door.

SEAL Special Strike Force
Alfa Platoon, SEAL Team Two
Near Habbush, Lebanon
2218 hours local time (Greenwich + 2)

They waited until well past dark to slip from their safe place.

They'd spent the daylight hours hiding in a storage shed behind a garage on the outskirts of Habbush. Hidden behind stacks of parts crates, rusted engine blocks, decaying tires, piles of chain and cable and rusted-out oil drums, they'd watched the day pass through the narrow gaps in the splintery boards that formed the shed's back wall. From there, they'd seen soldiers passing through in convoy, heading east, up the mountain face. Judging by their uniforms, they were government soldiers, troops answering to the Christian-rightist Beirut government . . . but that didn't make them the good guys, not by a long shot. Had they been Israeli—the IDF controlled this region, at least in theory—Randall might have attempted contact . . . but these were the people who'd orchestrated more than one massacre of civilians in the past few years, including the brutal slaughter of eight hundred civilians—mostly women and children—in the Sabra and Shatila refugee camps in southern Beirut five years before. The Christian Phalangists were at least as bloody-handed as the Shi'ite Hezbollah, and Randall was taking no chances on an encounter with either group.

Spinelli was just hanging on. He'd lost a lot of blood before they'd finally been able to pack the wound well enough to stop the bleeding, and he was drifting in and out of consciousness, drugged with morphine and weak from loss of blood.

There wasn't a lot they could do for him, though, and it was too risky going out in daylight. Habbush was on one of the country's main east-west roads, and that road paralleled the western end of a thirty-inch oil pipeline that stretched all the way across Lebanon, the southwestern corner of Syria, and all the way across Saudi Arabia to Dhahran and Bahrain on the Persian Gulf; an offshore terminal fed oil tankers gathering at the coast from Europe and the Americas. Because the pipeline was a strategic asset—and an obvious target for terrorists—it was heavily patrolled.

But at the pipeline terminus there would be a fair-sized dock area and plenty of boats and small craft. It was worth the risk if they could get down there. They just couldn't risk doing it in the light.

Once it was completely dark, however, they gently carried Spinelli out to the truck, which they'd parked under the shed's rotting eaves, and laid him on a mattress they'd found in the building. They'd wrapped Lieutenant Gallagher's body in a sheet of canvas and taped it up in a makeshift body bag earlier. Still disguised as militia—Christian or Islamic scarcely mattered now—they set off down the mountain road at a sedately inconspicuous pace.

McKenna's Arabic got them past two more checkpoints without incident. Passwords, it seemed, were not necessary if you could claim with enthusiastic shouts and gestures that you were looking for American commandos who'd attacked a camp in the Bekaa Valley, and who might still be in the neighborhood.

They reached the sea around midnight, but the port area at the end of the oil pipeline was crawling with troops, so they turned south and followed the coast road to the seaside village of Al Khudr. They chose one particular boat, a thirty-foot green-and-white fishing trawler with a high vertical prow and a small pilothouse set well forward. It was tied up by itself to a rickety pier on the north end of the marina area, with rubber tires slung over the sides as fenders to protect the wooden hull as it rocked in the gentle, Mediterranean swell. Eyes were painted on the prow, in Levantine fashion; the name *La Joie* was picked out on the transom in gold letters.

Silently, Randall, McKenna, Bowman, and Anderson walked out on the pier and slipped aboard the boat, while

Payton stayed with Spinelli in the back of the truck. They'd expected the boat to be deserted, but . . .

"Qui va la?"

French, after Arabic, was the most common language in worldly Lebanon. There were two civilians aboard, asleep in the nets at the boat's stern, an older man and a teenage boy, both terrified at the apparitions moving stealthily and armed about the deck.

"You will not be harmed," Randall told them in stilted, high-school French. Reaching into a pouch slung from his harness, he pulled out a heavy packet containing a roll of gold coins minted for just such a need. "But we need transport in your boat. We will pay you well. . . ."

There were initial protests, then avaricious bargaining . . . but clearly the fishermen's interest in the gold outweighed any ideological concerns they might have had. Swiftly, the SEALs brought Spinelli and the lieutenant's corpse aboard, while Anderson kept the wide-eyed civilians under guard. Within twenty minutes, *La Joie* was under way, chug-chugging clear of the breakwater, then swinging her blunt prow west, toward the open sea.

Little was said on the voyage. Randall's French was years rusty, but the fisherman and his son both spoke Arabic and a little English, so communication was no problem. McKenna sat in the stern, trying to use his Motorola to contact American aircraft in the area, quietly intoning "Starship, Starship, this is Free Sanction, do you copy" like a mantra. Randall went to work on the fishing boat's fish finder, a small electronics package in the pilothouse connected with a low-powered civilian sonar unit on *La Joie*'s keel. It was a simple enough task to find a way to disconnect a key wire in the control unit, then tap it against the contact in Morse code, sending out the cryptic signal "Free Sanction, Free Sanction" over and over again.

"Got 'em!" McKenna said at last, nearly two hours after their departure from port. By then, they were well past the twelve-mile limit, still cruising slowly toward the west. "An E-2C off the *Nimitz*. They know we're here."

The E-2C Hawkeye was the Navy's answer to the big AWACS aircraft flown by the Air Force, a prop-driven collection of sensitive electronic monitoring and detection gear beneath an enormous, revolving radome that looked like a flying saucer.

"Instructions?" Randall asked.

"They say to stay on this heading. We'll be met."

"Good enough."

It was just growing light in the east when Payton called to the others. "Periscope, port beam!"

They looked, and watched with numbed emotions as the periscope, mottled in camouflage gray-greens, slowly rose from the sea atop a feather of wake, followed in moments by the blunt, charcoal gray tower of a submarine's sail marked with the characters SSN 697. It was a Los Angeles class submarine, the *Indianapolis*, one of two attached to the *Nimitz* battle group.

The fisherman turned and looked at Randall. "You are Americans, *non?*"

Randall shook his head. "*Non*," he said. "*Russe*." Let them, and Syrian military intelligence, chew on *that*. He doubted that these civilians would know the difference between an American submarine and a Russian.

Sailors appeared on the submarine's forward deck, some of them armed with M-16s. Lines were tossed, and *La Joie* was brought alongside.

"*Merci, Capitaine*," Randall told the fisherman. "We appreciate the help."

"And we the gold," the man said with a gap-toothed grin. "We are available for charter any time!"

Spinelli died during the medevac flight from the *Nimitz* to Naples later that day.

Monday, 29 June 1987

Office of Naval Special Operations Command
D-Ring, the Pentagon
Alexandria, Virginia
0935 hours, EST (Greenwich −5)

"Gordon?"

"Admiral Goldman!"

"Don't get up." The admiral made a stay-put motion with his hand as he stepped into Gordon's office. He placed his briefcase on Gordon's desk. "I just thought you'd like to hear. Free Sanction made it out. The rest of them, I mean."

Gordon felt a wave of relief wash through him. "Thank God! Casualties?"

"Two dead. A couple of the others were dinged a little, but nothing serious." He frowned. "One of the dead was the team's Wheel. Lieutenant Gallagher."

"Damn. I'm sorry."

"It happens."

"Yes. But this time it was for nothing." Gordon had been chasing the events of the past few days around and around in his thoughts. It was hard not to take the blame for the op's failure. It had been his idea, his plan, after all. He wondered about the families of the dead men. It was one thing to have a father, a husband, a son die in exchange for some lofty goal—the liberation of Americans held by Middle East terrorists, for example.

But the team had gone in and turned up a dry hole. The hostages might have been at Objective Nevada, but they'd been moved before Free Sanction had arrived.

Worse, worse by far, was the knowledge that Hezbollah and Syrian troops had been waiting there in force, almost as if they'd set a trap for the expected arrival of American rescuers.

"It wasn't for nothing," Goldman said after a long moment. "We know that Waite was being held at Objective Nevada. One of our people saw where he'd left his name, and the letters CE."

"'CE'?"

"Church of England. Anyway, it looks like our intel was good. Just . . . a bit late."

"Either that," Gordon said, "or they knew we were coming."

"An ambush?"

"Remember how much political capital the Iranians got out of the failure of Eagle's Claw?"

"Sure. They weren't responsible for the failure, though."

"Oh, we did it all to ourselves. Too few backup helos in the op plan, an unexpected sandstorm, and a bunch of civilians joyriding out in the middle of the desert where they had no business being. And finally, the collision of one of the tankers with a helicopter." Gordon closed his eyes and tried to picture what it must have been like that night at Desert One, with America's one chance at rescuing fifty-two hostages in the balance. "But the Iranians took the crash and turned it into a great victory for the Revolution."

"You think Hezbollah wanted to do the same?"

"It's certainly a possibility, Admiral. One we ought to be looking at carefully."

"Failure doesn't necessarily imply enemy action."

"Of course not. There is a precise military-technical term for what happened at Objective Nevada the other night . . . and at Desert One, for that matter."

"And that is?"

"A cluster fuck. Pure and simple."

Goldman chuckled. "Not a bad term."

"But it shouldn't have been. Everything went exactly right. Every man did what he was supposed to do. But there were Syrian troops at the objective, not to mention a hell of a lot of militia. And they shouldn't have been there."

"Mmm. Maybe. Still, no student of military history can help but notice how many battles are won through sheer dumb luck. But that cuts both ways, you know. While one side is winning through luck, the other side is losing." He shrugged. "Sometimes the coin toss just comes up tails."

"And I'd like to be sure no one was playing with a jiggered coin."

"That's G2's show," Goldman reminded him. "They'll be looking at that op real closely, believe me."

Had it been a trap? Or coincidence? Right now there was no way to know, but Gordon knew that Intelligence would be digging into the possibility of a leak somewhere along the line of command from the Pentagon all the way down to SEAL Team Two.

He found himself wondering about the intelligence sources he'd heard quoted, though. HUMINT was so damnably frustrating. People were fallible . . . and fickle as well. An informer could be bought, or turned. Or planted by a clever foe.

And no matter what the cause, two good men were dead . . . and Frank Gordon had helped to kill them.

"I have something for you here," Goldman said, flipping open his briefcase. He extracted a manila string-tie envelope and handed it to Gordon.

Gordon had seen similar envelopes often enough in his eighteen years of naval service to know what it was.

Orders.

He accepted the package, and with one glance for reassurance at Admiral Goldman, unwrapped the string and pulled out the top page.

FROM: COMSUBSPECLANT
TO: CDR FRANK CHARLES GORDON
SUBJ: CHANGE OF DUTY

. . . YOU ARE HEREBY REQUIRED AND DIRECTED TO REPORT TO MARE ISLAND NAVAL STATION, VALLEJO, CALIFORNIA, NOT LATER THAN MONDAY, 6 JULY 1987, WHERE YOU WILL PREPARE TO ASSUME YOUR DUTIES AS COMMANDING OFFICER, USS *PITTSBURGH*, SSN 720. CHANGEOVER OF COMMAND WILL TAKE PLACE AT 1030 HOURS, MONDAY, 13 JULY 1987. . . .

His vision was blurring. He could scarcely read the words on the paper.

He held in his hands the fulfillment, the realization of twenty-three years of work, blood, training, dedication, and belief.

Frank Gordon had entered the Navy in 1969, upon his graduation from Annapolis. After his initial training at the U.S. Navy Submarine School at Groton, Connecticut, he'd had his first sea tour . . . aboard the submarine tender *Canopus*, which had spent most of her time tied up at a dock at the sub base at Bangor, Washington.

And because he'd run off with an admiral's daughter while he was still at Groton—the same admiral who was now standing there on the other side of Gordon's desk with a knowing grin on his face—it had looked as though Frank Gordon's career was never going to go anywhere more interesting than the leaden gray-skied purgatory of Bangor.

He'd gone the whole nuke career track. Every submariner officer who wanted to go anywhere wanted to go nuke . . . and most especially wanted to go with the nuclear fast-attack force—not the big, quiet, sneaking mobile fortresses of the SSBN boomers, but the swift and deadly sharks of the sea, the Sturgeons and, especially, the Los Angeles attack boats. That's where the prestige was. The glory. The promotions. The coveted chance at an eventual promotion to admiral and a flag command. He'd served aboard several boats, learning each department—engineering, navigation, weapons. He'd endured the interview every prospective nuke officer dreaded with Hiram Rickover, a man known as the Father of the Nuclear Navy . . . and a man who could have given Torquemada a few pointers in the tactics of inquisition. Rickover had passed him with a gruff "Not bad," high praise indeed from the father who could make or break any aspiring nuke officer's career with a single sarcastic word.

But after serving as XO aboard the ancient diesel boat *Bluefin* during the Iranian hostage crisis, he'd found himself, after yet another training billet, again on board the *Bluefin*, this time as her CO. Admiral Goldman had a long memory, and less than pleasant feelings for the brash ensign who'd eloped with his daughter just before her high-society wedding. The upward track of his career had begun lagging almost from the first, with missed promotions and less than strategic tours of duty.

It wasn't pleasant for any junior officer to think about, but the command ranks in the U.S. Navy, captain and above, were heavily politicized. A Navy commander on someone's shit list, an officer who didn't have some fairly impressive friends and patrons in high places, was lucky to make captain and would *never* make admiral.

It looked as though Commander Gordon was never going to rise higher in his chosen career, or command anything more prestigious than the *Bluefin*. Then, two years ago, he'd taken the *Bluefin* into one of the Soviet Union's innermost sancti sanctorum, the forbidden White Sea east and south of the Kola Peninsula. His mission, code-named Arctic Fox and still so highly classified it wasn't likely to see the light of day for another fifty years, had involved the transport and insertion of a Navy SEAL team near the Soviets' heavily guarded submarine base at Severodvinsk. At the end of that mission, he'd received the smallest ray of hope, again from Goldman, that he might yet find himself in command of a nuke. His estrangement from his powerful father-in-law had ended, thanks largely to Rebecca's interventions, he was sure, but also in part to his handling of his boat in those desperate hours within sight of the Soviet Empire's most closely guarded havens.

He was proud of what he'd done, proud, too, of his abilities.

And now, in his hands, was his reward.

"I . . . I'm not sure what to say, Admiral."

" 'Thank you' will do, son."

"Thank you."

"You're welcome. You've earned it." He paused, lips

pursed, as though considering what to say next. "Things haven't always been clear sailing between us, Frank. I regret that. And partly, too, you know, I had to be careful not to appear partial. Nepotism is an ugly, filthy thing, especially if it puts an unfit man in command of a Navy's ship or sub."

Gordon blinked. He'd always been focused so tightly on Goldman's anger over his elopement with his daughter he'd never considered the opposite tack, that Goldman was withholding the best billets because he didn't want to appear to be fostering his son-in-law's career.

It was an interesting new slant, one that put a whole new light on things.

"But your handling of the *Bluefin* in Arctic Fox," Goldman went on, "was nothing short of brilliant. I told you there might be a new command in it for you, after a year or two ashore. And here it is."

"I appreciate this, Admiral. I'll do my best."

Goldman made a sour face. "I had little to do with it, beyond signing off on the recommendation. As for doing your best, you'd damned well better if you know what the hell is good for you!" The smile robbed the words of their sting . . . or most of it.

"Does Rebecca know?" he asked. It was an odd position to be in. An admiral's daughter sometimes had near-instant access to information that could take some time trickling down the chain of command.

"Of course not. She could be a Russian spy!"

The words were both joke and rebuke. Of *course* no one in Goldman's position would discuss information as sensitive as who was going to be in command of a Navy submarine with anyone not authorized to receive that information, even if she was family. Gordon had just come close to insulting the admiral simply by suggesting such a thing.

"Just checking, sir," he said, trying to change his gaffe into a joke. "Navy wives have their own communications setup, you know. They pick up and transmit information at speeds faster than light, and no one can ever figure out just how they know what they know. I thought maybe I had the inside track, there."

"Well, you're right about that, but I'll leave it to you to break it to her." His expression had gone a bit cold. "Frank, is everything all right between you and Becca?"

He sighed. "Some rough seas, sir. Every marriage has them." He wondered what Rebecca had told her father.

"I know. But . . . this new command is going to take you back out to sea, son. And the word is, it'll be *soon*."

Gordon's eyes widened at that. "What? . . ."

"At this time, no comment. But break it to her gently, son."

"Aye aye, sir."

He snapped his briefcase shut. "Okay. I gotta make tracks." He extended a gnarled hand. "Good luck, son."

Gordon shook the hand. "Thank you, sir. Thank you for everything."

It wasn't until some minutes after Goldman had left that Frank Gordon thought of something else. These orders had been written two weeks before. Why had Admiral Goldman taken him into the Pentagon subbasement to watch the SEAL op in Lebanon that night? To teach him the seriousness of command responsibility?

Or to prove something more, something deeper, a something as deep and as cold as the depths of the Marianas Trench?

"Damn you, Ben Goldman," he whispered.

Thursday, 2 July 1987

Crew's Quarters, USS *Pittsburgh*
Pier 2, Mare Island Naval Submarine Station
Vallejo, California
1645 hours local time

The eerie shrill of a boatswain's pipe ululated through the
Pittsburgh's compartments from the bulkhead speakers, the
final quaver dying away as LCDR Latham's voice came on.
"Now starboard liberty section, muster on deck. That is,
starboard liberty section, muster on deck. Port section, now
sweepers man your brooms. Clean sweep-down, fore and
aft. The smoking lamp is lit in all authorized compartments."

"Liberty!" BM1 Scobey exclaimed, giving his necker-
chief's square knot a final tighten and tug. "Man, they're
playin' my song!"

"Yeah, but it ain't Honolulu, man," TM2 Benson replied.
He was taking a rag to his Korfam dress shoes, bringing
them to their accustomed mirror polish.

"*Nothing's* like Honolulu, Rog," BM1 Archie Douglas
said, grinning. "And promises in the Navy are just about

worth the cost of the teletype flimsies they're printed on. Get used to it!"

The crew compartment was crowded, the narrow passageway elbow-to-dress-whites-elbow with enlisted men preparing to go ashore. Scobey lowered his locker lid, which included the thin mattress and made-up sheets and blanket of his rack. Each man slept atop his own locker, a space only six inches deep, in which he kept his uniforms and few personal possessions during his enforced incarceration on board. The racks were stacked three high, each six feet long, three feet wide, and with twenty-four narrow inches between the top of the mattress and the bottom of the next rack above, a coffinlike space with the single virtue that each man could draw a set of curtains to provide a cloth-thin illusion of privacy when in his rack.

"It ain't right, though," Benson continued. "Promising us palm trees and hula girls, and sending us *here*!"

"Word is we'll be home-ported in San Diego soon enough," Douglas said cheerfully.

"Yeah," ET2 Jim Jablonski said. "Ballast Point isn't so bad. In fact, it's prime duty!"

"But it ain't Pearl Harbor, man," Benson said mournfully. "It *ain't* Honolulu."

"Will someone shut the damned broken record player off?" TM2 Mark Doershner said from a nearby rack. "It's fuckin' gratin' on me like fingernails on the blackboard, y'know?"

"Let's get topside," Douglas told them. "This is one liberty call I *don't* intend to miss!"

Dress white uniforms spotlessly resplendent, they trooped aft and up the gangway to the first deck, then up the ladder to emerge from the forward escape hatch just abaft the sail. It was warm topside, but with a leaden, overcast sky and the strong promise of rain. Afternoon in early July in San Francisco's northern Bay Area could be blistering hot, but a thunderstorm earlier that afternoon had cooled things down. Steam was rising in the damp air from the *Pittsburgh*'s deck, and from the pier alongside.

"Fall in for muster," Master Chief Fred Warren, the Chief of the Boat bawled. The crewmen lined up in two ranks, and Warren began calling off their names. The liberty inspection that followed was cursory and impersonal, as Lieutenant Commander Latham and Master Chief Warren walked swiftly up and down the two ranks, noting a couple of too-long haircuts and pointing out to RM3 Sanders that he had a rust spot on the sleeve of his jumper.

After that, the men were dismissed, filing down the gangway already rigged aft of *Pittsburgh*'s sail, and onto the pier. A number of civilians had gathered behind a roped-off area just off the dock . . . mostly women and kids. As the sailors trooped up the pier, more than one began jogging, and before long, the civilians were forcing their way past the rope barrier and racing down the dockside toward their men.

"Must be nice to have that waitin' for you, huh?" Scobey said, laughing, as one tall, leggy, auburn-haired woman threw herself into Seaman Hutchison's arms.

Another girl raced toward ST3 Kellerman, shrilling something that sounded like "Squeee . . ." at the top of her lungs. Kellerman scooped her up and spun her around, as she wrapped her short-skirted legs around his back.

"Hey, you two!" Douglas called out. "Get yourselves a room!"

"Don't worry!" Kellerman said, grinning. "We will. Boys, this is my fiancée, Loni Dayton."

"Nice to meet you," Douglas said, ignoring the fact that she was still glued to the front of Kellerman's white jumper, arms and legs wrapped tightly around his back.

"What the hell does 'squee' mean?" Boyce asked.

Loni shook her head, clearing away a stray strand of blond hair. "Squee," she said, is *not* just a word. It is a state of mind. You can squee when you're happy . . . or go into a major *squeeee* when you finally see someone you haven't seen in *entirely* too long! . . ."

"Squee, huh?" Benson said.

"Okay, *Squee*," Scobey said, tapping Kellerman on the arm. "You two wanna come with us into town?"

"No thanks, Big C," Kellerman said. "We've got things to do. . . ."

"He'd just cramp our style," Douglas added, grinning. "Have fun, you two!"

"Man, it must be nice," Benson said, watching Kellerman and Loni walk away, arms locked about one another.

"Ahh," Scobey said with a sneer, "if the Navy had wanted you to have a wife, they would've issued you one with your seabag! Let's go!"

A Navy liberty bus was waiting near the dock to take them across the G-Street Bridge and into town.

Twenty minutes later, Benson, Scobey, Boyce, Jablonski, and Douglas were walking down Trinity Street in Vallejo, looking at the flickering marquee lights, the tawdry buildings, the signs proclaiming tattoos, massages, uniform alterations, dry-cleaning services, food, alcohol, and various other forms of entertainment, all aimed at the Navy enlisted man freshly back from weeks or months at sea.

"So, where's the action in this town?" Benson wanted to know.

"You've never been to Mare Island?" Douglas asked.

"Never. I was with SUBRON 5, in San Diego."

"Well, there's the Wakky Key Club, over on Marin Drive," Scobey said with a broad grin. "It's a strip club, see, and the girls there are so—"

"Hey, hey!" Douglas said. "You're crazy! The Wakky's in Honolulu!"

"Honolulu!" Benson wailed.

"Yeah, I just wanted Rog to know what he was missing!"

"Actually," Douglas said, "there's nothing to do in Vallejo. No girls."

"No booze," Benson chimed in.

"No pussy," Jablonski said.

"No food," Boyce added, catching on to the game.

"Not much of anything, actually," Scobey said. "I think

it's a conspiracy. Probably has to do with Russian spies in the area. The government doesn't want the Russkis to find places where they can lead innocents like us astray."

"You know," Douglas said, thoughtful, "there *is* the old Tup 'n' Baa."

"What's that?" Boyce wanted to know.

"Submariner's bar," Jablonski said. "It's really the Ram and Ewe. They have it decorated like a submarine supply officer's wet dream!"

"Are there girls?" Benson wanted to know.

"Oh, there's girls," Scobey said. "But no grass skirts and no palm trees. . . ."

They found the Ram and Ewe, but Benson had an unpleasant feeling about the place as soon as they walked up to the door. Now it was Macy's Ram and Ewe, a seedy-looking and run-down place, badly in need of paint. A dozen big, gleaming motorcycles were parked in the lot beside the building, overlooking Mare Island Channel. A pair of too-thin women with harsh makeup, tight clothing, and flashy handbags leaned against the wall nearby.

"Doesn't look quite like I remember it," Douglas said, frowning.

"You've been here before?" Boyce asked.

"Oh, sure. Lots of times. The first was when I was shipping out on my first patrol, back in '79."

"Hey, sailor boys!" one of the women called. She was silver-blond, but with bright green streaks dyed in her crisply molded hair. "Lookin' for a date?"

"Maybe later, baby," Scobey called back.

"Maybe you'll buy us a drink?" the other said hopefully. Her hair was a more conservative flaming orange, which did interesting things to her purple lipstick and mascara.

"Sure," Boyce said. "Come on!"

"There's a nice place down the street," the green-blond offered.

"I'd kind of like to check this place out, guys," Douglas said. The redhead started forward, but the green-blond stopped her. "Shit, Liz. Not if they're goin' in there!" She eyed the sailors again. "Maybe we'll catch ya later, honey." They turned and walked off down the sidewalk, heels clicking on the pavement.

"What's with them?" Boyce asked.

"Ah, forget 'em," Scobey said. "C'mon. They've got food here and they've got booze. Let's get us some."

It was dark inside, smoky and not particularly clean. A number of bikers lounged at tables in the back, or stalked about the two pool tables with cues grasped in meaty hands like spears, steel and leather agleam in the weak light. The bikers weren't the only customers in the bar, but it felt like they were the ones who were in charge. Benson had the feeling that every eye in the place was on the quintet of sailors as they walked inside.

"They've done some new decorating, I see," Jablonski said, looking around. Pictures of motorcycles graced the walls, some shown off by bikini-clad girls. A forlorn-looking moose head hung above the bar. "Early biker punk, it looks like."

"Under new management, I imagine," Douglas added. "Damn! They had some really great stuff here!"

"Like what?" Benson wanted to know.

Douglas pointed. "They had a couple of old torpedo casings hanging from the overhead right there. Lots of submarine spare parts. Hull fittings. A commode lid from a sub's head. Battle lanterns. There was so much cast-off sub junk on the walls here that they said that an old World War II boat, the USS *Shellfish*, hadn't gone missing after all. She was hanging right here, in pieces, with so much other junk the Navy investigators never saw her."

"*Shellfish?*" Boyce said. "Never heard of that one."

"She wasn't real. But she makes for a good story."

They walked toward the bar, where the bartender watched with something less than open enthusiasm. Several bikers at the far end of the bar talked in low tones with one another, shooting hard, hooded glances at the sailors from time to time.

"One drink, fellas," the bartender said, his voice low and on the verge of pleading. "Just one. Then you'd better shove off, okay? This ain't *your* turf no more."

"It's a free country, ain't it?" Scobey growled.

"Take it easy, Big C," Boyce said. "We don't want trouble. C'mon. There's a table."

They sat down at a free table not far from the front door and a large window looking out onto the street. "Not real friendly here, are they?" Benson said. He watched the bikers in the back of the room return his casual glance with hard, cold stares.

"Gentlemen, we face an ethical dilemma," Douglas said thoughtfully. "If we were smart, we'd turn around and walk out that door right now, because we want to enjoy the rest of our liberty and not end up in a Shore Patrol brig because we got into a barroom brawl. But if we leave now, we let down the honor of our shipmates, the *'Burgh*, and the Navy."

"If you think I'm gonna let a bunch of fuzz-faced delinquents scare me off," Scobey said, "you got another think coming!"

"I don't know," Jablonski said. "They look like trouble with a capital *T*. These aren't your usual delinquents."

A waitress came up to their table. She was young, blond, and looked nervous. Her skirt was short and so tight she could hardly walk, and twice she stole quick glances toward the back of the bar, as though aware of all of those cold, dark stares. "H-hi. What'll it be?"

"Gimme a beer," Douglas said. "Stoneybrook, if you got it. Hey, what the hell happened here?"

"What . . . what do you mean?" she asked.

"This used to be a submariner's bar," Jablonski said. "Memorabilia all over the walls. Serviceman's place. What gives?"

The waitress shrugged her shoulders. "The old owner got bought out a couple years ago. New bunch came in. Times change, y'know?" She glanced toward the back of the bar again and swallowed hard. "Anything for the rest of you?"

"Hell of a change," Benson said. His eyes narrowed. The woman was *scared*. "Are you okay, miss? Do you need us to get the police?"

"I'm . . . fine. Thanks." She managed a smile. "You boys off the sub that just came in this morning?"

"That's right," Boyce said. "Fleet's in! Lock up the women and kids!"

She smiled again. "It can't be *that* bad!"

"This looks like a pretty tough neighborhood," Douglas told her. "Didn't used to be. Do you like working here?"

"Hey, times are tough. A girl does what she has to, and cocktailing and waitressing ain't so bad." She glanced back at the bartender, who was watching them closely and with obvious concern. "Look, you guys wanna order, or what?"

"I'll have a Bud," Jablonski said.

"Coke for me," Boyce said.

"I'll have—" Scobey began.

"Awwww, lookit the fairies in their cute little sailor suits," a big voice boomed from nearby. "Hey, guys! Get a load of the pansies!"

Scobey turned in his seat. "You want to turn the volume down, mister? I'm trying to order here."

"Fuck you, faggot!" the biker growled. He stood at least six feet tall and must have weighed 250, with a belly that hung over the waistband of too-tight leather jeans. His hairy chest and arms were bare under a leather vest, and a tattoo of a naked woman seated with her legs spread wide wiggled on his biceps when he flexed his arm. His beard, unkempt and wiry, reached to the top of his breastbone. Leather armbands, a black kerchief over his head, and wraparound sunglasses completed the unappetizing picture.

"What's the problem?" Douglas asked in a carefully reasonable tone. "We're not bothering you. . . ."

"Yeah? How do you know that, squid? You bother me just by existin'! And you're bothering the little lady, here!" He reached out with one thick arm and gathered in the waitress in a tight embrace. "Whassamatter, Sweet Cakes?" he asked.

"These sailor boys bothering you? Don't you worry! They ain't shit! I'll be real happy to protect you! . . ."

"Hey!" She elbowed him in the side hard, but without visible effect. "Lemme go, you pig!"

"You ever been loved by a *real* man, Sweetie? We can fix that!"

"*Leave me alone!*"

Benson was on his feet. "Hey!" he snapped. "Fuzzface! The lady said to leave her alone!"

Douglas closed his eyes. "Jesus Christ," he muttered, but then he was on his feet as well. Then other *Pittsburgh* crewmen rose, chairs scraping on the floor. Behind the bar, the bartender was furiously punching out a number on a telephone. The bar was suddenly so quiet they could hear the clicks of the bartender's fingers on the buttons.

The biker shoved the girl away and swung to face the semicircle of white-uniformed sailors. In the background, the other bikers were slowly forming a phalanx, moving toward the face-to-face showdown. Several wore leather jackets emblazoned with a flaming skull and the legend "Skullbangers."

"Faggots in your tighty whities!" he sneered. "I'll shove those cute little sailor hats up your asses so far you'll fuckin' choke on 'em!"

"We *don't* want trouble," Douglas said, his voice even. "Let us buy you a drink and—"

"You *got* trouble, faggot!" the biker screamed. His hand dipped into a pocket, then reappeared, a switchblade snicking open in a deadly flick of motion. "Take 'em, boys!"

Benson reached down, snatched up the heavy glass ashtray from the table, and swung it roundhouse, bypassing the outthrust knife and connecting hard with the side of the biker's head. Neither ashtray nor skull shattered, but the biker staggered heavily to the side. Scobey knocked the knife from his hand, sending it skittering across the floor.

An instant later, another biker rushed up and grabbed Benson by the jumper. Douglas picked up a chair and swung hard, crashing seat and legs into the tough's back and knocking him down. Benson grabbed a handful of tangled beard and pulled, hard, eliciting a wild yelp. Pivoting hard, he rammed his captive headfirst into the bar with a satisfying thud that didn't quite crack the oak paneling, but then some-one hit him in the back with a pool cue so hard the wood splintered, and the biting pain drove him to his knees.

The next few moments were a whirling kaleidoscope of noise and movement and pain. Benson staggered back to his feet, then went down again as a beefy fist collided with the side of his face.

For a moment, the other four *Pittsburgh*ers held the bikers at bay, standing shoulder to shoulder with chairs raised like a shield wall of old. Rushing forward with a yell, they drove their enemies back a few steps . . . but then the bikers recovered, grabbed the chair legs, and a wild tug-of-war ensued, a battle where the outnumbered and outmuscled submariners must soon lose. Fists flew, connecting with meaty thwacks and shrill yells.

The waitress was screaming. Other patrons were fleeing, squeezing through the open door and into the street. An alarm shrilled as some of the former customers slammed out through an emergency exit in the back rather than risk getting caught up in the free-for-all near the front door. The bartender was wading forward with a baseball bat, screaming obscenities . . . but one of the bikers plucked the weapon from the man's grip and hurled him back across the bar with a stiff-armed shove.

Together, Scobey and Douglas picked up their table and charged, crashing into the bat-wielding man and driving him down and under. Boyce took another biker down with a chair, but then was struck from behind and sent sprawling onto the floor.

Another civilian was on the scene now, a big, slab-muscled man with a gray mustache and a length of lead pipe wrapped in duct tape. "Break it the hell up!" he bellowed.

"Shut the fuck up, Macy!" one of the Bangers yelled back. "Get outta my way!"

Benson thought he could hear the approaching wail of sirens. "C'mon, guys!" he shouted. "Let's get out of here!"

But then someone had picked him up bodily and hurled him through the air. He struck the big plate-glass window and instinctively covered his eyes, knowing he was about to smash through and into the street . . . but miraculously the glass held and he hit the floor, his back shrieking pain.

Scobey hit the glass above him, and this time the pane gave way in a hurricane of whirling shards. Big C crashed through and into the street.

This, Benson decided, was definitely a time for the better part of valor. They didn't stand a chance against these monsters, and if they tried to stay and fight, they would be cut to pieces. Picking up the stunned Boyce, he staggered for the door, ducking as a beer bottle sailed past his head and smashed against the doorjamb. Jablonski and Douglas followed, fighting a rearguard action by throwing chairs, bottles, glasses, and anything else that came to hand at their foes.

But then a sudden rush by a trio of bikers blocked them from their exit. Benson let Boyce slide to the floor, and the remaining three '*Burgh*ers stood back-to-back, facing the menacing ring of leather and steel that was closing on them now from every direction. There were eight of the Skullbangers surrounding them, not counting two out cold on the floor. Not very good odds, Benson decided. The bartender and the man with the lead pipe—Benson thought he must be the owner of the joint—stood beside the bar, watching.

A little help would be a good thing just now, Benson thought. Then one of the bikers lunged, his face a hideous scowl as he barked paint-peeling obscenities. Scobey kicked him hard in the knee, dropping him, but then the others were piling on. Benson was hit in the side of the head and knocked down. The next thing he knew, several stinking, hairy bodies were piling on top of him, raining down blows with fists, bottles, and at least one set of brass knuckles. He curled up, trying to protect his head, neck, genitals, and kidneys all at once. His ears were ringing, and his mouth tasted of copper and salt.

Shrill whistle blasts cut through the bedlam, mingled with sirens. "Awright . . . *awright*!" someone was screaming. "Break it up!"

Several more hard blows landed, but then Benson was being hauled to his feet. His uniform jumper was blood-splattered and dirty. His side hurt like hell, and the room was spinning wildly. It took him a moment to identify the newcomers, a half dozen Shore Patrol, in helmets and armbands bearing the letters SP in white on black, swarming into the bar and separating the combatants.

"Cavalry to the rescue!" a bloody-faced Scobey shouted, though Benson had never heard the Shore Patrol ever called *that*. They waded in, black nightsticks at the ready.

"What the hell's going on!" an SP chief yelled with a voice like the trump of doom.

"Your people smashed my place the hell up!" the civilian with the lead pipe yelled. He pointed. "Look at my place! They smashed it up! Hassled my customers! Who's gonna pay, huh? That's what I wanna know! Who the hell's gonna pay?"

"Okay, mister, okay," the chief said, making calming motions with his hands. "It's all under control now, okay? We're taking them in. You can come down and press charges."

"I want this damage paid for!"

"It will be, sir. But you have to come down to the brig and press charges. . . ."

"Shit!" Benson muttered, rubbing his head. "I thought . . ."

"We're the scapegoats, Rog," Douglas said. He sounded bitter. "Business as usual!"

"Shit!"

The SPs roughly hustled them out of the bar. Outside, an SP van squatted in the street, red-and-blue lights flashing. Someone opened the back, and the five submariners were hustled in, and none too gently.

As they drove off, the chief was still trying to calm the bar's owner.

Six hours later, they were in the Shore Patrol's drunk tank at their Mainside headquarters in Vallejo. It was a small and crowded community wedged in behind steel bars, with two reeking, open toilets and the stink of alcohol, sweat, urine, and vomit.

"Man," Benson said, shaking his head, "this just ain't right!" He was sitting on one of the narrow cots in the cell, a cell now holding a couple of dozen sailors and Marines, with standing room only for newcomers.

"Never expected Vallejo to go the way of Shit City," Douglas said from the cot opposite his. Norfolk, Virginia, had acquired that particular appellation decades before, making a living off the Navy personnel who lived and worked there, but treating them like dirt. That bit of service-civilian animosity lay mostly in the past, now, but there were still plenty of places where the civilians kicked servicemen in the face every chance they got, even while they were pocketing their money for shoddy service and watered-down drinks.

"Yeah," Jablonski said, "I hear ya." His arm was bandaged and in a sling, and he was sitting on the bare concrete floor with his back against the bars. All of them had been treated for cuts, scrapes, and bruises at the small SP dispensary upstairs. None of them had seen Boyce since they'd been brought in, and no one seemed to know what had become of him. "I thought Reagan was making a big comeback for the military, y'know?"

"Aw, some things never change," Scobey said. "Take our money, kick us in the balls. It's a goddamned conspiracy."

"Makes you wonder, doesn't it?" Benson said. "Here we are, supposed to be the front line of defense against the communists, and we get beaten up by punks in a public bar, and the owner sics the SPs on us! There ain't *no* justice!"

"Aw, pipe down, runt!" one of the other prisoners groaned. Benson wasn't surprised to see another *Pittsburgh* crewman. TM2 Mark Doershner was something of a bully, loud, brash, and obnoxious, a self-proclaimed tough guy who got by on the boat by being very good at what he did. "No one wants to hear it!"

"What's the matter, Doershner," Scobey said, grinning. "Too much to drink?"

"Aww . . . there was something in the whiskey at Brunnli's, man. . . ."

"Yeah, yeah, that's what they all say."

"Fuck you, man . . ."

A pair of Shore patrolmen appeared in the green-painted passageway outside the cell. "Awright, listen up!" a First Class petty officer yelled. "Who in here is off the *Pittsburgh*?"

Benson struggled to his feet, as did Douglas, Scobey, and Jablonski. On the far side of the holding cell, Doershner began moving toward the cell door, along with several other enlisted men off the *Burgh*—YM2 Erskine, SN2 Patterson, EM3 Hannacker. As the SP rattled a set of keys in the lock, the eight of them squeezed past the others and filed out through the drunk-tank door.

"Follow me, people," the SP ordered.

The holding tank was in the basement. Upstairs, at the front desk behind the building's front door, Master Chief Warren was waiting for them, accompanied by a pretty young woman.

Benson felt a start of recognition. It was the waitress from the Ram and Ewe, dressed more modestly now in blue jeans and a short-sleeved print blouse. "There he is!" she exclaimed to the COB.

"Fall in!" Warren barked.

The sailors managed an untidy line. Doershner and his pals were clearly drunk; Benson and his three friends were much the worse for wear after the brawl, sore, bruised, and battered. Benson remembered Sanders getting gigged for a spot of rust on his sleeve; the four of them were wearing white jumpers liberally splattered with their own blood.

"Okay, what's the story?" Warren demanded.

"Sir," Douglas said, "EM3 John Boyce was with us. I think he was injured in the fight." He nodded at the watching Shore Patrol petty officers. "We haven't seen him since these people took him away."

"Boyce is okay," Warren told them. "He had some cracked ribs, so they took him to the hospital. He's back aboard the *'Burgh* now with a taped-up chest and a beaut of a black eye. What I want to know is what the hell happened?"

The woman crossed over to Benson and took his arm. "*This* man tried to help me, sir," she said. "Don't you dare punish him!"

"I can't promise that, miss." Warren placed his hands on his hips and looked at each of them. "Well?"

"We ran afoul of some of the locals, COB," Douglas said. "They'd taken over one of our usual hangouts."

"Who started the fight?"

"They did, COB."

"The manager says you people did it."

"Maybe because he figures the government'll pay up," Scobey suggested, "and the bikers won't give him squat."

"Or else he's afraid of 'em," Jablonski added.

"What about you guys?" Warren said, glaring now at Doershner, Erskine, Patterson, and Hannacker.

"We weren't even . . . there," Patterson said, hiccuping impressively in mid-sentence. Erskine appeared to be asleep on his feet.

Warren sighed. "I ought to leave the bunch of you to face mast with the SPs tomorrow morning," he said. "But Chief Dupres owes me a favor and I'm gonna call it in. Get your shit together and get out of here. We're going back to the boat."

"Hell, Master Chief," Jablonski said, "what do the SPs owe you?"

"Never mind. Just thank the luck of Davy Jones himself

that the SPs picked you up, and not the local cops. I don't have *nearly* as much pull with them!"

"Excuse me, Master Chief," Douglas said, as they emerged from the building and into the cool night air, "but how'd you know we were here?"

"Miss Radley, here. She called the front gate, asking to talk to the skipper of the boat that just pulled in today. That would be us. She sounded pretty excited, so they routed her call through to me and I came out to talk to her. Jesus, Benson. According to her, you were playing the white knight in town tonight."

"Not really, COB. . . ."

"Stow it. You guys aren't off the hook, not by six thousand leagues. I had to promise that you would all go up in front of the Old Man, and you damned straight will." He hesitated. "All of you are with me . . . except you, Benson. But be damned sure you're back aboard when liberty expires at zero-six-hundred hours!"

"Aye *aye*, COB!" Benson exclaimed.

He watched with something like awe as the Chief of the Boat ushered the other seven sailors into the back of a truck waiting on the street, clambered into the passenger's side of the cab, and roared off into the night. He felt the woman's arms wrap themselves around his.

"I guess I have you to thank, huh?" he said. "I don't even know your name."

"Carol," she told him. "Carol Radley. I'm just sorry it took so long. I had to wait until my shift was over at ten, and then I didn't know who to call."

"You did just *fine*, ma'am. Just *fine*." He felt her squeeze his arm, and he couldn't tell if she was coming on to him, or just being nice. "Uh, I really appreciate what you did for me and the fellas."

"Uh-uh. I have to thank *you*. I haven't seen bravery like that outside of the movies!"

"Wasn't bravery. I just wasn't going to let that guy get away with acting like that."

"Exactly my point. Come on."

"Where?"

"Back to my place."

"Huh?"

"I want to put something on those cuts and scrapes, and maybe some raw meat for that bruise on your jaw. After that, we'll see."

Dazed and wondering if he were dreaming, Benson let her lead him to her car. " 'Squeeeee,' " he said.

Sunday, 5 July 1987

En Route to Mare Island
1235 hours local time

It had taken almost three hours to get the kid to say something other than a tight-voiced "Yes, sir!" or "No, sir!" Commander Gordon had met him during the long flight out from Washington, when it had turned out that his assigned seat on the 737 was next to his own. Gordon had seen the kid's nervousness and started talking to him gently to see if he could get him to relax a bit. It wasn't that Gordon was feeling in a paternal way; he just didn't care for the idea of a four-hour flight with a nervous wreck strapped into the seat next to his.

At last, though—somewhere over the Great Plains—Gordon had begun to get through. Seaman Doug O'Brien was newly out of Submarine School at Groton, Connecticut, and was on his way to his first assignment. He wasn't wearing dolphins on his dress white blouse, yet, the badge that marked him as a submariner. That would come later, after he passed a probationary period of learning all there was to learn about working in each department on his boat.

"So . . . what boat are you assigned to, son?" Gordon asked him, once a more meaningful dialogue than simple affirmatives and negatives had been established.

"Uh . . . my ship is the USS *Pittsburgh*, sir. SSN-720."

"Uh-uh, son. Full aback. A submarine is always a *boat*, never a ship. Didn't you pick that up in sub school?"

"Well, they kept talking about 'boats,' yeah . . . but a buddy of mine told me they were setting me up for a kind of joke, see?"

Gordon nodded. "Well, sounds to me like it was your friend who was setting you up for the joke. Submariners are pretty dogmatic about being aboard boats, not ships. Same thing with Navy aviators."

"Sir?"

"To the men stationed aboard an aircraft carrier, the carrier is a ship. But to the aviators, the men in the carrier's air wing, she's a 'boat.'" He grinned. "Don't try to figure out the logic of it. Sailors have been using language their own way to define their special world for a couple of thousand years at the very least."

"Okay . . ." He didn't sound too sure of himself.

"So, anyway, you're about to join the *Pittsburgh*?"

"Yes, *sir*! She's at a place called Mare Island. That's somewhere near San Francisco, but I don't exactly know where."

Gordon chuckled. It had to be, of course. He didn't tell the youngster that he was headed for the same new duty station . . . as O'Brien's captain.

"Well, I'm sure she's a good boat," he said. "I know her skipper."

"You do?" O'Brien's eyes grew large.

"He was my roommate at Annapolis, actually, and the best man at my wedding. Mike Chase. A good man."

"Gosh! I keep hearing how small the Navy really is, sir, how you keep bumping into the same people. I guess that's true, huh?"

"You have *no* idea!"

Gordon could tell that O'Brien wanted to ask where Gordon was going, but was afraid to speak up. To a young seaman—nineteen, maybe eighteen years old—fresh out of boot camp and C-school, a ship captain was a godlike figure rarely glimpsed, and then with an awe approaching terror. The Olympian likes of commanders never socialized, never fraternized with enlisted mortals . . . none below the rank of E-5, at any rate. Gordon was afraid that if he admitted to who and what he was, the young man would swallow his heart.

Much of the rest of the flight they passed in silence, the boy watching the mountains slide by beneath the aircraft, while Gordon leaned his seat back and tried to nap. He thought about Becca again, and suppressed a stab of regret. How was he going to make this right with her?

He'd told her about the new assignment that evening, of course, the day he'd gotten his orders from Goldman. He'd taken her out to a favorite restaurant and sprung the news over a bowl of Maryland crab soup.

She hadn't seemed surprised. Her reaction was so lackluster, in fact, that at first he was certain her father had indeed told her all about it, and that she'd simply been waiting to hear it from him.

"The Navy wife's life," was all she'd said.

"You don't sound happy about it."

"Should I be? All my friends are here in Alexandria. Ellen and Margaret are settled in with their friends and school."

"It's summer, Becca. No school until September. If we're going to move, now's the time to do it, so we don't interrupt the kids' school year."

"And what if we don't want to follow you all the way across the country? Damn it, Frank, why can't you have a normal job that keeps you nine to five and doesn't send you off to the other end of the earth every six months?"

"You knew you were getting a sailor when you married me. You knew what it would be like." Damn it, she'd grown up in a Navy home, had hopscotched all over the world as her father had risen to the pinnacle of his career.

"And maybe I want something better for me! Better for my babies!"

"You're a Navy wife, Becca. . . ."

"You don't have to remind me! . . ."

Gordon lay back in the 737's seat and thought about the miles slipping away beneath him, taking him farther and farther away from Becca. He wanted to support her, but sometimes she was just so damned illogical about things. . . .

He could read the weather signs well enough to know that his marriage was in serious trouble right now. Becca's depression . . . he wasn't sure he could handle that and his career, not *now*, not when things were just starting to break his way at long, long last.

He loved her, loved her as much as it was possible for one to love another. And he hurt for her, and hurt because there didn't seem to be anything he could do to help.

In fact, everything he did just seemed to make things worse.

The plane touched down at San Francisco International Airport. As an incoming ship captain, he rated a car and driver—a young third class who met him in the terminal with a hand-lettered sign reading "CDR GORDON." A few moments later, he saw O'Brien, his young traveling companion, waiting at the baggage-claim belt.

"You want a ride out to the base, son?"

The youngster's jaw dropped. "Huh? I mean . . . sure!" The alternative was a long wait and a ride in a Navy bus. "Are you going out to Mare Island, too?"

"Sure am. Grab your bags and meet me over there by the door."

His driver retrieved Gordon's bag, and minutes later, bags slung into the trunk, they were in a gray Navy sedan winding out of San Francisco International and heading north up the Bay on the James Lick Freeway.

Picking up 80 in downtown San Francisco, they crossed the San Francisco–Oakland Bay Bridge, paid their toll, and then continued following 80 north.

Traffic was light, and twenty minutes later they were approaching the Carquinez Bridge, which spanned the mouth of the Sacramento River where it joined the Napa River from the north and spilled into San Pablo Bay, which comprised the northern reaches of San Francisco Bay.

Gordon had done some reading up on Mare Island ahead of time. As their car crossed the toll bridge into Vallejo, he pointed out the Mare Island Naval Shipyard to O'Brien, ahead and to their left.

"The island got its name back in 1830," he told the youngster. "A mare belonging to the leader of a Mexican mapping expedition was swept away by the current of the Sacramento River at the Carquinez Straits . . . right below this bridge. Somehow, it managed to make it to shore on the southern tip of the island. They called it Isla de la Yegua after that . . . Mare Island.

"The U.S. Navy arrived on the scene when David Farragut came in and took command in 1854. Today the base covers something like 2600 acres . . . a lot more at low tide. It's home to the shipyard, a naval station, the Combat Systems Technical School Command, the Engineering Duty Officer School, and something like twenty-three, twenty-four other commands. Several submarines are usually home-ported here . . . especially the ones assigned to sneaky-Pete ops in the western Pacific."

"Sneaky-Pete?"

"Covert operations. The missions the U.S. government does not admit take place."

"I always wondered about that, sir. I mean, you hear things, read things, sometimes, about stuff happening, like secret missions into Russia and places like that. I never really believed any of them, of course."

Gordon smiled. The kid was pretty naïve . . . and utterly

unaware that he was sitting next to the man who'd conned a U.S. sub into the heart of the USSR's White Sea.

"Things like that do happen, son. More often than you'd believe. But we don't talk about them. Submariners are a pretty closed-mouth lot to begin with."

"Uh . . . sir? Are you a submariner?"

"Open your eyes, son." He nodded slightly toward the gold dolphins riding his uniform jacket, just above the rows of colored ribbons.

"Oh! Sorry, sir. I didn't notice. I guess I didn't want to look like I was prying."

"The fruit salad is there to be read, son. As is the badge. Helps you know who you're dealing with. It's not rude to know something about your shipmate."

"I understand, sir. Thank you, sir."

Gordon sighed. He didn't think the kid really understood, even yet.

They rode in silence through Vallejo, along the typical Navy-town avenue with its uniform shops and tattoo parlors, locker services for civvies and magazine shops ripe with skin mags and crotch novels.

They turned left and crossed the G-Street Bridge above the sullen brown stillness of the Napa River, crossing onto Mare Island and stopping at the main gate, where Gordon, O'Brien, and the driver all showed their IDs. Gordon told the driver to drop O'Brien off at the enlisted barracks first, before taking him on to the Bachelor Officers' Quarters, BOQ.

"I guess they don't come much greener than that," the driver said, shaking his head as he removed Gordon's luggage from the trunk.

"We all have to start somewhere," Gordon replied. "And it's usually at the bottom. Thanks for the ride."

"My pleasure, sir."

He followed the driver into the BOQ, where he signed in at the front desk. *We all have to start somewhere*, he thought. *Where the hell do I start with my marriage?*

Tuesday, 7 July 1987

On board USS *Pittsburgh*
Pier 2, Mare Island Naval Submarine Station
Vallejo, California
0453 hours local time

"Now fire in the reactor room, fire in the reactor room!"
Klaxons blared, red lights flashed, lending an air of surreal
urgency to a scene already verging on nightmarish. *"All
hands, man your damage-control stations! That is, man your
fire and damage-control stations!"*

Panic flooded through Doug O'Brien's mind. A reactor
fire! And he didn't know what his duty station was, or where
he was supposed to be.

*"Now flooding in the reactor compartment, flooding in the
reactor compartment. Damage-control watch, report to
flooding stations. . . ."*

O'Brien sat bolt upright in his rack . . . and smashed his
forehead into the bottom of the rack above his, hard. "God
damn it," he exclaimed, dropping back to his thin mattress,
hands cupped over his forehead. "Shit, shit, *shit!*" Thrashing, he rolled through the curtain separating him from the
rest of the boat, landing on bare feet on the cold linoleum
tile deck of the crew's quarters.

Odd. The emergency Klaxon was no longer sounding. He
heard only the gentle hum of the *Pittsburgh's* ventilator system, the normal-sounding scuffs, bumps, and scrapes of
other men going about their duties elsewhere on the boat.

He was standing in the passageway beside his rack, in
Pittsburgh's crew spaces. There was no reactor emergency,
no flooding.

He was going to live. *Live!*

Had the emergency, then, been just a *dream*?

"Jesus! . . ."

"Hey, keep it down out there!" a groggy voice called from
one of the curtained-off racks.

He groaned and looked at his watch. Almost time for reveille. No time in any case to get back in his rack for another ten or fifteen minutes' sleep. He might as well get up and get moving.

Lifting the bottom of his rack, he opened up his personal locker and from the recess within pulled his shower thongs, soap case, and shampoo bottle, then skinned out of his T-shirt and boxers and removed his watch. Taking a towel, he flip-flopped aft to the shower head, where he stepped into a stall and began wetting down.

The nightmare, he recognized now, was one he'd been having a lot lately, ever since his first few weeks at Sub School in Groton, where the students were subjected to a steady run of alarms and drills, designed to get them to react, and react correctly, the instant something bad started to go down.

By the time he'd finished his shower and dried himself, the morning watch was rousting from their racks. *"Now reveille, reveille, reveille,"* a voice was calling from a speaker overhead. *"All hands on deck. . . ."*

And then, *"The uniform of the day is dungarees. The smoking lamp is lit in all authorized compartments. . . ."*

And O'Brien's second day of life aboard a Navy sub began.

He'd reported aboard yesterday, after spending Sunday night at a receiving barracks ashore.

Born in Rockville, Illinois, out on the flat and corn-shrouded prairie northwest of Chicago, Doug O'Brien had started out about as far from the sea and a sailor's life as was possible. His father worked in a John Deere dealership and never talked about his three years as an Army draftee in the late sixties. Certainly, there'd been no pressure on him at home to join the all-volunteer Navy, much less a volunteer elite within the Navy like the Silent Service.

But he'd wanted to be a submariner ever since he'd seen *The Enemy Below* as a kid. Sure, the submariners in that movie had been Germans, the *bad guys* . . . but somehow

Kurt Jurgens had made life aboard a German U-boat seem glamorous and exciting. O'Brien had been a small kid, and bright—two strikes against him when he went to school and began losing fights with bullies who beat him up for his lunch money or simply because they could.

Somehow, the image of the German sailors singing through the shattering thunder of a depth-charge attack had raised images of a camaraderie that the lonely O'Brien had never dreamed of before.

For you, *my friend, and* you, *my friend, and all of us together . . .*

The beatings his father had given him to punish him for losing the fights with the bullies had made things impossibly worse at home, especially after his mother had left and his father had started getting drunk every night. He'd run away from home on the morning of his eighteenth birthday and signed up with a Navy recruiter in Chicago that same afternoon.

Dressing in his dungarees, he made his way to the enlisted mess, only getting turned around and lost once. Unlike a supercarrier, even an L.A.-class submarine was essentially a sewer pipe with three decks, and it was pretty hard to lose your way.

The Crew's Mess was the largest single open space on board the boat, big enough for six tables with their attached seats, plus a counter leading into the galley forward, and an array of drink dispensers—various offerings of soda and the ever-present drink beloved of submariners for decades, the fruit drink known solely as "bug juice."

He took a metal tray from the stack and filed through the chow line, receiving hefty servings of scrambled eggs, bacon, fried potatoes, and sausage, with a glass of orange bug juice in the place of the time-honored tradition of Navy coffee. He'd never acquired a taste for the stuff, even though he'd wanted to like it in order to fit in with the other sailors almost from his first breakfast in boot camp at Great Lakes.

Much of the day before, his first day aboard, was still a

fuzzy blur made dim by strangeness, haste, and exhaustion. He'd been through an orientation program right here at this same mess table, where he'd learned that he would have to rotate through each department aboard the *Pittsburgh* to earn his "quals," beginning with the torpedo room. He would not win his coveted dolphins until all of his department supervisors had trained him, tested him, and signed him off.

Seconds after he sat down and started shoveling into the eggs, some of his new companions joined him. Boatswain's Mate First Class Charles Scobey—though everyone called him "Big C"—sat down on his left, while Torpedoman's Mate Second Class Roger Benson sat down on his right. Electronics Technician Second Class James T. Jablonski, his left arm in a light blue hospital sling, set his tray down one-handed and sat down on the other side of the mess table.

"So, get lost yet, nub?" Jablonski asked cheerily. "Nub," O'Brien had learned the day before, stood for "Non-Useful Body," a "newbie," a sailor fresh out of school and serving aboard a boat for the first time. It was an appellation he would not be able to escape until he'd signed off on his quals and won his dolphins.

"Not really."

"Well, nub," Scobey said, "don't sweat it. You'll be scrambling to get your bearings for a few days, but you'll catch on. If the Old Man or the Exec don't have you for breakfast first." The others laughed.

"You can forget most of what they taught you in Sub School," Benson said. "Living on a submarine isn't like living anywhere else in the world, 'cept maybe on board a ship out in space somewhere."

"Well, that's not exactly 'in the world,' is it?" Scobey put in.

"Shit, Big C, you know what I mean. Anyway, like I was sayin', you need to get used to a whole new lifestyle. Port 'n' starboard watches that go on and on for weeks, sometimes. Hot bunking."

"A 688 Flight II boat like the *Pittsburgh* doesn't have

enough racks for all of her enlisted people," Scobey told him. "So you'll be sharing your rack with someone else, with a schedule drawn up so that one of you is sleeping when the other's working."

"You've got a hell of a lot to learn," Benson told him. "All the tricks of the trade, as it were."

"Take the bug juice," Jablonski said with the air of a sage discussing arcane philosophies. He gestured grandly at the glass of orange liquid sitting on the table in front of O'Brien. "Now a true submariner knows that the *red* juice is the good stuff. The orange stuff, though . . . pah! Don't drink it. *Ever!* It'll rot your insides!"

"I saw an experiment done once," Scobey said, nodding. "Y'take a piece of iron—a flat metal fitting or plate. You tie it to a string and let it hang inside a glass of orange bug juice. Three days later, you haul it out and have a look. The iron plate's riddled full of holes, worse'n Swiss cheese! Imagine what it's doin' to your guts!"

"Works with the red bug juice, too," Jablonski said.

"I've seen that done with Coke," Benson put in. When the others scowled at him for taking their psych-out campaign off-topic, he added, "but it works really, *really* well with bug juice."

"Actually, the orange shit is great as an all-purpose solvent and scouring agent," Jablonski put in. "Real high acid content, y'know? Scours tiles and fittings better'n soap powder. Just don't ever use it on any 'J' or 'Y' type fittings."

"Wha . . . what are those?" O'Brien asked.

"Damn it, kid, don't you know anything?" Scobey exploded.

"What are they teaching you kids at Groton these days?" Benson asked, shaking his head.

"J and Y fittings are the ones with rubber seals," Scobey said, with the patient air of one telling the absolute truth to an absolute idiot, "and they lead to the outside of the boat. Things like seawater-intake valves and positive-pressure flushing flanges."

"Waste-dump outlets," Jablonski said, nodding. "Pressure-balance influx lines."

"Right," Scobey said. "If you use acid on them—and that orange shit *does* have a real high acid content, believe me!—it'll eat through the rubber, rupture the seals, and some chilly day when we're at a thousand feet they'll fail. You ever seen what happens when water comes in through a rup-tured seal, with a pressure behind it of five hundred pounds per square inch? It ain't pretty!"

"I scraped one poor nub off the bulkhead once," Jablonski said, shaking his head sadly. "Used a three-inch paint scraper and a sponge to get as much of him into the body bag as I could. Only found about this much, though." He held his hands out, shaping a shape the size of a basketball. "Five, maybe six pounds' worth. We decided to use a plastic trash bag from the galley instead of a regular body bag, 'cause there just wasn't enough left to make it cost-effective! You know, those regular body bags cost hundreds of dollars each."

"I remember that," Scobey said, almost mournfully. "There were bits of bone and teeth that were driven across the compartment and actually embedded in the steel bulk-head. Needed a dentist's drill and pick to dig them all out. . . ."

O'Brien's brows slammed together at that. "Hey!" he said around a mouthful of egg. "If that'd really happened, the *Pittsburgh* would've gone down and never come up again! You guys are pulling my leg!"

"How do you know it *didn't*?" Scobey said, leaning close by O'Brien's ear, dropping his voice to a melodramatic growl. "How do you know the '*Burgh* isn't a ghost ship . . . and that you were doomed to walk her decks with the rest of us the moment you set foot aboard her haunted decks! . . ."

O'Brien blinked, swallowed, then shook his head. "Geeze! You guys!"

He'd heard dark tales in Sub School about the hazing that went on with newbies aboard submarines. These seemed like pretty decent guys, though, and so far their hazing had been merely of the tall-tale variety.

ST3 David Kellerman brought his tray to the table.

"Squee!" Benson exclaimed. "How the hell are you?"

"'Squee?'" O'Brien asked, confused. Some submariner terminology was absolutely baffling.

"Don't ask," Boatswain's Mate First Class Archie Douglas said, joining the table.

"Oh, you can *ask*," Scobey said. "But if we told you, then Squee here would have to kill you. And we need you topside today on a working party."

"I thought I was supposed to start my quals in the torpedo room today."

Benson laughed. "You are, sort of. But the first thing you have to do is learn how to bring the torpedoes aboard. And before that, you have to take them off the boat. Can't have all that high-explosive shit just floating here beside Pier Two, waiting for some idiot to trip and fall and set the whole shebang off, and maybe take half of Vallejo with it."

"And getting torpedoes on and off the boat is a major evolution," Jablonski said, "because they haven't yet figured out a way to make a nineteen-foot-long Mark 48 torpedo go around corners in a submarine's companionways."

"Well, how *do* they do it?" O'Brien asked. "I know there's a forward torpedo-loading hatch, but I've never seen it actually done."

"What are they teaching you kids in school these days?" Douglas said, shaking his head sadly.

"Don't worry," Scobey said darkly. "You'll see. You'll see!"

Dockside, Mare Island Naval Submarine Station
Vallejo, California
0801 hours local time

Commander Gordon stood at attention, his right hand rigidly held with fingertips touching the right side of his uniform cap's bill. Commander Mike Chase stood to his right in an identical pose as they faced the flagpole above the dockside where a colors party was running up the flag. The last notes of the "Star-Spangled Banner" floated from a loudspeaker on the side of a nearby building. The two men dropped their salutes, and watched as the colors party formed up and marched away in parade-ground step.

"Still brings a lump to the throat, eh?" Chase said quietly.

"Always," Gordon replied.

Chase looked at the other man. Once they had been best friends, Annapolis roommates, about as close as two men could be.

A lot had happened in the twenty years since. For a time, Gordon had thought Chase'd been trying to sabotage his career. That had not been the case, but the distance between them had never closed up.

It was damned hard to find trust for a man once the old trust between them had seemed betrayed.

"So," Chase continued, as they turned and started walking toward the dockside. Seabirds shrieked overhead, circling, and bent white wings above the water. "When do you want to start going over the manifests?"

"Whenever convenient," Gordon replied. "Today, if you like."

"Not today," Chase said, smiling ruefully. "We're about to have an infestation of suits."

"Suits?" Gordon raised an eyebrow.

"Folks from Washington. Read Langley. I understand they want to debrief us on our last op."

"I see. What was the last op?"

"Can't tell you. Sorry."

"That classified?"

"That classified. And compartmentalized. And sanitized. And the key thrown away afterward."

"Hell of a way to run a Navy."

"My sense is that the Powers That Be are a bit nervous after the Walker incident."

The Walkers had been an entire family of Navy spies—

John Walker, who'd started selling secrets when he'd been a Navy officer in 1967, his defense contractor brother, his Navy lieutenant son, and his best friend, also a naval officer. They'd been discovered only in 1985, after they'd already done incalculable damage. The word was that the new Soviet subs coming off the ways right now, ultrafast and ultrasilent, were the product, in part, of the Walkers' espionage efforts.

"And I'm going to put to sea with a whole crew who knows more about where the boat's been recently than I do!"

"They may decide to fill you in," Chase said quietly. "With all the haste . . . with the suits swarming everywhere . . ."

"What?"

"I don't know. I just have the feeling the *'Burgh* is going to go right back into the lion's den again."

"And the next mission might have something to do with the last one?"

"Maybe."

"What makes you say that?"

"Nothing specific. Just a feeling, is all."

"Well, I don't want to come on board and spook the men," Gordon said. "Give me a call when we can get together and go over the books."

"Will do." Chase hesitated.

"What's the matter?" Gordon asked.

"Nothing really. Just a wonderment. I have to hold a captain's mast sometime this week. Five guys got into a fight in town the other night. Got pretty badly banged up."

"Sounds like they already got their punishment."

"That's true. But you know I can't let it slide."

"Of course not. What's the problem?"

"The problem is they had a raw deal handed to them on a platter. From what COB tells me, a biker gang decided to pick on them. They fought back. Predictable outcome."

"Ouch."

"The bartender wanted to press charges for damages. He knew he wasn't going to get it out of the bikers!"

"Yeah. I follow."

"COB got the men sprung, but the civilian establishment is still going to want to see justice done."

"So what have you done to the poor bastards so far?"

"Docked 'em liberty over the holiday. Though I *did* let the ones who wanted come topside to watch the fireworks over the Bay Saturday. But if they come up before me on mast, I'll have to dock 'em pay and give 'em extra duty. Seems a hell of a way to treat these boys, after what they've been through already."

And what they're likely to go through next. That shared but unspoken thought hung between them for a moment.

"Suggestion?" Gordon said.

"Shoot."

"Lose the forms."

"Eh?"

"Lose the forms. Since you're outgoing, they won't have any way to get hold of you, and I can play dumb. I'll refer them up the ladder all the way to Washington if I have to. If they want to sue the government, let 'em. By the time things straighten out, we'll be long gone to sea."

Chase nodded. "And from what I hear, you'll be home-porting down at San Diego after this. It'll be years before *Pittsburgh* sees Vallejo again."

"Sound workable?"

"Absolutely. I was hoping you'd think of that."

Gordon laughed. "I'd rather take care of our people than some parasite ashore."

"Amen. Well, I'd better go aboard and get squared away for our guests."

"I wish you luck."

"Thanks. We'll need it."

Chase walked down the pier, then stepped out onto the brow connecting the *Pittsburgh* with the dock. A small guard hut of strictly ceremonial utility had been erected on the *'Burgh*'s deck aft of her sail, along with a confusion of safety lines and temporary stanchions. A Navy sentry came to attention as Chase saluted the ensign aft, then saluted the OD.

A ship's bell dinged twice. "*Pittsburgh*, arriving," a voice said over a loudspeaker, the ancient declaration that the ship's captain had just come aboard.

But not for much longer, he thought. The knowledge that he would soon be departing *Pittsburgh* for the last time hurt like the anticipated loss of a loved one.

Tuesday, 7 July 1987

Topside-Forward Deck, USS *Pittsburgh*
Pier 2, Mare Island Naval Submarine Station
Vallejo, California
1120 hours local time

"Easy there . . . *easy!*"

Seaman O'Brien stood shoulder to shoulder with the rest of the working party, working under the combined direction of Lieutenant Walberg, the boat's Weapons Officer, or "Weps," the Chief of the Boat, and the supervisor of a gang of dockworkers all clustered around the weapons-loading hatch forward of the *Pittsburgh*'s sail. All of them wore life jackets and safety lines, which encumbered them a bit . . . but which were worth it when you considered the possibility of a false step or a heavy, free-swinging piece of machinery sending you ass over into the sea.

Pittsburgh carried a total of twenty-four of the big Mark 48 torpedoes, each a blunt-tipped pencil nineteen feet long and twenty-one inches thick, and weighing in at just over 3500 pounds. Sheathed in silver, with bright blue plastic protective nose shrouds, they gleamed in the morning sun as they slid slowly, magnificently, from the black depths of the submarine's forward hull.

Los Angeles class boats mounted four torpedo tubes, each of which went to sea warshot-loaded, plus room for an additional twenty-two reloads. Normally, however, one or two of the storage racks in the torpedo room were left empty, to allow the TMs to reach the stored weapons for maintenance, and to allow some extra room in the compartment for moving their long and massive charges about. All of those torpedoes were coming out of the *Pittsburgh*'s bowels for routine shoreside inspection and replacement.

O'Brien had learned how the huge torpedoes were maneuvered on and off the boat. The entire flooring of the second deck had been torn up and reassembled as a loading rack leading down from the weapons hatch through to the torpedo room on the third deck. Part of the third deck had been taken up as well, converted to a transit rack for maneuvering the torpedoes to or from their cradles.

O'Brien's work detail had started out working below deck in the torpedo room. From there, the redecoration had created what looked to O'Brien like a deep, sheer-walled canyon cutting straight through the heart of the boat forward of the sail. The berthing space with his rack and storage space was now part of an open slot three decks high, allowing the torpedoes, once lowered through a hatch just wide enough to receive them, with the crew's racks visible as part of the wall to either side. Each torpedo was manhandled from its cradle in the torpedo room and fed up into the loading rack, then gently maneuvered up the chute until it emerged, nose-first, from the loading hatch.

O'Brien had been reassigned after a time to the topside working party, helping to manhandle the torpedoes out of the hatch. Pulled by the considerable muscle of a cradle winch, but guided by the combined muscle power of the working party, each torpedo was pulled free of *Pittsburgh*'s embrace and locked into a cradlelike loading tray, which had been mounted on the upper deck forward of the loading hatch and elevated to a nearly sixty-degree angle.

Once clear of the hatch, the torpedo, snug now in the loading tray with its high, U-shaped flanges, was lowered until it was horizontal to the deck. Then it was attached to the business end of a towering, bright yellow crane on the pier alongside the submarine, which hauled it up and swayed it clear to a waiting torpedo cradle on the dock.

The evolution was a polished and smooth-running dance of men and machines; O'Brien was surprised at the efficiency of the design, which cleverly hid the loading equipment, racks, and guides as part of the boat's decks. A popular pastime for all enlisted men in the Navy was to gripe at the way things *didn't* work; this time, though, some careful thought and spectacular engineering had gone into the loading design. The entire process of unloading or loading *Pittsburgh*'s high-explosive toys—including the process of breaking down the decks and setting up the handling gear—took just twelve hours.

O'Brien found it interesting, though, that even in an age of push-button warfare, computers, and automatic machinery, the actual dirty work of manhandling torpedoes on and off a submarine still required considerable old-fashioned sweat and muscle power.

"Okay!" Master Chief Warren called. "Secured!"

"Let 'er go! Haul 'er up! Up! Up!" Weps called, and the torpedo they were currently working on was swayed free of the loading tray. Steadied by a half dozen lines held by men on the deck and on the pier, the torpedo was swayed clear of the deck, out over the dark water, and edged gently toward the waiting cradle ashore.

O'Brien and the others had a few moments, then, to rest. It was hot as the day pushed toward noon. The sun had burned off all of the fog that had lain over Mare Island and the straits between the base and Vallejo earlier that morning. Seabirds shrieked and wheeled; close about the *Pittsburgh*, a line of bright orange, pillow-sized floats bobbed with the swell, a containment device designed to prevent any accidental spillage of hazardous chemicals from contaminating the water.

Movement caught his eye ashore. Turning, he watched a trio of men in civilian clothing—dark suits, white shirts, dark glasses—walk down the pier, picking their way past the dockworkers, the yellow crane, and the crates and coiled piles of wire rope that made the pier a cluttered and watch-your-step journey. Reaching the *Pittsburgh*'s brow, they turned and came up the walkway, stopping to talk with the sentry and Officer of the Deck, who waited for them at the guard shack abaft of *Pittsburgh*'s sail.

"What the hell is going on there?" TM3 Gilbert asked, staring aft.

"Yeah," O'Brien said. "What are they made up as? FBI? CIA?"

"Ah, we have inspectors coming aboard all the time," Benson said. "Inspectin' this, inspectin' that. They're probably here to quiz the reactor gang, and maybe pick up a few hundred pages of reports, in quintiplicate."

A few moments later, the trio was led to the hatch by an enlisted rating, and they vanished down into the boat.

"Hey, hey, hey!" Master Chief Warren called. "Who told you people to stop working? Heads up! Another weapon on the way!"

With a sigh, O'Brien returned to the backbreaking work at hand.

He wondered, though, about those somehow sinister visitors now aboard the boat.

The work proceeded at a steady, wearying pace. They broke for dinner—the midday meal was referred to as "dinner," with "supper" served in the evening—and were back at work by 1300 hours. They had just finished swaying another torpedo out of *Pittsburgh*'s depths when a third class O'Brien hadn't met before came forward. "Seaman O'Brien?"

"That's me."

"You're wanted below. Now."

"What for?"

"Beats me. The skipper said to come get you. He didn't say why."

O'Brien looked at Walberg, who nodded. "Go ahead, son. When the Old Man barks, you jump!"

"Aye aye, sir. Thank you, sir."

He unclipped his safety line and followed the third class aft, past the sail and down the forward escape trunk ladder. Handing off his life jacket to another rating headed topside, he threaded his way forward, following the man to the Officers' Wardroom.

He hesitated at the threshold. The Wardroom was terra incognito for an enlisted man, especially one as green as he was. From behind the door, he could hear Captain Chase's voice raised in cold anger. "You know what I think? I think you're all crazy!"

The third class rapped on the door.

"Enter, damn it!"

The sailor opened the door. "Seaman O'Brien, Captain." He stepped aside so O'Brien could squeeze inside.

The Wardroom was luxuriously appointed by the standards of other parts of the boat, though it was about as roomy as a corner booth in the local diner. A tidy little pantry area aft included a coffeemaker and fixings. Most of the compartment was taken up by a single table surrounded by chairs. This was where the boat's officers ate their meals, did their paperwork, and relaxed.

Commander Chase sat at one end of the table, his expression one of barely controlled fury. Opposite sat the three civilians O'Brien had seen come aboard a short time before. One had a laptop computer open on the table, a device O'Brien had heard about, but never seen; the others had notebooks open before them, and manila folders stuffed with papers.

"O'Brien," Chase said, "these . . . gentlemen have some questions for you. They've also asked that they talk to you alone. Is that okay with you?"

"Uh . . . sir? What have I done?"

"So far as I know, not a damned thing. You're not in any trouble, but they do have some questions for you. Will you talk with them?"

"Sure. I mean, yes, sir. But—"

"Answer to the best of your ability, son. Tell them what they want to know." He stood up, but turned at the door before he left. "And I will talk with you three again when you're done!"

The door closed, and O'Brien was left alone with the civilians. They presented a vaguely comic aspect in their dark suit coats and ties, slightly rumpled by their descent down the boat's ladder. One was even still wearing his dark glasses, though the fluorescent overhead lighting in the compartment was scarcely hard on the eyes.

"Have a seat, please," one of them said, in tones not conducive to peace of mind.

O'Brien was afraid.

During his twelve weeks of boot camp at Great Lakes Naval Training Center, there'd been one serious problem for his company. The ARPOC—the Assistant Recruit Petty Officer Chief—had gotten into some serious trouble when he'd lost his bayonet.

Boot companies had an RPOC and an ARPOC, drawn from among the recruits of each unit and given certain limited command responsibilities. The Recruit Petty Officer Chief, besides the miniature chief's crow and knot he wore on his right shoulder, as opposed to the full rate and rank emblems worn on the left after graduation from recruit training, carried an old-fashioned dress cavalry saber as an emblem of his position. At parade formations, he was expected to salute with it . . . which was about all it was good for.

The ARPOC also carried a badge of office, an M-1 bayonet, its blade so dull it probably would have smashed, rather than cut, cheese.

One night, at about Week 9 of training, the ARPOC for O'Brien's company had gone bowling at the rec center on the base. Somehow, he'd managed to lose his bayonet. He'd accidentally left it behind after the game, and when he realized it was missing and returned to look for it, it was gone.

It seemed a minor enough crime . . . sheer clumsiness, and nothing more sinister. But so far as the Navy was concerned, a *weapon* had been lost, and weapons had to be accounted for.

The ARPOC—his name was Jack Hillel—had vanished. The other sailors who'd been with him that night, and O'Brien was one of them, had been taken one after another into the company commander's office in the barracks and grilled by a couple of gray-suited men from the FBI. The crime, as they called it, had been committed on a federal reservation, and, as such, was a federal crime.

Well, O'Brien had understood some of the concern, at least. Boot camp was a close association of over a hundred kids from every walk of life, including gangs and street kids from the inner cities. At that point in their naval careers, many of them didn't have much sense, and some were pretty wild, yet. And now, presumably, one of them had a knife, a potentially serious, even deadly situation.

The investigation had continued for a week. For that entire week, O'Brien and the others in his company had lived in dread of the consequences. It was possible that the entire company would suffer for Hillel's "crime," especially if the powers that were suspected that someone in the company had the bayonet and was hiding it.

In the end, nothing much happened. The word was that Hillel had been set back two weeks, transferred to another company. Nothing else was said about the bayonet . . . which was never seen again.

That interview with the FBI agents in the CO's office had been one of the worst moments in O'Brien's life up to that point.

The interview with the three men in the *Pittsburgh*'s wardroom, though, was worse, much worse.

And far more personal.

"You are Douglas Henry O'Brien," one of the men said, reading from a file full of loose sheets of paper.

"Yes, sir?"

"Aren't you sure?"

"Yes, sir. Who are you people?"

"Never mind that now." One of them pulled out a photograph and showed it to him. "You know this guy?"

It appeared to be a candid shot of a Navy commander and, yes, he did know the man. It was the friendly officer he'd sat next to on the plane flight from DC to San Francisco on Sunday. He thought the man had mentioned his name, but he couldn't remember.

"Yes, sir. He had the seat next to mine on my flight out here from the East Coast the other day."

"You know his name?" the man with the computer asked.

"Uh . . . I don't think so. I don't remember."

"You don't remember, huh?"

"Why did you take the seat next to him?" The first man demanded.

"Sir? That was the seat they assigned me!"

"The airline?"

"Yes, sir!"

"He had seat 14F," the computer man said. "You had 14E. And you claim that was just a coincidence?"

"*I* didn't ask to sit next to him!" O'Brien was becoming angry, now. "There were other Navy people on that plane!"

"O'Brien, do you have any idea who that man is?"

"No, sir. Should I?"

"Are you stupid or what?"

"No, sir! Damn it, what's this all about? Are you people FBI?"

"No, Seaman O'Brien. What are your duties aboard this vessel?"

"Until you people called me down here, I was helping unload torpedoes."

"Don't get smart, kid. What department are you assigned to?"

"Uh . . . I think it's going to be the torpedo room. I'm supposed to start my quals there."

"Quals? What are those?"

"My qualifications. Look, this is my first assignment to sea duty. I have to work in all the different departments aboard until I can show proficiency in all of them."

One of the men was shuffling through something that looked like a copy of O'Brien's service record. "Haven't you completed Sub School?"

"Yes, sir, I have. Doesn't mean I'm a submariner yet, though. Hey, listen. What is all this, anyway?"

"We'll ask the questions, Seaman O'Brien."

O'Brien found himself remembering the questioning he'd gone through during boot camp. Later, he'd told a friend about it, Kathy Gilquist, a woman he'd once dated who was in college now and planning on going on to law school.

She'd told him that he should have demanded to have a lawyer present. "They were violating your civil rights, Doug. You have the right to have an attorney present whenever somebody like that questions you. And you have the right to know what the charges are against you. If they haven't charged you, they can't hold you. Simple as that."

As simple as that, huh? Well, Kathy wasn't here, facing these people and their barbed questions.

"Have you ever seen this man?" one of his questioners demanded, holding up another photograph. This one was a somewhat blurry black-and-white shot of a pleasant-looking man in a sports coat and sunglasses, walking down the sidewalk in front of a sporting goods store. The man was a stranger.

"No," O'Brien said. "Look, I want a lawyer present."

His interrogators looked startled. "We were assured that you would be willing to cooperate with this investigation," one said.

"Am I being charged with a crime?"

"Not . . . at this time," another said.

"What crime are you charging me with?"

"It won't help you to adopt these sea-lawyer tactics, Seaman O'Brien."

"Tactics, hell! I want to know why you're trying to railroad me, here! I have a right to have a lawyer present! I have a right to know what you think I've done!"

"As we told your commanding officer, Seaman O'Brien, we are investigating a case that may have serious implications for our nation's security."

"Are you accusing *me* of being a *spy*?"

"We aren't accusing you of anything, Seaman O'Brien. We merely want your cooperation."

"I'm not answering *anything* else!"

"Why are you afraid to answer our questions?"

"What are you hiding?"

"Nothing, damn it!" O'Brien was scared now, and sweating heavily, but he was also angry. He hadn't thought this sort of thing happened outside of places like the Soviet Union. "Look, I don't want to talk to you guys anymore! I'm outta here!"

Rising from his seat, he marched to the door.

"Seaman O'Brien, I don't think you fully understand your situation."

"You could find yourself transferred to some place considerably less pleasant than San Francisco. Adak, Alaska, for instance, doing the penguin census."

"There are no penguins in Adak. Penguins live in the southern hemisphere."

"Don't get smart with us, kid. Polar bears, then."

"Sit *down*!"

They questioned him for some minutes more, asking now about his shipmates aboard the *Pittsburgh*, if he'd seen anything suspicious, and the like. O'Brien folded his arms and stubbornly refused to speak. Anything he said might be the wrong thing, something to allow the three to twist his words.

At last they stopped and quickly consulted with one another. "I don't think he knows a thing," he heard one mutter to the others.

". . . playing stupid . . ."

". . . don't think he's playing."

"Seaman O'Brien," the man with the laptop said finally, "are you aware of the provisions of the Official Secrets Act?"

"Huh? No . . ."

"You may in the near future find yourself deployed on a sensitive and highly secret mission aboard this vessel," another said.

"Failure to observe the letter of the law regarding the Secrets Act can result in a heavy fine and a long jail sentence."

"That is, assuming you survive."

"If we chose to take you for a helicopter trip out over the Pacific, for instance . . ."

"They would never find your body."

"Are . . . are you *threatening* me?"

"Simply making sure we understand one another, Seaman O'Brien."

"Please do not discuss this interview with other members of the crew."

"You may go now."

"Hey! Wait! I want to know—"

"Dis*missed*, Seaman O'Brien!"

Moments later, he was back on the boat's forward deck topside, rejoining the working party.

"Man, O'Brien," one said. "You look white as a ghost! What happened?"

"I'm not supposed to talk about it."

"Yeah, well, they don't call us 'the Silent Service' for nothing, do they?"

"C'mon, people," the COB said. "Who said you could stop working? . . ."

Enlisted Mess, USS *Pittsburgh*
Pier 2, Mare Island Naval Submarine Station
Vallejo, California
1730 hours local time

"So what did those guys want?" Benson asked. "They had you guys in there for hours, it seemed like."

"I'll tell you," Scobey said, shaking his head. "Those dark suits? The glasses? Them not sayin' who they were from? They were perfect MIBs."

"MIBs?" Douglas asked. "What the hell are you talking about, Big C?"

"Men in Black. Mysterious guys in black suits who always seem to show up when there's been an important UFO sighting. They question the witnesses, confiscate the film and any evidence, and tell everyone to forget what they've seen, and never tell anyone. They may be from some ultra-secret government organization. Or they could be ETs themselves, disguised as humans."

"Whoa, wait. Hold up a sec, Big C," Jablonski said. "Are you saying those guys were investigating a UFO sighting? Like . . . like little green men?"

"Nah," Benson said, "he's saying they *were* little green men!"

"Actually, they're gray," Scobey said. "And some of 'em look so much like you and me we'd never blink if we saw them in the corner 7-Eleven. But yeah!"

"Well, I dunno," Douglas said. "I've seen some pretty damned strange things in *my* 7-Eleven."

"Uh-uh," Mark Doershner said, leaning back on the bench and folding his arms. "I'm not buying that one. They kept asking me about our last mission. They especially wanted to know if any of *you* guys were acting suspicious. Nothing about flying saucers!"

"Huh. What'd you tell them?" Douglas asked.

"That I thought you all were Russian spies, but that I had you under close surveillance."

"Geeze! Russian spies! If they come after us, we're taking you down, too!"

Doug O'Brien entered the mess hall. Doershner nudged Scobey in the ribs. "So! Nub! How'd *your* little chat with our visitors go?"

"Uh, okay, I guess." He looked scared.

"What'd they ask you?"

"I-I'm not supposed to talk about it, okay?"

"No, it's not okay, nub! We gotta stick together on this! What happened?"

"Well, nothing, really. They wanted to know why I was sitting next to some Navy commander on my flight out last weekend. And they showed me pictures of people I didn't know and asked about them."

"Yeah? And what'd you say?" Doershner asked, pressing.

"Well, after a while I got tired of them threatening me, see? So I said I wanted a lawyer, that it was my right, and I told them I wanted to know what they were charging me with, if they thought I'd committed a crime."

"Whoa!" Douglas exclaimed. "Way to go, nub!"

"Yeah, the little shit's got real promise!" Doershner said, grinning.

"I still think we got a genuine case of MIBs here, gentlemen," Scobey said. "So, the way I figure it, now we have to work out which of us has seen a UFO!"

"A what?" O'Brien asked.

"A UFO. Flying saucer. You know, like Roswell? Those were government agents, son. Somebody on board has seen something, and they're trying to cover it up, see?"

"Must be a conspiracy!" Douglas and Jablonski chorused.

"Nah, I think you twerps've got it all wrong," Doershner said. "They was government agents, all right, but I think they were looking for something else."

"Like what?" Jablonski demanded.

"Well, what do you expect to find on board a nuclear submarine, huh?"

"Nukes?"

"A nuclear reactor, is what. I think those guys were from the AEC, checking up on the old *Pittsburgh*, here."

"What," Douglas said, looking alarmed. "You think there's been a leak? Contamination, maybe?"

"It's possible. I heard of this sort of thing happening before. The guys in black show up, start checking out the crew. One of them's a doctor, kind of sneaky-like looking each guy over for signs of radiation poisoning."

"Radiation poisoning!" O'Brien exclaimed. "What . . . what signs?"

"Oh, c'mon. You know. You heard it all at school. Nausea. The shakes. Vomiting blood. Oh, the first thing is, usually your hair starts falling out. Usually that happens before you start feeling bad, before you even know you've been contaminated."

"Wouldn't they evacuate the boat if they thought that?" O'Brien asked.

"Sometimes," Scobey said. "But, you know, if they don't want to cause a panic, they might not say a word."

"It's a conspiracy," Douglas said, and he winked.

**Captain's Stateroom, USS *Pittsburgh*
Pier 2, Mare Island Naval Submarine Station
Vallejo, California
1730 hours local time**

Mike Chase held the telephone to his ear. "Damn it, Admiral, these people are turning my command upside down! What the hell gives, anyway?"

"I'm sorry, Mike," the voice on the other end of the line said. "I'm not at liberty to discuss that with you."

Chase almost growled. The man he was talking to was Admiral Hartwell, commander of SUBRON 5 and just a few rungs above Chase in the chain of command. "It's a secure line, Admiral."

"And the information is compartmentalized. Strictly need-to-know."

"And maybe I need to know! They are using nothing short of Gestapo tactics on my people," Chase said, "and I won't have it!"

"Mike, simmer down. It's strictly temporary and completely pro forma. *Pittsburgh* is going out on another op soon, and there are people up the ladder who want to make sure your crew's loyalty is . . . unassailable."

"My crew's loyalty! Good God, Admiral! Has anyone told these Nazis that we're Americans? That we're on the same side?"

"Possibly, Mike, there are some . . . concerns in that quarter. Since the Walker case. . . ."

The Walkers. So that was it. Someone in Military Intelligence, or maybe the CI fucking A, was staying awake nights because of the Walker family spy ring, wondering what they may or may not have compromised.

"It's not right that my boys pay for that, Admiral. If they have a case under way, if they suspect one of my people, okay. But these terror-squad tactics are destroying morale and interfering with the efficiency of my boat. I will *not* sit by and watch my people attacked by these bastards!"

He heard Hartwell sigh. "Mike, there's not much I can do. We have some bigwigs coming up there to talk to your successor in a few days. These clowns are probably part of the show. All I can tell you is to button up and keep your head down."

"One of my men told them he wanted a lawyer if they were going to question him any more."

"Son of a gun! Sea-lawyer type?"

"Not hardly. Fresh out of school. A good kid, from what I've seen. Not a troublemaker. And he doesn't have an attitude. He just got pushed too far. I don't want him to get in trouble with these characters. And I don't want my command disrupted!"

"Okay, okay. I'll see what I can do. But I'm telling you,

this goes all the way up to Washington. It's not something SUBRON 5 has a thing to do with."

"If enough of us get up on our hind legs and fight back, Admiral, we'll make them back down. We don't have to tolerate this kind of treatment. And I will not see my men treated this way. They're professionals, every goddamned one of them, and they should be treated as such!"

"I hear you, Mike. And I'll see what I can do. But no promises. I'll see you Friday, and we can talk more then. Good-bye."

The line went dead, and Chase hung up the phone.

Government agents grilling the crew on security questions. If it wasn't so grimly serious, it would be hilarious.

He hoped they would all be laughing by the time the change of command ceremony took place . . . and the *Pittsburgh* was made ready for sea once more.

Wednesday, 8 July 1987

Topside, After Deck, USS *Pittsburgh*
Pier 2, Mare Island Naval Submarine Station
Vallejo, California
1510 hours local time

After a day and a half of stress and, at times, idiot terror, the *Gestapogruppe*, as the men aboard had begun calling the intelligence unit—the GG for short—had vanished ashore, taking their voluminously stuffed folders and notebooks with them. Quiet conversations among the crewmen interviewed had established no obvious pattern to their questions, save the injunction not to talk about their interviews with other members of the crew.

The guess was that the three MIBs, as Big-C Scobey persisted in calling them, were definitely from some branch of U.S. Intelligence community, quite possibly from the CIA, and that they were on nothing more significant—or amusing—than a fishing expedition.

"Sure, the way I figure it," Big C had said at noon chow, "is that the '*Burgh* is about to go out on another intel op like the last one, and they want to know they can trust us."

"Yeah," Douglas added, "or scare us all enough that we'll keep quiet about *whatever* it is!"

"Intimidation," Master Chief Warren said. "Sheer intimidation. I think the whole thing was a setup from the start. Get us all scared, or at least damned wide-awake. Then, when we come back from the *next* mission, all they have to do is step in and say, 'sign here.' Ten thousand dollar fine and ten years in Portsmouth Naval Prison for even breathing a word about what we've seen."

"Yeah?" O'Brien had said. "So . . . where are we going that's gonna be so all-fired secret?"

"Well, our last op was if-I-tell-ya-I-gotta-shoot-ya secret," Scobey said reflectively. "Hate to think what could be worse than that!"

"Uh-huh. And where'd you guys go last time, anyway?" O'Brien persisted.

"If we told you, nub," Scobey said, grinning, "then we'd have to shoot you. . . ."

Three hours later, Benson, Kellerman, O'Brien, Boyce, and Scobey were topside, working on garbage detail. At sea, garbage was carried topside and put over the side aft in special, weighted containers. If the boat was running submerged—her usual venue—the weighted containers were released from inside through a miniature and highly specialized version of a torpedo tube.

When in port, however, garbage was hauled topside and lugged ashore, where it was deposited in large, mobile Dumpsters brought to the pier and then hauled away again by garbage trucks. One hundred twenty men living together in closet-space proximity produced a *lot* of garbage, which had to be processed every day. If it went over the side while the boat was in port, it would—besides generating the active hostility of watch groups like Greenpeace—very swiftly beach the submarine on an artificial island of her own making.

The working party had been bringing plastic bags filled with garbage topside for the past ten minutes, handing it up the ladder of the forward escape trunk and bucket-brigading it aft to a growing pile astern. The next step would be to start hauling it down the boat's brow and tossing it into the Dumpster, waiting on the pier.

"How does it feel to be in the working classes again, Boyce?" Scobey asked with a laugh. As head of the working party, he was out of the line of actual labor, leaning against the aft corner of the sail with folded arms.

"Fuck you, Big C," was the equally cheerful reply. EM3 John Boyce was back aboard again, the obvious target now of the crew's barbed comments about goldbricking and the layabout life of ease. Diagnosed with concussion and possible skull injuries after the fight in the biker bar, Boyce had spent several days in a civilian hospital ashore, before being transferred to the Mare Island Naval Dispensary and his eventual release back to full duty.

"I wish," Scobey replied. "Not all of us have Benson's luck with women!"

"Yeah, I've been hearing about that," Dave Kellerman said, hauling another bag up through the gaping mouth of the escape trunk hatch and passing it on to Benson. "How about it, Benson? I hear you've managed to swing liberty tonight . . . *again*!"

"You should talk, Squee. You should talk!"

"Loni and I are engaged," Kellerman said. "But I hear you've been striking up a whirlwind romance ashore!"

"The waitress at the Tup 'n' Baa," Scobey said with a knowing wink. "I hear she was *real* grateful to Benson here after he stepped in to save the lady's honor that evening!"

"How grateful?" Boyce called up from the bottom of the escape trunk.

"Well, he came back aboard last night smelling of perfume and pussy. I'd say she was pretty damned grateful!"

"Lay off, guys," Benson said. He tossed the bagged garbage onto the pile on the deck. "Carol's a nice girl."

"Oh, a nice girl is it?" Scobey said. "I don't think I'm interested, then!"

Benson was about to respond when movement caught his eye to the south, past the pier close aboard on *Pittsburgh*'s port side.

"Hey! Guys!" he called. "Look there."

A submarine was coming into port.

She was a Sturgeon class, dark slate gray in color, her sail well forward on her long hull. She'd come around the southern point of the island out of San Pablo Bay, and was sliding gently up the channel now between Mare Island and Vallejo.

She wasn't wearing her hull number yet; American submarines did not carry the magnetic numerals mounted on either side of their sails above the dive planes unless they were in port or engaged in what was jokingly known as a photo op. Still, each boat had its own telltale characteristics, signs of wear or hull scratches, fingerprints enough that other crews familiar with her could usually tell which one she was.

"*Parche*," Scobey said. "She must just be coming back after the op."

Boyce and O'Brien had come up the ladder and on to the after deck to see. "What op?" O'Brien wanted to know.

"Our last op," Kellerman said. "We were working . . . someplace with the *Parche*."

"Yeah," Boyce said. "We went in and made noise, got the whole bad guy fleet coming after us. And the ol' *Parche* over there just snuck into where she was supposed to go as quiet and as sneaky as you please."

"You see the broom?" Scobey added.

"Sure do."

Since World War II, a broom secured to the forward periscope housing or the weather bridge atop a submarine's sail during the return to port had meant the boat had successfully carried out her mission . . . effecting a "clean sweep" of enemy targets. Submarines still raised the emblem today, even though their missions no longer included the torpedoing of enemy targets.

The heads and shoulders of two men were visible in the

weather cockpit, atop the forward edge of the *Parche*'s sail, just ahead of the periscopes and the broom, raised bristle-end high. One of them saw the working party watching from *Pittsburgh*'s stern, and waved. As working party supervisor, Scobey came to attention and saluted, holding until one of the tiny figures atop *Parche*'s sail returned it.

"Well, well," Benson said, nodding at the pier. "Someone else is interested in *Parche*'s return."

A gray government vehicle had just driven up to the beginning of Pier Two, and a quartet of MIBs was clambering out, adjusting jackets, straightening ties, donning hats and sunglasses. While one took up a position at the shore side of the pier, the other three trotted down the pier's length, obviously hurrying to be in position by the time the *Parche* pulled in and put her mooring lines over. A handful of Navy personnel in dungarees were already waiting as the shore-side line-handling party. They watched with evident amusement as the suits hurried into position.

Parche, meantime, was backing down in the main waterway, rudder hard to port as she swung her tail out into the Napa River Channel, bringing her blunt prow in toward the other side of Pier Two, just opposite from *Pittsburgh*'s berthing space. Sailors stood on her deck, lines ready. A tugboat stood out in the channel, having guided *Parche* in to the dock area, and standing ready should she need an assist, but it was clear that Captain Perrigrino was an old hand at these maneuvers, and could carry them out unassisted.

"C'mon," Scobey said. "Let's start hauling this garbage ashore." His grin and his manner demonstrated clearly that he was interested in other things than filling the pierside Dumpster just now. Though he was in charge of the working party, he reached down and picked up a couple of the big, plastic bags and started for the *Pittsburgh*'s brow, trooping down the gangway with a metallic clatter as the rest of the work detail picked up bags and followed in his wake.

They were met at the pier end of the brow, however, by one of the suits. Benson wasn't sure, but he was pretty certain that it was one of the men who'd interviewed him the day before . . . the one with the fancy laptop computer. "You can't come down here," the man told Scobey.

"Why not?" Scobey replied. He hefted the garbage bags. "Working party. Besides, *they're* down here." He nodded at the line handlers.

"Don't give me crap, sailor," the suit said. "Get back aboard your ship and go below!"

"I'll need authorization from my commanding officer to abandon my work detail," Scobey said. "Here." Casually, he tossed one of the garbage bags at the man, who instinctively reached up and caught it. "If I can't come onto the pier, maybe you could take care of this?" He tossed the second bag, making the man drop the first.

"Yeah," Benson said, coming up behind Scobey and tossing both of his own bags. "Make yourself useful, why don'tcha?"

Scobey turned and squeezed past the line of sailors on *Pittsburgh*'s brow, heading back for the ceremonial guard shack for the OOD. The rest of the men kept filing down the brow and tossing garbage at the suit, who by this time had dropped the one bag he was holding with a disgusted look and refused to catch any more. He planted himself at the pier end of the brow and stood there, arms crossed, as though daring any of *Pittsburgh*'s sailors to come ashore.

Laughing, the 'Burgh sailors went back aboard and sat down on the aft deck, watching *Parche*'s arrival.

"You men go below!" the suit called up at them, pointing.

"Hey, we're under orders!" Benson called back. "We can't just up and leave without orders to do so!"

"*Ja!*" Jablonski called. "Und ve are chust following orders! *Verstehen?*"

The suit glowered, but had no way to enforce his edict. The 'Burgh men kept their seats as the *Parche* gracefully nosed up to the pier, then walked her stern in. With only a single screw, the maneuver took some fancy boat-handling skills. She had thrusters for fine-tuned station-keeping and movement, but it was a mark of considerable pride and sea-manship to edge up to the dock on screw alone. They could see her skipper, Commander Perrigrino, watching from the weather bridge and calling down orders to the control room through a headset phone.

With a final churn and backwash as the *Parche* killed her maneuvering way, the submarine drifted the last few feet to-ward the dock as line handlers in *Parche*'s deck crew tossed mooring lines to their counterparts ashore, who caught them and began pulling the vessel home. Lines were made fast to bollards on the pier, while deck cleats were uncovered on the *Parche*'s deck and shipboard lines secured. The entire evolution took only a few moments, and was performed with an effortless and casual ease born of long experience, train-ing, and practice.

"Welcome home, *Parche*!" Boyce yelled through cupped hands.

"Damn it, that's a breach of security!" one of the suits ashore yelled. "Get me that man's name!"

"Uh-oh," Benson said. "You'd better get below."

"Yeah," Kellerman agreed. "We never knew you, never saw you before in our lives!"

"And we will disavow all knowledge of your actions," Jablonski added.

"Right." Boyce vanished down the hatch.

It was amusing, really. The intelligence officers, if that's what they were, obviously wanted to keep a lid on the fact that it was the *Parche* coming in to port . . . and yet it was likely that half of the military personnel on Mare Island, and a fair-sized percentage of the civilians over in Vallejo, not only knew her name but had known for some time already that she was coming in. The intelligence network that Navy wives alone commanded was as impressive as anything ever fielded by Naval Intelligence.

Scobey, meanwhile, had returned from below. "Don't let 'em rattle you, guys," he said. "Mr. Walberg says they can't tell us what to do on Captain Chase's boat!"

"Hey, yeah," Benson said. "That's right. The skipper is king on his own boat. *They* can't tell us what to do!"

"Not with Fightin' Mike Chase, anyway," Scobey said, laughing. "The Old Man'd have 'em all for breakfast, sunglasses and all!"

Together, the two submarines loomed above the pier, the dark, whale-shape forms of their hulls motionless beneath the upward stab of their sails. The Sturgeons had been the standard U.S. Navy attack sub from the late 1960s through the seventies. Three hundred two feet long, with a beam of 31 feet, they were fifty-eight feet shorter overall than their Los Angeles class successors, and two feet narrower, and had a submerged displacement of almost 2000 tons less. Though they carried only about twenty-five fewer men than an LA boat—107 as opposed to 132—Sturgeons were actually considered much more comfortable to serve aboard than their later, bigger replacements. More of a Los Angeles boat's interior space, compared to a Sturgeon's, was taken up by electronics and a bigger sonar suite, the BQQ-5 which replaced the older BQQ-2. The simple fact that you had to hot bunk in an LA boat, and that that was rarely necessary, if ever, aboard a Sturgeon, was proof enough of the available crew space on board.

A few moments after tying up at the dock, a brow was rigged between the *Parche* and the pier. Two of the suits went aboard almost as soon as the brow was secured, and could be seen engaged in some fast and furious conversation with several of *Parche*'s officers.

"I wonder if they're going to have GG show-and-tell aboard the *Parche*, now?" Benson wondered.

"Sure. Before any of her people can go ashore and get laid by Russian spies," was Scobey's reply.

"I wonder if we should warn them?" Jablonski said.

"Ahh, they'll find out soon enough," Kellerman said.

"No, it's the principle of the thing," Benson said. "They're brother submariners, right? It would be fun just to tweak the bastards, just for the hell of it."

"Sounds good to me," Scobey said. "How?"

"Well, we could get Johanson in on this." PO2 Johanson was one of *Pittsburgh*'s divers. "Or one of us could swim over there. Like after dark. With a message."

"I'm liking this better and better," Scobey said.

Thursday, 9 July 1987

Briefing Room, Station Headquarters
Mare Island Naval Submarine Station
Vallejo, California
0940 hours local time

"Thank you for coming, Commander," Admiral Hartwell said.

Frank Gordon stepped into the air-conditioned coolness of the briefing room, a secure, windowless, concrete-walled chamber beneath the modest three-story facility that housed the headquarters of most of the various Mare Island commands.

It sure wasn't like I had a choice, Gordon thought, but he smiled and nodded. "Not a problem, sir. May I introduce my Executive Officer, Lieutenant Frederick Latham."

Mike Chase was already there, seated at the conference table next to Admiral Hartwell, the CO of Submarine Squadron 5. On the other side of the table were several men whose suits suggested intelligence officers. One was a tall, almost gaunt man with silver hair and a patrician manner. He was impeccably dressed in a Savile Row suit, and would have looked more at home in a gentleman's club in London or Boston than in a Navy briefing room with its Spartan furnishings and pale green cinder-block walls.

As Gordon was taking a seat at the long briefing table, two more men entered, both Navy commanders. One was wearing dolphins above the rows of brightly colored ribbons on his whites.

"Good," Admiral Hartwell said, rising. "We can begin."

"Perhaps, Jules," the older man said, "we should start with introductions."

"Of course . . . sir." The admiral began making introductions for those who needed them. Mike Chase, *Pittsburgh*'s former CO, and Gordon, her next. Commander Richard Perrigrino, the skipper of the *Parche*. Commander James Edward Travers, of Naval Intelligence, who'd been aboard *Parche* as a passenger during her last deployment. Jules Hartwell himself, commander of SUBRON 5.

The only one of the other intelligence officers given a name was the older man in expensive clothes—John Wesley Cabot, introduced as "a senior intelligence officer from Langley, Virginia."

Langley meant the Agency, of course, the CIA.

"Thank you, Jules," Cabot said. "Before we begin the briefing proper, I'd like to speak briefly with Commander Chase, if I may."

"By all means."

Gordon studied the man carefully, since he seemed to be—or seemed to think he was—in charge of the proceedings here. Gordon was reminded of an old, old saying extant in the Boston–New England area, a land where legions of Cabots and Lodges had ruled for generations, where the Cabots, especially, had a history of serving in the church as ministers. Lodges, the old saying went, spoke only to Cabots, and Cabots spoke only to God.

"First of all I have to ask you, Commander Chase," Cabot said in a whispery voice with a strong Harvard accent that changed *first* to *fust*, and *ask* to *awsk*, "if you are aware of covert and possibly illegal efforts by men of your crew to communicate with the crew members of the *Parche*?" He pronounced the vessel's name "Patch," and Gordon was reminded of the Harvardese line about "pahking your cah in the cah-pahk."

"Illegal? No, sir. I'm not aware of anything like that."

"It was our hope to completely cordon *Parche* and her

crew off from, um, outside influences. It appears we have been unsuccessful."

"Unsuccessful in what way?"

"Intelligence agents went aboard the *Parche* early this morning to conduct interviews, much as they conducted interviews of your men, Captain Chase. But each and every one of the men interviewed stubbornly refused to answer all questions, even so far as confirming their identity. They claimed, each and every one of them, that they were not allowed to talk to any unauthorized personnel, and that if my people insisted, then they would do so only with an attorney present . . . at government expense."

Gordon held back a chuckle, and he could tell Mike was suppressing a barely controllable grin. "And what makes you think one of my men was involved, sir?"

"It's the only theory that makes sense! Your crew knew what had happened aboard *this* ship. It only seems reasonable that they would try to let *Parche*'s men in on the secret."

"That strikes me as excessively circumstantial, Mr. Cabot," Chase said. "Unless you can prove such an allegation—"

"Of *course* we can't prove it! But I suggest that you let your people know, Commander Chase, that this sort of behavior constitutes a *serious* breach of security regulations. It is not impossible that we could have the entire crew of the *Pittsburgh* up on charges."

"What charges, sir?"

"Suborning authority! Conduct prejudicial to national security! Violation of security oaths!"

"Frankly, I doubt that you could get blanket charges of that nature to stick," Chase said calmly. "And I doubt your willingness to prosecute them in what would quickly become an open forum."

"What do you mean, 'open forum'?"

"Only that you can't lock sailors up forever, and sailors love to talk. The story would get out sooner or later. Newspapers. TV. . . ."

"TV!"

"It's possible. Especially if they thought they were being railroaded. Especially if their *commanding officer* thought they were being unjustly treated."

"That would be a violation of your oath as a naval officer, Chase."

"My oath, Mr. Cabot, was to the Constitution of the United States."

"There are the Official Secrets Acts. And obedience to duly appointed authority in your chain of command."

"And I and my men will not do anything to jeopardize national security. But you people can lean on that horse only so long before its legs finally give way. I suggest that you not test it."

Cabot scowled. "I had hoped, Commander, that you would be more cooperative."

"What are you going to do to me, take away my boat?" He spread his hands and laughed. "Commanding a submarine was all I ever wanted out of life. I've done that, now, and I'm not going back. So beach me or drum me out of the Navy, but quit making empty threats and stop harassing my crew!"

"I . . . see," Cabot said. He pursed his lips. "Well, at least you are honest with me, speak your true mind. But I fear that your loyalty to your country may be questionable."

"*You take that back!*"

"Mike, easy," Hartwell warned.

"I'm not going to take that kind of shit from *anyone*," Chase said.

"Mike—"

"Do you *hear* this crap? He sounds like a CIA recruiting poster out of the 1950s. I am a loyal American. I wouldn't be wearing this uniform if I was not."

"Mike, none of us question that. . . ."

"*He* does. And if he doesn't believe me, let him lay charges against me, right here, right now!"

"Commander Chase, I apologize," Cabot said, surprisingly. "Your loyalty is not in question here. I submit that this is not the time or place for airing this sort of unpleasantness. Commander, if you wish to discuss this with me further, in private, I will be happy to do so.

"However, time is short, and we need to proceed to the real purpose of this briefing." He raised his voice. "Commander Travers? If you please. . . ."

"Lights, please," Travers said, rising.

The room lights dimmed. A projector switched on behind the big screen, illuminating it. Visible now was a photograph shot through a periscope camera, obviously shot through a light-intensifier lens, with brights painted in yellows and whites, and darks in greens and blacks. Date and time stamps in the lower right-hand corner marked the photo as having been taken at 0447 hours local time, on the twenty-fifth of June.

Gordon's eyes narrowed as he peered at the image. That he was looking at a Soviet submarine was obvious. There was something about the look of a Soviet boat's hull that was unmistakable. The sail on this one, though, was longer and squatter than other Russian boats Gordon had seen.

"We are looking here at a Soviet attack submarine," Travers said. "We first ran into this boat when she was on sea trials two years ago. Following the NATO tradition of naming Soviet boats after the maritime alphabet, she was designated as 'Mike.'"

Of course. A Mike. Gordon had seen some blurry intelligence photos a year and a half ago, shortly after he'd come on board at the Office of Naval Special Operations Command. There'd only been one boat, though . . . at least until now.

"That first Mike was obviously a research prototype," Travers went on, as though reading Gordon's thoughts. "She sported some extremely sophisticated features . . . as fast, we think, as an Alfa, and possibly as deep a diver. What makes her a considerable advance over the older Alfa, however, is her extreme silence. Our people believe she may be at least as silent as a Flight I Los Angeles."

Gordon heard the collective intake of breath—from Mike, from Admiral Hartwell, from LCDR Latham. He felt the shock, too. The first twenty-four Los Angeles boats off the ways had been extremely silent by American standards. With the *Atlanta*, SSN-712, first of the uprated Los Angeles Flight II boats, the class had gotten even quieter. The Russians had had nothing to match American quieting technology. Their boats were noisy; the ugly little Alfas, especially, banged through the deeps like railway cars, the pumps on their liquid-sodium nuclear reactors pounding away like sound simply didn't matter.

Along with so much else, the Walker family betrayal had warned the Soviets as to just how much noise their boats were making, and given them hints in how to quiet future generations of submersibles. The result had been the quiet Typhoons and Sierras, and the ultra silent Akula, which *Pittsburgh* and the old *Bluefin* had stalked in the White Sea two years before.

And now there was the Mike. . . .

"We thought she might be one-of-a-kind," Travers continued. "This Mike, however, showed up in an unexpected place. Her sound signature is different from Mike One, and we have named this one Mike Two. As you can see, she was photographed two weeks ago. The location, incidentally, is not in the Baltic or White Sea, where Mike One was launched. This is off the Siberian port of Magadan, in the Sea of Okhotsk."

He went on to discuss Operation Silent Dolphins, explaining how four Sturgeon class intel boats had parked off Magadan and Sakhalinskiy Zaliv, off of Petropavlovsk, and in the Zaliv Petra Velikogo close to Vladivostok, Nakhodka, and Vostochnyy. The *Pittsburgh* had entered the Sea of Okhotsk and deliberately exposed herself, in intelligence terms, allowing the encircling Soviet forces to spot her and give chase.

"We've run this kind of scam before," Travers said. "It's an excellent way to pick up electronic intelligence. At the same time our Sturgeons were watching and listening, putting up radio antennae to snag any excited, unguarded transmissions among the various Russian ports. We also had a couple of SIGINT aircraft circling in international waters east of Kamchatka, and NSA assets listening from Hokkaido, in Japan. By any definition, Silent Dolphins was an astonishing success. The Soviets, it seems, are not that good at following radio protocol for encoding sensitive transmissions. We had a lucky break along those lines four years ago, when KAL 007 accidentally strayed into Soviet airspace. We actually taped the voices of Russian MiG pilots scrambling to intercept."

And over two hundred civilians died, you son of a bitch, Gordon thought. *Some lucky break! Damn it, he made it sound as though that tragedy had been a* convenience.

"This time, though, we made our own luck by provoking a Soviet response in waters they consider to be their own. And, we got a bonus. We spotted this Mike. We had no idea she was there, or that she'd been launched."

"Thank you, Commander," Cabot said. "And now, gentlemen, it's time to follow upon our intelligence coup in the Sea of Okhotsk. With information provided from Operation Silent Dolphins, we are preparing to launch a new covert op in this same area—Operation Swift Deliverer. Next slide, please."

The image of the Mike was replaced on the screen by a full-color, topo-relief map of the circular embrace of the Sea of Okhotsk. Cabot rose and approached the screen, unfolding a whip-thin aluminum pointer with which he tapped the screen lightly. "In ten days, *Pittsburgh* will return to the Sea of Okhotsk, gentlemen. She will enter the region as before, by slipping through the Kurils, avoiding Soviet seabed sonar sensors and surface patrols. She shall proceed to this point, on the Siberian coast north of Sakhalin Island, where she will deliver a special package, a small team of agents in our employ . . . here, in the Sakhalinskiy Zaliv. This package will be brought aboard your vessel just before you sail. A small team of Navy SEALs will be taken aboard at Adak, Alaska, along your course due east, to facilitate the actual transfer of personnel.

"These agents are tasked with learning whether the Mike we have seen in these waters was manufactured at the submarine yards at Novolayevsk. The *Pittsburgh* will wait submerged offshore and monitor local communications traffic. The SEAL divers will take this opportunity to put seabed sensors in place in the narrow channel between Sakhalin and the mainland, and also to establish taps in seabed telephone cables. Since the phenomenal success of Operation Ivy Bells a decade ago, we've learned a few new wrinkles to this game.

"Finally, after our agents ashore have completed their mission, some will return to the *Pittsburgh*, while others remain to proceed with other intelligence operations within the Soviet Union. *Pittsburgh* will egress the Sea of Okhotsk at her commander's discretion, either through the Kurils or south into the Sea of Japan, and, from there, proceed home.

"Full details will be included in your written orders, which will be hand-delivered aboard the *Pittsburgh* by early next week. We have included you, Commander Chase, in this briefing so that you can personally brief *Pittsburgh*'s new commanding officer on conditions and likely Soviet responses in the Okhotsk Operations Area.

"Is this clear?" It took Gordon a moment or two to realize that the silence was in the expectation that he might have something to say. His very first deployment in his long-dreamed-of command . . . and he was going to be taking her into a lion's den, and one that only last week had been set on its ear by American intruders.

It was not exactly the sort of mission that encouraged thoughts of promotion or an advancing career. For something like this, it would be an achievement simply to survive.

"I appreciate your confidence in me and my new command."

There was not a lot else he could honestly—or diplomatically—say.

Monday, 13 July 1987

**Pier 2, Mare Island Naval Submarine Station
Vallejo, California
1505 hours local time**

My God, it's him. It really is him. . . .

Seaman O'Brien stood at attention in the second rank of
Pittsburgh's crew, listening to the change-of-command ceremony on a warm and blustery Monday afternoon. The formation was drawn up on the pier, facing the *Pittsburgh*; the
twin podiums set up on the sub's forward deck, and the
'Burgh's brow were festooned with red, white, and blue
bunting, and a blue backdrop had been rigged behind the
podiums to support the Navy Seal and to serve as a neutral
background for the photographers.

To O'Brien's right was an audience area, consisting of
rows of folding metal chairs hauled out from the base for the
occasion. At his back was the *Parche*, with a fair number of
her crew gathered on her deck and on her sail-top weather
bridge to watch the festivities.

"In the long tradition of naval service," the admiral who

seemed to be running the show was saying, "the ceremonies revolving around the passing of command from one ship captain to another have held a special and vitally important place. . . ."

The man had been introduced as Admiral Hartwell, the commanding officer of Submarine Squadron 5, but he didn't sound as though he were especially excited about being there. He was reading from a prepared speech. The two other officers up there behind the patriotically colored bunting set up around the torpedo-loading hatch sat on their chairs and tried to look relaxed, as Admiral Hartwell's voice droned on from speakers set up on the pier.

O'Brien was still in shock from meeting the man who was going to be his commanding officer, the boat's new skipper . . . and O'Brien's companion during the four-hour flight across country two weeks ago. He'd only seen Gordon that morning, when he'd come aboard for an inspection with Captain Chase. O'Brien had been in the torpedo room going over his qual requirements with Lieutenant Walberg and the COB when Gordon and Chase had stooped through the torpedo-room hatch.

"Attention on deck!" COB had called out.

"As you were," Chase had said. "Surprise inspection."

And it *was* a surprise. Generally, word of a snap inspection was passed by various covert means from department to department, giving at least a few moments' warning. O'Brien had already learned how that dodge worked from personal experience.

Gordon had smiled when he'd seen O'Brien.

"Seaman O'Brien, isn't it?" he'd said with a wink. "How are your quals coming along, sailor?"

"Uh . . . just getting started, sir."

"I'll want this man standing watches down here as soon as possible, Lieutenant," he'd told the others. "He's a smart man, and I want him up to speed as quickly as possible."

"Aye aye, sir," COB had said, looking a bit startled.

O'Brien couldn't take his eyes from the man, now. Commanders and ship captains were such godlike creatures from the perspective of an E-3 fresh out of C-School. And this guy had actually *talked* to him for the better part of four hours. . . .

He must have known he was going to be O'Brien's CO, and he hadn't said a word, hadn't pulled rank, hadn't acted like anything except a friendly and interested naval officer sharing a few hours of boredom on a transcontinental flight.

What kind of submarine captain was he going to make?

Hartwell's "few remarks" came to an end at last, and Captain Chase stood at one of the podiums to give his speech. Overhead, seabirds wheeled and screeched and called, as small whitecaps began kicking up on the waters of the straits separating Mare Island from Vallejo.

O'Brien remained stiffly at attention. His feet were starting to get numb, and he resorted to an old trick learned in boot camp . . . wiggling his toes hard within the embrace of his spit-shined dress shoes, and alternately tensing and relaxing the muscles of his calves, to keep them from cramping.

Commander Frank Gordon had talked to *him*.

Incredible. . . .

USS *Pittsburgh*
Pier 2, Mare Island Naval Submarine Station
Vallejo, California
1541 hours local time

"I stand ready to be relieved, sir."

"I relieve you, sir."

"Very well. The boat is yours. Good luck with your new command."

Mike Chase extended a white-gloved hand, and Gordon accepted it. The small band on the pier struck up "Anchors Aweigh," as the handful of civilians in the folding chairs nearby applauded. Gordon and Chase stood at the podium on *Pittsburgh*'s forward deck for a moment more as photographers snapped pictures. Admiral Hartwell stepped forward and shared a place in several shots, the three men grinning as they repeated handshakes and shoulder claps for the press. A stiff breeze blew across the Mare Island Strait, ruffling the surface of the water and eliciting a *whoosh* sound from the speakers as it whispered across the microphones, followed by a squeal of feedback.

It seemed a strange way to begin a secret mission, with a change of command in the full glare of publicity, but then to break with ceremony and tradition would have been to invite comment . . . and suspicion.

The formal ceremonies were over. There would be a reception and dance that evening in the big recreation hall, but the deed itself was done.

Frank Gordon was now in command of a Los Angeles class nuclear attack submarine.

The ship's complement was drawn up in ranks ashore, to the right of the seated crowd, standing quietly at attention. The actual change-of-command ceremony was brief and simple, but vitally important in the routine of Navy life. Since the days of wooden hulls and canvas aloft, ceremonies like this one had served as a visible ritual whereby the absolute authority of command was transferred from one man to another, ensuring that every man aboard was fully aware of the authenticity of the new captain's orders and the legality of his command. While a naval captain no longer held the absolute command of life and death over his crew, he was still, within carefully proscribed limits, the law aboard ship.

And the men had to trust him absolutely, since it was his decisions that determined the success or failure of their mission, and, quite possibly, whether they lived or died.

Gordon was just glad the dog-and-pony-show part was over with. Two years of giving Special Ops briefings in the Pentagon had long ago gotten him over any fear he might have had about public speaking, but it was still a chore he disliked. *Politicking* was how he thought of it. Trying to buy people, to manipulate them with pretty words.

But his brief speech was over. He'd spoken of the verities, of duty and honor, of sacrifice and trust. His men needed to trust him implicitly, but that trust was two-way. He would need to trust them as completely, as deeply, if this new command of his was to be a success.

"Well done, boys," Hartwell said, as they stepped away from the podium. Ashore, the band had reached the triumphant conclusion of its closing piece. The crowd was standing now, breaking into small knots. It wasn't a large group—twenty-five, maybe thirty people. The *Pittsburgh*'s crew only comprised 120 men, and not that many of them had family living here at Mare Island or within a reasonable drive.

The boat's COB was dismissing the formation. Most of the men began filing back aboard up the gaily decorated brow. A few remained with the visitors, mostly women and children, wives and kids, with a few older couples, proud parents.

Gordon tried picking a few faces out of the crowd. He'd spent the past several evenings going over personnel records, memorizing names, rates, and positions, and now he was trying to attach faces to the descriptions. In the coming months, it was going to be vital that he know each man—not only by name and face, but by what could be expected of him.

He saw the new kid, O'Brien, and smiled to himself. It looked like the nub was just getting over the shock of realizing just who it was with whom he'd shared that flight out from Washington.

He already knew a surprising number of the men aboard . . . but then, the Navy was a tight little community, and the Silent Service was smaller and tighter still. Lots of men found themselves serving together with old shipmates, given time enough. BM1 Archie Douglas, for instance, was one of *Pittsburgh*'s old hands. According to his dossier, his

first cruise had been that memorable op aboard the old
Bluefin in the Persian Gulf in 1980. Gordon remembered
him well. The kid had dived in after an injured SEAL while
the boat had been on the surface under attack, and won a Silver Star for the act.

Gordon had been XO on the *Bluefin* during that op, under
none other than Commander Mike Chase. *Geeze*, he
thought, *it's like old home week.*

That one over there, the third class in the arms of a star-
tlingly pretty young woman with long hair, was ST3 Dave
Kellerman, one of his sonar techs. Nearby was SM/2 Rodriguez, with his wife and two-year-old daughter. Entries in
his record suggested he was one of the best sonar men in the
service. Rodriguez was due for rotation ashore pretty soon,
and *Pittsburgh* would be losing him. It would be a good
idea, Gordon thought, to have Rodriguez and Kellerman
work particularly closely together, if the watch schedules
could be swung that way, to make sure Kellerman was up to
Rodriguez's standard. He made a mental note to talk to
Latham about that.

Pittsburgh's Executive Officer was another potential
worry, something that was going to require his attention.
Latham, too, was nearing the end of his tour as *Pittsburgh*'s
XO. According to his records, he was up for consideration
for a command of his own. In fact, the Promotion Board
should have made him a full commander, sent him to Command Orientation, and given him his own boat.

The question was whether Latham harbored any grudges
or bad feelings thinking that *Pittsburgh* should have been
his. Fred Latham was another of *Bluefin*'s officers, and had
served with Gordon before. Like Gordon, he was a bit behind the point on his service career curve where he should
have been, had he not missed a promotion opportunity a few
years back. There were only so many sub-driver billets to go
around in the Navy, with many more qualified officers standing in line to take them. Miss the selection board process
a time or two, and the next available billet would go to

a younger man coming up the rank ladder behind you.

How did Latham feel about that? Gordon needed to know, needed to get to know the man well. The boat's XO was responsible for everything inside the submarine's pressure hull, including, specifically, the crew and all of the crew's individual and personal problems. If he did his job and did it well, Gordon would have a happy, efficient, and well-run boat. If he did not, this coming cruise could turn into sheer hell.

"Good job, boys," Admiral Hartwell said.

"Well, they didn't throw anything at us," was Gordon's reply.

"So, shall we see to the final handover details below?" Chase asked.

"Of course."

"I have to get back to headquarters," Hartwell said, "but I'll see you both at the reception tonight. Deal?"

"Deal, Admiral."

"Congratulations again, Gordon. It was a long time in coming."

"Thank you, sir."

They escorted the admiral aft to the brow, where he was joined by some of his staff. "SUBRON 5, departing," a voice called from the loudhailers, accompanying the clang of the ship's bell and the squeal of a boatswain's pipe.

With the admiral safely ashore, Gordon followed Chase down the forward escape trunk ladder into the boat. As they made their way forward through the control room, now *his* control room, Gordon wondered what Chase was thinking, what he was *feeling*.

Through the control room and forward to the captain's cabin.

"I think we're done with all the busywork," Chase said, opening the door and ushering Gordon through. He gestured toward the wall safe. "Your orders were delivered by courier this morning. They're in there."

"Thank you."

"Anything else I can tell you? Any other questions you might have?"

"You can tell me about Okhotsk."

Chase sighed and dropped into a chair, leaving the chair behind the compartment's small desk free. Gordon walked around behind the desk and sat down. It wasn't as though this were a new thing for him. He'd commanded a submarine before, the *Bluefin*.

Did the sense of newness, of sheer *wonder* never go away?

"Probably not a lot that you can't get from the standard oceanographic charts. It's big, it's deep, it's cold. Ice-covered October through May, usually. Something like six hundred ten thousand square miles. Except for a little fishing traffic along the coasts, it's mostly a restricted preserve for the Soviet Fleet. They've got sonar arrays stretched on the seabed between each of the Kuril Islands and across La Perouse Strait, all the way from Sakhalin to the northern tip of Hokkaido. They have a PLARB bastion there, so it's real tightly controlled and patrolled." PLARB was the acronym for *Podvodnaya Lodka Atomnaya Raketnaya*, the Soviet equivalent of American boomers, ballistic missile submarines. Soviet naval strategy called for keeping their naval ICBM assets in safely contained and heavily protected areas, or "bastions," secure from prowling American hunter-killers.

"Did you run into any sign of their bastion forces in Silent Dolphins?"

"Hell, we ran into their whole Siberian fleet! But we weren't there long enough to pick up any of their attack subs, if that's what you mean." Bastion areas, according to what was known of their strategic doctrine, would be patrolled by attack boats—Alfas, Sierra IIs, Victor IIIs, Akulas.

"Yeah. I'm not that worried about their surface ASW assets. You need a sub to catch a sub."

It was an old saying among submariners, trite, but no less true for that. In World War II, most sub hunting had been

done by surface vessels—destroyers and destroyer escorts—
and by aircraft. In the fifties and sixties, however, that had
changed. Hunter-killer submarines—as opposed to the ponderous guided-missile boats, the SSBNs like modern-day
Soviet Typhoons or American Ohios—were designed primarily to find enemy submarines and, in wartime, sink them . . .
especially the enemy's ballistic-missile subs that hung as
such terrible threats above home cities and populations. If
war came, some HK assets would be deployed against the
enemy's merchant shipping and surface naval forces, no
doubt . . . but their first and by far most important target
would be his submarines.

To that end, SSNs on both sides of the Iron Curtain continued to train and, when possible, to spar with one another. A
common game in the larger game of Cold War maneuver was
to find the enemy's boats wherever they might be patrolling,
sneak in close and unheard, and pick up what intelligence
you could from passive sonar, signals intercepts, and the like.
Hell, frequently, when the other guy heard you, a real battle
developed, complete with maneuvers . . . and terminated not
by the sudden launch of torpedoes, but by a loud active sonar
ping that, in effect, called out "Tag! You're It!"

Mike Chase continued talking, describing what he'd seen
of Soviet ASW assets in the Sea of Okhotsk three weeks before. "It's all in my after-mission report. I'm sure they'll dis-
till it down and include the skinny in their briefing for you."

Gordon snorted. "Yeah, maybe. But sometimes the cult of
secrecy gets so thick around here, they won't tell you the
name of your own boat or what color she's supposed to be
painted."

"I know what you mean. But I'll see if I can get you a
copy, just in case."

"Fantastic! I'd appreciate that."

"Anything else?"

"Any major discipline problems I should know about?"

Chase shook his head. "They're all great kids. The best.
Absolute professionals, every one of 'em. COB went back

and had a quiet talk with the owner of that bar ashore, by the way. The fight last week? We're paying him for damages out of the boat's fund, and he's dropping his charges."

"That's good. I'd hate to leave that unresolved."

"Still a shame. That bar was an old submariner's haunt for a lot of years. Sounds like the SPs are going to have to put it off-limits, now that that gang has taken it over."

"Won't be the first time."

"Roger that."

"And the men involved?"

"I'm deferring to you. Your problem. But I recommend you take it easy on them. They weren't to blame."

"Understood. I'll have to review the Shore Patrol reports, of course, but I don't see any point in being the bad guy, here."

"Anything else?"

"Can't think of anything, Mike. I know you're giving me a good boat."

"The best, Frank. Absolutely." He extended a hand. "Good luck."

"Thanks a lot. You have your new orders yet?"

"Oh, yeah. I'll be conning a desk for a while down in San Diego. After that, I expect they'll be talking to me about senior service college, and maybe a major shore command. But hell. After driving a boat like the *'Burgh* . . ."

Gordon looked up at the bulkhead, then the overhead. *His*, now. "I know what you mean."

SEAL Team Three
Third Platoon, Attached Special Operations Group
Adak, Alaska
1412 hours local time (Greenwich –11)

Lieutenant (j.g.) Kenneth Randall swam with long, easy strokes of his flippers. Even though it was only a little past noon, the water was murky enough to make visibility a bitch. He had an underwater lantern attached by a lanyard to his left wrist, but the silt in the water served only to make the beam dazzlingly opaque. He relied instead on his eyes, peering through the high-tech mask that covered his entire face. He could just make out the bottom a foot or two ahead.

The water was frigid, though he honestly didn't feel the cold that much. His wet suit insulated him well with a layer of water warmed by his own body between the rubber and foam layers of the suit. Even in July, the water temperature in this region never got much above forty-five degrees or so. Without protection, a swimmer would die of hypothermia in minutes.

He checked his wrist compass to make sure he was still following the correct bearing. In this kind of silty gloom, it was possible to swim aimlessly in circles and think you were going in a straight line, just like a man lost in an Arctic whiteout. Yeah. The reported sighting ought to be just ahead.

"Trout One, this is Trout Two. Do you copy, over?" Nelson's voice was a bit garbled over the earpiece buried in the depths of Randall's dive hood, but recognizable.

"Trout Two, this is One." The full-face mask let him speak into the small radio microphone by his lips. He just had to be careful not to put too much pressure into the mask by talking, and risk breaking the pressure seal from the inside. He held the corner of the mask tight against his face as he spoke. "Go ahead."

"I think I found the objective. Track's pointed straight at the beach."

"Copy, Two. I should be there in a few moments. Hold your position."

"Copy, One. Holding."

Navy divers had been experimenting with various types of underwater radios for decades, with varying amounts of success. The trouble was that water was almost impenetrable to radio, so even modern units like this still-experimental one were only good for pretty close range—distances out to a few tens of meters or so. There was the promise of a whole

new family of underwater communications gear piggy-
backed onto blue-green laser beams, which treated the ocean
like a pane of transparent window glass.

Randall had trouble believing that even that technomarvel
would work well in conditions as crappy as *these*.

There it was. It had to be.

Careful not to touch the bottom—one careless flick of a
flipper would stir vast clouds of silt into the water which
would not settle out for hours—he moved closer, then hovered. Reaching for the underwater camera slung from his
waist, he raised the plastic housing, aimed, and clicked the
shutter. Film advance was automatic. He took three more
shots, just to be safe.

The subject of his photographic study was two sets of lin-
ear marks on the seabed just below . . . a pair of long rows of
marching indentations in the soft muck running side by side
about ten feet apart. As Trout Two had suggested, they were
aimed straight at the beach.

He could see the shadow of his dive buddy above the
tracks to his right, in the direction of shore. Carefully, he
turned and followed, reaching GM1 Tom Nelson's position a
moment later.

"They look fresh," Nelson said, his voice breaking up a
bit over the radio circuit.

"Hard to tell. This goo would look fresh no matter what."

"Yeah, but currents and stuff would erode the markings.
These are razor-sharp."

"Okay, Tonto. You're the ace tracker, then. Let's do some
tracking."

"Right you are, *kemosabe*, sir."

They turned toward the shore and began gently kicking
along side by side. The water here was nearly thirty feet
deep, but shoaling rapidly. Overhead, the murk gradually
grew lighter, until a silvery, flashing swirl of daylight began
penetrating the silt. Ahead, light and dark churned and
chopped, and the two SEALs could feel the insistent tug of
the surf.

"Okay," Randall said, moving upright and holding his position with gentle motions of his arms. "We go in hot . . . just in case."

"Copy."

They dropped their lanterns and unclipped their weapons, H&K submachine guns specially designed for work in salt water. They removed muzzle plugs and breech covers, then started swimming in.

Randall's head broke the water as his knees hit the bottom. Shoving his mask up high on his head, he took a careful look around before letting the next inrushing wave pick him up and body-surf him forward another ten feet.

The beach was sere and lifeless, as lifeless as the gray mountains shouldering behind the dunes into a gray and leaden sky. Aptly named Split Top, one of the handful of genuine mountains on Adak was just visible on the horizon through the rain-laden haze to the east.

There wasn't a lot to Adak. A tiny island, one of the larger of the Andreanof Islands in the middle of the Aleutian chain, the place occupied a point almost precisely midway between East and West—2,062 miles from Seattle and 2,070 miles from Tokyo, as a hand-painted directional sign set up on the base pointed out. There were no native trees, no native civilian population. *All* that Adak boasted was a naval station, the site of NSGAA, the Naval Security Group Activity Adak. About two thousand naval personnel were stationed there, along with approximately a thousand dependents.

Randall lay in the surf, studying the beach. It was all rock and gray, volcanic ash. There was a lot of ash cover on the island, for Great Sitkin Volcano was located just thirty-six miles to the northeast, while Kanaga was to the west, just across Adak Strait. The gray muck and silt on the seabed surrounding the ocean was the accumulation of thousands of years' worth of volcanic fallout.

But that muck had captured the underwater tracks that had first captured a hiker's attention. Two days before, a young sailor stationed at the air station had been hiking along the western shore of the island above Adak Strait, not far from Cape Yakak, when he'd come upon strange tracks along the beach. The incoming tide had destroyed those tracks within the next couple of hours, making it impossible to pinpoint exactly where they'd emerged from the sea . . . or where they'd returned. Since the special SOG-SEAL unit had just flown into Adak to await transfer to a nuclear sub and their next op, the captain commanding the Adak station had asked if Randall and his people would take a look.

The beach was deserted, and Randall moved up out of the surf, still keeping a careful eye out for any unwelcome presence on the beach. Though the tracks sighted by the sailor had been created two days ago—the tide gave them a good indication of exactly when—it was possible the intruders had come back more recently . . . possible, in fact, that the intruders were still there.

"Ground looks pretty churned up above the high-tide line," Nelson pointed out.

"Yeah. Let's check it out."

"Whatcha think. Crawler Subski?"

"I'd bet money on it. *We* don't have anything like this."

There'd been stories for years, now, ever since the early eighties, of sightings of track marks exactly like these on sandy beaches along the Alaskan coast. Similar sightings had been made on the beaches of Finland and Sweden as well. Though no official statement had ever been released by the Navy, it was almost certain that the Russians possessed some sort of unusual submarine or amphibious crawler, one that traveled underwater, but did so by crawling along the sea floor on tracks like a sealed and pressurized tractor or tank. No one had ever actually seen one of the beasts, but there was little doubt about its existence.

And it had to be the Russians. Siberia, after all, was only about seven hundred miles northwest of Adak.

Most likely, though, the vehicles, which some in the SEAL community had dubbed Crawler Subski, were brought in as passengers on a Russian cargo or special operations submarine. The mother boat would drop the intruder off a few miles offshore, and wait to pick it up upon its return.

But . . . return for what? That was the biggest question Naval Intelligence still faced in regard to the mysterious beach visitors. It wasn't as though Adak was a high-priority target. . . .

Adak had been born as a result of the Japanese occupation of two Aleutian Islands—Attu and Kiska—some hundreds of miles to the west during 1942. With the advent of the Cold War, any base positioned strategically relative to the Soviet Empire had been of value. If the Cold War ever turned hot, Adak might serve as an advance airbase for operations against Kamchatka or northeastern Siberia.

But what could the Soviet tracked intruders have possibly been looking for?

"Hey! Lieutenant Randall! Something here."

Randall moved farther up the beach, passing the high-tide line and joining Nelson where the sand and ash grew soft, just before the inland dunes.

"Whatcha got?"

"Looks like they came in and had a fucking *picnic*!"

A black plastic trash bag lay half-buried in the ash. Spilling from the open mouth were napkins, dirty paper plates, some paper cups, and assorted ripe garbage, including fish bones. A couple of empty bottles—vodka bottles—lay nearby.

"This is too weird for school," Randall said. "They pack up their crawler aboard a special ops submarine in Petro, say, and come all the way up here, deploy their vehicle, come ashore on American territory . . . to have a picnic? It makes no sense!"

"They might have been eavesdropping on Adak Naval Station," Nelson suggested. "Might even have climbed Split Top over there for a straight line of sight to the base communications center."

"Still doesn't explain them leaving their lunch here on the beach. Unless . . ."

"Unless what?"

"Well, there've been rumors, scuttlebutt about American submarines sneaking into Russian coastal waters, right?"

"Sure."

"Suppose they left this here deliberately?"

"Why?"

"To say, 'Hey! We can play these games, too!' "

"Seems pretty far-fetched."

"Yeah? You come up with a better answer."

"Dunno. They might've done it on a lark. Or as a bet or a dare. Maybe they never figured we'd spot their tracks and come looking."

"If they didn't want to be found, they would have taken their garbage with them," Randall said evenly. "That's the way it's done."

"Well, it's the way *we* do it. Maybe they're just pissing on the fire hydrant."

"Doing what?"

"You know. Marking territory, like dogs."

"Interesting image. Well, we'll let the Intelligence boys sort through this."

"Are we going to take it back?"

"Negative. We'll mark it with a beacon, and let the higher powers come and play in the garbage." Kneeling, he pulled a transponder from a waterproof pouch and planted it in the sand next to the spilled trash. "My guess is that they'll turn this whole beach into an archeological site, and go over it with penknives and toothbrushes, looking for clues . . . cigarette butts, bottle caps, girlie magazines, that sort of thing."

Nelson looked out at the gray sea to the south. "Yeah. And some Russian sub driver'll be out there watching through his periscope, laughing himself sick." He pitched his voice in a broad, mock-Russian accent. "Gullible Amerikanski!"

"Well, we won't be here," Randall said. "We'll be in Siberia, saying 'gullible Russki' to them! C'mon. Let's go."

Together, the two SEALs trudged back down the beach toward the water.

Monday, 13 July 1987

Weather Bridge, USS *Pittsburgh*
Mare Island Naval Submarine Station
Vallejo, California
0640 hours

Commander Frank Gordon, captain of the USS *Pittsburgh*, looked over the forward deck, watching as the line handlers stood at their posts. Damn it, what was holding up the show? He'd intended to be under way by 0630 hours.

Fog blanketed the strait and Mare Island; astern and to the north, Vallejo was almost lost in the gray soup, though Gordon could make out the wet shapes of the nearer buildings, and see a few car headlights moving up and down Sonoma Boulevard.

A sea lion barked mournfully in the water to starboard, as though nursing hurt feelings. Gordon had sent the sailor on deck watch forward an hour ago to shoo a pod of the big animals off of *Pittsburgh*'s bow, and they'd lumbered off into the water in ill-tempered slow motion. *Sorry, fellow,* Gordon thought with a wry grin. *We've all got to get up and get moving early today.*

Damn it, where *were* they?

The past week had been a fury of activity. Torpedoes had been reloaded back aboard, and then the tedious process of bringing food and other stores aboard the boat had begun. No one could say how long *Pittsburgh* would be gone on this mission, so stores for two months had been piled high on the pier, then fed a can or a cardboard box or a jug at a time down through the forward weapons loading hatch to be stowed somewhere aboard. The *'Burgh*'s pantry spaces were filled first, and after that, stores began stacking up in every corner and stretch of unused space, including some of the heads and low-traffic passageways. Submarines taking supplies aboard for a six-month voyage looked anything but military when they first set out. Their crews had literally to eat their way through some of the supplies to get to deck metal and bare linoleum.

He looked at his watch. Was this the way the Agency ran things on ops in the field? Did they have so many electronic gadgets they couldn't look at their wristwatches from time to time?

He saw two sets of headlights flare on the dock and heard the multiple slam of car doors. A moment later, a small group of men hurried down the pier.

Four had the look that Gordon long ago had come to recognize as that of men well trained and practiced in the military arts. They wore black combat utilities, vests, and gear, and carried black-nylon satchels. Two of the men were bearded, which suggested that these were not SEALs or other U.S. Special Forces commandos, but something else.

Accompanying them were two other men—the tall and saturnine Mr. Cabot, and another civilian who had the look of an aide. These last two stopped at the end of *Pittsburgh*'s brow as the other four clattered their way up to the boat's after deck, where the OOD took them in hand and sent them down the forward escape trunk hatch.

Cabot's "special package," the agents *Pittsburgh* would be putting ashore on the Siberian coast.

On the pier, Cabot raised a hand in farewell. Gordon gravely saluted him, then picked up the handset that linked him with the control room. "Mr. Latham? Has the package arrived?"

"They're being taken for'rard to the torpedo room now, Captain."

"Very well. Let's make all preparations to get under way."

"Make all preparations to get under way, aye, sir."

He flipped a switch on his comm console, connecting him to Torpedoman's Mate Chief Bart Allison on the deck. "Chief? We're ready to roll. Secure the brow."

"Secure the brow, aye, sir!" crackled from the speaker. Allison was wearing a radio headset, which removed the need for shouting orders back and forth.

The deck crew, their orange life jackets bright in the murk, moved swiftly to unfasten the shipboard end of the brow. Ashore, the dock gang hauled on the brow and swung it clear of the boat.

"Brow is cleared away."

"Single up lines, fore and aft. Stand by to cast off."

"Single up, fore and aft, aye."

The deck crews on the sub and on the pier worked together, casting off lines until only a single mooring line forward and another one aft secured the *Pittsburgh* to the dock.

Gordon took a last look around. If anything, the fog was a bit thicker now than it had been moments ago, but he could make out the shapes and lights of two harbor tugs aft, one almost dead astern, the other upriver a bit. The two sail lookouts stood in their own sail-top openings aft of the weather bridge, looking to port and starboard. His best eyes, though, would be fog-penetrating radar. Someday, perhaps, satellite navigational aids would be good enough that a sub could be gentled up to the dock even when the dock was completely invisible in fog or rain. For now, though, they had to rely on the old and time-tested methods, radar, sound, and basic Mark I Mod 0 eyeballs.

In most other tight docking areas around the world, harbor tugs actually brought submarines all the way in and out. It wasn't that boat captains weren't *trusted* as such . . . but each submarine represented a not-so-small fortune in delicate sonar gear and electronics, and an accidental bump against a bollard could send a good many hundreds of thousands or millions of tax dollars into dry dock, and deprive the United States of a valuable defense asset.

The quarters were just too tight between the Mare Island slips to admit tugboat and sub. But they were waiting in the main shipping channel to catch him should something go wrong.

And that would be the ultimate embarrassment for an ambitious young nuke skipper, not to mention a serious speed bump for his career. He glanced down at the pier again. Cabot and his shadow were still there . . . along with another figure, wearing khakis. Mike Chase. It looked like the *Pittsburgh*'s old skipper had turned out to see her off. And there was another officer as well, with a lot of gold braid. Admiral Hartwell, then, had come to see them off as well.

No, it wouldn't be good at all to fumble this one. . . .

"Cast off aft."

"Aye aye, sir. Cast off aft."

Gordon heard the chief's voice raised. "Aft line handlers! Cast off!" The line arced gracefully through the wet air, to be caught by handlers ashore.

He looked across at the *Parche*, on the other side of Pier 2. He could see his opposite number there atop *Parche*'s sail. Perrigrino tossed a jaunty salute, and Gordon returned it. A number of *Parche*'s sailors had come up on deck to watch. Damn, was the whole world going to be looking over his shoulder?

"Lookouts, check astern."

"Clear astern, sir."

"Maneuvering, bridge," he said. "Rudder to starboard. Come aft, dead slow."

"Rudder starboard, aye! Come aft, dead slow, aye!"

With the rudder over and the screw turning, *Pittsburgh*'s stern began walking out away from the pier. He watched the line handlers aft brace themselves against the gentle motion. All of the safety railings had been stricken and stowed below, so it was somewhat dangerous to be on the boat's open and rounded deck. A diver in full wet suit and swim gear stood on the deck just in case he was needed for a rescue, and a Coast Guard cutter waited farther upriver to follow *Pittsburgh* out into the bay, just in case someone fell overboard.

When *Pittsburgh* had swung out at a nearly forty-five degree angle from the pier, her rounded bow almost touching the dock, Gordon said, "Forward line handlers! Cast off forward!"

"Casting off forward, aye, sir!"

"Conn, give me three blasts of the horn."

"Three blasts, aye aye, sir." The shrill blast of *Pittsburgh*'s horn cut through the fog, two short hoots signaling that she was backing down.

"Maneuvering, rudder amidships. Continue aft, dead slow."

"Rudder amidships, aye aye, sir. Maintain aft revs, dead slow, aye."

Gently, gently, the submarine's 360-foot length backed away from the pier, sliding backward into the Napa River Channel between Mare Island and Vallejo. The river was only about a quarter mile wide at this point, just enough room to get into trouble.

"Captain," the port lookout called. "The *John Andrew Keith* is coming close abeam to port."

Gordon turned. One of the harbor tugs was maneuvering in close to pass the *Pittsburgh* a line. "I see him. Maneuvering, Bridge. Reverse engine. Bring us to ahead slow."

"Reverse engine, ahead slow, aye aye, sir."

With a slight shudder through her hull, *Pittsburgh* slowed her backward crawl, stopped, then began sliding forward. A line was tossed across the submarine's forward deck by a linesman aboard the *Keith* and made secure to a recessed cleat alongside *Pittsburgh*'s sail.

"Maneuvering, Bridge. Bring the rudder two points to port. Engine, all stop. We get to ride for a way, here."

"Bridge, Maneuvering. Rudder two points to port, aye. Engine at all stop, aye aye, sir."

The powerful little harbor tug, basically little more than a pair of powerful diesel engines with a red-painted superstructure around them, began picking up speed, hauling the *Pittsburgh* like a barge slowly downstream. The second tug and the Coast Guard cutter followed astern.

He heard the thud-thud-thud of the tugboat's engines alongside, the brooding low of a foghorn, the shrill clang of a buoy. He tasted salt on the air, felt the shiver of *Pittsburgh*'s hull as she made way through the water, fast enough that her bow wake was curling up over her prow and wetting the forward deck. It was, for Gordon, a jubilant moment.

It wasn't until frozen instants like this one that he realized how much he missed the sea when he was apart from her. For two years he'd been locked away in the Five-Sided Squirrel Cage, trapped in the D-Ring labyrinth.

He was at his best when he was at sea, whether he was commanding a nuke or a diesel, or simply an officer of the watch. He gave a wry grin, realizing how sentimental he was getting about sea duty . . . and he wasn't even out into San Pablo Bay yet!

For just a moment, the fog lifted a bit, and Gordon's eyes were drawn to the dock below the piers, where a concrete abutment with a safety rail extended a short ways out into the water. A small crowd of people was there, women and children, mostly, watching the *Pittsburgh* go to sea. Some waved, while others simply . . . watched.

Families and loved ones of the men aboard. His jubilation

ebbed, still there, but subdued now by the realization of the awesome responsibility he commanded.

Damn. *How* did the Navy wives always know? They had an intelligence network that would make the CIA hang its collective head in shame, if it knew. The announced sailing time for the *Pittsburgh* had been noon; as sailors had come back aboard from liberty through the night, they'd been quietly told that sailing had been moved up to 0630 hours, partly as a security concession to Cabot, partly, too, because Gordon wanted to avoid a confrontation with Greenpeace. The militant environmentalist group liked to picket the sailings of nuclear subs, and had been known to do some pretty pinheaded stuff, like steering Zodiacs into a submarine's path.

It looked like they'd managed to fool Greenpeace . . . but not the wives of the sailors on board. They watched silently as the *Pittsburgh*, tucked in close alongside her escorting tug, slipped quietly through fog-misted waters toward the southeastern tip of Mare Island. Gordon could almost feel the force of their prayers.

He turned, looking aft, trying to see if Mike Chase was still visible. He wasn't. Pier 2 was already hidden by the bulk of the *Parche*, and, as he watched, even her dark, square-sailed mass faded away into the mist.

He had now the command he'd always wanted. True, the mission was an exceptionally tough one; the possibility for failure, disgrace, even death was high. But he knew he had an edge . . . the men who sailed with him.

Gordon looked down at the civilian crew of the tug, a casual and relaxed lot who looked like they had more in common with the salty and sometimes raggedly turned-out submarine crews of World War II than with the sailors aboard his own command. Some were trading friendly insults with the life-jacketed sailors of the 'Burgh's linehandling party. There was unspoken camaraderie there. Men who lived, worked, fought, and died on the sea shared a common brotherhood, whether they were Navy or civilian, submariner or surface.

The sea had an uncanny way of leveling the men who served on her.

Past the point, they swung to starboard, steering southwest, and the tug cast off her tow. *Pittsburgh*'s deck crew secured the last of the lines and deck fittings. The sub's hull numbers had already been taken down, and her flag transferred from the jack staff aft to a mast alongside the periscope housings atop the sail, age-old indicator that the vessel was now at sea.

The crew filed below, and Gordon had the comm watch signal to the Coast Guard cutter that their lifesaving services were no longer needed. With a last, friendly honk of its horn, the *John Andrew Keith* parted from the *Pittsburgh*, veering off to port and fading away into the fog. The other tug and the escorting cutter were already headed about and moving back toward the Mare Island Channel and Vallejo.

Half an hour at eight knots brought them all the way across San Pablo Bay, beneath the span of the bridge bearing Highway 580 near San Quentin, and into the northern reaches of San Francisco Bay proper. Twenty minutes more took them past the monument of Alcatraz and on out through the glorious red-orange arch of the Golden Gate Bridge.

"Lookouts, secure the colors and go below," he said. The two lookouts gathered in the flag, then dropped through the hatch at their feet and clambered down the ladder through the sail and into the control room. Gordon took a last look around. As *Pittsburgh* picked up speed, the bow wake lashed up and over the prow in great, rolling arcs, kicking up a bit of white foam around the foot of the sail. It was nearly 0800 hours now, and the fog was lifting, with broad slashes of early-morning light cutting through the tattered remnants of overcast from a crystal blue canopy above.

Through his binoculars, Gordon could see a pair of tiny Zodiacs flying Greenpeace colors, racing toward the *Pittsburgh* from the direction of Sausalito. Evidently the word had been passed, and they were still trying to catch the boat for a symbolic protest . . . but the sub already had far too great a lead.

He grinned at the distant rubber boats. "Better luck next time, guys." Slinging the binoculars around his neck, he dropped down the hatch, sealing it above him. Emerging in the control room, he nodded at Latham, who crisply announced, "Captain on deck!"

"Thank you, XO. Diving Officer, let's take her down. What's the depth beneath keel?" The channel through the Golden Gate was deep . . . fifty-nine fathoms, if he remembered the charts correctly.

"Depth beneath keel now . . . three-one-zero feet, sir," Lieutenant Francis J. Carver reported. He was seated portside forward, between and behind the two enlisted men manning the boat's helm and dive plane station.

"Very well. Flood main ballast, Mr. Carver."

"Flood main ballast, aye, sir."

"Down bubble fifteen degrees. Make depth one hundred feet."

"Down bubble fifteen degrees. Make depth one hundred feet, aye."

The faint, restless shuddering of water sliced by steel gradually faded as the deck tilted gently beneath their feet. Moments later, there was no sensation of movement at all, as the *Pittsburgh* entered her accustomed environment . . . and hunting ground.

"Depth six-zero feet," Carver reported. "Depth eight-zero feet. Leveling off at one hundred feet." The deck came back level, as the *Pittsburgh* slid invisibly from the Bay and out into the open ocean.

He picked up the microphone at the periscope walk. "Sonar, Conn."

"Sonar, aye, sir."

"Keep a sharp ear out, boys. I would be very surprised if Ivan didn't have a shadow waiting for us out here. I'd just as soon he not know where we're going."

"We're listening, sir. Nothing so far but transients, surface traffic, and biologicals."

"Very well. Call me if you hear anything."

"Aye aye, sir."

"Mr. Latham."

"Sir."

"We'll take her out fifty miles or so. I want a full run of angles and dangles before we set course for the first way point."

"Very good, Captain."

Gordon took a deep breath.

Yes. This felt *right*. . . .

Enlisted Shower Head, USS *Pittsburgh*
West of San Francisco Bay
0940 hours

This was *wrong*, damn it. Badly wrong.

O'Brien had had the duty last night, standing watch on deck with a rifle from 0400 hours to 0600 hours. Having to walk along the *Pittsburgh*'s forward deck toward those monstrous, bulky marine mammals, their snouts half hidden by rolls of fat, had been one of the oddest moments of his life. "*Shoo! Shoo!*" he'd shouted, and wondered if he was going to have to get authorization to fire a couple of shots, to scare the beasts off.

Damn it, they didn't *have* monsters like that in Rockford, Illinois, none with such intelligent eyes, anyway, or such arrogance. The most difficult animal O'Brien had yet had to manage were the cows on his uncle's farm.

They rolled away from him at his approach, however, sliding into the water. It was amazing how ungainly sea lions were on a solid deck . . . and how graceful in the sea.

In any case, his watch had ended before the guests they were expecting had arrived. He now had twelve hours of downtime when he could relax, study, catch a shower, and hit the rack when Seaman Montgomery, the guy he was hot bunking with, got up for his stretch of duty at 0930 hours, so his rack was free. He was standing in the enlisted head shower stall, water streaming from his body, a bottle of shampoo in one hand, a handful of hair in the other.

No, there was definitely something wrong. His hair was Navy-haircut short, of course, but he had a full head of it. As a civilian, he'd worn it quite long. But it seemed to be coming out in clumps as he lathered up his scalp.

My hair is falling out. My hair is falling out. And what makes hair do that?

I'm aboard a nuclear submarine at sea, sleeping a few feet from an atomic reactor, and I'm wondering what might make my hair fall out. My God. . . .

It couldn't be radiation poisoning. It couldn't be. There would be alarm bells . . . people yelling and screaming . . . They'd be sealing off the aft spaces, evacuating the crew.

They had instruments monitoring that sort of thing, didn't they?

O'Brien was so scared, his knees were starting to tremble and feel weak, and his stomach was twisting.

Nausea! . . . Didn't radiation poisoning also give you nausea too? God, what if he started barfing up blood?

Sick call. I gotta go to sick call and have a doc check this out.

He couldn't remember. Did Los Angeles boats rate a full medical doctor? Or did they just have an independent duty corpsman? He wanted a real doctor to look at him, not a damned pecker checker.

"Hey, Navy shower in there!" someone yelled from outside. "Take it easy on the water supply!"

"Uh . . . sure! Sorry!" Reaching up, he turned off the water. Submarines manufactured their own fresh water—as well as generating their own oxygen—from seawater, but with so many men crowded into such a small space, only so much water could be generated per hour, and the people aboard still had to ration it. Showers aboard submarines consisted of a brief spray to wet down, followed by lathering with the water turned off, followed at last by a rinse. You did *not* stand in the stream and soak.

After a moment of wondering what to do next, he turned the water on and stepped into the cold, hard stream. Soap lather spilled from his hair and stung his eyes. He tried to wash the lather out . . . and succeeded in pulling out more of his own hair.

Radiation poisoning! It had to be!

He had to tell someone . . . but . . . shouldn't they already know? He didn't want to appear to be panicky.

But his hair was falling out, damn it!

Somehow, he completed his shower and toweled off. He was going to have to see the boat's doctor, and fast. *He* would know what to do.

Stepping from the shower head, he grabbed his towel and flip-flopped his way back toward the enlisted berthing spaces. Doershner, Scobey, and Douglas were standing together in the narrow passageway talking, and he had to squeeze past them.

"Hey! O'Brien!" Doershner said. "What's the matter with you? You look terrible!"

"Uh, nothing," he mumbled. " 'Scuze me."

He lifted the lid to his personal compartment, which, of course, he now shared with Montgomery. He was stowing his sandals, soap case, and shampoo when the captain's voice came on over the loudspeakers. "Now hear this, now hear this. All hands prepare for angles and dangles. Secure all loose gear, and keep movement about the deck to a minimum. That is all."

Angles and dangles? He'd heard the term before, at Sub School, but he couldn't quite place what—

And then the deck tilted sharply beneath his feet, and O'Brien knew he was going to die.

Torpedo Room, USS *Pittsburgh*
West of San Francisco Bay
0955 hours

Roger Benson leaned against a rack support and grinned at the four passengers. "You boys never been on a submarine before, huh?" he asked, not exactly helpfully.

The four passengers, "packages," as they'd heard the skipper refer to them, were seated on the bunks set up in the torpedo room, alternately clutching at the black-nylon bags containing their gear and the rack supports for their bunks, as the submarine deck dipped, rolled, and tilted beneath their feet.

TMC Bart Allison stepped through the watertight doorway into the compartment, cheerfully standing upright against the list of the deck, which at the moment must have been close to thirty degrees. He held a large mug of steaming coffee in his hand. "Our guests getting settled in all right, Benson?" he asked.

"I guess so, Chief. They still don't have their gear stowed, though."

The *Pittsburgh*'s bow began coming up. Both Benson and Allison adjusted their stance naturally and easily, flexing their knees a bit to take the attitude change. Several other sailors in the torpedo compartment grinned knowingly at each other.

One of the bearded guests clutched his bag and goggled at Allison. "Sir," he said in a thick, Slavic accent, "is this happening on submarine . . . *always*? . . ."

"First of all," Allison said, "I'm not '*sir.*'" He tapped his crow with two fingers. "I'm a chief. That means I work for a living. Secondly . . ." He paused, and then his leathery face split in an unpleasant grin as the boat's deck continued to tilt, bow-high, until the deck was again at a thirty-degree angle from the horizontal. "Secondly, what do you mean 'happening'? Is something wrong, fellas?"

"It's the damned boat," one of the Americans said, grimacing. His face had a distinctive green cast to it. "Is it gonna be like this all the way to fucking *Siberia*?"

"Well, that's hard to say," Allison said. He paused reflectively and took another sip of coffee. "Depends on the weather, partly. Stormy seas topside can make for a rough passage, you know."

"But . . . but . . ." the other American said. "I thought it was always calm at the depths where submarines operated!"

The torpedo-room deck dropped back to level again, but now they could feel the gentle throb as her engine brought her up to speed. A moment later, the boat heeled to port as her rudder went hard over in a sharp turn.

"Normally that's true," the chief agreed, taking the maneuver without any outward sign at all. "Still, sometimes it can be pretty rough. I remember one time aboard the old *Seawolf*, back in '70, must've been, when we—"

"*Please*, sir, Chief," the Russian said, "not to tell us colorful sea stories at this minute. Your captain is carrying out high-speed maneuvers. I feel this . . . the sharp turn just now. Is it . . . is it that we are engaged with Russian submarine, *da*?"

"Well, sometimes we have to make some pretty hard maneuvers," Allison said, sneaking a wink at Benson.

Benson grinned. "You know, the captain doesn't tell us much down here," he said with matter-of-fact nonchalance. "We could be smack in the middle of the biggest submarine dogfight since the Battle of the Atlantic right now, and unless he orders us to launch a torpedo, we'd never know a thing about it." He jerked a thumb at the torpedo tubes, two set to either side of the compartment, angled out slightly, rather than set dead ahead in the forward bulkhead. The round hatches were closed and dogged, with ominous signs hanging from each:

WARNING
WARSHOT
LOADED

"As you can see," Benson continued, "we're loaded for bear. All tubes loaded and ready to shoot!"

"We should really see about getting your bags stowed,"

Allison said. He raised a hand and snapped his fingers. "Hey! Martinez! Doershner! Willis! Give a hand here."

The second Russian clutched his bag a bit closer. "These contain . . . explosive material."

"Yeah?" Allison said, curious. "Like what?"

"Grenades. Ammunition. Plastic explosives. Tools of the trade, yes?"

"Well, you shouldn't have 'em all stowed together like that. Give them to our people, we'll check 'em, bag 'em, and stow 'em for you."

"But you do not understand. Explosives . . . very dangerous . . ."

"Which is why I want to see to it that they're properly stowed, okay, Ivan?"

"Name is Sergei Mikhailovich."

"Right. Anyway, Sergei, you don't need to worry. We know all about handling explosives."

"*Da?* But . . ."

Allison reached down and rapped sharply on the nose of one of the big Mark 48 torpedoes, carefully stowed in its cradle immediately beneath the bunk that Sergei was sitting on. "See? You boys are sleeping with six hundred fifty pounds of high explosives in each of these warheads!"

Sergei flinched as Allison rapped on the torpedo, but surrendered his bag to TM2 Doershner. The others did as well.

"Okay, boys. This is your bunkroom for the length of the voyage. Used t'be, in the old Navy, that enlisted men slept in the torpedo room all the time. Nowadays, though, we don't do it unless we absolutely have to."

"Because the men don't like sleeping surrounded by torpedo warheads?" the second American suggested.

"Nah. If one of these babies went, it would take us all out. The guys in the torpedo room would be the *lucky* ones, since they'd all get killed in the blast, and not have to worry about getting sealed in some after compartment, slowly sinking into the depths until the pressure imploded what was left of the hull. Nah, nowadays, it's the torpedoes that are sensitive.

You get people sleeping on and around them, leaning on them . . ." He reached out and struck the warhead again with the flat of his hand. "Bumping into them. These damned things are delicate, y'know? Not like the old steam torpedoes we used to have! So we try to keep people away from them unless it's absolutely necessary."

"So . . . why are we put here?" Sergei asked.

"Because the boat is crowded, and we don't have anyplace else to put you! Don't worry. Just stay the hell out of the way of the boys on duty in here, and jump when they say jump. Okay?"

"*Da*. We comply. . . ."

"Good man." He looked up toward the overhead. "Well, feels like the skipper's done with angles and dangles."

"With angles . . . and what?" Sergei asked.

"Angles and dangles, son. See, the first thing the skipper does out of port is check the boat for watertight integrity. He has the Diving Officer pump water in and out of the trim tanks to give us perfect neutral buoyancy, make sure we're perfectly balanced. He also runs an inspection on every compartment, checking to make sure they're all watertight and that no machinery is making any unusual or abnormal noises. Then he takes us through a bunch of maneuvers called angles and dangles. If anything on this boat is improperly stowed, that'll find 'em out!" He pointed to a corner where cartons of food had been securely lashed to the deck behind a torpedo cradle. "If we got into a *real* turn-and-burn with a Russian sub, we wouldn't want that shit flying around the compartment, right?"

A few moments later, in the passageway aft of the torpedo room, Benson and Allison had a good chuckle. "They may be the Agency's best and brightest," Allison said, shaking his head, "but they wouldn't last out six months in the Silent Service!"

"Idiots, bringing bags of loose explosives aboard like that. Shouldn't they have checked it all at the pier for proper stowage?"

"Yeah, yeah. Some of their stuff already came aboard last night. But nobody told us they'd be bringing their own toys on board with 'em, and they came aboard so late there wasn't time. No harm done."

"Except to their peace of mind," Benson said. "They were getting pretty shook-up in there!"

"Ahh. A little messing with their minds won't hurt them, none. Why should they be treated any differently from everybody else on board, right? And it does wonders for *me*. C'mon. If you're not doing anything useful, I got work for you."

"Right, Chief."

He followed Allison up the ladder to the second deck.

Monday, 13 July 1987

Enlisted Mess, USS *Pittsburgh*
1205 hours

"Man, O'Brien," Archie Douglas said, setting his tray down opposite his. "You look terrible! What's the matter, you didn't get enough sleep last night?"

"He had the duty topside, oh-four hundred to oh-six hundred this morning," Scobey explained. "He's just running a little short on rack time, is all."

"No, guys," O'Brien said. He looked at his tray, a hamburger and fries and red bug juice, and his stomach twisted ominously. He didn't think he was going to be able to eat. "Look, I don't want to scare anybody, or anything—"

"Hey! That's mighty nice of the nub," Scobey exclaimed. "He doesn't want to scare us!" The others at the table laughed.

"No, listen! I think . . . well . . ." Reaching up, he grabbed a tuft of hair on his scalp and tugged. Some remained in place, but some came away in his clenched fingers, too, pulling free with a brittle, itchy feel. "I think I've been exposed to radiation?"

"You had your dosimeter checked?" Douglas asked, all trace of levity gone now from his voice. Every crewman carried a small plastic badge, worn or carried in a pocket, in which a strip of film was kept. Periodically, the medical department collected the film and developed it, making certain that no one aboard had received more than the legally allowed dosage of background radiation.

"Uh, not yet. I figured I'd go to sick bay and talk to the doc—"

"Sick call is at zero-eight-hundred hours, son," Douglas said. "And you've got things to do today. Like your qual studies?"

"But I thought this was serious. . . ."

Douglas reached over and cupped O'Brien's forehead in one hand, peeling his left eyelid up and peering into his eye. He repeated the exercise on the right eye. "Don't see no jaundice. A little bloodshot. What do you think, Big C?"

Scobey looked at O'Brien's eyes as well. "Hard to tell . . . you feeling sick any other way, kid?"

"Uh, sick at my stomach. . . ."

"Vomiting?"

"No. . . ."

"Well, you might just have a touch of *mal de mer*."

"Huh?"

"Seasickness, son, seasickness. It'll pass."

Douglas grinned. "You probably just got your insides jolted around during angles and dangles this morning!"

"I . . . I'd forgotten about that. I was feeling pretty sick at first. Then I remembered hearing about how the skipper puts the boat through all sorts of maneuvers to shake stuff loose. But I was already feeling queasy then. I really think I ought to go to the doc."

"Nerves, son," Scobey said. "Just nerves. And if you have quals to do, you'd best get yourself at 'em, right? If you fall behind on your study schedule, it's a real bitch, let me tell you!"

"But I haven't had *time*!" O'Brien wailed. "They keep

putting me on watches and special duty and stuff. And I really think I'm sick! . . ."

"You're not sick," Scobey said gruffly. "Just nerves. First time at sea, first time locked up in a sewer pipe a hundred feet under the surface. You'll get over it."

"But what about my hair! . . ."

Scobey shrugged. "Did your dad lose his hair?"

"Huh?"

"Was your dad bald?"

"Well, yeah. . . ."

"There you go, then. It happens. You can always get a hair transplant."

"My dad didn't go bald until he was in his fifties! What about the radiation?"

"Hey, what did they teach you in Sub School?" Douglas asked him reasonably. "We've got unscheduled ORSE checks every so often, right? We had one two weeks ago, as soon as we came into port. If there'd been any radiation danger, any leaks, they'd have picked it up, right?"

"Well . . . yeah . . ."

"If there was a leak," Scobey said, "there would be alarms going off. You hear any alarms?"

"No. . . ."

"There you are, then. This boat is sound and solid. I don't know about your hair problems, but it's not a radiation leak . . . and you'd better belay that kind of talk if you don't want to get into trouble as a rumormonger. You have any idea what the Old Man'd do to someone who was spreading wild stories about radiation leaks on this submarine?"

O'Brien shook his head.

"Well, I just *hate* to think what he'd do. So . . . learn to trust your shipmates, okay?"

"Yeah, Big C. Okay."

"Right," Douglas said. "We'll tell you if you're dying or not!"

"That's *real* reassuring, Archie," Jablonski said, joining them. "What kind of stories are you telling the nub, anyway?"

"Ahh, first-time-out jitters. O'Brien here thinks he's losing his hair."

Benson sat down as well, eyeing him critically. "Well, he
looks like he's got a bad case of the mange, but I don't know
that he's losing *all* of it."

They continued discussing his condition . . . and the dangers of spreading unfounded rumors about radiation leaks
on the boat . . . a federal offense, according to Jablonski.

O'Brien decided that he didn't want any food, and gave
his tray to Douglas. "Let's just drop it, okay fellas?"

"Suits me," Scobey said. "Hey! Benson! You look like the
proverbial cat that ate the proverbial canary. What gives?"

"Well, I know where we're headed."

Douglas shrugged. "Who doesn't? Siberia, right?"

"Yeah!" Benson said. "How'd *you* know?"

"I was in the control room this morning. All the charts at
the chart station are places on the eastern Siberian coast.
Magadan. Sakhalin. The coastline between the Amur and
the Uda Rivers. I think we're going back to Oshkosh for another try."

"What'd you hear, Benson?" Scobey wanted to know.

"Chief Allison and I were with the packages during angles and dangles," Benson replied. "I think they were a little
shook-up, you know? Anyway, one of 'em blurted out something he probably wasn't supposed to. He asked, 'Is it gonna
be like this all the way to fucking *Siberia*?'"

The others chuckled.

"Well, we all knew we were probably headed east again
anyway," Douglas pointed out. The word was that we were
dropping our 'packages' off somewhere over there, and they
don't look like they're intended for delivery to Beijing. It
had to be either Oshkosh or Petro."

"Could've been Chukotskiy," Benson said, referring to the
peninsula that marked the easternmost tip of Siberia, close
up by Alaska.

"Doubt it," Douglas said, shaking his head. "Nothing
much up there in the way of naval assets except Anadyr, and

there's not much there but coastal-defense stuff. No, I'd bet on Magadan, or maybe the mouth of the Amur. There's a lot of shit going on there."

"Damned tight and shallow at the Amur," Boyce said, scowling. "Shallow water, lots of seabed sonar, and a lot of Red Banner Fleet ships and subs, in a lot of bases. Don't know if I like the sound of that."

"You guys sound like you've done this before," O'Brien said. The discussion had taken his mind off the fear. He found that his mind was wonderfully focused, sharp and clear, fastening on each word they said.

"Oh, we play this game all the time," Douglas said. "You have no idea."

"It's not the sort of thing to talk about," Scobey warned. "Know what I mean?"

"Sure. 'Silent Service.' But . . . you guys don't mean we might actually go inside Russian territorial waters?"

Scobey laughed. "Kid, one time, in the Baltic, we were so fucking close to the beach, the skipper let some of us take turns lookin' through the periscope, y'know? We could see girls sunbathing half-nekkid on the rocks west of Kaliningrad."

"C'mon, Big C! You're making that up!"

"Got pictures to prove it."

"What, periscope shots? From the scope camera?" Douglas laughed. "Now I *know* you're full of shit!"

"Can we see the pictures?" Benson asked.

"Sure, but it'll cost ya."

"Cost us! How come?"

"What, for a peek at nekkid broads? Especially Russian nekkid broads? Five bucks."

"Shit. *Playboy* costs half that!"

"*Playboy* isn't *Russian* nekkid broads."

"Yeah," Douglas said. "They're American. Which means no mustaches and tits that don't sag to their knees."

O'Brien looked at Benson. He looked thoughtful, and perhaps a bit worried. "Benson? What's the matter?"

"Ah, nothing. Nothing, really. It's just, well, I keep wondering at the ethics of what we're doing."

"What do you mean, ethics?" Scobey asked. "We're protecting our country. Right boys?"

Douglas gave him a high five. "Fuckin'-A, Big C."

"Are we? Are we *really*? I mean, yeah, it's one thing to follow their submarines and make sure they're not trailing our boomers. If a war started, we'd have to nail their boomers *and* their hunter-killers real fast. I understand that.

"But what do we get by going all the way in to their coast, inside their territorial waters? I mean, well, how would we react if a Russian Victor III snuck up the Chesapeake and parked itself off Baltimore Harbor? That sort of thing would really piss us off, you know?"

"What makes you think they haven't?" Scobey said ominously.

"Well, if they have," Benson said, "then I'm pissed!" He spread his hands, his voice earnest. "They have no right to do that . . . any more than we have the right to play games in their waters!"

"Right?" Douglas asked. "Who said anything about 'right'? The Cold War is still a war, my man. Casualty lists aren't as high, but people do die, battles are fought, and casualties are taken!"

"It's almost a sure bet," Scobey said, "that the Russians had a hunter parked off San Francisco Bay, just waiting to pick up a boat coming out of Mare Island. If they did, then you can bet they're following us right this moment, nice and cozy in our baffles, just a few hundred yards off our screw."

O'Brien looked at Douglas. "Is that true?"

"It's possible. And if they're there, don't worry. The skipper'll lose 'em."

"But facts is facts, Benson," Scobey went on. "They do it. We do it. Nobody likes it, but it's part of the way the game is played."

"Damn it, it's not a game. Not if people get killed. Not if a mistake, by us or them, could bring somebody's finger down on the firing button and light off World War III!"

"You sound like you've thought a lot about this," Douglas said.

"Yeah. I have."

"Maybe you should think about going up on the roof."

"Yeah," Scobey said. "Service in the boats is for volunteers only. You don't like it, you can ship out."

"I didn't say I wanted that," Benson replied. "I just wonder sometimes if what we're doing is right."

"Sometimes," Scobey replied, "it's just possible that *right* has a lot less to do with this thing than *survival* does. Know what I mean?"

"I know. And what if the people playing this game, as you call it . . . the politicians, the generals, the Joint Chiefs, whoever else is sitting back there in Washington moving little plastic game pieces around on a big map of the world . . . what if they really do think it's a game and miscalculate? Our survival is still on the line.

"And, damn it . . . I trust you guys with my life. But do I trust those armchair strategists in Washington? The White House? The State Department? Some vodka-sodden jerk at a desk in the Kremlin? Some scared punk of a kid from some Soviet Socialist Republic none of us has ever heard of, sitting at the fire-control system for an RBU-6000 ASW rocket launcher aboard one of their sub hunters?

"Do you trust them with your lives? 'Cause that's what it comes down to. And I'm not sure I do trust 'em. *Any* of 'em."

Benson stood suddenly, picked up his tray, and returned it to the galley. Douglas and Scobey watched him go. "You think he's okay?" Douglas asked.

"Ah, he'll get over it. Mission jitters."

"I got 'em too," O'Brien said as he stood. "I'd better go get some rack time while I can. If I'm lucky, I can get three hours in before I have to go on duty."

"Grab a few Zs for us, while you're at it," Douglas said.

"And don't worry about the hair," Scobey added. "I'm sure it's *perfectly* normal."

The others burst out laughing, and O'Brien hurried away faster, embarrassed.

And scared. . . .

**Sonar Room, USS *Pittsburgh*
1445 hours**

"So what do you have, Rodriguez?" Gordon asked.

He was standing in the sonar compartment forward of the control room. Two sonar techs, Rodriguez and Kellerman, were seated at the long console with its monitors, each displaying arcane scryings painted on black in green light. Gordon could read the waterfall, as the main cascade was called, but it took a real expert, one with a master's ears, to pick faint patterns of repetition or artificial noise out of the sea of hissing, popping static all around them.

"Something, Skipper," Rodriguez said. He held up a finger as he listened intently to his headset. "There." He whipped off the headset and handed it to Gordon, who pressed it to his ear. "Listen to that."

What Gordon could hear quite easily was a loud, throbbing rumble overlying a steady whooshing noise, but he had the feeling that Rodriguez hadn't called him in here to listen to the noise made by his own boat. "I hear our own prop wash," he said. "What—"

"Not the wash, Captain," Rodriguez said. "Listen past that, deeper. See if you hear something else behind the hissing noise."

Gordon closed his eyes and stretched, trying to feel the sound as much as hear it. He could almost catch something . . . there!

"Kind of a fast chirping or popping sound," he said. "Not very loud, but it's regular. Like something mechanical squeaking. . . ."

"*Very* good, sir!" Rodriguez said, eyes opening wide.

"With ears like that, you should have been a sonar man."

"So what am I listening to?"

"Cavitation, sir. Not ours. Somebody else."

"A Russian boat?"

"Unless you think we're being stalked by one of ours, sir."

"No war games scheduled for this cruise." Gordon handed the headset back. "What's the cavitation from? At ten knots it's not like he's going too fast."

"My best guess? His screw is just a little bit off center. It's wobbling. That, or one of the blades is bent a little bit, and causing the screw to turn unevenly. Whichever it is, it's causing little pockets of vacuum to pop just ahead of the screw."

"How far aft?"

"That I can't tell you, sir. My guess would be five hundred to a thousand yards, but it's *only* a guess. We're streaming our BQR-15 at eight hundred feet, and that's where we're picking this up. What I'm hoping to do is get a side profile on the bastard. As it is, we've got him bow-on, and I only pick up the cavitation once in a while, when he falls off a little bit and I can 'see' his stern."

"You want a better look at him?"

"If we can manage that, yes, sir."

"I'll see what we can arrange. Our first job, though, is going to be to lose this bozo. I don't want him tailing us all the way to our objective."

"That would definitely be a bummer, sir."

"Where'd you pick him up? Or, rather, where'd he pick us up?"

Rodriguez glanced at the big clock on the bulkhead above the sonar screens. "I logged him as Sierra-one at 1120 hours, sir. That's when I first notified you."

Gordon nodded.

"But it's a damned big ocean. My money would be on this guy sitting right outside the Golden Gate waiting for us. We came cruising by, happy as clams, rigging for angles and dangles, and he picked us up."

"My guess too, Rodriguez."

"Sorry I didn't get him sooner, sir."

"Hey, the rule book says you guys are completely deaf astern. It's a miracle you picked him up at all out of all that hash. Well done!"

"Thank you, sir."

Gordon ducked through the curtain and walked back to the control room. Latham watched him with a shuttered expression. "Something, Captain?"

"We definitely have a tail. I'm going to look for a way to scrape him off."

"Do we have any other boats out here? They could scrape him off for us."

"No, damn it. I wish we did." Standard tactical doctrine—employed especially in the case of boomers going out on patrol, was to scrape off any Soviet tails using a second boat. Acting as decoy, or simply running interference, it would cut between the Soviet boat and its quarry, making enough noise that the tailed boat could quietly slip away.

Unfortunately, another Los Angeles wasn't available, not this time. Gordon had discussed the possibility with Cabot and with Hartwell the previous week. "Needless security risk," Cabot had said bluntly. "We don't want everyone in the Navy to know you're going out on this mission."

Great, Gordon thought. *Just great! We'll keep our mission so secret no one will know about it except the Russian Navy! . . .*

He wondered if his counterparts in the Russian submarine fleet had the same sorts of frustrations as he.

"Diving Officer! What's the depth below keel?"

"Seven-seven-five feet, Captain, and dropping. We're over the edge of the shelf."

The waters here overlay an interesting topology. At this point along the California coast, the continental shelf was narrow, and quite steep. This close to the San Andreas Fault, the shelf dropped away as steeply as the contorted mountainsides above San Francisco itself. The *Pittsburgh* had been traveling northwest, on a heading of 310 degrees sixty miles from the Golden Gate Bridge when the shadow had been discovered.

During the past half hour, the bottom had dropped away suddenly, from less than two hundred feet to over a thousand, a plunge into the cold blackness nearly as precipitous as a sheer cliff.

Two hundred feet, a bit more than half of *Pittsburgh*'s length, gave a boat as long as a Los Angeles almost no depth-maneuvering room at all. But a thousand—that was different.

He picked up a microphone and keyed it. "Sonar, Conn."

"Sonar. Go ahead, Conn."

"Hold on to your ears, boys, and reel in our tail. We're going to do some maneuvering, here."

"Thank you for the advance notice, sir."

"My pleasure. Don't start taking it for granted."

He walked over to the Diving Officer, who stood just behind the helmsman and planesman. "Okay, gentlemen. This is what we're going to do. . . ."

Control Room
Russian Attack Submarine *Ivan Rogov*
1456 hours

His name was *Ivan Rogov*, after a man who was a former wartime *kommisar* and later Chief of the Russian Navy's Central Political Department. Designated as Projeckt 945B within the Soviet Admiralty, he was third of the new Barrakuda class of attack submarines, vessels known to NATO and the West as the Sierra II. Within Russian nomenclature and tradition, a ship or submarine was always a *he*, never a she.

The *Ivan Rogov*'s commanding officer was Captain First Rank Viktor Dubrynin, an eager up-and-coming officer from

Odessa who knew the sea well. For almost two weeks, he'd been lurking at the ambush point just off the entrance to San Francisco Bay, hoping for just such an encounter as this. According to GRU intelligence reports, many American intelligence missions, those fielded by submarine, originated at the Mare Island facility tucked away in the northeast corner of the bay. Penetrating those crowded, shallow, and undoubtedly well-protected waters was not a sane mission, not with American ASW technology as good as it was . . . though Dubrynin could dream. Once, indeed, he'd trailed an oil tanker up the Chesapeake Bay, penetrating the Americans' East Coast inland waterway as far as the mouth of the Potomac River. He'd taken numerous periscope photographs of shipping and navigational landmarks in the area and brought his boat safely out and home. For that daring feat, he'd been proclaimed a Hero of the Soviet Union.

Viktor Dubrynin was, without question, one of the best of the Russian submarine commanders, best of an elite brotherhood. He took extreme pride in everything he did, in each mission, in each deployment.

His orders this time were passing strange, almost bewildering, in fact, though he was a good enough naval officer and a good enough communist to know that orders, even strange ones—perhaps even *especially* strange ones—were to be obeyed without question. And these orders came direct from the headquarters of the Red Banner Fleet itself, bearing the name of none other than Admiral of the Fleet V.N. Chernavin, the Union's Deputy Minister of Defense and Commander in Chief of the Navy, and it was countersigned by Admiral of the Fleet V.V. Sidorov, commander of the Pacific Fleet.

The orders, when boiled free of the flowery language, were to intercept any American submarines exiting San Francisco Bay and follow them without revealing *Ivan Rogov*'s presence. The American submarine was expected to cross the Pacific Ocean by a great circle route and attempt to enter Soviet waters somewhere along the Kuril Islands.

Dubrynin was to maintain surveillance contact with the American sub, to report its position at periodic intervals, and to assist in the vessel's capture when it was forced to the surface.

Assist in its *capture*? . . .

He wondered, of course, where the intelligence came from behind this mission. Someone had a pretty clear picture, it seemed, of at least part of current American submarine espionage activities, clear enough to know that a penetration of the Sea of Okhotsk was being planned. Dubrynin had heard about the debacle a few weeks ago when an American submarine, a Los Angeles class and just possibly the very submarine he was now trailing, had entered the Sea of Okhotsk, been spotted by regional fleet elements, and somehow managed to escape just as ASW units were closing in for the kill. An embarrassing situation all around, and not one promising long or honored naval careers for some.

So far, the mission had been almost absurdly easy. The two weeks of waiting had been tediously boring, of course, but most submarine deployments were like that . . . endless tedium capped, sometimes, by a few minutes of stark terror.

"Captain, Sonar!" The Sonar Officer was a young *leytenant*, Vladimir Krychkov, reputed to be one of the best sonar listeners in the Fleet.

"What is it, Krychkov?"

"Aspect change on target, Captain. He appears to be turning to port."

"*Da*. Clearing his baffles, then." Or . . . "Sonar! Is there any indication that he has spotted us?"

"Negative, Captain. Not at this time. The maneuver is being carried out slowly, almost leisurely. There are no sounds of torpedo doors being opened, or of machinery."

"Helm. All stop."

"*Da*, Comrade Captain. All stop."

Both Russian and American submarines went through the routine, every so often, of "clearing the baffles," turning in a large circle and taking a careful listen with hull and bow sonars for any unwanted guests in the area, especially astern, in the baffles, where a vessel's sonar was notoriously hard of hearing.

But the *Ivan Rogov* was an unusually quiet boat, for a Russian. Using quieting technology only recently obtained through intelligence sources, the Barrakuda class boats were widely regarded as the most silent submarines yet launched by the Soviet Navy, at least the equivalent of their Sturgeon class . . . and quite possibly as silent as their early Los Angeles boats.

With his engines off, with *all* machinery that might communicate vibrations to the surrounding ocean off or isolated on special, insulated pallets, the *Rogov* drifted in near-perfect silence, a "hole in the water," as his American playmates sometimes called it.

"Sonar, Captain. Report on target."

"Target aspect continues to change. He is now forty degrees to port of original bearing, still turning. Now forty-five . . . fifty degrees."

"Range to target!"

"Estimate six hundred meters, Captain. Captain . . . he is turning very sharply. Engine now making turns for twenty knots . . . no . . . twenty-five. Sir! He is accelerating!"

"Helm! Come left forty-five degrees!" He would turn into the American's turn, positioning himself so that he could remain bow-on to the target. This would keep his own sonar profile narrow . . . and would give him the edge if torpedoes began to swim.

Dubrynin was torn. He wanted to be in sonar, listening to the American's antics for himself . . . yet he *had* to stay here, when the situation could turn deadly at any instant.

"Captain! Sonar! The target . . ."

"What is it Krychkov? Sonar! Report!"

"The target appears to be bow-on and coming straight toward us, making turns now for twenty knots! Target may be descending. . . ."

"*May* be? Tell me!"

"Target appears to be descending. Making turns for thirty-three knots. Range now estimated at three hundred yards . . . and closing! . . ."

"Great God. . . ."

He hoped *Rogov*'s political officer hadn't heard that peculiarly uncommunist exclamation. Then he decided it didn't matter. The American captain must be crazy, deliberately risking a high-speed collision at sea.

"Helm! Come hard left! Up diving planes fifteen degrees!"

The *Rogov* responded, but *slowly . . . slowly. . . .*

What the hell was the American doing?

This wasn't the way the game was supposed to be played. . . .

Control Room, USS *Pittsburgh*
1458 hours

"Sonar, Conn! Can you hear him?"

"Negative, Captain! We're deaf at this speed!"

"Stand by, then."

What Gordon was trying to do was dangerous, though not, he thought, excessively so. While it was always a bit hairy with more than one boat making unexpected maneuvers in the same area, it was a big ocean, and five hundred yards was over four times *Pittsburgh*'s length overall. *Lots* of room . . .

"Passing one-five-zero feet!" the planesman called out. Moments before, Gordon had ordered the diving planes set to eighteen degrees down bubble, and the deck was canting beneath his feet. They needed to go *deep*. . . .

The scary part about playing chicken was not knowing what the Russian captain would do. If he zigged when the *Pittsburgh* zagged—or dove when she dove—there could be a very expensive debris field scattered across this part of the Pacific seabed.

Stepping up onto the stage beneath the two side-by-side periscope housings, Gordon moved to the starboard scope and hit the control that activated its low-light optics.

The port-side periscope was a Type 2 attack scope, capable only of daylight optical resolution. The starboard scope, however, was a Mark 18 search scope, a wonder of optical and electronic technology capable of a wide variety of tasks. It included low-light settings that could be projected onto TV monitors throughout the boat, and a 20mm camera for taking either still or motion pictures through the scope.

The Mark 18's head could be angled up, allowing either air searches or, when submerged, it could be used to watch the bottom of the ice when the boat was maneuvering in Arctic waters. At times, it had been used to film the bottoms of Soviet warships at close range, and even inspect the hulls of Russian submarines.

"Passing two-zero-zero feet, Captain."

Periscopes normally were useless underwater; below a very few hundred feet, no light at all penetrated the depths. Even at the *Pittsburgh*'s current depth and using low-light optics the surface was little more than a featureless, green glow. Gordon pressed his eyes against the plastic shield, however, watching for . . .

There! A shadow fell across the Mark 18's field of view, just for an instant. Briefly, Gordon cursed himself for not engaging the camera . . . but the other boat was far enough above that any pictures he'd gotten would have been uselessly fuzzy and distance-blurred.

Catching a glimpse of the other boat was sheer luck, but proved his instincts as to where the Russian would be were accurate. He could also tell from the angle of the other boat as *Pittsburgh* slid beneath its keel that the Russian skipper was now turned hard to port, trying to meet the '*Burgh*'s sudden turn and sprint.

"Helm! Hard right rudder! Come to zero-zero-five degrees. Continue descent to six hundred feet!"

"Hard right rudder to zero-zero-five degrees, aye. Make depth six-zero-zero feet, aye."

He grabbed the periscope housing as the hull groaned in protest.

Monday, 13 July 1987

Control Room
Russian Attack Submarine *Ivan Rogov*
1459 hours

"*Michman* Antonov!! Stand ready by the ballast lever!"
Unless he could be sure the American was diving, he wanted
to be ready to blow ballast and surface.

"Helm! What's happening?"

"Responding, Comrade Captain . . . but he's as sluggish
as a pig. . . ."

"Engine room! Increase revolutions to twenty knots!"

"Make revolutions for twenty knots, yes, Captain!"

He could actually *hear* the other vessel now, a steady
throbbing pulse transmitted through the bulkheads. *Rogov*'s
deck heeled over to port as the Barrakuda class submarine
turned hard away from the oncoming American.

"Sonar! Give me bearing and estimated range to the
American!"

"Sir, we're deaf. At this speed, I couldn't hear an explosion outside the hull!"

Damn, and damn again!

"Helm! Maintain this turn. I want to come back parallel with the American's new course."

"*Da*, Comrade Captain!"

The rumbling of the other vessel was much nearer now. He could feel it beneath his boots through the *Rogov*'s steel decking. Jesus Christ . . . he was passing directly beneath the *Ivan Rogov*!

Control Room, USS *Pittsburgh*
Eighty Miles Northwest of San Francisco
1459 hours

The maneuver was easily the match of any pulled earlier that morning during the angles and dangles evolution, a hard left turn at high speed. The hull shuddered, and gave an ominous creaking sound, as the deck tilted sharply underfoot.

Had he guessed right?

"Depth reading, Mr. Carver."

"Eight-five-zero feet beneath the keel, Captain," the Diving Officer reported. "We are now passing two-five-zero feet. . . ."

"Now on course zero-zero-five, Captain."

"Maneuvering! Engine to dead slow. Just give us enough revs to keep us moving."

"Engine ahead dead slow, aye, sir."

Silently the *Pittsburgh* continued to nose ahead, on a new heading, now, her screw just turning over as she descended into the inky depths northwest of the continental shelf drop-off.

Control Room
Russian Attack Submarine *Ivan Rogov*
1459 hours

And then . . . the rumble of the other submarine faded off astern and to starboard, as the *Rogov* continued his hard, high-speed turn. Dubrynin saw at once what the American had done . . . lose himself within *Rogov*'s baffles, then change course. He would maintain his sprint for a few moments to get clear . . . and then . . .

"Engine room! Slow to eight knots!" Faster than that and they would remain deaf. Damn it all, he needed to *hear.* . . .

"Eight knots, aye, Captain."

"Sonar! Do you have him?"

"Wait one, please, Comrade Captain."

Seconds dragged on, interminable. Dubrynin found he was sweating heavily, his uniform shirt drenched. "Sonar!"

"Sir, I fear we have lost the American. I cannot register him on any of my screens."

"Lost him! How?"

"Sir, it is only conjecture, but I believe he made another hard, high-speed turn either beneath us or just astern, moving onto a new heading when we could not hear the course change. He then cut his engine and is drifting."

"You mean . . . you mean he is still close by?"

"*Da*, Comrade Captain. But close by . . . where?"

Where indeed? It was a terribly large ocean, and a submarine was a very small chip adrift in all that water.

There seemed to be nothing to do but to break off the pursuit . . . or to drift and wait, listening.

Dubrynin knew he would never be able to adequately explain simply breaking off the chase.

"Helm, all stop!"

"All stop, *da*!"

"Maintain current attitude and course. We will drift. Sonar room!"

"*Da*, Captain!"

"Find the bastard. Find him!"

"Yes, Comrade Captain. We will do our best."

"Never mind your best. Just *find him*! . . ."

Control Room, USS *Pittsburgh*
Eighty Miles Northwest of San Francisco
1503 hours

"Conn, Sonar."

"Go ahead Sonar."

"Conn, we've just dropped through a thermal. I can't hear Sierra One at all now."

"Very well. Keep listening."

Pittsburgh continued her downward course, sliding now past four hundred feet. The thermal the sonar watch had just reported was a boundary layer between warmer, upper waters and the much colder and less salty waters beneath. Such thermals reflected and bent sound waves in odd ways, creating deep channels that allowed sonar signals to be picked up across hundreds of miles . . . but also forming shields that allowed a submarine on one side of the layer to remain perfectly invisible to a searching boat on the other. At six hundred feet, she leveled off, continuing to move gently north.

"Sonar, Conn. Did you get anything during our pass?"

"Just a little, Captain," Rodriguez replied, "just before you put the pedal to the metal. Got enough to get a make on him from the library. He's a Sierra II, probably number three in the class."

"Pretty good work, pegging him as a Sierra from the initial contact!"

It was a weak joke. All initial sonar contacts were identified as "Sierra," with a sequential number listing the number of contacts through the course of the mission. It was pure coincidence that the boat following them was *also* a

Sierra . . . in NATO's international signal alphabet nomenclature for Soviet submarines.

But he heard Rodriguez chuckle. "Actually, I heard her skipper jingling loose change in his pocket. Only Sierra skippers do that. . . ."

"Okay, Rodriguez. You tell me if you so much as hear anyone sneeze back there."

"Aye aye, sir. We are commencing sneeze watch."

An hour passed, dragging by slowly, with nothing to break the monotony, though in this case, nonevent was definitely good. The longer they eluded the Sierra's questing ears, the more likely they were to get away unheard.

The bad guys could still catch them if they decided to dive below the thermal. Gordon knew better than to try to outdive the other boat. A Los Angeles class submarine had an operational depth of just under 1500 feet . . . and a maximum depth, the "crush depth," so endearingly named, of 2460 feet. Recent Soviet designs, however, their Alfa interceptor, the Akula, and the Sierra II, were capable of reaching extreme depths . . . partly because of the aluminum-hull designs pioneered by the Alfas and Akulas, but possibly, too, because they were willing to push the engineering envelope a bit more than were American submariners. Sierras were thought to have operational depths of six hundred meters, nearly two thousand feet . . . with a maximum depth of a thousand meters, or over thirty-two hundred feet.

There were some voices in the Pentagon who felt that the Sierras, which didn't have the aluminum-hull construction of the Alfas and Akulas, probably had operational depths of no more than 450 meters, about the same as a Los Angeles. Gordon wasn't about to test that theory, though, especially since Sierras almost certainly had towed arrays that could be lowered through deep thermals to detect submarines hiding below them. Whether the Sierra up there went sub-fishing that way, or came down to pay them a personal visit didn't really matter. Now that Gordon had the other guy off his tail, it was a simple matter to choose a depth and remain silent or nearly so, knowing that the other skipper's chances of picking them up again under these circumstances were very slim indeed.

An hour passed . . . and then two. Eventually, Gordon gave the order to increase revolutions to twenty knots, and the *Pittsburgh* accelerated, coming onto a new course, headed northwest.

Control Room
Russian Attack Submarine *Ivan Rogov*
1800 hours

Dubrynin had been forced at last to admit that the American had slipped away. After three hours of careful searching, including dives to five hundred meters to search beneath the thermal layer, he'd turned up nothing more interesting than some migrating gray whales.

The American had dived beneath the thermal, then slipped away at three or four knots, making so little noise the *Rogov* had not had the ghost of a chance of hearing.

Long experience had taught Dubrynin that American submarine captains were good; this one, he thought with wry admiration, was fucking fantastic.

There would be a rematch. He would find this American captain again, and the next time, he would be ready for the encounter.

"Up planes, ten degrees," he ordered. "Bring us to periscope depth."

Nubriev, the political commissar, looked at him curiously. "What are your plans, Comrade Captain?"

"Plans? What is there to plan? We will go to periscope depth, raise a mast, and report to Petropavlovsk that we have lost the target. We will tell them that the American is on the way, and that we will be there to intercept him in the Sea of Okhotsk, as written in our orders."

"You think, then, that we can still catch this American?"

"We know where he is going, Comrade Nubriev. And we will be there waiting for him when he arrives.

"What more do we need to know?"

The gray shape of the *Ivan Rogov* slid upward toward the distant light of day.

Wardroom, USS *Pittsburgh*
180 Miles Northwest of San Francisco Bay
1845 hours

"Gentlemen," Gordon said. "Thank you for coming."

"Like we had a choice?" Master Chief Warren said, and the others laughed. They were in the *Pittsburgh*'s Wardroom, a compartment almost filled by the dining table, with booth chairs around two of the bulkheads. This was where *Pittsburgh*'s officers took their meals, and where ship's business was conducted when it required the presence of more than three or four people. Gordon's stateroom—a compartment smaller than most American jail cells—usually served as the Captain's Office, but larger gatherings simply demanded space enough to allow breathing.

This time, there were six present besides Gordon—Latham; Carver; Walberg; the Navigation Officer, Lieutenant Sean Garrison; the Engineering Officer, Lieutenant James Ostler; and Master Chief Warren as the representative of the enlisted crew. The final member of the assembly was the civilian spook who'd identified himself only as "Mr. Johnson," almost certainly a pseudonym. Bearded, balding, and pinch-faced, he looked wildly out of place in blue coveralls, a garment worn by boat officers and universally known as a "poopie suit."

With the seven of them around the table, Gordon couldn't help but think that if anyone yelled "Fire!" they were all going to be in very serious trouble.

"First of all," Gordon told them, "I want to thank each of you for a job very well done. Brushing off that Sierra earlier was a bit rough as a shakedown. The men did a superb job. Fred, COB, I'd like you both to pass along my 'well done.'"

"Will do, sir," Fred Latham said.

"Sure thing, Skipper," Warren added. Latham, as the boat's XO, was responsible for everything that happened within her bulkheads. As such, he was the official link between captain and crew within the Navy's chain of command.

The Chief of the Boat, however, as the senior enlisted man on board, was the practical, day-to-day link between the men and the officers. Most enlisted men would go to Warren with a problem before they would approach an officer, and a "well-done" from him often meant more than the XO's formal benediction . . . or even the personal thanks of the captain.

Gordon turned and punched up the combination to the wardroom safe. Inside was a manila envelope, tied shut with string and sealed by a DOD secret sticker.

"Orders, gentlemen. We all know more or less what's happening. They briefed me, and I briefed you. But these will give us the specifics."

The COB handed him a penknife. He broke the seal and opened the envelope. He pulled out the top sheet and began to read aloud.

FROM: COMSUBPAC
TO: CAPTAIN, USS *PITTSBURGH*, SSN 720
RE: ORDERS

TO BE OPENED ONLY AFTER VESSEL IS AT SEA.

1. USS *PITTSBURGH* WILL SET SAIL FROM MARE ISLAND NO LATER THAN 1200 HOURS PST MONDAY, 13 JULY, 1987, AND PROCEED NORTHWEST TO WAYPOINT ALFA. EMBARKED ON BOARD WILL BE FOUR SPECIAL PERSONNEL UNDER NURO ORDERS AND AUTHORIZATION, WITH THEIR EQUIPMENT. UNDER NO CIRCUMSTANCES ARE THESE PERSONNEL TO BE

QUESTIONED OR HARASSED FOR INFORMATION. THE NATURE OF THEIR MISSION IS TOP SECRET, AND DETAILS OF THAT MISSION, AS WELL AS ANY INFORMATION REGARDING THEIR PRESENCE ON BOARD *PITTSBURGH*, FALL UNDER THE PURVIEW OF THE OFFICIAL SECRETS ACT.

2. WAYPOINT ALFA IS LOCATED AT 50° 50' 30" NORTH LATITUDE, 176° 43' 10" WEST LONGITUDE, AT OR ABOUT SIXTY MILES SOUTH OF ADAK, ALASKA.

3. UPON ARRIVAL AT WAYPOINT ALFA, *PITTSBURGH* WILL COME TO PERISCOPE DEPTH AND SEND A CODED TRANSMISSION, SPECIFICATIONS AS SET FORTH IN APPENDIX 1. SAID TRANSMISSION WILL INDICATE *PITTSBURGH'S* READINESS TO SURFACE AND TAKE ON NEW PERSONNEL.

4. UPON ARRIVAL AT WAYPOINT ALFA, YOU WILL MAKE RADIO CONTACT WITH A TRANSPORT AIRCRAFT, IDENTIFIED BY A CODED TRANSMISSION AS SET FORTH IN APPENDIX 2. AFTER POSITIVE IDENTIFICATION, *PITTSBURGH* WILL SURFACE AND TAKE ABOARD PERSONNEL DROPPED IN THE AREA BY HELOCAST. AS IN (1), THESE PERSONNEL, COMPRISING AN OPERATIONAL ELEMENT OF NAVY SEAL TEAM 3, OPERATING UNDER THE AUTHORITY OF BOTH SPECIAL OPERATIONS COMMAND AND NURO, ARE NOT TO BE QUESTIONED AS TO THE NATURE OR DETAILS OF THEIR MISSION.

5. *PITTSBURGH* WILL THEN SET COURSE FOR THE SEA OF OKHOTSK, ENTERING THE REGION VIA THE CHETVERTYY KURIL'SKIY PROLIV, MAP REFERENTS, APPENDIX 3. YOU WILL OPERATE IN SUPPORT OF NURO AND SEAL TEAM 3 PERSONNEL, RENDERING ALL POSSIBLE COOPERATION CONCOMITANT WITH THE SAFETY OF YOUR VESSEL AND CREW.

6. *PITTSBURGH* WILL ENTER THE SAKHALINSKIY ZALIV UNDER COVER OF DARKNESS ON THE EVENING OF 19 JULY, 1987, AND APPROACH AO COSSACK, AT 53° 40' 15"

NORTH LATITUDE, 141° 10' 12" EAST LONGITUDE, APPROXIMATELY TWENTY MILES NORTH OF BOLSOJE VLASJEVO. USING NAVIGATIONAL AND VISUAL SIGNALS AS OUTLINED IN APPENDIX 4 , YOU WILL ESTABLISH CONTACT WITH A RESISTANCE GROUP ABOARD A CIVILIAN FISHING BOAT OPERATING IN THE SAKHALINSKIY ZALIV. THE SEAL ELEMENT WILL AFFECT THE TRANSFER OF SPECIAL OPS PERSONNEL TO THE CONTACT BOAT AND IN MAKING CONTACT WITH THE RESISTANCE GROUP.

7. *PITTSBURGH* WILL REMAIN IN THE VICINITY OF AO COSSACK FOR 48 HOURS WHILE AWAITING THE COMPLETION OF THE OPERATION ASHORE. DURING THIS TIME, SEAL TEAM 3 PERSONNEL WILL ENGAGE IN UNDERWATER OPERATIONS OFF THE COAST NEAR THE COASTAL TOWN OF PUIR, DESIGNATED OBJECTIVE MONGOL. YOU ARE REQUIRED TO ASSIST THE SEAL TEAM, THROUGH MANEUVERING AND TRAVEL, IN ANY WAY THAT THEY MAY REQUIRE TO ACCOMPLISH THEIR MISSION.

8. AT THE END OF THE 48 HOUR PERIOD, TWO OF THE SPECIAL OPERATIONS PERSONNEL WILL RETURN TO *PITTSBURGH* ABOARD A CIVILIAN FISHING BOAT. YOU WILL TAKE THEM AND ALL SEAL PERSONNEL ON BOARD AND RETURN TO U.S. NAVAL STATION, MARE ISLAND TO OFF-LOAD RETURNING SPECIAL PERSONNEL AND FOR FORMAL DEBRIEFING.

9. BE ADVISED THAT INTELLIGENCE REPORTS INDICATE THAT A NEW SOVIET ATTACK SUBMARINE OF UNKNOWN BUT HIGH CAPABILITY, DESIGNATED "MIKE 2," IS OPERATING IN THIS AREA, PROBABLY OUT OF THE PORT OF MAGADAN. THE *PITTSBURGH* SHOULD AVOID ANY CONFRONTATION WITH MIKE 2 THAT WOULD JEOPARDIZE ANY PART OF HER PRIMARY MISSION. HOWEVER, INTELLIGENCE PLACES A HIGH VALUE ON RETURNING ANY INFORMATION POSSIBLE ON THE MIKE CLASS, INCLUDING SONAR

READINGS, MAGNETIC ANOMALY SCANS, AND VISUAL INSPECTION OF THE HULL. *PITTSBURGH* SHOULD ENDEAVOR TO PROVIDE THIS INTELLIGENCE IF PRACTICABLE DURING THE PURSUIT OF THE PRIMARY MISSION.

10. ALL RADIO COMMUNICATIONS ARE RESTRICTED TO THOSE CONTACT PROTOCOLS SPECIFICALLY DESCRIBED IN THE APPENDICES OF THIS DOCUMENT. *PITTSBURGH* IS NOT TO ATTEMPT OTHER COMMUNICATIONS WITH SHIP OR SHORE FACILITIES AT ANY TIME DURING THE MISSION, UNTIL AFTER EXIT FROM THE SEA OF OKHOTSK AND CLEAR OF ALL SOVIET STATIONS AND VESSELS. THIS RESTRICTION INCLUDES FAMILYGRAMS AND ALL OTHER ROUTINE RADIO TRAFFIC.

(SIGNED) BENJAMIN GOLDMAN, RADM
OFFICE OF NAVAL SPECIAL OPERATIONS COMMAND

"What the hell is NURO?" Lieutenant Walberg wanted to know.

"Naval Underwater Reconnaissance Office," Latham said. "It's a scam."

"What makes you say that?" Gordon asked.

"It's theoretically a fifty-fifty operation between Naval Intelligence and the CIA, only the Agency's always able to buy the pot."

"What do you mean?"

"Well, it's supposed to be a joint venture, Naval Intelligence and CIA, right? Headed by the CNI, with the CIA's DDO as his number two, and roughly equal numbers of personnel, CIA and Navy. But it's actually almost all CIA, using Navy assets and money."

"Cute," Walberg said.

"Sure. The CIA pulled the same trick back in the sixties when they set up the NRO, the National Reconnaissance Office. It was supposed to allow the sharing of intel from Air

Force spy satellites. But where the Air Force couldn't afford to put that many people into the new program, the CIA could send all it wanted. Before long, the NRO was turning out good intel, but it was all Central Intelligence Agency stuff . . . and the Air Force was paying for a lot of it."

"You're saying the CIA is doing the same thing here?" Warren asked.

"Of course. NURO is run by the Chief of Naval Intelligence, but he can't afford that many people to operate the place. But the Agency's always happy to help out. Isn't that right, 'Mr. Johnson'?"

Johnson didn't meet Latham's gaze. He appeared to be intensely interested in the piping of the overhead in the far corner. "I wouldn't know about any of that," he said. "But I submit that this subject is *not* one for public discussion."

"Come on, Mr. Johnson," Ostler said, grinning. "No secrets *here*."

"The organization and purview of NURO is a matter of national security," Johnson said, "and not a matter for public debate."

"Is it national security?" Latham asked with a bitter quirk to his mouth, "or is it that the Agency just doesn't want any more oversight?"

"Come on, people," Gordon said. "We're supposed to be on the same side. Sean? You have the charts?"

"Yes, sir," *Pittsburgh*'s Navigation Officer said. Alerted ahead of time by Gordon, he'd brought along an aluminum carry tube containing several charts. Pulling them out and unrolling them on the table, he pointed to the first one, which showed the pearl-string line of the Kuril Islands, from Cape Lopatka at the tip of Kamchatka all the way to Hokkaido.

All of the charts were marked SECRET. Normally, they would be kept covered by a blotter, and revealed only to select members of the boat's crew. Gordon glanced at Johnson, suppressing as he did so a momentary twinge of distrust. The man's security clearance was astronomically higher than Gordon's. Still, a submariner's ingrained worship of security, his unwillingness to share *anything* with outsiders, was tough to overcome.

"Okay," Garrison said. "The Chetvertyy Kuril'skiy Proliv is this gap in the Kurils, between Paramusir and Onekotan. Deep-water channel . . . averaging five hundred feet. It's one of the main entrances into the Sea of Okhotsk . . . which worries me a bit. I'm wondering why our orders are so specific about where we go through."

"It's the northernmost deep-water channel through the Kurils," Gordon said, arms folded, "and the closest to a direct-line course for us coming down the great circle route along the Aleutians. However, I'm not going to worry too much about that line in the orders, gentlemen. Captain's discretion. If there's too much traffic at that entrance, if I so much as get a bad feeling about what's there, then we go south . . . to this passage north of Raykoke, or even all the way to the Proliv Bussol'. You might have those charts ready, Sean, just in case."

"Aye, sir. Already have 'em pulled."

"Good man."

"Once into the Sea of Okhotsk, things aren't so bad," Garrison continued, opening another, larger chart. "We've been there before. No surprises. We have this nice, deep arm of the sea running northwest toward Ostrov Iony—that's 'Saint Jona's Island,' though the Soviets don't recognize saints. Brings us up to the northern tip of Sakhalin.

"Here's where it'll get hairy, though. Sakhalin Island is this long, skinny one right running north–south right off the Siberian coast. At its closest, here at Lazarev, the Tatarskiy Strait is only a few miles wide. There are rumors—unconfirmed—that Stalin had slave labor digging a tunnel between the mainland and Sakhalin during World War II. It's *narrow*.

"North of there, we have this big, circular bay between northern Sakhalin and the northern tip of the Maritime Provinces. Sakhalinskiy Zaliv—Sakhalin Bay—is about eighty miles across, wide-open to the north . . . but it narrows sharply to the northern opening of Tatarskiy Strait.

There's an underwater oil pipeline here, at Puir, connecting Nikolayevsk and the North Sakhalin oilfields at Okha. Water depth is estimated at forty to fifty feet, depending on the local tides.

"Puir is here, right on the opening to the Tatarskiy Strait. Nothing much there. Pipeline and communications facilities. Probably some small naval facilities. Lord knows what the SEALs are supposed to do there."

Johnson was still studying the overhead piping, Gordon noticed.

"Now, right around the Puir headland is the mouth of the Amur River," Garrison continued. "And ten miles up the Amurskiy Liman—the Amur Estuary—is the city of Nikolayevsk-na-Amure. Major port. Major naval facility. Major shipbuilding complex. Very heavily guarded. They obviously chose the placement of their sensitive naval facilities to make it damned difficult for us to slip in and photograph it from a periscope. We have some fair satellite photographs of the area, of course, but almost no data on the underwater topology, depths, presence of ASW nets or minefields, that sort of thing."

"That close to Nikolayevsk," Gordon said, thoughtful. "ASW coverage and coastal patrols are going to be a bitch." He looked at Johnson. "And we have to sit there in shallow water for two *days*?"

"How deep's the water north of this Bolsoje place?" Carver wanted to know.

"Bolsoje Vlasjevo," Garrison said. "Depending on how close ashore we get . . . seventy, maybe eighty feet."

"Shit," Carver said. "That's practically periscope depth!"

"We're gonna be a damned cockroach on a dinner plate," Warren added.

"That's going to be another captain's discretion," Gordon said. "I don't see why we can't come in and drop off our packages at midnight, then move back up here to the north, where we have some maneuvering room."

Johnson gave him a hard look at that. "Your orders, Captain, are to wait for us until we're done doing what we have to do ashore."

"My first order is to support you and yours, as well as Lieutenant Randall's SEALs, to the best of my ability *without* compromising the safety of this vessel."

"If you got into trouble while you were joyriding off somewhere in the Sea of Okhotsk," Johnson said, angry, "you wouldn't be able to come back in and pick us up!"

"If we get spotted by a Russian Krivak," Gordon said evenly, "or if we trip a seabed sensor, we're not going to be able to pick you up either, because we will be *dead*."

"Damned straight," Latham said.

"We'll be there to pick you up, don't worry," Gordon told the NURO spook. "I can promise you that our moving into deeper water will *not* increase the chances of our being caught. Quite the opposite, in fact."

"I thought you could just sit on the bottom," Johnson said.

"Not in an LA boat," Carver told him. "We have thrusters and we have delicate sonar equipment on our keel. We can hover pretty close above the mud, but we can't go sit on the bottom like a Sturgeon or an old World War II boat. No way."

"The bad part of it, sir," Warner said, "is that if we're right down near the bottom in seventy foot of water, the top of our conning tower is about twenty feet deep. On a bright, sunny day, an aircraft flying overhead would see us like a big, dark, cigar-shaped shadow under the water."

"Like the man said," Gordon added, "a roach on a dinner plate. Kind of easy to notice, know what I mean?"

"I will protest this violation of your direct orders," Johnson said.

"You go right ahead and protest, Mr. Johnson. We're specifically forbidden from making radio contact with anyone, except for the signals protocols in these orders. Hell, we're not even going to be able to allow the crew Family-grams this time out. So you just write down your protest, put it somewhere safe, and deliver it to the proper authority when you get back to Mare Island!"

"The SEAL operations in the Tatarskiy Strait may require our presence," Latham reminded them. "We'll need to coordinate with the SEALs, to see how far we can withdraw back into open water. But," he added, looking at Johnson, "I agree that we cannot remain in shallow water during daylight hours."

"We're going to be busier than a one-legged man in an ass-kicking contest," Gordon observed. "But we can do it. Do the rest of you concur with the plan, as revised?"

The others nodded or voiced their agreement. It wasn't as if the command of *Pittsburgh* was anything close to a democracy, of course, but Gordon believed in letting his officers participate in the command process as far as was possible.

"Okay," he went on. "What do we know about this Mike?"

The COB leaned forward, eyes eager. He was always at his best when he could show off some portion of his encyclopedic stores of knowledge, everything from specs on other submarines to tall, tall sea stories. "Well," he said with an easy drawl, "that's a bit of a challenge, isn't it, sir? Your Mike is a pretty sharp boat, if half of what we think we know about her is true. She's a direct descendent of the Alfa, and that means trouble right there. Aluminum hull, we think. Liquid-sodium reactor . . . and that would be second or third generation, not the crap that screwed up their very first Alfa prototype.

"Four hundred feet long, overall. Thirty-nine-foot beam. Seven thousand eight hundred tons' displacement on the surface, and about ninety-seven hundred tons submerged. Big sucker, bigger than us. Biggest SSN in the world except for the Soviet Yankee, and that's because it's a converted SSBN, a boomer. Top speed unknown, but probably in the neighborhood of thirty-six to thirty-eight knots underwater, a bit slower on the surface."

"Bigger than us, and faster," Carver said, thoughtful.

"The bad news," Gordon said, "is that the Mike is significantly quieter than earlier Soviet subs. Sounds like they worked the bugs out of the Alfa's noisy propulsion plant. It's at *least* as quiet as a Flight I Los Angeles, and that means big trouble."

"I find it fascinating," Latham said, "that the Soviets are experimenting with so many different designs. We're pretty much locked into the Los Angeles class attack boat, which is a direct follow-on from the Sturgeon and Permit classes. We're modernizing the same design, with Flight II boats like the *'Burgh*, and we'll have it again when the Flight III boats come on-line, but all of the LAs are basically the same. The Soviets, though, have the Alfas, Sierras, versions I *and* II, Akulas, and now this new Mike. Must be nice to be able to throw money at any military project that comes down the pike."

"Well, a lot higher of a percentage of their gross domestic product goes to the military, you know," COB said. "I guess we could do the same, if the American people didn't *also* want paved roads, social security, and free-lunch programs at school."

"Screw that," Ostler said. "Soviet boats are meltdowns waiting to happen. Everyone knows the U.S. has a perfect operating record with sub reactors. The Russkis have lost . . . how many, now? Two? Three? That we know about? At least ours *work*."

"Gentlemen, let's attend to the business at hand," Gordon said, dragging the conversation back on course. "Do you have any comments about . . . this?" He waved a hand above the charts of Sakhalin Bay, taking in the whole mission, and its dangers.

There was no reply for several heartbeats. "It's a bitch," Warner said at last. "A royal, fucking-A-one bitch."

"Second that," Latham said. "Someone back in the Five-Sided Squirrel Cage is living in a dream world."

"Is it your opinion that the mission is *impossible*, XO?"

"Not . . . impossible, sir. . . ."

"But highly improbable," Garrison put in. "We're going to be in a tight box, in shallow water, and exposed for a lot longer than is healthy."

"Can we do it?" Gordon pressed. "I'm the newcomer here, remember. Captain Chase knew this boat cold. He knew each of you and the people in your departments. I can't imagine him accepting an order that he knew to be flat-out impossible . . . for their sake. I need your honest assessments."

"You're not thinking of turning back. . . ." Johnson said, his brow creasing. "This mission is important."

"I'm sure it is, Mr. Johnson. So are the lives of my men. So is the safety of this submarine, which, incidentally, is my responsibility. No nuke-driver accepts suicide missions. It's not in the job description."

"We can do it," Garrison said, peering again at the Sakhalin Bay chart. "*If* we can move in and out of this shallow area, so we're not sitting there in plain sight in the daylight. And if we can avoid their seabed sonar nets and any other surprises they've rigged for us."

"The boat is up to it, certainly," Latham said.

"And the crew," Warren added. "They're hot, prepped, and eager to please."

"Maneuvering is in A-one condition, Captain," Ostler said. "But you knew that."

Gordon nodded. He'd been making almost daily inspections of the engineering department for the past two weeks.

"Please God we won't need them," Walberg said, "but the Tomahawks and Mark 48s all test out optimal. We've got teeth, if we need them."

"As you say, let's hope it doesn't come to that. Okay, gentlemen. Thank you for your input. This mission is a go."

He thought now that he knew what Caesar had felt while crossing the Rubicon.

There was no going back now.

15

Friday, 17 July 1987

SEAL Team Three
Third Platoon, Attached Special Operations Group
Fifty Miles South of Adak, Alaska
1412 hours local time (Greenwich −11)

"Three minutes, ladies!" Randall called out, bellowing to be heard above the clatter of the UH-1N's rotor. "Check your gear!"

There were only four of them, instead of the usual squad of seven. SOG operations frequently required customized fireteam and squad deployments. Besides Lieutenant (j.g.) Randall, there were TM Chief Donald McCluskey, GM1 Tom Nelson, and RM1 Rodney Fitch. All wore wet suits, masks, and fins, and lugged heavily laden satchels carrying the rest of their gear. The Huey Slick had been traveling south for the past fifty miles, searching for a featureless spot on a vast and wave-ruffled ocean.

Conditions were not especially good—low overcast, scattered showers, limited visibility, and winds gusting to forty knots.

Randall took his seat next to Fitch, seated on the edge of the cargo deck, feet on the helicopter's starboard-side skid, with the mingled wind and prop wash blasting around his ears like a hurricane. Somehow, the chopper pilot had to find a pencil-thin sliver out there in all that gray and whitecap-streaked water.

Still, they'd received pretty precise coordinates at Adak Naval Air Station before they'd lifted off, precise enough that the copilot had just given him the three-minute warning. He checked his watch; two minutes ten, now.

"I still want to know what genius thought I looked Russian!" Fitch yelled.

"Don't sweat it. If you get questioned, just tell 'em you're looking for your prayer rug!"

Fitch was black, though with skin tone light enough that he could pass for an inhabitant of one of the central Asian republics. And he *did* speak fluent Russian.

"Besides," Randall added, "you volunteered, remember?"

"Must have been temporary insanity, Lieutenant. You and me both know it never pays to volunteer!"

"Should be coming up on the drop point pretty quick. . . ."

"There!" Fitch yelled. "Just off to starboard! Y'see it?"

Randall leaned out a little against his safety harness. Fitch had damned good eyes; it took a moment or two for Randall to spot the telltale feather of a periscope wake against the whitecaps and spindrift. As they watched, the dark gray rectangle of a submarine's conning tower broke the surface, then rose, as plumes of white spray burst around it.

The Huey dropped toward the deck, until its landing skids were skimming just twenty feet off the water.

"Okay!" the Huey's pilot called back to them. "You're good to go!"

"Thank you, Lieutenant!"

"Any time! Good luck!"

"Okay!" Randall yelled to the other SEALs. "Gear . . . then go!"

From either side of the helicopter, large bundles of the

team's equipment were heaved out into the wet air, to plummet into the waves below. An instant later, all four SEALs leaped out as well, two to either side of the aircraft, in a maneuver known as helocasting.

Randall dropped with his arms folded across his chest, his legs crossed, and his head tilted far forward, as he'd practiced innumerable times. He hit the ocean hard, and was instantly engulfed by the bitterly cold water. Kicking hard, he broke the surface, blowing and gasping. The water was frigid on the exposed parts of his face; the waves were a lot rougher than they'd appeared from the air, carrying him up, up, and up, then swiftly down again as the wave rolled past. He'd maintained his bearings, however, and was able to strike out in a vigorous crawl, swimming for the submarine intermittently visible through the surging waves.

A wave broke over him, salty green and freezing. Then he broke through to the surface again, and the submarine's hull was almost within reach. A line fell across his outstretched arm; he grabbed hold and let himself be pulled the rest of the way in.

Clambering up the side of a submarine in heavy surf wasn't easy, but training and sheer strength let him haul himself aboard at last, to lie gasping on the steel deck. Someone stooped over him in a bright orange life jacket, connecting a safety line. "Request . . . permission to come aboard . . . sir. . . ." he gasped out.

"Granted," the voice replied. "Though I'm not a fuckin' *sir*. . . ."

Ten minutes later, all four SEALs were aboard and safely in the enlisted mess, cups of hot coffee in their hands, warm blankets flung over their shoulders.

"I very much hope this is an American submarine," Randall said after taking a hard swig of coffee. "I didn't see a flag coming down, and it would be embarrassing if you were Russians."

"*Prisvetstvie*," a bearded man said, grinning. "*Dobri dyehn'!*"

"*Da*," another said. "*Vi ryehzyehrverahvahli nomyehr?*"

"Yes, I have a reservation," Randall replied. "*Very* funny. But the guy who dragged me aboard topside gave it away when he welcomed me aboard."

"That would be me," a sailor said, raising a finger, "but I speak perfect English."

"I'm Commander Gordon," a lean, angular-looking man said, stepping forward, "and don't let Douglas or these other hooligans tell you otherwise. Welcome aboard the *Pittsburgh*, gentlemen."

"Good to be aboard, Captain," Randall said. "Thanks for the lift."

"Not a problem. You boys picked a pretty rough day for it."

"Not our idea, believe me, sir."

"I should introduce these gentlemen," Gordon said, gesturing at four of the men in the mess hall, including the two who'd spoken such perfect Russian. "Sergei Mikhailovich Putin and Anatol Grigorovich Kasparov, late of the Union of Soviet Socialist Republics. And George Smith and John Johnson, of the USA."

"Good to meet you, Lieutenant," Smith said. He was thin and cold, with an assassin's hooded eyes. "*Medved'*," he added, the Russian word for bear.

"*Povushka*," Randall replied, giving the Russian word for trap and completing the recognition code.

"Good to know who your friends are, huh?" Johnson said. He was shorter, with a neatly trimmed beard.

"Lieutenant (j.g.) Randall," he said. "My men—McCluskey, Fitch, Nelson."

Gordon's eyes narrowed. "Did you say Lieutenant Randall?"

"Yes, sir."

"Kenneth Randall?"

The SEAL hesitated before responding. "May I ask if we know one another, sir?"

"We'll talk later, son," Gordon said. "Douglas here will

take you all forward to the torpedo room and see that you get settled in, get dry clothes, and get what you need to be squared away. You'll be bunking in there until we reach our destination, which should be in another three or four days. Make yourselves at home. There's not much room to stretch, but the chow's good, and the company is congenial. Enjoy your stay."

"Thank you, Captain."

He wondered though, how this man knew him. His presence here was supposed to be classified. . . .

Captain's Quarters, USS *Pittsburgh*
Sixty Miles Southwest of Adak, Alaska
1530 hours

"Enter," Gordon called in response to the two sharp raps on the door. It opened, and Lieutenant (j.g.) Randall stepped in. He'd showered and donned clean, dry clothing, the blue one-piece jumpers worn by officers aboard the *Pittsburgh*, known as "poopie suits."

"You wanted to see me, Captain?"

"Yes, Lieutenant. Have a seat."

"Thank you, sir."

"I was wondering if you were the Lieutenant Randall who was the 2IC on a SEAL raid in Lebanon last month. The Bekaa Valley, looking for the American hostages."

Randall's eyes narrowed to hard slits. "Sir, I'm really not at liberty to talk about that."

Gordon sighed, then nodded. "I understand, Lieutenant. I'd just like to say—hypothetically, of course—that if you were the man on that operation, well, I'm damned glad you made it back."

Randall nodded slowly. "And . . . just hypothetically, of course, if I had been that man . . . how the hell would a submarine skipper know about that?"

"Hypothetically, he might have been holding down a desk at the Pentagon last month, before taking command of a sub. It's possible he worked at the Naval Special Operations Command Office, planning little excursions like the one into the Bekaa Valley.

"And as long as we're making this all up, we could, just hypothetically, assume that sub driver has been wondering if he was responsible for the deaths of two good men."

"I . . . see." Randall looked Gordon up and down. "You don't look like the typical REMF. Not what I always picture them like."

REMF was military slang for a rear echelon mother-fucker, a peculiarly juicy term for hacks, yes-men, ticket-punching brass, politicians, malingerers, wanna-bes, and a whole zoo of hangers-on, part and parcel of the enormous logistical tail of every military deployment . . . necessary, some of them, even most of them, but personnel far from the whisper of bullets or the thin stink of gun smoke and fear.

"I *was* a REMF. But mostly I drive submarines for a living."

"You planned an op in the Bekaa? What was it called?"

"Operation Free Sanction."

"Huh. You know, there was a time or three when I really wanted to kill you, sir."

Gordon noticed that Randall had dropped the pretense. "I imagine that's so. But I wasn't responsible for abandoning you out there."

"I know, I know."

"Nor was the micromanaging my idea. They brought me down to their Agent Double-Oh-Seven bunker that night. Until then, I didn't even know they'd accepted the plan. I'd drawn it up, submitted it, and never heard about it again, until that night."

"But you were watching over our shoulders, huh?"

"Most of it. They . . . *we* lost track of you when you went back for First Squad. What I wanted to know was what went wrong?"

"You didn't know?"

"They didn't tell me. I was surprised at how many bad guys were on-site . . . and I know the objective turned out to be a dry hole. Waite wasn't there."

"No. He'd been there, and probably pretty recently. But they'd moved him out and moved half the damned Syrian Army in. We weren't fighting militia that night, Captain. It was Assad's best, his crack troops." He leaned forward, his hands clasping one another. "Sir, I think it was a trap."

"As in . . . they knew you were coming?"

"They knew we were coming. They moved the hostages out and the Syrian Guard in. And they held back until we'd committed ourselves. It was God's own luck we got out. Two of us didn't."

"But who? How?"

"I'd kind of like to know that myself, Captain."

"And why?"

"That seems pretty obvious, doesn't it? Uncle Sugar had a real setback, image-wise, when Eagle's Claw went sour at Desert One. Remember those photos of Iranian soldiers cheering above the wreckage of our crashed helos in the desert? Think of the propaganda mileage Assad and his backers in the Kremlin could get if they could parade a captured SEAL platoon through the streets of Damascus."

"I see what you mean."

"I'll tell you the truth, sir. I've got a bad feeling about this mission, too."

"Such as?"

"It has all the makings of a cluster fuck, Captain. Security so tight none of us can even talk to one another, but signs indicate that Soviet intelligence is stepping up the power a notch. A few days ago, two of us investigated some mystery tracks on a beach at Adak."

"Mystery tracks?"

"Probably a Soviet marine tractor, a kind of submarine with tank tracks . . . or maybe a true submarine that can crawl as well as swim. There've been reports of the things in

Alaska and Scandinavia for years. Anyway, it looks to hell like one went ashore at Adak . . . and just when we were there, waiting for our ride."

"Coincidence?"

"Maybe. SEALs don't get old believing in coincidence, though. Let me ask you this, Captain."

"Shoot."

"Did you get out of port clean?"

Gordon gave him a humorless smile, tight-lipped. "Negative. We picked up a tail."

"But you had someone to scrape it off?"

"Actually . . . no. Security concerns were such that we didn't have another boat to run interference for us. We shook him off with some fancy maneuvers off San Francisco."

"Hmm. Interesting."

"You've got that paranoid look to you."

"How do you know what I look like when I'm paranoid?"

Gordon shrugged. "Something about the eyes."

"I see too many coincidences running through here. It'd make anyone paranoid."

"Just because you're paranoid," Gordon quipped, "doesn't mean they're *not* all out to get you."

"You got that right. Did you have anything to do with the planning of this op?"

"No." Gordon's eyes widened. "Wait. Are you saying the ambush in the Bekaa Valley and this mission are connected somehow?"

"No. Not at all. I *am* saying that we have some very high-level leaks, possibly at the Agency, possibly in the Pentagon. Frankly, I smell a rat . . . a rat that looks to me like a mole."

"I take your point. The question is, what can we do about it?"

Randall leaned back in his chair, eyes closed. "Captain, I don't think there's a fucking thing we *can* do. I have my mission orders. You have yours. We follow the plan as best we can . . . and see what shakes out. Sir."

"Sure." Gordon nodded. "In other words, if we're walking

into a trap, we stick our necks out and shout, 'Here we are!'"

"You have a depressing way with words, Captain."

"Thank you. I like to think it's one of my better features."

Saturday, 18 July 1987

Sick Bay, USS *Pittsburgh*
One Hundred Ten Miles Southwest of Adak, Alaska
1710 hours

"Okay, so what makes you think you have radiation poisoning?" HMC Ronald Pyter was an old-Navy hospital corpsman; when he wore his dress blues, the gold hash marks, each one representing four years of service, seemed to go clear up his sleeve, from wrist to elbow. He ran *Pittsburgh*'s tiny sick bay and dispensary like a benevolent and somewhat mellow tyrant, dispensing advice as often as pills.

O'Brien sat on the opposite side of the steel desk from Pyter. "Well, my hair is falling out in clumps. . . ."

"We already checked your dosimeter," Pyter said. "I showed it to you. You are not picking up anything close to a dangerous level of radioactivity."

"But my hair . . ."

"Doug," Pyter said, surprising O'Brien with his use of his first name, "do you trust me?"

"Yes, sir."

"I'm not a sir. Call me 'Doc' or 'Chief.'"

"Yes, s . . . Chief." He wasn't sure if he did or not at this point. But it was the right thing to say. "I trust you."

"Okay. Have you been nauseous?"

"First day or two, yes . . . Chief. But I've been okay since then."

"Right. And . . . you've been to Submarine School at New Groton, right?"

"Yeah! Of course!"

"Okay, just checking. So you know about radiation alarms, ORSE inspections, and all of that. Or maybe you just slept through those lectures. Do you really think a radiation leak serious enough to make one of the crew members sick could go undetected? Or that senior crew members would cover such a thing up if it happened?"

"No, Chief. I just thought . . . I don't know, that maybe there was just a patch of radioactivity on a tabletop, or something, you know? Like I touched it and got it on my food or something."

Chief Pyter sighed. "Radiation doesn't work that way. Oh, granted, somebody could have sprinkled plutonium dust in your rack or something like that, but can you tell me why anybody would do that?"

"No, Chief."

"You have to trust your shipmates, son. Even when they yank your strings to make you twitch." He paused, letting that sink in. "If there was a radiation emergency on this boat, it would contaminate forward compartment by compartment. And as soon as the alarms sounded, we would seal off the contaminated areas from the rest of the boat. Does that make sense?"

"Yes. . . ."

"Next we would surface and try venting the affected compartments to the open air. If it was serious enough—and at that point it probably would be—the captain would evacuate the boat.

"You do not have radiation symptoms, son. Do you hear me?"

"Yes, Chief." He was trying to reorder his thinking. For an entire week he'd been living in dread, convinced he was dying. For several days, he'd been kept too busy to come down to sick bay and see anyone. And for the past couple of days, as his hair grew so patchy that several officers and petty officers had commented on his unkempt appearance, he'd simply been too afraid and too ashamed to say anything.

Not that that made any sense. But it had taken a definite act of willpower to demand that he be allowed to come down to sick call and see Chief Pyter.

Only now was he beginning to let himself relax into the idea that he wasn't sick.

And yet . . .

"Okay, Chief. If it's not radiation, what is it? I mean . . . Chief Allison told me the other day I looked like I had the mange. But that's a *dog* disease, isn't it? Do I have mange?"

"Uh . . . no. It's not mange."

"Then what is it?" He reached up and pulled another tuft of hair out. "What's *wrong* with me?"

"Mmm." Pyter looked at O'Brien for a moment. He had a bushy mustache and light blue eyes that twinkled merrily when he was amused . . . like now. Damn it, what was so funny?

"Doug, you look to me like a squared-away sailor, all your shit in one seabag, know what I mean?"

"Thank you, Chief." That was not praise he'd heard before, and he sat up a bit straighter now for it.

"Don't mention it. You're always well turned out . . . uniform clean and neat. Good personal hygiene. . . ."

"Well, they stressed that hard, both in boot camp and in Sub School. Locked up in a tin can with a hundred twenty other guys . . . you keep yourself clean or they just might hold a blanket party."

Blanket parties—a relic of the old Navy, but not condoned any longer in this more sensitive era—were part of the hazing folklore in boot camp, a kind of boogeyman story about how offending recruits might find themselves dragged off to the head inside a blanket and given a shower that included caustic soap and a bristle brush.

"You shower every day?"

"Of course, Chief!"

"It's not 'of course.' You'd be astonished how many sailors are oblivious to their own ripe aroma. Especially after being at sea for a spell. You shampoo your hair every day?"

"Sure, Chief. I mean, it's part of the routine, right?"

"Uh-huh."

"So . . . when did you notice your hair was starting to fall out?"

"I don't know. I guess, maybe, a week or so after I came aboard."

"Uh-huh. And . . . have you discussed radiation poisoning with anyone else aboard?"

"Well . . ."

"It's okay, son. This isn't a mast, and I won't report you."

"Okay, I talked about it with some of the guys when it first started getting bad, y'know? But they said I could get in trouble for spreading rumors. None of them thought that's what I had either. But they didn't sound real convinced, know what I mean?"

Pyter chuckled. "I know exactly what you mean." He looked thoughtful for a moment. "You have any college, son?"

"No, Chief. My family couldn't afford it, and my grades weren't all that great to begin with."

"But you know how fraternities will haze pledges before they get to be part of the club?"

"Oh, sure. And they told me at Sub School I'd probably get the treatment."

"Uh-huh."

When Pyter didn't elaborate, O'Brien's eyes widened, and he felt a sudden rush of anger. "Wait a minute! . . ."

"Are you starting to get the picture, son?"

"Are you saying the guys are doing this somehow? Just to play a practical joke on the new guy?"

Pyter leaned back, his twinkling gaze on the overhead for a moment. "Doug, submariners are an elite community. No, a *fraternity*, a true brotherhood of blood and steel. You're part of a tradition that goes back to guys waiting out Japanese depth-charge attacks in stinking, steel coffins . . . hell it goes back eighty-seven years to America's first true submarine, the *Holland*, back when nobody knew if it was coming up again once it went down. Or to the Confederate *Hunley* going up against the Yankee *Housatonic*, with sixteen men aboard who knew they probably wouldn't survive the explosion when they rammed their spar home . . . or even back to David Bushnell in 1778, turning the hand cranks on a little tar-sealed barrel called the *Turtle* as he tried to get close enough to the British man-of-war *Eagle* in New York Harbor that he could try to attach a bag of gunpowder to the enemy's keel. His wooden screw wouldn't bite through the *Eagle*'s copper-plated bottom, unfortunately, and the attempt failed." He waved a hand. "Beside the point. Bushnell was the first recorded submariner. He started a brotherhood of men willing to undergo some serious danger, hardship, and privation in order to carry out their missions.

"Now, submariners are a choosy lot. They want to know the men serving with them are the very best. Over the years, they've evolved some pretty sneaky ways to initiate others into the brotherhood. Some of their tests are downright vicious."

"You're saying this . . . what's happening to me, is a test?"

"Sort of. They're putting you through the sort of stuff they had to go through when they were nubs. It becomes a tradition, a part of your life aboard the boats. Doesn't make it easier, doesn't even make it right. But it's going to happen. You can squawk and complain and probably never be fully accepted by the rest of the crew . . . or you can just go along with it, take your lumps, have a good laugh when it's over . . . and maybe plan how you're going to get the next newbie who sets foot on board the *Pittsburgh*.

"Because that *will* happen, you know. Individuals come and go aboard the boats, but the boats remain. There'll always be another poor new guy to dump the shit on."

"I guess it's not so bad then, huh?"

"It happened to me, a good twenty years ago. All of your buddies have been through it. As a kind of initiation into an elite? No, it's not so bad." He grinned. "Did you get your invitation yet?"

"My invitation?"

"King Neptune's party. Tonight."

"Oh! I didn't think that was an invitation. More like a command." He reached into the breast pocket of his dungaree shirt and pulled out a folded-up piece of paper, handing it to Pyter. "Douglas gave it to me yesterday."

USS *PITTSBURGH* UPON ENTERING
THE DOMAIN OF THE GOLDEN DRAGON
NOTICE AND LISTEN, YE LANDLUBBER

I ORDER AND COMMAND YOU TO APPEAR BEFORE ME AND MY ROYAL COURT ON THE MORROW TO BE INITIATED INTO THE MYSTERIES OF MY SPECIAL ROYAL DOMAIN. FAIL TO APPEAR UPON PAIN OF BEING GIVEN AS FOOD TO THE SHARKS, WHALES, SEA TURTLES, POLLYWOGS, SALTWATER FROGS, AND ALL LIVING CREATURES OF THE SEA, WHO WILL DEVOUR YOU HEAD, BODY, AND SOUL AS AN EVERLASTING WARNING TO LANDLUBBERS WHO ENTER MY DOMAIN WITHOUT WARRANT.

KNOW YE THAT YOU ARE CHARGED WITH THE FOLLOWING SERIOUS AND MOST REPREHENSIBLE OFFENSES: EXCESSIVE LIBERTY, NOT SWEARING AND CURSING LIKE A PROPER SAILOR, REPEATED SEASICKNESS, JACKING OFF IN YOUR RACK, TALKING BACK TO YOUR BETTERS, AND BEING IN GENERAL A SCROUNGY, WORTHLESS, MISERABLE WORM OF A NUB, WHO IS SO LOW THAT WHALE SHIT APPEARS TO YOU LIKE UNTO SHOOTING STARS.

THEREFORE, APPEAR AND OBEY OR SUFFER THE CONSEQUENCES!

DAVY JONES
SECRETARY TO HIS MAJESTY
THE GOLDEN DRAGON OF THE EAST

Pyter glanced at it, smiled, and handed it back. "You know what this is all about?"

"Huh? Oh, sure. It's like crossing the equator for the first time, only this is the International Date Line. Order of the Mystic Eastern Dragon? Something like that."

" 'Something like that.' You scared?"

"Well, I'm not looking forward to it, if that's what you mean. Some of the old hands have been trying to scare those of us who haven't been through it before. I know it'll be unpleasant. Scared? No, not really."

"Doug, it's the same as your being accepted as a submariner. People have been crossing the equator and the date line for a good many centuries, now. And it's an old, old tradition to have the guys who've already been there, done that, to put the new guys through the wringer. To initiate them. It's embarrassing, sometimes painful . . . mostly fun if you're willing to let go and join in. And next time, it'll be you wielding the paddle.

"And by going through with it, you're symbolically joining in with sailors who've braved the high seas and storms and hardships and long separations from loved ones and all of that clear back to . . . hell, I don't know. I've heard some of the Shellback stuff goes clear back to the Romans."

"I never knew the Romans crossed the equator."

"Maybe they didn't. They weren't any great shakes as seamen. Not like the Phoenicians. Doesn't matter. They had ceremonies, *rites of passage*, all their own." He chuckled. "You know, if this stuff was *easy*, it wouldn't feel as good once you were in the club!"

"I guess not."

"This sort of hazing gets dropped on every nub from the moment they set foot on board their first submarine. It won't be forever, it's *usually* not dangerous, and at the end of it you're an accepted member of the community."

"So, what did they do to make my hair fall out?"

Pyter looked uncomfortable. "I've been trying not to say. I wouldn't want to ruin their joke."

"Chief, they've had me thinking I was going to die for two weeks now!"

"Well, let me put it this way. *I* have to live on this boat, too!"

"You're afraid they'll get even if they know you told me?"

"Not afraid, exactly, but it's not the sort of hassle any sane man looks forward to."

"Yeah, and you've been initiated. What'd they do to you, Chief?"

"Oh, the usual Mickey Mouse shit. Sending me off looking for left-handed spanners and blue skyhooks. And they pulled the hair routine on me, too. I think it's routine now for just about anyone shipping out aboard a nuke or a boomer."

"So how'd they do it?"

He smiled. "A little bit of Nair, or some other woman's hair removal cream, slipped into your shampoo bottle. They start out with a little, and work it up until you're going about half-and-half Nair and shampoo. That way, you don't notice the change in the texture and the lather so much."

"I thought I was just dealing with hard water or something."

"Aboard a submarine? You've got to be kidding!"

"They just wanted to scare me?"

"And make you part of the pack. And remember. You did *not* hear it from me!"

"I understand, Chief. Thanks a lot."

"Anytime, son." He grinned. "You know, normally I go along with the charade. Tell the poor son of a bitch that I don't *think* it's rad poisoning . . . but maybe he should take these pills for a few days, just to make sure. Then I give him a pack of aspirin."

"God . . ."

"Looked to me like you'd been through enough already! Anyway, you want some advice, son?"

"Sure."

"You'll be accepted as one of the gang faster, and more completely, if you find a way to turn the tables on them."

"Huh? What do you mean? Like putting Nair in *their* shampoo?"

"No. I mean by going along with the gag, and maybe even by turning it back against them. Shows you're in on the spirit of the thing."

"I think I get it. Thanks, Chief." He thought hard for a moment. "Ah . . . *hah!*"

"Something?"

"Just an idea. Say, Doc, you wouldn't happen to have a straight razor here, would you?"

Sunday, 19 July 1987

Enlisted Mess, USS *Pittsburgh*
One Hundred Fifty Miles West of Adak, Alaska
1805 hours

"Jesus Christ, kid, what happened to *you*?"

Benson gaped at O'Brien. He'd scarcely recognized the nub, whose scalp was clean-shaven and polished, gleaming brightly beneath the overhead fluorescent lights.

"The Cult of Death," O'Brien said, his sepulcher tones low and measured as he sat down at the table, his food tray before him. "We have, verily, accepted our fate and are numbered now among the dead. . . ."

Douglas opened his mouth as if to say something, closed it, opened it again. "The Cult of *what*? . . ."

"The God of Radiation hath decreed it," O'Brien said, his eyes rolling back in his head. "I am the dead. . . ."

Scobey looked nonplussed. "Well, I guess the twenty-four-dollar question is, can the dead still *work*?"

"Until the final parting of the veil, until the final crossing of the River of Death, verily even so long as the spirit inhabits this shell, it shall perform the duties required of it."

"Shit!" Douglas said. "I think you lost your brains when you shaved your head!"

"No!" Scobey said, laughing hard. "No! This is great!"

"Zombie torpedomen," Benson said, laughing. "Does that mean we can work 'em double watches?"

"You know, I think we might be onto something here."

"I didn't know zombies had such a healthy appetite," Douglas said, nodding toward O'Brien's tray.

"No," Boyce said, "that's how you make zombies, you know. Feed 'em orange bug juice and sliders, hot off the galley grill. Turns 'em into stone, just like that!"

Scobey pinched O'Brien's arm, hard. "He ain't stone. Just zombified."

"He must've found your secret still in the torpedo room, then, Big C," Douglas said, "and been tapping the inventory. That stuff would pickle anything."

"I told you, I ain't got no still, I don't care what the tradition is."

"The radiation hath penetrated the forward compartments, and taken the first converts. But soon, verily, there shalt be more, and the Cult of Death shall increase, and verily we shalt take over the world. . . ."

At this point, Scobey, Benson, and the others all broke into hysterical laughter. "I think . . . I think we should get him a robe," Scobey said. "You know, like a magician-priest-Druid kind of thing! This is great! . . ."

"Nah," Boyce said. "He'd look too much like Uncle Fester. *The Addams Family?*"

"He doesn't need to worry about getting gigged for no haircut, man," Benson added. "That's for damned sure!"

"Yeah," Boyce said, "and we can use his head as a mirror when we get up. It'll save us all kinds of time."

"Mirror, hell," Douglas said. "I'm gonna use his scalp for a freakin' reading lamp!"

Supper continued, with most of the commentary revolving around bald jokes, mystery radiation, and the Cult of

Death. Benson and Scobey had both decided that they wanted to be members, though Douglas had pointed out that if they were going to do that, they would have to shave their heads as well, and no one would be able to tell them apart.

"In death," O'Brien had intoned, arms crossed over his chest and eyes rolled back, "is ultimate anonymity! . . ."

As they were carrying their trays back to the galley, Scobey clapped O'Brien on the shoulder. "You're okay, kid," was all he said.

Monday, 20 July 1987

**Enlisted Mess, USS *Pittsburgh*
Two Hundred Ten Miles West of Adak, Alaska
0010 hours**

"Bring forth the Crunchy Dragon Snacks!"

O'Brien had been grabbed out of his rack in the middle of the night, had his hands bound behind him, a pillowcase jammed over his head, and he'd been dragged in his boxer shorts the long way around up to the Crew's Mess. He'd been doused in a bucket of frigid seawater to "wake him up," then made to crawl on hands and knees through a passageway-turned-obstacle-course with fishnets and lengths of plastic piping.

Now he was standing and shivering with the other soaked nubs of the boat, newbies who'd never crossed the International Date Line before . . . Montgomery and three others who'd come aboard at Mare Island.

The Crew's Mess had been transformed, with spotlights and blue and green filters to give it an eerie, deep-sea atmosphere, and with seaweed, shells, and nets hanging everywhere—along with plenty of Japanese lanterns for a colorful, surreal touch.

The place was packed with grinning sailors, and even the

boat's "special packages" and the Navy SEALs watched from the safety of the galley. Captain Gordon was present, but strictly as an observer, leaning against the forward entrance to the Crew's Mess, a cup of coffee in his hand.

Things had been arranged, though, to focus attention on the throne forward.

Master Chief Warren—O'Brien was pretty sure that's who it was from his size, age, and build—made a spectacular Golden Dragon, wearing gold bikini briefs, swim fins, and a truly bizarre, long-horned dragon mask made of what looked like papier mâché. He was painted all over with gold paint, and with scales picked out in black Magic Marker. He wore gold-painted gloves with black claws, and a kind of crown made of seaweed and starfish. He was seated upon his throne—a commode from a submarine head decorated with plywood, fishing nets, and a lot of paint—and held in his hand a scepter improvised from a plumber's helper.

To either side were the "Ladies of the Court," Boyce and Benson, wearing black mop-head wigs, gold bikinis with tissue-stuffed bras, and with heavy eye makeup to give them a vaguely Oriental look. Archie Douglas was the Dragon's Special Executive Secretary in an outlandish costume that included an archaic quill pen with an immense plume. Other members of the court included Father Time—Scobey in a sheet and a long white beard—and various senior NCOs as the Seven Days of the Week.

The linoleum deck before the throne had been painted with a thick, dotted line. The word "Sunday" was painted on the Dragon's side of the line, just in front of his throne; the word "Saturday" was painted on the deck on O'Brien's side of the line.

Stepping between the nubs and the Dragon, Douglas knelt, head bowed. "O mighty *Draconis orientalis rex*, thou great, wise, noble, and *hungry* Golden Dragon of the East! The prisoners and worthless nubs come before you now, in humble supplication, begging forgiveness of their sins, and induction into the great, royal, and most secret ranks of those who have sought thee across the Mystic Line."

The dragon stood suddenly, bellowing forth a shrieking, wailing howl. "Read to us the listing of their sins!"

Rising, Douglas accepted a parchment scroll from Chief Allison, unrolled it, and began solemnly intoning the list of charges and offenses—the same offenses that had been listed on O'Brien's invitation, with a few new ones thrown in for good measure.

"These are charges most serious indeed!" Still standing, the Dragon pointed a wickedly curved claw at the nubs. "Know ye, miserable nubs, that it is *never* wise to meddle in the affairs of dragons, for you are crunchy and taste great when dipped in chocolate sauce!" Reaching out to either side, he grabbed Boyce and Benson by their waists, drawing them close, eliciting girlish squeals. "Know, too, that dragons are horny beasts, who like to *play* with their food!"

The next hour was sheer misery for the nubs. They wallowed in lime Jell-O, they crawled on hands and knees through a paddling gauntlet, they were drenched in chocolate sauce and spray-coated with whipped cream.

And they were subjected to a barrage of questions about what day it was on which side of the line, each contrived to trip them up in tumbling illogic and imponderables.

"Tell me if you can!" the dragon bellowed in his most imperious manner. "If it be Sunday in Tokyo, on *this* side of the line, and Saturday in San Francisco on *that* side of the line . . . well, doesn't that mean it's also Sunday in Ceylon, while it's also Saturday in Chicago? And if *that* be true, isn't it also true, then, that it's Sunday in London while it's Saturday in New York? And doesn't *that*, then mean, that it is Sunday in the middle of the Atlantic Ocean, and also Saturday in the middle of the Atlantic Ocean? . . .

"By which, of course, we see that all days are one, and time is an illusion . . . and you are all AWOL because you've already missed your watches tomorrow! . . ."

"Captain!" Douglas called out. "We have to put these men on report!"

"I'll take that under advisement, Mr. Secretary," Gordon replied, laughing.

The Dragon extended a gold and scaly arm, pointing at O'Brien. "You! Baldy! Get down on your belly and squirm your way across the Date Line to me, that you may be recognized!"

O'Brien dropped onto the deck, which was already slick with lime Jell-O, and started crawling. The crowd was chanting, "Go, nub, go! Go, nub, go! . . ."

"Crawl into tomorrow, miserable worm!" the dragon commanded.

"Captain, Sonar!" Kellerman's voice cut in, and instantly the crowd went silent.

Gordon went to a bulkhead intercom and pressed the switch. "Sonar, Captain. Whatcha got, Kellerman?"

"Contact, Captain, bearing two-zero-three, making turns for twenty knots. Sounds like our friend Sierra One is back . . . but he may just be passing us by."

"On my way." Gordon speared Rodriguez with a look. The sonar tech was one of the days of the week—Wednesday, as it happened—and was wearing a sheet. "Lay up to the Sonar Shack, Rodriguez. I want you on that baby."

"Aye aye, sir."

"COB, sorry, but I need you in the control room."

"Right, Skipper." The golden dragon removed its fearsome head and gloves, leaving them on a mess-room table. The ritual began to break up as both participants and onlookers headed for duty stations. Or to places where they could simply stand by. O'Brien got up off the deck, translated suddenly back to the familiar world of duty stations, boredom . . . and occasional moments of stark terror.

He decided to make his way forward to the torpedo room. If anything was going to happen, he wanted to be in on it, and that was his current training station.

As he hurried forward, though, squeezing past other crewmen moving swiftly through *Pittsburgh*'s passageways, he found himself wondering what their Soviet opposite numbers in that other submarine would think if they saw *Pittsburgh*'s crew now. . . .

Sonar Shack, USS *Pittsburgh*
Two Hundred Miles West of Adak, Alaska
0145 hours

"He's definitely moving away, Captain," Rodriguez said. He was still wearing his sheet and a name tag that read "Wednesday," and presented a less than completely military look. But his voice was all crisp professionalism. "He's making turns for twenty–twenty-five knots, and he's in a hell of a hurry. I doubt that he can hear a thing at that speed."

Gordon nodded. "Okay, Wednesday. Stay on him as long as you can, and let me know if anything changes about the target. Aspect, speed, anything."

Rodriguez grinned. "You got it, Skipper."

Gordon left the sonar room and made his way back to the control room.

"Sorry to interrupt the show, Captain," Latham said.

"Not a problem. It's his fault," he said, nodding toward their unseen adversary somewhere beyond the port bulkhead and forward, "not yours."

He walked aft to the plotting tables. Latham and Master Chief Warren joined him. "I'm interested in this guy," Gordon told them. "You notice anything strange about him?"

"Well, he's in a hurry," COB said. "Not going flat out, but fast enough that it's obvious all he wants to do is get home in a hurry."

"On this course, where would home be?"

COB's eyes narrowed as he studied the chart. "Maybe Petro. Pretty good chance, in fact. If not, then he's headed for Oshkosh, and that means one of the other sub bases in there. Magadan, maybe, or Vlad."

"Funny, isn't it? He comes all the way to 'Frisco and picks us up. Starts shadowing us. Then we lose him. He pokes around on that side of the Pacific for a few days, presumably looking for us . . . then up and tears like hell for home. Why?"

"You're saying he's going to warn them?" Latham asked, sounding puzzled.

"No. He could do that by coming shallow and sticking up a radio antenna. What if he's still hunting us?"

COB's eyes narrowed. "If that's true, it means he knows where we're going. You know, Skipper, I don't really like the implications of that."

"Nor do I, COB. Nor do I." Part of Gordon kept thinking that he was getting way too paranoid. It simply wasn't reasonable to suspect that the Russians were somehow luring *Pittsburgh* into a trap . . . that they knew where she was going, and were preparing for her arrival.

On the other hand, he was now captain of a several-hundred-million-dollar piece of United States government property. If he had reason, any reason at all to suspect an attempt to damage, capture, or otherwise dispose of that property, he was going to sit up and take notice.

Unfortunately, the mission he'd been handed required that he take his boat into one of the narrowest, most closely guarded stretches of water in the world, then bring her out again, a risky enough proposition no matter what the enemy knew or was trying to do.

If they knew *Pittsburgh* was coming, the job was damned near hopeless.

Wednesday, 22 July 1987

Torpedo Room, USS *Pittsburgh*
Sea of Okhotsk
1315 hours

"Right," Chief Allison said. "What happens when the skipper calls down, 'Snapshot, two-one'?"

"Uh . . . it means the enemy has fired a torpedo at us," O'Brien said, "and we're going to try to launch one back before we're hit. We'll fire tube two, then tube one, and do it without waiting for a complete firing solution."

"Correct. What's 'polishing the cannonball'?"

"Polishing Baldy's head," TM2 Doershner put in.

"Ignore the jerk," Allison said. "Answer the question."

"That's where the Weapons Officer is working and working and working on a firing solution," O'Brien said, "trying to make it better and better, to the point that you might lose your opportunity for a shot. *Not*," he added, "a smart idea."

"Never mind the commentary, nub," Allison said. "Just answer the damned questions."

O'Brien grinned. Chief Allison's caustic and often profane comments were an accepted part of life now, a guarantee that all was right with the world. "Aye aye, Chief."

He was still a nub, but he was an *accepted* nub. Shaving his head had proven that he could take a joke, and even turn it back on the perpetrators. The hazing had decreased significantly since they'd crossed the Line, and with a few exceptions, people called him by name now instead of "Nub," "Useless," or "Hey, you." He sensed the transformation as a kind of internal flowering, an inner growth or expansion that left him feeling like one of the guys . . . and damned good.

The torpedo room, as always, was crowded, holding as it did not only the regular compartment watch, but four SEALs and four spooks, who had to hot bunk over the Mark 48s in a system guaranteed to make sure none of them got much sleep.

One of the SEALs, the black guy seated on a rack above a torpedo, chuckled.

"What's so funny, frog-face?" Allison demanded.

"Polishing cannonballs," Fitch replied, grinning. "That's a good one."

"Like taking too long to take your shot," Nelson, another SEAL, said.

"So . . . what is idea, here?" Sergei asked. "Is some kind of class, yes?"

"All nubs have to pass their qualifying exams in each department aboard the boat," Benson replied. "He's finished with Sub School, but it'll take him another year to make a *real* submariner out of him."

" 'Nub'?" Johnson asked.

"Non-Useful Body," TM2 Doershner explained. "On a submarine with a hundred and some crewmen, you don't have room for *any* nonessential personnel. Right now, Baldy here is a waste of perfectly good oxygen. But he'll learn."

"Everybody aboard knows at least something about every other job. The cooks know how to fight fires or give first aid. A torpedoman can stand a quartermaster's watch . . . or lend a hand in the reactor compartment aft. This is no place for supernumeraries."

"You mean, folks like us," Mr. Smith, the other American agent said, grinning.

"Well, now that you mention it," Chief Allison said, "yeah."

"What amazes me," Sergei said, shaking his head, "is how much responsibility ordinary seamen have aboard American submarine. In my country, officer runs torpedo room. Officers only man sonar watches. Officers only man key posts in control room. American sailors are trusted with more information, more responsibility than in Soviet Union."

"American sailors are better educated," Doershner said.

"No, this is not true," Grigor, the other Russian national, replied. "What is true is bureaucracy tends toward . . . how you say? Top-heavy."

"Well," Allison said, "we have that problem, too, in Washington. But on board the *Pittsburgh*, it's the enlisted men who make things happen."

"We know more, too," O'Brien put in. "I heard they never tell Russian enlisted men anything. But on an American sub—"

"Yeah?" Doershner said. "What do you know about this mission, nub?"

"I know we're headed for Oshkosh," O'Brien replied. "And probably we're going to be poking in and around real close to the coast, somewhere around northern Sakhalin Island, maybe."

"That is not a topic for discussion!" Johnson said, sitting upright so suddenly his head rammed the bottom of the rack above him like a bell. "*Shit!*"

"You okay, there, Mr. Johnson?" Chief Allison asked.

"Yeah." Gingerly, he rubbed his head. He shot an angry glance at O'Brien. "You're not supposed to know things like that!"

O'Brien shrugged. "I heard it from one of the quartermasters," he said. "He sees the charts, works with 'em every day."

"It's common knowledge on the boat, Mr. Johnson," Benson added. "Hell, we all know where we're headed, more or less. And the fact that you guys are on board tells us we're gonna slip in close to the shore."

"I'm going to have to speak to the captain about this."

"Aw, can it, Mr. Johnson," Chief Allison said. "Who are we gonna tell, anyway?"

"That doesn't matter. Does every man on this ship know the details of our mission? Fuck! He—"

"This secrecy shit is getting on my nerves," Lieutenant Randall said. He'd been sitting on one of the aft bunks, listening, saying nothing, which made the interruption that much more startling. "Look, we have three different groups here. CIA—"

"Who says we're CIA?" Johnson demanded. He seemed startled at the revelation.

"C'mon. You're not Military Intelligence, and certainly not Naval Intelligence, or you wouldn't call this vessel a 'ship.' I suppose you *could* be NSA. The 'Never Say Anything' boys might have active field operations units no one knows about, but generally they're concerned with electronic intelligence and not gathering intelligence from the field, SIGINT instead of HUMINT. The CIA's Directorate of Operations is pretty well known for the games it plays, though. And you boys were all trained at Camp Perry, I was told."

"What's Camp Perry?" O'Brien asked.

"They call it 'The Farm,' " Randall replied. "It's a big, closely guarded compound, mostly woods, in Virginia just outside of Williamsburg. The Agency runs it as a training camp for agents and field officers, including, among other things, a complete mock-up of an Eastern European town, complete with a border crossing. Some SEALs have trained there for special ops we don't talk about."

"You shouldn't be talking about *this*," Johnson said, angry.

"If you're not CIA," Randall asked pleasantly, "why are you upset? This information is *not* classified, by the way. It's been circulating in books available to the public for the past five or ten years at least. But the Agency still doesn't like to talk about it, right, Mr. Johnson?"

"Lots of people train at The Farm," Smith added, "under Agency auspices. That doesn't mean we are CIA."

"Okay, okay," Randall said, raising a hand. "It doesn't matter. What I was trying to say is that we have three groups of people here—you spooks, whatever alphabet-soup agency you really work for, our submariner friends here, and us SEALs. All three of us are on the same side, and all three of us know how to keep a secret." He winked at O'Brien. "This *is* the Silent Service, right, son?"

"Yes, *sir*!"

"Listen," Benson said abruptly. "I've got a question, something that's been bothering me for a long time, okay? And maybe you guys can answer it for me."

"If it's not classified," Randall said, his tone bantering. It sounded as though he enjoyed yanking Johnson's chain.

"Yes, sir. I understand that. But, well, it's more philosophical than practical, if you know what I mean."

"Whoa, there," Doershner said. "We got us a genu-wine philosopher on board!"

"Stuff it, Doershner. It's like this. Ever since I joined the boats, I've heard stories about American submarines moving into Russian and Chinese waters, getting in real close, I mean, right up to their port cities, sometimes. I've heard stories of SEALs and Navy divers going in to actually examine Russian ships up close, or tapping underwater cables. I heard they did that right here in Oshkosh, where we're going."

"It was only because a traitor sold secrets to the Russians that anyone knows about that," Smith said.

"Whatever. On our last mission out here, the 'Burgh went into Oshkosh and provided some sort of distraction. I haven't heard any skinny on what the mission was all about, but scuttlebutt has it that we were providing a diversion for some other classified operation in the area, maybe getting the Russians to chase us instead of some other boat, if you know what I mean."

"Damn it, sailor, you are *not* supposed to—"

"Let him talk, Johnson," Randall said. "We all know more than you people would like us to. Let's hear what he has to say."

"I'm just wondering," Benson said in a rush, as though trying to get the words out before someone stopped him, "what *right* we have to do these kinds of things. I mean, what if a Russian submarine came into San Francisco Bay, and sent divers up the Mare Island Channel to look at our boats? Wouldn't we be damned mad about that? Wouldn't we demand an apology, or something?

"And if we caught a Russian sub in there, wouldn't we try to sink it, and maybe start a *war*? I mean, it would be like an invasion or something, wouldn't it?"

"That's the way the game is played, kid," Johnson said with a shrug.

"Yeah, we've been doing this sort of thing since the late

1940s," Chief Allison said. Johnson gave him a dark look, but he kept talking. "American subs have been operating in Russian waters since the fifties. Old news."

"What makes you think the Russians haven't been doing just that?" Randall asked.

"You mean . . . they are?" O'Brien asked, shocked.

Randall appeared to turn something over in his mind, as though trying to decide what to say. "Um, let's just say that there are cases where the Soviets have entered our territorial waters, even come ashore on our territory. And we've done the same. But intelligence gathering is absolutely vital. Think of it this way. We have two guys who don't like each other, each one with a loaded pistol up against the other guy's head. The first guy is thinking something like, 'I don't want to fire first, but if I think he's going to fire, I'll have to fire first.' And the second guy is thinking exactly the same thing.

"Now, if the first guy knows what the second guy is thinking, he won't shoot. He might even take a bit of pressure off the trigger. If someone who knows the second guy comes and whispers in the first guy's ear, 'don't worry, he's just as scared as you are, and won't shoot unless he thinks you will,' well, that might make the first guy relax, just a little. Maybe he might even suggest the two of them talk about their differences . . . maybe get the other guy to agree that both of them should aim their pistols up in the air instead of at each other's heads.

"Of course, a lot of intelligence work has to do not so much with what the other guy is thinking as what he has. How good his ships and submarines are. How well his supply network and logistics work. How fast his response time is to a threat. The more we know about what he's capable of, the less likely we are to panic, assume he has an overwhelming advantage, and pull the trigger."

"Hear, hear," Chief Allison said, laughing. "And the submarine service leads the way, defenders of world peace!"

"Truck drivers," Johnson and Randall said in unplanned

unison. The two looked at each other, and then laughed. Most of the men in the compartment joined in.

"Spooks!" Chief Allison said with a snort. "You wouldn't get there without the truck drivers, that's for damned sure!"

"It still just doesn't seem right," Benson said as the laughter died. "I mean, you keep hearing, on TV and stuff, about how one mistake could touch off a nuclear war. Well, doesn't it make sense not to provide the other guy with an excuse to start shooting?"

"There *have* been shots fired," Randall told him. "And people have died."

"There've been mistakes, too," Allison said. "Lots of times when one side's submarine was following a boat from the other side, got too close, and bumped. Hell, just last year, the *Augusta* bumped into a Russian missile sub in the Atlantic . . . and there's a story going around about a British boat, the *Splendid*, that got too close to a Soviet Typhoon right inside one of the Russian's bastions. The Typhoon brushed the *Splendid*, and snagged one of her towed sonar arrays."

"There've been incidents, sure," Randall added. "But they've been smoothed over. Both sides know how important it is not to overreact." He shrugged. "Maybe it's even done some good. Now that Gorbachev is in power in Moscow, the Russians have seemed a lot more willing to talk."

"You don't look convinced, Benson," O'Brien said.

"I dunno. I just keep wondering what we'd do if a Russian sub got caught in the Chesapeake Bay."

"Sink her, of course," Chief Allison said. "The idea is to sneak in and not be caught."

"But if it's a game, like Mr. Johnson says. . . ."

"It's a very serious, very *deadly* game," Randall said. "And all results are final."

"I find it fascinating," Sergei said, "that your sailors can question orders."

"American sailors are not robots, Sergei," Chief Allison said. "We're allowed to think what we want."

"It seems like anarchy way of doing things. . . ."

"Torpedo Room, Conn," a voice cut in over the intercom. "Chief Allison, you there?"

"Allison here, Mr. Walberg."

"Heads up down there. We're having to maneuver. We have multiple targets, and things could get tight."

"Aye, sir. We're ready, warshots loaded."

When no further communications were forthcoming, Allison looked at the others, shrugged, and hung up the microphone. "On the other hand," he said, "sometimes they don't tell us nothin'!"

A few moments later, they heard a gentle but persistent throbbing sound that seemed to be coming from ahead and above. All eyes went to the overhead as the sound grew louder, stronger, and slowly churned overhead.

"ASW frigate," Doershner said softly.

"Nah," Allison said, listening. "Bigger. Cruiser. Maybe a Kresta. . . ."

A sharp, metallic ping echoed through the torpedo room, a shrill chirp that left behind wavering, fading echoes.

"Whoever he is," Doershner said, "he's hunting active."

"What . . . what is that?" Smith wanted to know.

"Active sonar, Mr. Smith," Allison said. "He sends out a pulse of sound, and listens to the echoes that come back. One of those echoes is us."

"Then he knows we're here?"

"Maybe. And maybe the skipper's managed to tuck us in close enough to the bottom that we're lost in the ground clutter. Or maybe that ping is from an emitter trailing below a thermal, and the echoes'll be lost and scattered."

"So what do we do?" Johnson asked. He was clearly frightened.

"Is same in all submarine navies," Sergei said with a fatalistic shrug. He locked eyes with Allison, who nodded. "We wait . . . and pray."

Another ping rang through the compartment like a high-pitched, tolling bell.

Wednesday, 22 July 1987

Control Room, USS *Pittsburgh*
Sea of Okhotsk
1316 hours

Gordon stared overhead as a second ping rang through the *Pittsburgh*'s hull. The waiting, as always, was nerve-wracking to the point of insanity. *If he's going to nail us,* he thought, *now's the time.*

Lowering his eyes, he caught Latham's steady gaze from forward . . . no fear, but, possibly, a slender touch of recognition, as though he'd been here before, as though he were somehow measuring Gordon's performance. The measurement was neither intrusive nor challenging, merely . . . curious.

Gordon winked. Latham's mouth pulled back in the slightest of smiles.

And then the churning throb of the vessel overhead— Sierra One-three, the thirteenth sonar logged thus far on *Pittsburgh*'s voyage—was receding astern, unhurried, unchanging.

Missed us again, you bastards, Gordon thought, a bit fiercely. Long, strained moments followed, as *Pittsburgh*'s control-room watch strained, motionless, listening to silence.

"Conn, Sonar," Kellerman's voice called over the IC. "Contact is fading. No change in aspect." There was a hesitation. "I think he missed us, Captain."

"Sonar, Conn. Keep your ears peeled, Kellerman. He could have a tail-end Charlie keeping him company." Sometimes, a large Soviet ASW vessel would be followed at a distance by a smaller vessel, or an ASW aircraft, listening for possible targets that might have thought themselves safe once the loud and obvious threat had passed. It was an old trick, one used by the Americans and British as well.

Minute followed minute, however, with no further contacts.

"Mr. Carver, bring us to periscope depth."

"Periscope depth, aye, Captain."

Pittsburgh was lurking near the bottom in shoaling water, three hundred feet down, just south of the island of Paramusir, one of the northernmost of the Kuril group. Gliding silently ahead, she rose from the depths toward the dappling, shifting light of day.

In fact, notions of day and night were largely immaterial and unnoticed aboard a submarine, which might go for weeks or months without rising even to periscope depth. Watches aboard submarines were deliberately set to an artificial eighteen hour day as soon as the vessel left port, allowing for a six-hour-on, twelve-hour-off routine for the watches. At any given moment on board, the best way to tell whether it was day or night above the eternal night of the ocean depths was to take a look at the control room. If it was "rigged for red," with red lighting to preserve the night vision of men who might need to peer through the periscope, then it was night.

The information scarcely mattered. Submariners prided themselves in living in their own little world, cut off from the world above.

"Leveling off at periscope depth, Captain."

"Very well." Gordon stepped up onto the periscope dais, taking his place at the port-side scope, the Number 18. "Sonar, Conn. Any contacts?"

"Conn, Sonar. Negative contacts close by, sir. But it's pretty shallow, here. I'm getting lots of scatter. And we're picking up a fair amount of confused noise at extreme range, bearing two-one-zero through three-one-zero. Might be commercial traffic, sir."

"Not out here, it isn't," Gordon replied. "Up scope."

The Number 18 was called that because it had a magnification factor of eighteen times . . . far better than that of its predecessors. The improvement allowed a submarine to see surface targets in detail at ranges impossible for earlier systems. Leaning on the handles, he rode the scope column as it slid upward from its deck housing, walking the scope in a slow circle as it broke the surface. Midday sunlight glared and scattered off a smooth but rolling sea.

No aircraft . . . no silently waiting surface predator positioned to pounce on an unwary intruder. To the west, however, right on the horizon, Gordon could make out a clutter of tiny silhouettes. "Mark," he said, centering on the first.

"Bearing two-one-five," Latham said, reading the bearing off the scope compass.

"Krivak class, southerly heading, range ten miles. New target, mark."

"Bearing two-two-one."

"Kresta class, southerly heading, range ten miles. New target, mark . . ."

They continued the observation, Gordon picking out and identifying targets while Latham noted each contact and checked the bearing. Gordon had the camera running, making a visual record.

"Down scope," he said at last. He looked at Latham. "Southern route," he said.

"Sounds like they're waiting for us."

"It's possible." Stepping down off the dais, Gordon

walked to one of the navigational tables aft of the periscope walk. One of Garrison's charts was spread out on the light table, with *Pittsburgh*'s zigzagging course and hourly positions plotted in blue grease pencil, with contacts and bearing lines noted in red. He pointed. "That flotilla up there appears to be coming down along the west side of Paramusir Island . . . about here. They could be lying in wait, hiding behind the island. Or . . ."

"Or?"

"Or it could be routine maneuvers. We don't know, and I dislike paranoia as much as the next man. But we're *not* taking chances."

"I'm with you there, Skipper."

"Down scope!" The periscope slid with an oily silver gleam into the well. "Take us down to two hundred feet."

"Two hundred feet, aye aye, Captain."

"Make our course one-eight-five."

"Helm to course one-eight-five, aye, sir."

Latham grinned at Gordon. "Captain's choice, sir?"

"What's the fun in being captain if you don't have it?"

"Damned if I know. But our passengers are going to be pissed."

"Mr. Johnson might be, at any rate. But even he wouldn't want us charging right through a cordon of Soviet ASW ships."

"He is a stickler for following the book, sir."

"Well, we'll worry about him if we have to later." He turned, checking each station in the control room, studying the intent gazes of the personnel at the controls. "I'm going to my quarters," he told Latham. "Call me if there's any change."

"Aye, sir."

Making his way forward, he opened the door to his cabin and stepped inside. He took his seat behind his desk, pausing a moment to look at the small photo of his wife and daughters in its plastic frame. They seemed so hellishly far away just now.

On a normal voyage, he would have been allowed to send and receive personal messages—at least the 150 words of a Familygram. He wondered how Becca was doing.

The notion that command was a lonely life was hopelessly clichéd, but true nonetheless. He was terribly worried about his wife, but saw no way to help her short of leaving the service . . . and command. And this was what he was born for. He could live his own life, or how she wanted him to, with a normal job, a normal career, with normal hours.

Which way to go? Which way *could* he go, and stay true to himself?

Weather Bridge
Russian Attack Submarine *Ivan Rogov*
1440 hours

Surfaced at last, the *Ivan Rogov* made his way into the main approach channel to Tauyskaya Guba, with small, wooded Zav'yalova Island sliding aft along his port side. It was hot and humid—the Maritime Provinces could swelter during midsummer—but the breeze coming off the submarine's bow was cool, and Captain First Rank Dubrynin leaned into it, savoring the salt taste and freshness after over a month locked away in the ocean's depths. It was like being released from prison . . . and with the promise of a return to Katarina's arms.

They'd moved to Magadan from the military suburbs of Leningrad almost a year ago. Dubrynin had embraced the transfer, of course, since it had meant promotion, and a literally once-in-a-lifetime chance to command an attack submarine, the *Rogov*. Katarina, however, had been miserable at first, forced to leave friends and family for a land as alien to her as the far side of the moon. There'd been talk of her staying in Leningrad, perhaps of her moving back into that tiny apartment with her mother, father, and younger brothers.

He'd convinced her at last to come, however, and he was sure now that the decision had been the right one. She was making friends among the other navy wives at the Magadan base, learning to love the stark beauty of the mountains behind the city, so different from the flat horizon beyond Lake Lagoda.

At his side, *Starpom* Vladimir Tupov, his Executive Officer, pointed north across the water. "It appears, Comrade Captain, that the *Krasnoyarskiy Komsomolets* is making ready to depart."

Dubrynin raised his binoculars and studied the dockside of the submarine base. Sure enough, he could see the *Krasnoyarskiy Komsomolets*, mooring lines cast off fore and aft, and a naval tug positioned abeam, ready to move him out into the channel.

"It seems soon after Anatoli Vesilevich's last excursion," Dubrynin said. "I wonder if he's been ordered to the chase?"

"It seems likely, Captain. The *Krasnoyarskiy Komsomolets* is a fine ship. Our very best . . . excepting the *Ivan Rogov*, of course."

"Of course." Dubrynin chuckled. "Although the State might withhold him from the battle, for that very reason."

"That hardly seems likely, does it? The alert was for a single American submarine this time, not a wolf pack, as they deployed against us last time."

"Ah, Vladimir Ivanovich, there is no accounting for some of the decisions of our leaders. The State moves in mysterious ways. . . ."

The *starpom* remained silent at this near blasphemy. He was a stolid and unimaginative sort, unable to accept the possibility that the *Rogov*'s leaders might be as fallible or as venal as the next man. Most Russians took the vast and often cruel clumsiness of the government for granted—that acceptance was a part of the Russian character long preceding the October Revolution—but a few, Vladimir Ivanovich among them, maintained a fanatical blindness to the State's failings.

But the *starpom* was young. He would learn, as Dubrynin had.

"Captain, this is Pavlenko," crackled over the weather-bridge speaker.

"Go ahead." Boris Pavlenko was *Rogov*'s senior communications officer.

"Sir! Radio message from headquarters! We have new orders!"

Dubrynin exchanged bemused glances with Tupov. "We're not even back to port yet!" Tupov exclaimed.

"It was to be expected, Vladimir Ivanovich. Let's get below."

The two submariners clambered back down through the sail access into the control room.

Within minutes, the *Ivan Rogov* was coming about, heading once again for the open Sea of Okhotsk.

Thursday, 23 July 1987

Control Room, USS *Pittsburgh*
Sakhalinskiy Zaliv
2230 hours local time

"Up scope."

The Type 18 periscope slid into the overhead well as Gordon rode the optics up. As the periscope head broke the surface, the IR optics picked up the image and relayed it not only to Gordon's eye, but to TV monitors in various quarters of the control room. Under infrared, the sky was featureless black, the waves a thick and nearly featureless gray. Slowly, he walked the scope about, watching the compass readout numbers at the top of the scope readout. The control room was rigged for red, a dim and eerie darkroom illumination that gave a faintly satanic cast to the officers and men working there.

They'd turned south and run parallel to the Kurils at thirty knots, turning west at last at a point 120 miles south of Paramusir Island, a place where the island chain thinned to a straggle of tiny, barren and uninhabited rocks, Shiaskokan, Matua, and tiny Raykoke. Slowing again to ten knots to reduce their sound signature, they slipped through the passage just north of Raykoke, ever conscious of the fact that the Russians had probably seeded all of the channels with sonar listening devices similar to the U.S. SOSUS net.

They encountered no major surface activity, though twice they heard the distant throb of a ship—the first slow and ponderous, almost certainly a freighter, the second higher-pitched and faster, possibly a Grisha I light ASW frigate.

Then came the long, exposed run northwest across the Sea of Okhotsk itself, 650 miles to Mys Yalizavety at the northern tip of Sakhalin, then slowed to a crawl as they rounded the cape and slipped through rapidly shoaling water into the Sakhalinskiy Zaliv—Sakhalin Bay.

They'd averaged twenty knots for the crossing, sometimes dashing at *Pittsburgh's* full underwater speed of thirty-five knots, but stopping frequently to listen . . . and sometimes crawling at a painful five knots to avoid the notice of hunters above. In all, it had taken almost thirty-five hours, but the timing had let them slip into the shallow waters of the bay well after dark.

It seemed as though the Sea of Okhotsk was unusually busy. Sonar had racked up another twelve contacts since entering the Sea of Okhotsk. According to the boat's log, her last mission in these waters only a few weeks ago had encountered relatively little traffic until she'd deliberately surfaced to attract Soviet attention. Perhaps the heavy patrols were simply a reaction to the American sub's penetration so recently. Or perhaps the Soviets were engaged in fleet maneuvers.

"Sonar, Conn," he said. "What's the bearing on Sierra Two-seven?"

"Conn, Sonar," Rodriguez's voice came back. "Sierra Two-seven now bearing two-zero-four. Estimated range, six to eight thousand yards."

Gordon leaned into the periscope eyepiece again, trying to pierce the darkness. This was the spot where they were supposed to meet their Russian contact. Sonar had reported a contact in the area—Sierra Two-seven—and reported that it sounded like a trawler or fishing boat, with a single screw making turns for five knots.

But . . . was it the contact, code-named "Stenki" after a historical Cossack leader? Or a KGB or MVD border patrol boat? *Pittsburgh* was now prowling southeast along the Siberian coast, barely thirty miles offshore. Technically, they were still in international waters, but that technicality was so slender Gordon wasn't going to hang a wish upon it, much less a 6,900-ton submarine. The Sea of Okhotsk was a Soviet sea, open only to their military traffic and a few—a *very* few—commercial vessels operating close inshore. It was known that the Sea of Okhotsk was one of the Soviet Navy's bastion areas, heavily guarded regions where their Typhoons and Deltas and other SSBN boomers lurked, under the watchful protection of surface fleet elements and attack SSNs. It was also the downrange target area for Soviet missile tests for launches from central Asia. It was no wonder Moscow didn't like American intruders in these waters.

And here, within the shallow Sakhalinskiy Zaliv, was close aboard one of their most sensitive shipping channels, the marine highway leading from one of their most secret ports at Nikolayevsk, down the Amur Estuary, then north into the Sea of Okhotsk.

Gordon wondered again if the highly secret operation involving his four packages was somehow targeted against Nikolayevsk. It seemed likely. Most other ports and shipbuilding facilities were close enough to the open sea that U.S. submarines could come very close indeed, in some cases entering the harbors themselves to identify and photograph Russian subs and warships.

There . . . a fleck of green-yellow brightness, momentarily visible between the rolling surge of the waves. Something was giving off a lot of heat, visible as a fleck of brightness against the blacks and grays of the night.

"Down scope. Helm, come to two-zero-four. Make turns for eight knots."

"Helm to two-zero-four, aye. Making turns for eight knots."

Minutes dragged past. When Gordon again ordered "Up scope," and leaned into the eyepiece, he could make out the ghostly shape of the trawler ahead, a cluttered relic of a fishing boat, its diesel engine glowing brightly in the infrared. It appeared to be loitering, its engines barely turning over, less than five thousand yards away.

He still needed to verify that it wasn't a Soviet AGI trawler, one of their vast fleet of slow and decrepit-looking former commercial craft outfitted with the electronics allowing them to serve in a reconnaissance and electronic surveillance role. AGI trawlers were stationed worldwide, hanging about missile test ranges and major ports and bases, shadowing U.S. ships during fleet maneuvers and training exercises, carrying out, in fact, many of the surveillance missions American submarines had been tasked with during the past thirty years.

He checked the time . . . 0255 hours. It was time. . . .

A bright light winked on from the trawler's bridge, flashing rapidly in Morse.

"He's signaling," Gordon said. "K . . . V . . . R . . . N."

"Message confirmed," Latham said. "That's our man."

"Log it," Gordon said.

"Aye, sir."

He continued studying the other vessel for another several moments, searching for something, anything amiss or suspicious. There wouldn't be, of course. He had to trust his orders, which had told him in exacting detail that he would meet a small commercial craft like this one at this spot, transmitting the code characters K-V-R-N every half hour, at five till and twenty-five after the hour.

"What's the depth under keel?"

"Eighty-nine feet, Captain," Carver replied.

He felt like he was sitting in a box. A very small box. "Okay. Let's get this over with and get the hell out. Alert the divers and tell them they're good to go."

"Aye aye, sir."

The sooner they delivered the packages and got out of there, the happier Gordon would be.

Forward Escape Trunk, USS *Pittsburgh*
Sakhalinskiy Zaliv
2301 hours local time

Randall leaned back against the cold, green-painted steel of the escape trunk. He was packed in with Mr. Johnson so tightly it was nearly a lover's embrace. "You ready?"

Johnson nodded, a bit nervously, Randall thought. Both wore wet suits, masks, and flippers. They wore Draeger LAR V closed-circuit rebreathers over their chests, the twenty-four-pound units almost touching as they faced each other in the trunk.

"Okay," Randall said. "Remember to breathe out on your way up."

Again a short, jerky nod for an answer.

Randall reached up for the WRT valve and turned it, then opened the vent that regulated the pressure inside the escape trunk. He kept his eyes on Johnson's face the whole time. As he understood it, the four operatives had gone through a thorough class in rebreather and submarine lock-out procedures at Camp Perry, Virginia, the CIA's training camp for field-ops agents.

But a few weeks of training was no substitute for experience . . . or SEAL training, which emphasized long hours of practice in tight quarters underwater, and in the infamous SEAL drownproofing, which was designed to reduce or eliminate a man's normal fear of drowning. Escape trunks on submarines were so tiny that even SEALs sometimes felt a touch of claustrophobia when they were locked inside, and the water started rising.

The water was gushing in, now, swirling about their feet . . . and on up their legs. Johnson was breathing in short, hard gasps, now, as he lowered his mask across his eyes and placed his mouthpiece between clenched teeth.

"Relax, Mr. Johnson," Randall told him. He tried to reach up and reassuringly pat the man's shoulder, but the space inside the escape trunk was too restricted. "Just a walk in the park."

Another nod.

"Slow your breathing. Long, slow breaths."

Again the nod . . . but Johnson's breathing did steady a bit.

SEALs were sometimes tapped for this sort of mission— "baby-sitting," they called it, helping field operatives of any of several intelligence services to get from the submarine to the shore. Each SEAL on this op was responsible for one of the CIA men; and Johnson belonged to Randall.

The escape trunk was two-thirds full now, and Randall closed the vent. The water kept rising, however, the pressure building, until at last it churned and bubbled up past their chins. Reaching high, Randall hit the blow valve, then opened the outer hatch. Water surged over their heads, and Randall squeezed his mask tight on his face, then cleared it. Working more by feel than by sight in the dark water—the light in the escape trunk hardly seemed to penetrate the water at all—he guided Johnson up the trunk and out into the open water.

Emerging from the thirty-inch hatch was like escaping from prison. Suddenly, the ocean yawned about him, black and empty. Don McCluskey had already locked out, along with Sergei. Randall could sense the other men as shadows above the deck forward, just behind the looming black cliff of *Pittsburgh*'s sail.

He closed and dogged the deck hatch. Nelson and Smith would be coming through next, followed by Fitch and

Grigor. Touching Johnson lightly on the leg, he started up, kicking slowly, making sure the CIA operative was coming along.

This was the riskiest part of the procedure. Draeger rebreathers had been chosen over standard SCUBA gear for the obvious reason that they didn't make as much noise—a critical consideration in this area that might well be criss-crossed by Soviet sonar and sound detectors. But Draeger units were dangerous at depths much below thirty-five feet, and *Pittsburgh*'s deck was that deep or deeper than that when the submarine was at periscope depth. If the sub moved any higher at all, its sail would break the surface, and instantly register on a dozen Soviet search radars blanketing the entire region.

Together, Randall and Johnson rose for the surface, visible as a kind of rippling, ultramarine movement in the darkness straight overhead, contrasted against the black, wedge-narrow cliff of the submarine's conning tower. He could sense Johnson beginning to tighten up, and moved closer. A common panic reaction to the claustrophobia of working underwater at night—not to mention the claustrophobic hell of being locked into a submarine escape trunk—was for the swimmer to hold his breath as he kicked wildly for the surface.

But at thirty-five feet, the human body was being squeezed by the pressure of all of the water piled up above him, and the air in his lungs was compressed as well. Strike out for the surface without breathing out, and that air would expand . . . violently. . . .

Johnson started to kick, stroking for the surface. Randall grabbed hold, pulled him close, and drove the rigid fingers of his right hand into Johnson's side, just to the left of the small oxygen bottle riding below his Draeger chest pack.

The blow couldn't carry much force underwater, but it was hard enough to startle Johnson, who lost his mouthpiece and expelled a large belch of air bubbling toward the surface. He thrashed for a moment, until Randall placed the mouthpiece back between his teeth and he began breathing again. He nodded, and the two resumed their ascent, more slowly this time.

This, Randall thought, amused, *is why they have us baby-sit. I hope he's better at spy stuff than he is at diving!*

Moments later, their heads broke the surface. McCluskey and Sergei were nearby, illuminated by the faint green glow from a chemical light stick, and clinging to the lifelines on a beach-ball-sized float bobbing in the swell.

No words were spoken, though the chances of being over-heard were remote. The sky was overcast except for a few thin patches through which a few stars and the silver glow of a setting moon in the west were just visible. A bell was ring-ing somewhere in the distance at irregular intervals—the bell atop a navigation buoy, most likely. The water was oily, chill, and carried a faint industrial stink with the normal smells of salt and seaweed.

And he could also hear the throb of a diesel engine to his left. Turning in the water, he could just make out a shape, slightly less dark than its surroundings, moving with the swell of the waves. A single white navigational light gleamed at one end, casting pale reflections on the water. That would be Stenki, their destination.

McCluskey was already unshipping the IBS, "Inflatable Boat, Small" in the Navy lexicon, which had been stored as a tightly wrapped package raised to the surface by the float, but which was expanding now as it inflated from its attached CO_2 bottle. As the rubber boat flopped open, the two SEALs released the last of the lines keeping it folded up, then held on to it as it reached full size. They helped Johnson and Sergei roll into the raft, then clung to the safety lines on the side to keep it from drifting away. Nelson surfaced with Smith a few moments later, as the SEALs unshipped the small, 7.5-horsepower outboard motor and fastened it on the stern mount.

Working in the swell, with no anchor or safety lines, was a tricky operation. If a sudden surge caught them unprepared and the outboard motor went to the bottom, they and the mission would be screwed—an inglorious end to this exercise in daring and wet darkness. They secured it with lanyards, just in case, and worked carefully to bolt it down tight on the mounting brackets.

Nelson and Smith had surfaced with another bundle of equipment, this one a waterproof satchel holding weapons and the CIA team's special gear. This was transferred to the raft, while Randall began bundling the swim gear and rebreathers together and securing them in the bottom of the boat, then breaking out their weapons. The SEALs were packing H&K MP5 submachine guns, specially modified to operate reliably despite immersion in seawater.

Randall glanced up into the dark sky. This time out, there was no spy aircraft recording his every movement for transmission back to some Pentagon basement. He imagined the REMFs and chair-warmers would be peeking in via satellite—there were a number of military reconnaissance satellites aloft that could give fair resolution even through light cloud cover.

But whether they could see him or not, at least there would be no micromanagement this time. Randall smiled, and suppressed the wry urge to flip a middle finger at the sky. Even the best spysats couldn't resolve *that* much detail.

By the time Fitch and the second Russian, Grigor, surfaced, they were ready to cast off.

The whole operation had been practiced again and again before the team had been flown to Adak. Still without words, the SEALs fired up the motor, which was carefully muffled to give off only the softest of purrs, then cast off the last line securing the IBS to the float, pulled the valve on the float to collapse and sink it, and swung the tiller about until the heavily laden IBS was nosing across the waves toward the waiting trawler. The IBS was normally rated as a seven-man raft; it was jam-packed with eight and their gear.

Randall couldn't shake a certain darkness of spirit. It was an unsettling feeling, motoring into the empty night this

way. When they'd practiced this maneuver at the amphibious base at Coronado, the float had been attached by a safety
line to a mock-up of a submarine conning tower. This time,
though, there was no lifeline, and the terrible risk that if anything went wrong, they were going to have a damned hard
time finding their way back to the *Pittsburgh*.

More unsettling, though, were the *human* factors. Johnson
and his comrades, so precise, so methodical, so melodramatic in a low-keyed way. They might have been playing
some sort of involved and preposterous game.

He tried not to let himself think about the might-bes, concentrating instead on the mission as it had been planned out
and rehearsed. The *Pittsburgh* would be waiting for them
when—*when*—they returned.

At least they'd damned well better be. The four SEALs
were a hell of a long way from home, in a place—the kid
Benson was right about this—where they had no right to be.
The submarine was their only ticket out of here, the only
thing between them and death or a cell in Moscow's dread
Lubyanka Prison—or a slave camp in the Siberian Gulag.

That waiting trawler up ahead could so easily be a trap for
the CIA agents.

But, of course, that possibility was one reason the baby-
sitters were here. The packages needed the extra bit of experienced help getting to the surface . . . and they just might
need some firepower at the contact point. SEALs were very,
very good at providing firepower, in large and devastating
doses.

He just hoped that it wasn't going to be necessary.

Thursday, 23 July 1987

Control Room, USS *Pittsburgh*
Sakhalinskiy Zaliv
2312 hours local time

"Up scope."

Gordon peered into the periscope eyepiece again, walking the scope in a slow, steady circle. There was no sign of the SEALs and their charges, no trace of their black raft against the dark sea. Under IR, though, they should have been visible if they were still close by. Human body temperature, even muffled by wet suits and combat gear, contrasted sharply with the cold water.

But there was nothing, which meant that they were on their way. In the distance, still at a bearing of two-zero-four, was the phantom shape of Sierra Two-seven, dimly marked by a light on her stern.

He still wondered at the possibility of a trap. Like most Navy men, Gordon had a less-than-perfect respect for the capabilities of the various intelligence agencies, at least at the gold-braid level. They tended to be self-sustaining, self-justifying, and self-serving, unwilling to admit mistakes, accept oversight, or acknowledge responsibility when things went wrong. The eighties had brought forward one spy scandal in the American intelligence services after another, making the ancient joke about "military intelligence" being an oxymoron more apt than ever. The Walker family in the Navy, Aldrich Ames in the CIA's Directorate of Operations, Ronald Pelton in the National Security Agency . . . what other moles or agents still operated unnoticed within the inner sanctums of the CIA, NSA, or in sensitive positions with the military?

"Down scope."

Latham looked a question at him, his face bathed in the red glow of the control room. "They're away," Gordon told him. "Mr. Carver, what's the depth beneath our keel?"

"Depth beneath keel forty-eight feet, sir."

He exchanged a glance with Latham.

"The waiting's always the hardest part, sir."

"Yeah. I just don't like sitting here feeling like a whale in a bathtub. Helm, bring us around to three-five-five, ahead dead slow."

"Helm to course three-five-five, ahead dead slow, aye, sir."

"I want us pointed in the right direction," he told Latham, "in case we have to scoot."

"Good plan, sir."

"Sonar, Conn. Any further contacts?"

"Conn, Sonar. Negative on new contacts, sir."

"Okay. Then we wait."

Lt. (j.g.) Randall
Objective Stenki
2348 hours local time

The port side of the trawler loomed up out of the night, a gray wall of peeling paint, splinters, draped nets, and tires tied to the gunwales as fenders. The name, in large Cyrillic lettering on her stern, was *Katarina*. Randall cut the IBS's engine, letting the boat drift free, coming broadside to.

The SEALs already had their H&Ks out and ready, the first round chambered. There didn't seem to be any activity aboard the fishing boat, which didn't speak well for their watchkeeping abilities.

"Yuri?" Sergei called softly. "*Padahyedeete!*"

Several dark shapes materialized along the gunwale, AK-47s in hand. Randall heard the snick of bolts being drawn, and breathed a deep and death-cold *oh, shit. . . .*

"*Ktah eedyat!*" a deep voice called from the fishing boat's bridge.

A demand that they identify themselves.

"*Yanvehr l'yahd,*" Sergei called back. January ice.

"*Vesna ottepel'*" the voice on deck replied, giving the countersign. Spring thaw.

Then the AKs were being raised, and a line flicked down out of the night, splashing in the water alongside the IBS. The SEALs grabbed the line and hauled the boat alongside the trawler, as helping hands reached down to help the men on board.

Fitch and McCluskey stayed in the IBS, while Randall and Nelson went on board. Randall hadn't been sure what to expect . . . but the five men waiting on board, except for their weapons, looked like fairly typical fishermen anywhere in the world, in jeans and pullovers, T-shirts, and slickers. Most were bearded. One wore an odd-looking white sailor's beret with a blue pom on the top, a relic, apparently, of earlier days in the Russian Navy. Another wore a heavy leather apron, the sort worn by butchers or fishmongers.

All in all, they didn't look much like KGB types . . . or Russian military, for that matter. A pile of fish on the afterdeck, and the associated stink, added to the reassurance of the scene.

"*Dobre vecher,*" Sergei said, smiling. "*Vih Stenki?*"

"*Da*," the biggest of the sailors said. Then, in grinning English, he added, "Welcome aboard!"

Johnson turned to Randall. "You can go now."

"They are welcome too!" the boat's captain boomed. "We show good time, *da?*"

"We have work to do," Johnson replied. "And so do they."

"*Da, da.* Well, we are on our way, then. Before the patrols come, *da?*"

"You're sure everything is all right?" Randall asked Johnson.

Johnson lowered his voice. "Russian underground," he said, quietly so only Randall could hear. "Antisoviet, but you can't always pick the quality of your friends, if you know what I mean. But we'll be okay."

"We'll be here in forty-eight hours," he told the *Katarina*'s captain.

"*Da! Da skaravah!*" See you soon.

"*Da v'danya*," Randall replied. The captain's eyes lit up and he guffawed. "Your Russian is being good like mine English, *da?*"

Randall followed Nelson back down the side of the trawler and clambered into the raft, much roomier now that four of its passengers were gone. Together, the SEALs helped pass the rest of the agents' equipment up to the trawler's deck. Then with a final round of *das v'danyas*, the trawler's diesel engine fired to life, the SEALs engaged their outboard, and the two craft parted, the Russian trawler toward the invisible coast to the south, and the IBS for the place where they'd left the *Pittsburgh*.

The friendly calls in the night, he found, were not all that reassuring. He was pretty sure they were legitimate, despite his earlier concerns; if they were part of some kind of Soviet antiespionage sting operation, their chance to bag four SEALs was slipping away right now. But he was less than impressed with his glimpse of the underground, if that's what these fishermen were. The loud, overly friendly, overly exuberant attitude of the captain had been such an obvious put-on, especially when contrasted against the taciturn, almost surly glares of the other four. If he'd had to guess, he'd have classified those five as dockworkers. Or as common thugs, rather than fishermen.

He hoped Johnson and the others knew what they were doing.

Now, though, came the tough part of the operation . . . finding a submarine that was going out of its way to remain invisible in all this ocean. They motored back along their outbound course, but there was no way to retrace their course precisely, not with the vagaries of wind, wave, and current.

The SEALs had brought a small piece of technology, however, to help them in the search. After reaching what was probably the approximate location of the submerged boat, he broke open a plastic case stowed in the IBS's stern and produced a device the size and shape of a yo-yo, complete with an electrical cord for a string. Attached at the other end was a box with a button. McCluskey took the yo-yo and lowered it over the side. Randall pressed the key—*click, click-click, click* . . . repeating the sequence at irregular intervals, and stopping after five times.

Sound, of course, traveled quite well underwater, and sound was a submarine's worst enemy. If *Pittsburgh*'s sonar could pick up Randall's signals, it was a sure bet that any Soviet underwater listening devices would as well.

The signal, though, was deliberately simple, the Morse letters E-I-E. To the uninitiated, they might sound like random noise, would probably be overlooked entirely.

Rodriguez aboard the *Pittsburgh*, however, would be listening for exactly that signal, and his computer could be set to sort the clicks out of any background garbage more precisely than even the best-trained human ear.

With luck, *Pittsburgh* was already very near, and getting closer.

It would have been simpler, of course, to have secured the float by a safety line to *Pittsburgh*'s conning tower and homed in on that . . . but if a Russian ASW patrol had shown up and *Pittsburgh* had been forced to run, float and line vibrating in the conning tower's wake would have created an unmistakable and easily tracked sonic signature.

And so they had to do it the hard way.

After perhaps five minutes had passed, he pressed the button again. *Click, click-click, click.* And repeat. And wait a longer period of time, and repeat.

McCluskey touched his elbow. "There, sir."

Dimly seen in the overcast darkness, but very faintly luminescent in the oily waters, a single periscope rose from the swell, its surface dappled a camouflage dark gray on medium gray. They motored closer, and Nelson rolled over the side, taking a line with him which he secured to the boat's sail just beneath the surface. The others began donning their rebreather gear and making ready to collapse and secure the IBS.

It was going to be damned good to be safely home once more.

Friday, 24 July 1987

Control Room, USS *Pittsburgh*
Sakhalinskiy Zaliv
0040 hours local time

"Divers are aboard, Captain," Latham reported.

"Let's get her out of here," Gordon told the XO. "I want a bit more space between keel and bottom."

"That'll feel damned good, sir. It's pretty tight in here."

"Maneuvering, Conn. I want turns for twelve knots."

"Conn, Maneuvering. Turns for twelve knots, aye aye."

The four SEALs entered the Control Room from aft, wet, and looking both tired and a bit bedraggled. Gordon caught Randall's eye as the other three filed past, heading forward and down to the torpedo room. "How did it go, Mr. Randall?"

"Well enough, I guess, sir," Randall replied. "They looked like a pretty rough bunch. Streetfighters and brawlers, rather than fishermen, is my guess." He shrugged. "But everything seemed up and up. They knew the passwords."

"I suppose the spooks know what they're doing."

"You don't sound all that sure, sir."

"This vessel is at stake, Mr. Randall."

"I understand, sir."

"It's 0040, Mr. Randall," Gordon said, glancing at the big time readout on the forward bulkhead. "It'll be tight getting you in to do any useful work at your AO tonight, and still have time to get clear before daylight."

"Frankly, sir, I think we need some downtime. We did our swimming thing for tonight."

"Understood." What Randall and the other SEALs had just done—locking out, deploying an IBS, making contact with Stenki, returning to the *'Burgh*, and locking back aboard—and all with the possibility of combat or missing the pickup hanging over them—was enough stress for anyone for one night, even a SEAL. "Get some sleep. We'll plan an approach to Objective Mongol tomorrow."

"Thank you, sir."

"Conn, Sonar," sounded over the intercom.

"Sonar, Conn. Go ahead."

"Multiple contacts, sir, bearing two-nine-five through three-three-zero. I have three . . . no, make that four contacts. Designating Sierra Two-eight and Sierra Two-nine. The other two are old friends, Captain. Sierra Two-one and Sierra Two-four. I make them as light ASW assets, frigates or large patrol boats. On a southerly heading . . . making turns for about fifteen knots."

"How far?"

"I'm picking this up through a CZ, Captain. Hard to say, but my guess is thirty to thirty-five miles."

A convergence zone.

Sound waves propagated well through water, but the colder the water, the slower the wave. Cold water tended to bend the moving sound wave downward, refracting it the same way a lens refracted light.

Increasing water pressure, however, tended to refract the wave back up . . . though at a much lesser rate than the decreasing temperature. Eventually, though, the wave headed back toward the surface . . . to be bent downward once more when the pressure was low and the temperature dropping.

The result was a kind of a sine wave through the ocean, between the warm surface layers of the water and the ice-cold depths. A listening sonar could detect undersea sounds from astonishing distances, *if* that sonar was in the convergence zone of the sound, with the wave passing through that depth at that point. If the listener was a little ahead of the wave, or a little behind it, in the empty trough between crests, the sound would pass by and never be detected.

The oncoming Soviet vessels posed no immediate threat. They were an hour away or more, at least, and *Pittsburgh* would be long gone from the area by the time they could arrive. In any case, their due-south heading was not directly toward the *Pittsburgh*, but toward a point some miles to the west. Nor could they hear the American boat. While convergence zones worked both ways, the Russians were moving too fast to be able to hear much, if anything, through their sonars.

But Gordon couldn't help wondering what they were doing, and why. Light ASW assets . . . on routine patrol? Unlikely. A patrol would be conducted at speeds low enough to allow them to use sonar.

Moving into position for an ambush, perhaps, an ambush directed at the *Pittsburgh*? Or—disquieting thought—at the resistance fishing trawler, and the CIUA men aboard her?

Whatever they were, they were *not* good news.

Control Room
Russian Attack Submarine *Krasnoyarskiy Komsomolets*
Sea of Okhotsk
0130 hours

"Engineering!" Captain First Rank Anatoli Vesilevich Vetrov shouted into the microphone. "More power!"

"Sir," Filatev, the Engineering Officer replied, "we are at one hundred ten percent now, and I can hold it here for only a short time. The cooling assembly . . .

"I want one hundred fifteen percent on the reactor *now*, damn you, or I'll see you in Hell! . . ."

The *Krasnoyarskiy*'s captain was aware of the silence on the control deck, of the eyes fixed on him as he leaned against the housing of the vessel's Number 1 periscope. He sensed the fear there. *Good. . . .*

"One . . . one hundred fifteen percent on the reactor, Captain. I will require the order in writing."

"It's logged," Vetrov spat, and he clicked off the intercom.

"Stations!" he bellowed at the watching bridge crew. "We will not catch the American dogs with you gawking like schoolchildren! There are still billets within the Gulag for men who shirk their duty!"

He caught the hard gaze of *Starpom* Felix Nikolaevich Salekhov, his Executive Officer, and watched the other man's mouth harden into a thin line. No matter. Vetrov required no man's approval. He required only obedience . . . and results.

Vetrov closed his eyes and felt the rising throb in the *Krasnoyarskiy*'s steel decking, felt the silent shudder through his hull as his pace through the depths increased. It required daring to command one of the State's newest and most deadly attack submarines, and he would show the old men at Fleet headquarters in Vladivostok that he had the daring it took.

Anatoli Vesilevich had been in the Navy for twenty-five years, nearly all of them in submarines. He was, as they said, well connected in the service. His uncle on his mother's side was none other than the now-legendary Admiral of the Fleet of the Soviet Union S.G. Gorshkov, the man who'd single-handedly dragged the Soviet Navy out of the Dark Ages during his tenure from 1967 until his retirement just two years ago.

Vetrov allowed himself a wolfish grin. One of old Uncle Sasha's personal crusades had been the elimination of the nepotism and favoritism corrupting the entire Navy from top to bottom. He'd made an issue of not helping those of his relatives who were also in the service, especially those who, like Anatoli, were on the fast command track.

Small matter. Gorshkov might have been a full member of the Central Committee, a deputy minister of defense, and the Admiral of the Fleet of the Soviet Union, but there were some facts of life in Russia that not even *he* could change, not completely. Anatoli Vesilevich was ambitious, and he had a keen eye for politics . . . and for power, which was much the same thing. He'd fought for command within the State's submarine service, and his family connections had prised open tightly locked doors more than once. One did not need to call God in order to invoke His power. The mere knowledge that a quiet word in a certain quarter could end a career, ruin a reputation, or result in transfer to coastal patrol duties in Novaya Zemlya was more than sufficient.

Even so, it had not been easy. Diplomacy had never been one of Vetrov's stronger points—with his family connections, why should he need it?—and he'd made more than a few enemies in his climb up the ladder of rank and command. That unfortunate incident in '77 with that base commander's young, pretty, and very bored wife at Severodvinsk, for instance, had come close to leaving him beached, and his first command the following year had been a creaking rustbucket of an SK, a conventionally powered boat of the type the Americans called *Foxtrot*.

He'd needed to pull quite a few strings after that to get transferred beyond that bastard's reach, to the Soviet Red Banner Pacific Fleet, and the headquarters station at Vladi-

vostok. His next command had been of a Kal'mar class
PLARB—the West called them Delta Is—first of the Soviet
Union's true ICBM missile boats and the largest submarine
in the world when it was first launched in 1972.

There was enormous prestige in being commander of a
doomsday machine, one of the *Rodina*'s PLARB missile
boats, which could incinerate western cities within a few
hours' notice. But Vetrov had hungered for more. PLARBs
were vastly powerful and their command carried with it considerable prestige, but Soviet strategic and tactical doctrine
limited them to the closely guarded bastions in Okhotsk, the
Barents and Kara Seas, and beneath the Arctic ice. A
PLARB skipper was hemmed in by regulations and the prying of his *zampolit*, his political officer. In fact, he was little
more than a deliveryman, a truck driver at the wheel of an
extraordinarily expensive and dangerous vehicle almost entirely directed by others.

It was the difference between the pilot of a Tupelov Tu-26
strategic bomber, and the pilot of a high-performance MiG-29
interceptor. Vetrov was, by nature, a hunter, a predator . . .
and one did not exercise such instincts cowering in a bastion, shielded by ice and protected by others.

Still using his web of connections throughout the Fleet,
connections that would have been impossible without the
mere existence of his powerful uncle, he'd managed a transfer to the hunters. In 1983, he'd won command of the *50 Let
SSR*—the name translated as "Fifty Years of the Soviet
Union," and under his captaincy the vessel had garnered an
impressive list of efficiency awards and honors, including
one awarded *personally* by none other than Uncle Sasha
himself.

He'd commanded two more attack boats since . . . including one of the hot little interceptors NATO called Alfas—the
Zolotaya Ryba, or "Golden Fish" as Russian submariners
called him, because of his incredible development costs.
He'd nearly ended his career then, as well, when an American Los Angeles submarine had picked him up on sonar and

dogged his baffles once when he'd been on patrol guarding a PLARB bastion in the Chukchi Sea. He'd tried every trick he knew to shake the Yankee . . . and nothing had worked until, at last, he'd been forced to outrun it, which, of course, meant he'd had to leave his assigned patrol station.

The matter had been satisfactorily covered up, however. And now, finally, he was captain of the *Krasnoyarskiy Komsomolets*.

The Americans, he been told, called the vessel Mike. He was the largest and most deadly hunter-killer submarine in the world—displacing 9,700m tons submerged, and with a 122-meter length that dwarfed the Americans' Los Angeles boats. Slower than an Alfa, which could make forty-five-knot dashes submerged, he was still able to manage a respectable thirty-eight knots, faster than any Western submarine. He was better armed, too, with both 533mm and 650mm torpedo tubes forward, and launch tubes for the SS-N-21 cruise missile, equivalent to the American Tomahawk, as well.

Krasnoyarskiy Komsomolets and his brothers were still experimental, technically test platforms for a whole array of new technologies and design elements. Privately, many captains believed the boat to represent design elements stolen from the Americans, but Vetrov ridiculed that idea publicly with every opportunity he found. The Soviet Union was capable of creating dazzling new weapons on her own, without recourse to theft or dealings with traitors.

And if, as the whispers claimed, *Krasnoyarskiy Komsomolets* had been stolen from American Los Angeles class vessel plans and specifications . . . why had he been deployed on *this* mission, to track, cripple, and capture one of their Los Angeles boats? . . .

A boat that was, he was confident, in every way inferior to his own.

It was difficult sometimes to read between the lines of one's orders, but these had been clear enough. An American SSN had been tracked entering the Sea of Okhotsk, and was now operating off the northern mouth of the Tatar Straits, in the vicinity of Litke and Puir, and uncomfortably close to the big shipbuilding base and naval port up the Amur at Nikolayevsk. His orders were *extremely* specific: The American intruder was to be forced to the surface, trapped against the Far Eastern coast, and captured at all costs—captured, *not* destroyed.

There might well be technological secrets to be gleaned from such a prize, but Vetrov knew that the *real* prize here would be the political humiliation of the old enemy, the United States, and the final vindication and triumph in the Soviet Navy's long struggle with the American foe.

And for Vetrov, personally, there would be revenge for the affair in the Chukchi Sea. There were men in the high command—*those old men in Vladivostok*—who felt he owed his current position entirely to the influence of his famous uncle. He'd been called incompetent, lickboot, climber, and worse.

He would show them. He would show them *all*. . . .

"Captain! Reactor now at one hundred fifteen percent," his Executive Officer informed him. "We are making turns for thirty-eight knots!"

"Excellent," he replied. "We are going hunting, Felix Nikolaevich. We are going hunting after the most deadly game of all!"

Enlisted Mess, USS *Pittsburgh*
Sea of Okhotsk
0250 hours local time

O'Brien glanced at his watch and, for the first time during the cruise, had to stop and think hard about whether it was almost three in the afternoon . . . or three in the morning. He'd not been through the control room for a number of watches, now—his duties simply hadn't taken him up to the deck immediately above this one in longer than he could remember.

He had a feeling it was morning. He had that hollow-behind-the-eyes feeling he always got when he was up in the middle of the night, standing the mid-watch, or staying up all night during his school years. With his rhythms now regulated by *Pittsburgh*'s eighteen-hour day, he tended to feel a bit log-headed all the time.

He hoped the condition was temporary. He felt like he was tired all the time these days, but wasn't sure whether that was because of having to adapt to the shorter day-night cycle, or because with his regular duties, his watch schedule, and the studying he was doing for his torpedo-room quals, he simply wasn't getting enough sleep.

"Hey, Ben? Is it day or night?" he asked, still staring at his watch.

Benson looked up from his coffee. "What does it matter?"

"C'mon, you've got one of those number watch thingies. . . ."

"It's called *digital*, Baldy. You have numbers on your wrist, too. It's just that they're old-fashioned analog, and don't come in nice, discrete packets like mine." He looked at his wrist. "At the tone, the time will be . . . 0250 hours . . . and thirty seconds . . . ahhnnn."

"Zero-dark-thirty, right." He nodded, glad to have his inner clock vindicated. "Thanks."

"Why do you want to know?"

"Oh, I don't know. I still remember sunlight once in a while. I like to imagine that it's up there, shining right now, even if I can't see it."

"Still shining on the other side of the planet, Doug. Not that it makes a bit of difference."

"What's the matter, Ben? You sound down."

Benson shrugged. "Ahh. I just get to wondering why I put up with this shit."

"Life in the boats?"

"That ain't so bad. You get used to it."

"The people?"

"Most of them are pretty good guys." He managed a small grin. "Most of 'em."

"Doershner?"

"Ahh, Doershner's a jerk. He gets on your nerves, sure, but he's mostly harmless."

O'Brien chuckled. Most of the men on board had been reading *The Hitchhiker's Guide to the Galaxy,* an oddball, comic science fiction book almost as popular among the crew as the usual collection of crotch novels. There was something about the work's quirky, off-the-bulkhead humor that appealed to the men. "Mostly harmless" was one of the book's happily memorable lines.

"So what's the problem, man?"

"Nothing." His face revealed the lie behind the blunt-spoken word. "It's just, well, the usual shit, I suppose."

"What are we doing here, and all that?"

"Don't you wonder about it sometimes, Doug? Why they put us out here in the Russians' backyard?"

"Hey, it's what we do! It's why we're here."

"Is it?" He shook his head. "I'm not so sure. I've been thinking about this a long time. A long time. And it gets worse each time I go out. I think I'm gonna get out."

"What, out of the Navy?" O'Brien asked, puzzled. "How?"

"No, out of the Service. This is a volunteer outfit, you know. You don't have to stay if you can't take it."

"Aw, man! You can't do that!" Of all the men aboard, O'Brien probably felt closest to Benson.

Benson looked at him coldly. "Just watch me, Doug. Just watch me."

"But you can take it. I've seen you. You get on board a boat better than I ever could!"

"That's not the point. If I was aboard a destroyer, I wouldn't be sneaking around in the USSR's territorial waters, and maybe starting a war or something."

"The Old Man said we were outside of their waters. We only recognize the international twelve-mile limit, and he said we were, like, thirty miles or so offshore."

"We've had this talk before. That's not the point." He

folded his arms. "It's this damned back-and-forth with the other guys, like it was some kind of obscene game. It's not enough that both sides have nuclear arsenals that could wipe out the whole human race several times over. It's not enough that a fucking computer error or a burned-out twenty-nine-cent transistor could blow us all up someday. No, *we* have to go stand eyeball-to-eyeball with them and rattle their cage. Well, I've had it. Next time we put into port, I'm outta here."

O'Brien felt as though Benson were attacking him somehow. Because he didn't feel the same way? Because he was supporting a position Benson felt was morally wrong? He was uncomfortable with the thought, and wasn't sure why.

"Well, I'll miss you, Ben."

Benson sighed, eyes closed. "I'll miss you. Hell, I'll miss this life. It's pretty good, in a lot of ways. The people are good to work with. I'm not sure how well I'd fit in aboard a target."

"Kind of strange, thinking of holding exercises with you trying to find us."

"That's the way of it, kid. Set a fox to catch a fox. That's how they recycle sub drivers, you know."

"Yeah. What time you going on duty?"

"Sixteen hundred hours." He gestured with the coffee. "This is breakfast."

"Me too. Think we'll get used to it?"

"Me, I'm thinking about getting used to a real, solid, twenty-four-in-a-day day, y'know what I mean? Aboard ship, or at a duty station ashore, somewhere. That'll be the life, man."

"You'll hate it."

"Don't tell me that. Let me enjoy my fantasies." He looked hard at O'Brien. "You should come with me."

"Nah."

"Why not? You were pretty miserable when this cruise started out, as I recall."

"Same's any other nub, I guess. I don't know. I feel like I'm starting to fit in."

"A whole year before you get your dolphins. That's a long time."

"I don't want to go this far, and back out. Besides, I feel like I have a lot more in common with the guys, now."

"Well, let me know if you change your mind."

"Sure."

The conversation lapsed after that.

O'Brien already felt as though he had less in common with his friend than he'd had before, a sense that Benson was a *them*, like the SEALs on board or the spooks, as opposed to an *us*.

The feeling was more than a little unsettling.

Friday, 24 July 1987

In the Tatarskiy Proliv
Between Puir and Rybnovsk
2215 hours

To say that it was dark was the grossest understatement. Randall looked about and realized that the effect was precisely like SCUBA diving in a pool filled with ink. When he switched off his powerful little underwater flashlight, he literally could see nothing . . . not even the rim of his own face mask.

Even with the light on, his visible world was limited to a misty glow of swirling, drifting particles, a snowstorm illuminated by the beam. The bottom was a featureless layer, tabletop smooth, of gray silt and organic sludge, deposits laid down over centuries by the outflow of the Amur River and by the indiscriminate dumpings from dozens of factories along the banks. The surface was so fine that a single careless flick of the flipper could send it all swirling up in a vast, opaque cloud, and it was long minutes before the detritus settled out again, or was carried away on the northbound current.

He felt a tug on his safety line and looked to his right. He couldn't see Nelson on the other end of the line, and that length of nylon was only five feet long. He kept moving.

Beneath him was the curved, rusty, silt-coated surface of a thirty-inch oil pipe. The pipe had been laid across the seabed at the northern end of the strait to carry oil from the fields at Okha in northern Sakhalin across to the mainland, then up the banks of the Amur River. He checked his watch. Twenty-one minutes at depth. They were okay so far.

During the late afternoon, *Pittsburgh* had left the deep waters in which she'd been lurking, to the north, creeping down mile by inching mile into the southernmost reaches of the Sakhalinskiy Zaliv. While Captain Gordon had been scrupulously careful not to violate Russian national waters the previous night, when they'd made contact with Stenki, such niceties had not been possible this time. The mission plan called for the SEAL divers to survey the northernmost reaches of the slender strait between Sakhalin Island and the mainland . . . including checking on the location of an oil pipeline, locating Russian sea-floor listening devices and photographing and mapping them, and doing some other basic UDT survey work.

But the SEAL swimmers' range was sharply limited without an SDV, a SEAL Delivery Vehicle which could extend the range and reach of divers underwater. The *Pittsburgh* was hovering now just a couple miles north of this point, in waters uncomfortably less than eighty feet deep.

Randall and Nelson had taken the first survey run; Fitch and McCluskey would come out later, after they returned. Their bottom time was limited, and there was only so much they could do in their allotted hour.

He was using a Mark VI semi-closed-circuit SCUBA rig, equipment that matched the advantages of rebreathers—the bubble disperser all but eliminated the telltale cloud of bubbles associated with open-circuit units—with the deep-diving capabilities of straight SCUBA gear. With the Mark VI he could dive to a maximum working depth of 180 feet, not that he'd be trying anything close to that on this op; working for half an hour at 180 feet required a total of fifty-three minutes of decompression time, divided among three stops along the way up . . . and the *Pittsburgh* didn't have a decompression chamber.

Best of all, it was *quiet*—not just an advantage but an out-right necessity when working around enemy sonar equipment.

He checked his depth gauge. Sixty feet. According to the Navy dive tables, he could stay at this depth for a full hour without having to decompress. Stretch the bottom time to an hour ten, and he would need a two-minute stop at ten feet before going on.

In fact, he wouldn't be going to the surface, since *Pittsburgh*'s forward escape trunk would never be shallower than about forty feet, thanks to the height of the sail. For short decompression times, or to simulate a wait at depth on the way to the surface, he and Nelson could endure the escape lock.

But if ever there was a guaranteed way to give a guy claustrophobia, locking him into that coffin-sized pipe face-to-face with another six-foot, two-hundred-pound guy was it.

The depth reading verified that there was a shallow ridge stretched across the channel at this point. Surface vessels could make the passage all right, but submarines would have to transit on the surface . . . and there was no way that an American boat could pull that off.

Randall felt two sharp tugs on the line, insistent this time, and deliberate. They were wearing the same full-face masks they'd had in Alaska, with the radio transmitters, but were not wearing receivers or battery packs this time out. There was too much chance that their transmissions would be picked up by all of the Soviet electronics in the area.

He stopped, then moved toward his swim buddy, playing his light on the bottom.

There. Planted on the seabed a few feet from the oil pipeline, almost obscured by drifting muck, was a device rising from the bottom that almost looked like part of the construction. It was separated from the pipe, however, and appeared to be mounted on a concrete block, visible in the mud only because of its squared-off, obviously artificial shape.

The device itself appeared to be a polished aluminum sphere held clear of the sea bottom by a slender pipe. At the base were some canisters, boxes, and wiring, all of it heavily coated with silt. Nelson pointed with his light. A heavy cable, thick as a man's arm, was just visible running in one side of the object's base, and out the other.

They came in many sizes and shapes and could be hard to identify, but it was pretty clear what this one was for. It was a small sonar pickup, something akin to the American SOSUS arrays that tracked Soviet submarine movements in and out through the choke points into the world's oceans.

Hovering in place, taking care not to disturb the silt, Randall pulled out his camera, a tiny thing packed into a transparent plastic box the size of a hardback book, and fitted with mechanical controls so that the whir of a motor wouldn't trigger an alarm. He began taking photos from several angles, while Nelson made notes on a slate.

Idiots. Randall grinned as he took the pictures. They'd planted the damned thing in the shadow of the pipeline, effectively crippling its sonar "view" toward the north.

Not that American submarines were ever likely to work their way this far into the Tatar Straits again. The waters here were simply too shallow, too restricted, the possible rewards nonexistent. U.S. subs trying to hunt down Soviet vessels exiting Nikolayevsk in wartime would be far better off lying in wait for them among the Kuril passages, or in the Sea of Japan. With the possible exception of a SEAL raid to sabotage the oil pipeline with a few well-placed limpet mines, Randall couldn't think of *any* good reason for an American submarine to be here.

He thought about that as he took the last photograph, then

reattached the camera to his harness. Damn . . . why *had* the *Pittsburgh* been sent here? Oh, poking around submerged pipelines, photographing and mapping seabed sonar arrays, and surveying approaches to a major shipping lane were all very SEALie things to do, all pumped full of the warrior's spirit and fairly dripping with adrenaline. But there was no hard, military or intelligence reason that this survey had to be carried out.

Certainly not one requiring the risk of a Los Angeles class submarine.

The two SEALs resumed their silent swim along the pipeline. Visibility was clearing slightly as they moved deeper into the center of the strait, where the current was stronger. Before long, the shaft of illumination from Randall's lamp pierced eight or ten feet into the murky snow-storm before being swallowed by night.

Randall was under no illusions about the necessity for military intelligence—or of commando operations such as this one. He wouldn't have been a SEAL if he had been.

Kenneth Randall's father, a Marine, had been killed in Vietnam, a casualty of the assault outside the Citadel in Hue during the Tet Offensive. A six-year-old's desperate attempts to understand why Daddy wasn't coming home again had led, inevitably, it seemed now, to a lifelong search for answers, first in the history of a war few of his friends even knew existed, then in the determined study of global politics.

Throughout the seventies and the early eighties, it had seemed genuinely possible that Russia, the "Evil Empire" as President Reagan had recently named it, was on the way to dominating the world—politically and militarily, if not by outright conquest. A staunchly conservative Ohio Republican, Randall *knew*, with absolute conviction, the danger to his country presented by Communism. He'd considered becoming a Marine, like his father, but ultimately decided that the Navy SEALs—the Navy's premier commando outfit that had first proven itself in Vietnam—offered him the chance of taking an active role in the ongoing, largely behind-the-scenes quasi-war against the Soviets.

During the past year, Randall had deployed to a number of far-flung trouble spots across the globe, and he'd encountered nothing to shake his conviction that the Russians would eventually take over if they weren't confronted *now*, with guts and resolve.

Randall rarely talked about it. SEALs didn't discuss politics—not with those outside the SEAL community, at any rate. Besides their inborn, security-conscious reticence to discuss what they did with *anyone*, they knew the Teams could be hurt by any association in the public's mind with Rambo and similar Hollywood myths. The news media didn't help, not when they tended to fawn over leftist causes and celebrities while routinely presenting the right as demented, fanatical, and under the thumb of religious extremists.

He and his fellow SEALs went about their duties with a steady and consummate professionalism, confronting the Soviet threat in the best way they knew how—training hard, obeying orders, and looking within and to their own community for support, rather than to a largely ignorant and uncaring civilian culture.

Sometimes, in melodramatic moments—say, during a bull session in the barracks at Coronado—they thought of themselves aloud as guardians of Western civilization. They knew how ridiculous such a concept might seem to the newspapers or even a majority of American citizens. And yet . . .

Randall still remembered the sight of those mystery tracks on the beach at Adak. Some people might think this whole thing was a game, but he knew just how deadly serious it was.

The bottom was dropping sharply now, as the SEALs entered a deep, V-shaped valley. The pipeline, he saw, continued straight across the valley like a bridge, suspended in the dark and murky water. Shadows—something strangely regular, caught his attention at the valley's bottom. He tugged on the safety line and pointed; Nelson nodded, and the two began to descend.

The valley bottom was at seventy-eight feet, some fifteen feet beneath the pipeline in the darkness overhead. The silt here was firmer, less powdery . . . and was deeply etched by curiously regular markings which Randall had seen before.

They looked like the prints left by tank treads, pressed into the mud. They had to be newly made, too, because the current and drifting silt would swiftly cover any markings on the bottom, probably within a matter of hours. Thoughtful, Randall hovered above the track marks and pulled out his camera again, taking several pictures from different angles, while Nelson held the light to throw distinct shadows with high contrast.

A miniature crawler sub, probably the same make as the machine that had left the marks on the beach at Adak. After taking the last picture, he reached down and gently poked at the mud where it had been pressed down by the crawler's weight. The compacted mud dissolved in a flurry of silt. These tracks were fresh . . . perhaps less than an hour old. And—now that he thought about it—he could hear something in the distance, a kind of metallic purr made high-pitched and strange by transmission through the water.

It was difficult to tell direction under water, but he thought the sound was coming from *that* way, from the north. *Pittsburgh* lay in that direction, but he didn't think he was hearing the American submarine. This, whatever it was, was far too noisy . . . and closer.

He pointed again, and Nelson nodded agreement. Together, the two men began swimming along the valley floor, moving north. If there was something up there, they wanted to get a glimpse of it . . . and maybe even a photograph or two. And it was time to start heading back for the *Pittsburgh*, before they had to start paying time penalties on the decompression tables.

They swam for five minutes, the sound from ahead growing louder all the time. The valley appeared to slice cleanly through the ridge, opening on the other side onto a broad, flat plain, sensed more than seen in the cloudy murk.

Nelson stopped, pulling upright, and pointed. Ahead, Randall could make out a glow in the darkness, a misty light against which something large and black was silhouetted. Both SEALs switched off their own lights then, and the blackness of the undersea night closed in around them once more, enveloping them completely except for the eerie looking silver-white glow up ahead, like headlights in dense midnight fog.

Navigating by the light, they kept swimming. They were closer to the light source than they realized; almost immediately, the light resolved into the glare of a pair of headlamps. Though clearer here in the main current through the strait, with visibility at perhaps twenty-five feet, the water was still so silt-laden that the outlines of the thing backlit by the headlamps were blurred, as though they were looking at it through a thick fog.

Still, Randall could get a general impression of the thing. The lamps on the vehicle's bow cast a silvery nimbus of light and cast peculiar shadows, jet-black and ominous. As the SEALs swam around the left side of the thing, they could see that it was roughly cylindrical, perhaps five yards long and half that high, raised higher off the mud by the massive tracks and suspension. Oddly, it possessed twin screws aft, a cruciform rudder, and diving planes, as well as a tiny conning tower with a hatch; Randall hadn't imagined that the vehicle might swim like a conventional submarine, as well as crawl on the bottom, but it clearly possessed the means to do so.

And as a final, lethal touch, two torpedoes were mounted on the hull, up high, to either side of the conning tower. They were a lot smaller than Mark 48s, probably 406mm ASW torps, a type carried by Soviet helicopters and light patrol craft. *Crawlerski subski*, it seemed, packed a sting.

Randall did some fast thinking. That type of torpedo, just sixteen inches thick, packed a seventy-kilogram warhead . . . not enough to sink a vessel as large as the *Pittsburgh*, but powerful enough to do her some very serious damage. Was the crawler sub's appearance here coincidence, or something more sinister?

Pittsburgh was certainly picking up the sounds from that thing. It wasn't moving at the moment—simply sitting still, but an engine on board was idling. As the SEALs got closer, Randall saw a pipe or hose extending from the rear of the conning tower toward the surface. A snorkel, then, allowing a diesel engine to run while the submarine was submerged without swiftly poisoning the air for all on board. The upper end was probably kept at the surface by a ring bladder or flotation collar.

What the hell was the crawler doing here? Was its presence coincidence, or did it have something to do with the *Pittsburgh*?

Consulting with hand gestures, Randall and Nelson untied the safety line that had kept them together in the heavy silt. The current, stronger now, was moving them slowly past the Russian machine, along its port side. Side by side, they started working their way closer to the hybrid monster, careful to stay out of the illumination of its headlamps.

From abeam, they could see the overall design more clearly, and Randall began taking photographs. The rounded forward end of the cylinder was glass or plastic, though it reflected light and darkness with an opaque, mirrorlike silver sheen, and they couldn't see in. A pair of manipulator arms were mounted to either side of the cockpit, each equipped with a small video camera and light. The vehicle had been designed to carry out underwater construction, repair, or maintenance. Possibly they used it for seabed construction at oilfields like Okha.

But . . . why the torpedoes?

An instant later, Randall was too busy for questions, as powerful hands grabbed him from behind, and a hand wielding a diving knife snaked out of the night toward his face.

Sonar Room, USS *Pittsburgh*
Sakhalinskiy Zaliv
2231 hours local time

"Any ideas yet on Sierra Four-five?" Gordon asked.

Rodriguez was seated at his console, leaning forward, eyes closed, right hand lightly touching the headset he wore. For a moment, watching him, Gordon had the feeling that Rodriguez wasn't really there in *Pittsburgh*'s sonar shack, but somewhere else . . . his mind and focus and being projected out into the black and watery universe beyond *Pittsburgh's* hull. The green-lit cascade of the sonar's waterfall drew its arcane lines and wiggles on the display screens before him, but Rodriguez appeared to have forsaken the visual world entirely, in favor of one composed entirely of sound.

ST3 Dave Kellerman sat at Rodriguez's right. He was also listening through headphones, but his eyes were on the waterfall . . . or on Rodriguez. His silence suggested that he'd been left far behind by his more experienced—and talented—mentor.

"I would have to say it's a diesel engine," Rodriguez said after a small eternity of minutes had dragged by. "Pump noises, and a reciprocating engine—cylinders and pistons. What it *sounds* like, Captain, is a tractor. I know that's impossible. . . ."

"Not necessarily. The Japanese have used tractors with sealed cabs for underwater work for years. I think those are diesels. They use long hoses from the shore or a boat so they can breathe."

"Could be something like that, I suppose," Rodriguez

said. "A Russian oilfield machine, maybe? But what would it be doing out here?"

"Checking that oil pipeline, maybe," Gordon replied. "Or it's something new out of Nikolayevsk, and it's out here on trials or for testing."

Rodriguez reached behind him and made a quick entry on a computer keyboard. "I'm going to run it through the library anyway, and see what comes up. I've never heard anything like this, but there might be something in the record."

All American submarines carried a computer record of the myriad sounds acquired and stored by generations of previous submarine voyages, as well as clips from ASW sonars and seabed SOSUS nets worldwide. In general, any sound could be broken down into one of four broad categories. There were the biologicals, sounds made by the world of life around them—whales singing and shrimp mating and fish making some of the most bizarre sounds ever recorded on the planet. There were the geothermals, also natural sounds, but these produced by nonbiological sources—steam hissing and shrieking under pressure just above a seabed river of molten lava, the clatter of an avalanche, the grumbling sounds of magma moving beneath the thin skin of a deep ocean trench, the outrush of hot water from sea-floor thermals.

The other two categories embraced man-made sounds. The general category included thousands of recordings of everything from fishing smacks to supertankers, and other artificial sources as well—the clank of warning bells on navigational buoys as heard from underwater, for example, or the noises of an oil-rig drilling operation.

The final category was warships, a listing of every ship and submarine so far cataloged, from friendly, neutral, and potentially hostile sources. Using the library, a sonar crew could swiftly ID any given target . . . and could often pick out characteristics of an individual vessel, *old friends* as Rodriguez sometimes called them. A good sonar man like Rodriguez often could pick the individual differences that separated one Russian Typhoon, for example, from another, by a system that seemed more magical—or at least parapsychological—than otherwise. A boat's sonar library, however, gave quick, sure matches to almost anything the vessel's sonar might encounter.

"How about the other Sierras?" Gordon asked.

"We've got three main groupings now, Captain," Rodriguez told him. One to the west . . . that first batch we picked up yesterday, heading south. It looks like they've gathered off of Vlasjevo, four vessels, all small, coastal patrol stuff."

Gordon nodded. They'd followed the progress of those sonar contracts for most of the past twenty-two hours. Whether they'd moved in on Stenki, or were simply part of a routine patrol was still unknown, but it didn't look good for Johnson and Smith and the two Russian agents. At the moment, there was little that could be done.

"The second is moving toward us slowly from the north," Rodriguez continued. "Three large contacts, five small ones. Range thirty to forty miles, best guess. I keep losing them outside of the convergence zones, but they seem to be maintaining a heading dead on toward the Straits."

"Or toward us. And the third group?"

"Sierra Three-three and Sierra Three-four. They're close enough now I can hear their captains jingling change in their pockets while they walk the bridge. A pair of Grisha IIIs. Range approximately five miles. They seem to be idling, not doing much of anything."

A tone sounded from the library, accompanied by the clatter and hiss of the printer spitting out a sheet of paper. Rodriguez snagged the sheet, glanced at it, and handed it to Gordon. "Sounds like we have a match for a Swedish UUO, sir."

Gordon read the printout. More than once in the past fifteen years, the Swedish Navy had picked up unusual sounds off their coast, sometimes deep inside their territorial waters. Sometimes, the sonar contacts were visually identified—as when a Soviet diesel sub ran aground in Swedish waters recently. More often, the contacts were lost . . . and few were completely identifiable.

Apparently, the Swedes had more than once tracked contacts in and around their naval facilities at Karlskrona and the island of Gotland that had sounded suspiciously like underwater tractors. Similar contacts had been tracked along the Alaskan coast a few years back as well. Naval Intelligence speculated that the contacts represented a very small Soviet submarine with tracks like a tank, designed for beach reconnaissance and amphibious operations. Never identified—at least, not in reports that Gordon had seen—the contacts were called Swedish Unidentified Undersea Objects, or UUOs.

He handed the printout back to Rodriguez. "Is this contact getting closer?"

"Doesn't seem to be, sir. Range is maybe fifteen hundred yards. It was moving when I first picked it up a few minutes ago, but it's been stationary since."

Gordon visualized the chart of the area back in the control room. The UUO, whatever it was, was in the general area of the pipeline the two SEALs had gone out to investigate. Chances were, they would hear the thing themselves and check it out.

He just wished there was something more material he could do to help them. At the moment, though, all he could do was what submariners did best . . . sit and wait.

In the Tatarskiy Proliv
Between Puir and Rybnovsk
2231 hours

Randall clung to the hand with the knife, tucked hard, and somersaulted, pulling his attacker over his back as he rolled. Breaking free, he twisted around as his flippers hit the muddy bottom, stirring up a boiling cloud of silt.

The other diver recovered and came at him again, knife hand extended. The guy was clad in a wet suit, like the two SEALs, but of unfamiliar design. He was big, heavily muscled, and wearing what looked like first-line military underwater breathing gear, either a rebreather or a semi-closed-circuit rig like Randall's with a hell of a good disperser.

Out of the corner of his face mask, Randall saw that Nelson was also locked in hand-to-hand combat with another diver. He could spare no attention for his partner, though, because his own attacker was lunging at him with the knife.

Randall blocked the thrust and got the man's arm in a bonebreaker lock; his attacker countered, though, with a leverage move that flipped Randall away with almost contemptuous ease.

The other diver was strong. Randall was pretty sure these guys must be Spetsnaz, *Spetsialnoye Nazranie* or "forces at designation," the Soviet military equivalent of U.S. Special Forces and SEALs put together. They were a highly trained elite operating under the Russian *Glavnoye Razvedyvatelnoye Upravlenie*—the GRU, which ran most Soviet military intelligence operations. If so, he and Nelson were up against men as well trained, possibly, and certainly as deadly as Navy SEALs.

His opponent lunged again; Randall responded by deliberately dragging his flippers through the silt on the bottom, creating an inky cloud as effective as a squid's defensive jet of black ink. Instead of ducking, he twisted to the side, grabbed the Spetsnaz swimmer's outthrust arm, and pulled himself in close, using his free hand to drag his own Mark I SEAL knife from its scabbard.

The other swimmer twisted, breaking Randall's hold, and slashed backhanded with the knife. Only the fact that the two men were moving more slowly in the dense medium of the water gave Randall the time to roll clear.

Hands grabbed him from behind, one around the chest and upper arms, the other coming down on his head, the hand grabbing for his mask. A *third* Russian diver . . .

Again, he tucked and rolled, this time catapulting himself and this new foe over in a tight, hard somersault that threw the man on his back into the first diver in a tangle of legs and arms.

Randall had trained long and deeply in several martial arts. His official SEAL training had emphasized a Korean martial form called Hwrang-do, but he'd studied jujitsu and aikido as well.

Though the moves and countermoves couldn't apply underwater—the medium was too dense, and there was no way to gain leverage from the floor—certain principles did, among them the fact that a man actually had an advantage over two opponents that he lacked when facing only one. Being better off fighting one-against-two seemed counterintuitive, but made sense. His two opponents couldn't communicate with one another, would have trouble synchronizing their moves and attacks, and might even get in one another's way.

And that was exactly what he'd just done to them, dropping the one Spets diver on top of the other. For a critical second or two, they thrashed, trying to right themselves, get untangled from one another, and launch another attack. And that second was all that Randall required.

Before the two could separate, Randall lunged with his knife at a barely visible target, aiming the point of the blade at the second diver, at the angle of his jaw and his throat. Razor-honed steel sliced through wet-suit rubber and foam . . . and a black cloud flowered, adding to the murk. Grabbing the man's head, he used the added leverage to slice deeper, harder, finishing the job. Pulling the blade free, he pivoted to face the first swimmer, almost invisible now in mud, blood, and night black gloom.

The first diver had taken advantage of the second or so while Randall was killing his partner to reorient himself, and prepare his own thrust. His knife hand flashed close beside Randall's mask, and he felt the blade catch and pull on his equipment.

He slashed a parry, cutting rubber and flesh. The knife hand withdrew, and in that moment Randall closed, grasping the other diver's face mask and air hose, pulling them off and away.

Bubbles chirped and warbled, exploding into the silent near darkness. Randall actually heard the other man bellow, the sound muffled by the water as the Spets diver thrashed and churned, trying to find his air hose and mask. Randall lunged again at the man, now completely distracted from the fighting and, a moment later, the diver was drifting toward the mud, faceup, with bubbles and a stream of black blood issuing from his mouth.

Spinning, knife at the ready, Randall searched for Nelson and his opponent, but could see almost nothing in the gloom save the glare of the Russian submarine's lights. He could see shadows struggling, a few feet away, and began swimming toward them, knife ready.

He drew breath . . . and nearly choked on the seawater that filled his mouth and began filling his mask. He could hear the ringing of bubbles on his left, and, reaching up, felt the severed air hose on his own equipment.

He was about to drown, unless he could think of an alternative . . . and damned quickly. . . .

Friday, 24 July 1987

In the Tatarskiy Proliv
Between Puir and Rybnovsk
2232 hours

Randall jerked upright, groping for a mask rapidly filling with salt water. He tried to clear his mask, and failed.

The right air hose on his mask was the intake, with a valve that opened when he breathed in. The left hose was exhaust, and was supposed to open when he exhaled. The Spets diver had cut the left hose, and the exhaust valve had jammed open with the inrush of water.

He couldn't worry about that now, however. He could sense the struggle in the silt-laden water ahead, where Nelson and the third Spetsnaz diver were rolling over and over in a desperate struggle. Clinging to the air already in his lungs, he kicked hard, lunging forward, emerging from the cloud just in time to see the Russian diver bury his knife up to the hilt in the side of Nelson's skull.

Nelson's legs kicked spastically, then stilled. Randall screamed into his water-filled mask and slashed out, cutting the Russian's arm, then thrusting and stabbing, trying for his air hose, his mask, for any vulnerable target.

The Russian lost a valuable second trying to pull the knife free from Nelson's head, then turned to face Randall's wildly slashing attack. Randall's blade caught him under the chin, biting deep. The man's head went up, his mask filling suddenly with dark blood, as he reached for his throat; more blood flowered into the sea around his throat and hands.

Randall delivered a killing thrust between the diver's fourth and fifth ribs, then, sheathing his blade, he turned to examine Nelson. The SEAL was sinking slowly, arms limply extended in front of his body, the knife still buried in his skull.

Shit, shit, shit! . . .

Reaching out, he pulled Nelson's mask off, removed his own, then pressed the other SEAL's mask to his own face and cleared it, taking in several deep breaths. He began un-buckling the harness for his own diving rig. He would use Nelson's instead; his swim partner wasn't going to need it.

Before he could begin removing Nelson's gear, however, he heard a metallic clank. Rotating in the water, he could just make out the shadow of yet another diver emerging from the conning-tower hatch of the Russian crawler sub. Light spilled upward into the silty water, stage-lighting the swimmer's torso and masked head. The other man raised something bulky in his hand . . . and then a needle-sharp contrail stabbed through the water with a sound like ripping cloth.

The projectile shrilled within inches of Randall's head, and he felt the slap of concussion as it passed.

Reacting without thinking, Randall dropped Nelson's mask and swam as hard as he could toward the Russian sub, now a vaguely lit blur against a vaster blur of dim light. Salt stung his eyes, but he ignored it, racing for the cover of the crawler's track assembly. Again came the tearing-cloth sound, and something skimmed just above Randall's back.

The Russian diver, he thought, was using some sort of

projectile weapon designed for underwater combat . . . and his best guess was that it was something like the old Gyrojet.

The U.S. military had experimented with pistols firing rocket-propelled bullets back in the 1960s, but given up on them because of one serious design flaw. A regular bullet emerged from the gun with a muzzle velocity that could only drop as it encountered air resistance or—in the case of a bullet fired under water—water resistance. Gyrojets worked just the opposite. It took time for a miniature rocket, once ignited, to accelerate to a velocity that could kill the target, which meant they were less than lethal at point-blank range. The Navy had worked with several designs for covert underwater work, however; Randall had worked with one of them himself on a test range. Whatever its other flaws, a Gyrojet's projectile could travel a lot farther in water than a bullet, and several top-secret spin-offs had been employed over the years in an attempt to arm SEALs and other elite commandos for underwater combat.

Still holding his breath, Randall took cover beneath the swell of the Russian vehicle's hull, close beside the port-side tracks. Pausing only a moment to unsheathe his knife again, he launched himself up and then over the curve of the hull, lunging for the dimly seen shape of the other diver.

He had only an instant's glimpse of the Russian Spets swimmer, his legs still inside the open airlock set into the top of the vehicle's squat conning tower. The man was raising the bulky-looking underwater pistol for another shot when Randall collided with him.

They grappled above the yellow-lit, open hatchway, Randall grasping the Russian's right hand and the gun, the Russian clutching Randall's right hand and the knife. Randall used his forward momentum to knock the Spets diver over backward, bending him back over the edge of the open hatch. A third time the sound of ripping cloth shrilled, accompanied this time by a heavy blow to Randall's left side.

The pain followed a moment later, shrill and burning, but he kept wrestling the Spets swimmer back, gripping the man's right wrist and bending it backward until the fingers opened and the rocket-projectile weapon dropped into darkness.

Releasing the man's empty hand, Randall clawed the mask from the other diver's face and ripped at the mouthpiece clenched between his teeth. Bubbles exploded in his face and he could hear the man's strangled, drowning scream. The Spets swimmer thrashed and struggled, but Randall held him pinned in the hatch, blocking his attempts to reach his air hose or Randall's face. The Russian's grip on his right wrist increased, exploding into blinding pain, and Randall lost his knife.

Randall's lungs were bursting. He couldn't simply outwait the Russian; he was willing to bet that the Spetsnaz drownproofed their own recruits just as the SEALs did, and conditioned them until they could hold their breath for long minutes underwater. Randall had already been exerting himself for a good thirty seconds or more since his last breath. In a breath-holding contest with this guy, he would lose.

Somersaulting over the Russian's head, he grabbed the flailing, bubbling air hose with his left hand, turning so that he was now behind the Russian, his feet braced against the Soviet sub's conning tower, yanking the other man over backward. He tried to pull the air hose to his face to steal a quick breath, but the Russian twisted in the hatch and pulled the air hose and mouthpiece away.

With horror, Randall saw the air hose tear wide open with the rough handling. Bubbles filled the water, blinding them both. The Russian was groping at his waist, trying to draw the knife scabbarded there.

Randall beat him to it. He could see the knife, while the Russian was trying to reach it by touch alone. That tiny advantage was enough; he grasped the hilt, found the catch-release, and drew the blade with a sharp snick of steel on plastic. The Russian raised his arms, trying to block him, but the SEAL slipped the blade home, puncturing the wet-suit-covered skin of the man's left armpit, driving it in hard and deep. The Russian struggled, blood pouring into the water, but his thrashings quickly became weaker. Randall withdrew the blade, then cut the struggling man's throat with a single sharp, clean slash.

His lungs burning, Randall pulled the body clear of the hatch and sent it drifting into the darkness at the sub's starboard side. Feet first, he dropped into the yawning, yellow-lit opening, pulling the hatch shut above him as he moved down, squinting as he tried to find the controls he knew must be there. Turning the hatch locking wheel until the dogs engaged, he turned in a steel compartment somewhat shorter than a coffin, looking for the vent, blow valve, and WRT and sea flood valves.

Physics, he reasoned, worked the same on Russian submarines as on American boats, and they should share similar controls. Good design demanded those controls be placed where he could see them, where they would not be blocked by his own shadow cast by the single small lighting fixture in the trunk.

Then again, these were the people who planted a sonar unit where it couldn't see past a thirty-inch seabed oil pipe.

There . . . up high, a series of four valves, and they were even signed. *Voshdooh pavlenye*—that was air pressure, the equivalent of a blow valve. *More navodnyat'*—sea flood? *Vodoeem navodnyat'* was the WRT flood, which meant that *Vipuskat'* must be vent. . . .

Blow valve first. He turned it, fighting desperately the need, the *demand* to draw breath. He felt the pressure on his eardrums growing, and swallowed hard to equalize. The largest valve was unlabeled, but it must be the WRT flood valve. He turned it, opening the connection to the submarine's Water Retaining Tank. The pipes rumbled and rattled, and he quickly closed the blow valve. As the sound died away, he closed the WRT valve, then opened the vent valve.

Air was being forced into the escape trunk. The surface

bubbled and churned as it dropped past his head. Turning his face upward, he gulped down a deep, desperately needed breath . . . and another . . . and another.

He might be giving himself a case of the bends, but all he could do was try to slow his breathing, keeping each breath as normal as he could once the gasping stopped.

The interior hatch was in the wall in front of him, five feet tall and rectangular, with rounded corners. No window, thank God. If there was anybody left on board this thing, they'd most certainly heard the racket when he started draining the airlock and were waiting for him to come out.

Reaching down into the water, he slipped off his swim fins. If he was going to face another Spetsnaz trooper, he didn't want to trip over his own flippers and fall flat on his face. As he bent, the pain in his side struck him like a hammerblow. He looked, and saw blood welling up from a deep slash in his side, and the grating sensation told him he had a busted rib. The Russian's Gyrojet projectile must have been kicked out of the gun like a conventional bullet, with enough kick to cause some serious damage. It didn't feel like it had entered his body, though; it felt as if it had glanced off the rib, breaking it as it passed.

The pain nearly brought him to his knees, and each succeeding breath hurt worse.

A small speaker set over his head crackled. "Gennadi?" a voice called, tinny and rough. "*Vih tudah?*"

Reaching up, gasping again at the pain, he touched the intercom switch. "*Da!*" he called back. He didn't have to fake the pain-rough edge to his voice, the disguising gasp. "*Da! Ya raneen!*"

Telling the Russian on the other side of the watertight door that he was wounded might explain any strangeness in his voice, and just might make the other guy lower his guard for a moment.

The water was being forced now past his legs. He reached up and grabbed the locking wheel to the inner hatch and felt someone turning it from the other side. He grasped his knife and waited, fighting the pain and weakness. A moment later, the dogs opened and the hatch swung outward with a clang. Water still in the airlock rushed over the combing and onto the steel deck beyond.

Inside, a young Russian sailor, wearing the red-and-white-striped T-shirt of the Soviet Naval Infantry, clung to the open hatch. His eyes bulged when he saw Randall, who took a step across the combing, lunging with the knife.

The Russian was too agile, and Randall too weighed down by his wound. He missed and nearly fell as the Russian yelped and backpedaled.

Randall had an instant's glimpse of the submarine interior, a cylindrical, steel-walled compartment cluttered with pipes and valves, wiring bundles and instrument panels, air tanks and supply lockers. A pair of narrow bunks were stacked up to starboard; beyond was a control room, of sorts, a padded shelf just big enough for a man to lie flat on, extending forward into the silvery hemisphere of the plastic viewing bubble. The air stank, a foul, gagging fog of diesel fumes and oil, gasoline and sweat. The Russians' snorkel system must not be completely efficient.

The Russian sailor was clawing at one of the racks, where a military-style belt and holster were hung from the frame. He slid a pistol—a deadly little Makarov automatic—from the holster just as Randall collided with him.

They fell together, slamming into the racks, Randall grappling for the other man's gun hand. The Russian was smaller than Randall, and didn't move with the fluid, graceful training of a Spets. Probably he was just a sailor, the submarine's driver, perhaps . . . but that Makarov was the perfect equalizer. If Randall, weakened by the wound in his side, couldn't disarm the man . . .

The pistol went off, the explosion close beside Randall's head, deafening and shocking. The detonation was still ringing when Randall heard the stuttering *ping-ping-ping-pang* of the ricochet, as the bullet bounced wildly about the interior of the vessel.

Both men ducked instinctively; Randall, by chance, was staring across the Russian's shoulder at the plastic viewing bubble when the ricochet ended with a final, sharp *crack*, accompanied by a brilliant white star's appearance dead center in the bubble.

With a final surge of fast-draining strength, Randall picked the Russian up and slammed his back against the metal framework of the bunks. The man shrieked. Randall pulled him forward, then slammed him once more, hard enough to snap his spine. The Makarov clattered to the deck. The Russian's eyes glazed, and his head sagged; Randall dropped him like a sack of meal, then delivered a single quick mercy thrust with the knife.

The narrow steel compartment appeared to be spinning, and it took a moment for Randall to figure out that the spinning was in his head. Carefully, he made his way forward, lowering himself belly-down onto the thin padding of the pilot's couch to inspect the damaged canopy.

Not good. Not good at all. A needle-thin jet of water was spraying into the compartment through a tiny hole in the center of the starred plastic. As he watched, the starring worsened, a craze of cracks spreading out from the impact. He heard the snap of yielding plastic above the thin, high hiss of water.

He began searching about the compartment for something, anything, with which to seal the crack. Sealing putty . . . a rubber patch . . . hell, *chewing gum* . . . but all he could find was a roll of heavy gray tape, something like duct tape. He tried applying that to the crack, but it slid uselessly from the wet plastic and stubbornly refused to stick.

He heard another crack, and the stream of incoming water grew thicker. That canopy wasn't going to hold for very much longer.

And Randall was rapidly running out of options.

Sonar Room, USS *Pittsburgh*
Sakhalinskiy Zaliv
2234 hours local time

"We've got trouble, Skipper," Rodriguez announced. "Sierra Three-one, Three-two, and Three-three have just gone active. They're moving this way, banging away like metalsmiths in a boiler room."

"Did they hear us?"

"I don't think so, sir. It looks like they're spreading out in a line and just moving south blind. Uh . . . they might be trying to drive us."

"Which implies they knew we were here all along. *Damn*. . . ."

"If we wait here too long," Latham pointed out, "we'll be trapped against the coast."

"We still have divers out, Mr. Latham."

"New contacts," Rodriguez said. "Bearing zero-three-zero, range . . . estimate thirty miles. Multiple contacts, can't sort them out yet. . . ."

Gordon could picture the strategic situation. *Pittsburgh* was at the bottom of a bowl . . . and three separate groups of Soviet ASW ships were positioned across the bowl's mouth, while a fourth group charged in to stir things up.

If they didn't leave, and quickly, they would be trapped.

But Gordon was unwilling to abandon any of *Pittsburgh*'s own . . . even passengers.

You didn't abandon shipmates, no more than SEALs left their own wounded behind.

In the Tatarskiy Proliv
Between Puir and Rybnovsk
2252 hours

Randall used the last of the surgical tape he'd found in the first-aid kit, snugging it tight against his chest. That kit, which he'd found secured to a bulkhead and marked with a red cross, had provided him with gauze, scissors, and a goodly amount of white tape. All he needed to do, really, was staunch the bleeding a bit, and tape his ribs tightly enough that he didn't puncture a lung.

The pain was manageable—barely. He pulled the top of his wet suit back into place and zipped it up, moving experimentally. Yeah . . . not bad at all. If he focused his mind hard, he could beat the pain down. There were syrettes of what was obviously morphine in the first-aid kit, but he wasn't going to touch those. He needed a clear head . . . especially since he was going to have to go back outside. The thin stream of water from the cracked canopy was hissing still, and the deck was already covered to a depth of five or six inches, lapping in dark, bloodied waves about the broken body of the Russian sailor.

The problem was what to do next. *Pittsburgh* was a mile or more away. He had no SCUBA gear—correction, there was undamaged equipment on at least two of the bodies outside, including Nelson's, but to get it, he would have to lock out of the Russian sub—a process that took several minutes at best—and still have air enough to swim out and find it, in total darkness and swirling mud.

And if he didn't find it, and quickly, he was dead; he wouldn't be able to hold his breath long enough to lock back inside once more.

On top of it all, the wound in his side would slow him, and would certainly make it all but impossible to draw the deep breaths he would need to oxygenate his blood. The mere thought of taking a deep, chest-expanding breath made him wince.

So . . . what was left? He could try driving the submarine closer to the 'Burgh, but he had his doubts that he would be able to operate something as complex as a submarine tractor. His Russian was good enough to puzzle out the Cyrillic labels over the valves in the airlock, but operating heavy machinery would be damned chancy at best. Besides, how was he supposed to navigate? The *Pittsburgh* was doing her best to keep quiet and out of trouble; he could drive this thing around in the darkness and murk until doomsday and not get close enough to see her . . . and if he switched on the crawler's sonar—he was pretty sure that that was the active sonar switch—and if he could interpret it, chances were the *Pittsburgh* would assume bad guys were hunting for them and move well clear.

Damn it, there had to be *something* he could do. If he couldn't go to the *'Burgh*, maybe he could bring her here . . . or at least McCluskey and Fitch. Randall and Nelson were due back aboard just about anytime now; when they were late, the other SEALs would be champing at the bit to come find him.

Would Gordon let them? He would have to weigh Randall's recovery against the safety of the vessel. He might rule out a rescue attempt as too risky, and Randall wouldn't blame him at all.

Damn, damn, damn. He couldn't think straight. The pain in his side was gnawing at him, and shock was setting in, leaving him light-headed, trembling, and fuzzy-brained.

The need to do something other than wait and watch the incoming water drove him back to his feet, and into a determined search of the Soviet crawler's interior. The vessel was cramped, obviously designed for a crew of one or two, and no more than two to four passengers, and even that many would be crowded inside this narrow tube with a claustrophobic coziness that made *Pittsburgh*'s torpedo room seem as roomy as the wide-open spaces. Most of the bulkhead space not occupied by pipes, valves, and wiring conduits was taken up by storage cabinets of various descriptions, including lockers for canned food, bottled water, tools, charts, a camera, spare parts, survival gear, life jackets. What he was hoping to find, however—another set of SCUBA gear— was not there, though he did find the lockers, now empty, that had held the tanks, wet suits, and other diving gear worn by the four Spets swimmers outside.

He finally found a possible jackpot tucked into a rack beneath a fold-down chart table, a pair of emergency breathing masks and air bottles. They were handheld—the bottles were only a foot long and four inches wide—with a trigger valve and a rubber mask at the business end. Similar devices were used on board American vessels; during a fire in an enclosed space, they could keep a man breathing long enough for him to find his way out of a smoke-filled compartment.

It wouldn't deliver air under pressure—not the pressure of the sea at a depth of eighty feet. It might not work at all . . . or it might kill him. But if it worked, it would give him a few minutes of air . . . enough, possibly, to have a chance at finding the SCUBA gear outside.

On the other hand, he would need light to find the bodies. His own underwater flashlight had been dropped somewhere along the line . . . probably during the hand-to-hand action when Nelson had been killed. Without light, he had little chance of finding the bodies, and the needed gear they wore.

Well, then . . . could he turn the Russian crawler ninety degrees? He knew about where the bodies were—fifteen or twenty feet off the port beam. If he could rotate the crawler that far, its headlamps might give him the illumination he needed.

But there was that problem of maneuvering again. Moving forward and lying once more on the couch, ignoring the spray of icy water, he studied the controls for several minutes before shaking his head with frustrated exasperation. It would take a *lot* of experimentation . . . and a wrong move while he was playing with the controls could set him in lurching charge to God knew where . . . or upset the delicate balance among the ballast and trim tanks and put the vessel hard over on its side.

Well . . . at worst, he could use the emergency air mask to make it to the surface. He would have to go slow and be sure to breathe out all the way up, but he ought to be able to make it. Eighty feet wasn't far.

But he didn't like that idea, not one bit. A SEAL *never*

surrendered . . . and surfacing would be tantamount to sur-
render, since about all he could do once up there was cling to
the snorkel float and wait for a Soviet warship to spot him
and pick him up.

No. That wouldn't do at all. If he were lucky, they would
put a bullet through his brain right then and there, but he
knew they wouldn't waste such a valuable asset as a captured U.S. Navy SEAL. He would be interrogated. Eventually they would break him—he'd been taught that *all* men
can be broken, given time—and there were things locked
away in his brain that the KGB would be very interested in
indeed.

Maybe he could swim for the Siberian coast . . . maybe he
could make contact with the Russian resistance . . .
maybe . . . maybe . . . maybe . . .

No. Too many maybes, and his wounded side would keep
him from moving very far, or very quickly. Unless he found
a way to communicate with the *Pittsburgh*, he would die
here.

The question, then, was how to communicate with the
Pittsburgh. Radio was out, of course, even if he knew *Pittsburgh*'s operating frequency, even if they were monitoring
equipment that usually wasn't in operation when they were
submerged. Radio waves simply wouldn't penetrate that far
underwater unless they were pretty low frequency and high-
powered. Sonar would do the trick—sound traveled tremendous distances in the sea, and much more quickly than in
air . . . but the Russians *would* hear it. Even sonar listening
devices badly placed in the shadow of an oil pipe would pick
up *that* kind of signal, delivered at close range.

Still, sound appeared to offer him his best chance. A good
loud bang—say, by smacking a bare piece of the crawler's
hull with that spanner wrench over there—would definitely
reach the *Pittsburgh*.

The problem was how to convey any useful information,
without being heard by the Russians. They knew Morse code
as well as he did, and would be drawn like flies to shit if he

started hammering out anything like a regular code. And yet it had to attract the attention of the *Burgh*'s sonar crew.

All assuming, of course, that the *Pittsburgh* was still there. He looked at his watch: 2320 hours. He was way overdue. Was the *'Burgh* even still in the area?

Well, there was one thing he could try. . . .

Control Room, USS *Pittsburgh*
Sakhalinskiy Zaliv
2323 hours local time

"You gotta let us go out and look for them," Chief McCluskey said. Belatedly, he added a growled "Sir!" McCluskey was a big, barrel-chested man with a bullet head and hair trimmed down to the consistency of a light fuzz, and the scowl he wore now could have curdled milk at twenty paces.

"And where would you look, Chief?" Gordon replied, keeping his voice reasonable, conversational. "It's a big ocean and the middle of the night. What are you going to do, trace out Randall's planned recon route? You could pass five feet away from him and never know he was there."

McCluskey opened his mouth to reply, then seemed to think better of it, clamping his jaws shut. Beside him, Fitch shook his head. "Man, we can't leave 'em behind, sir."

"I don't intend to. Not if I can help it. *But* . . ." He stressed that last word hard, and let it hang there in the air of the control room for a second or two. "But we're not going to go about this in a haphazard way. It's obvious they ran into some sort of trouble out there, or they would have been back aboard by now, right?"

"Yes, sir." McCluskey's words were a most reluctant admission.

"They might have encountered a patrol, Russian swimmers. I can't imagine what else they might have run into . . ."

He stopped. "Actually, now that I think about it . . ."

"What is it, sir?" McCluskey asked.

"Sonar picked up a contact out there. Close. We think it's a Russian crawler. It's possible they ran afoul of that."

Fitch and McCluskey exchanged glances. "They might use something like that to guard or maintain their oil pipeline," Fitch said.

"Exactly. Now, if you two just go swimming out there after them, I run the risk of losing both of you as well. And I have another problem. We've got Russian ASW ships closing on us, banging away on their sonar like drivers at a tiger hunt. From the look of things, they know we're in the area. And that, gentlemen, is *not* good. Among other things, it means we don't have much time."

"So . . . so what do you intend to do, Captain?" McCluskey wanted to know.

"I intend to move south, toward the sonar contact . . . but very, very slowly. I'm going to have Rodriguez listening for anything that might give us a clue. If your people are in trouble, they have sense enough to make noise that we can pick up."

"Well, they might not," McCluskey said, "if they thought that making noise would put the sub at risk."

"I can appreciate that. What I suggest is that you two suit up and get in the escape trunk. And wait. If we pick up anything that sounds unusual, we'll let you know over the 31MC and send you out. But only then. We can't afford the time to have you quartering a couple square miles of seabed out there looking for them. Clear?"

"Clear, sir. But, if I might say—"

"Conn! Sonar!"

"A moment. Sonar, Conn. Whatcha got?"

"Sir, can you come up?" Rodriguez said. "We're picking up something weird."

"On my way." He glanced at the SEALs. "Suit up. This might be it. XO! You've got the conn!" Turning away, he hurried forward toward the sonar shack.

Saturday, 25 July 1987

In the Tatarskiy Proliv
Between Puir and Rybnovsk
0015 hours

Clang . . . clang-clang . . . clang . . .

Randall's arm ached with the effort, but he continued wielding the spanner, striking a bare patch of cold, green-painted metal that communicated directly with the ocean outside. He'd been hitting the bulkhead for almost an hour. Trying to maintain the same rhythm, a regular one-two-one pattern, but broken in such a way that Russian listeners wouldn't realize what it was.

Clang . . . clang-clang . . . clang . . .

E . . . I . . . E . . .

The same Morse call the SEALs had used to summon the *Pittsburgh* on the surface last night.

Old MacDonald had a farm. E . . . I . . . E . . . I . . . Oh. . . .

He shook his head, trying to clear it. The pain in his side was a little better, so long as he didn't move around or exert himself, but he was still feeling a bit muzzy.

Water continued to enter the crawler. It was almost three feet deep, black and oily and icy cold, lapping around the mattress of the lower bunk. With a sharp, rasping crackle, the main light in the cabin flared and went out, accompanied by a stink of chemicals as the seawater drowned the batteries. It wasn't completely dark. An emergency light aft continued to cast a wavering, fitful glow over the rising black water.

The diesel engine was still turning over, sealed behind a watertight door aft, just past the airlock. The main lights outside were still on, but he didn't know how much longer he could rely on them. If anybody aboard the '*Burgh* heard his hammering, they would need the crawler's lights to find him.

How much longer did he have?

Clang . . . clang-clang . . . clang . . .

Funny. It was just now occurring to Randall that he'd single-handedly boarded and stormed an enemy military vessel at sea. The Navy had boarded plenty of civilian ships in the drug war, so they didn't count. The last time that had happened had been . . . when? The capture of the U-505 during World War II?

No, the Marine boarding of the *Mayaguez* in '75 must count, even though the freighter was both a civilian vessel and deserted. Everyone had thought it was occupied by well-armed Cambodians at the time.

Well, his capture of *Crawlerski Subski* was the first capture of an enemy *submarine* since World War II, that was for damned sure. And there wasn't a single damned way he could think of to turn that interesting bit of trivia to his advantage.

Clang . . . clang-clang . . . clang . . .

And, now that he thought about it, the U-505 had already surfaced and surrendered when sailors had gone aboard to disarm the explosive charges the German crew had set to scuttle her. He'd had to take this boat in hand-to-hand combat, board and storm, knife clenched in the teeth . . . *yahrrrrrr!*

That hadn't been seen on—or beneath—the high seas since . . . when? The Civil War? The War of 1812?

He wished his knowledge of naval history was a bit better. He wanted to know.

Clang . . . clang-clang . . . clang . . .

If he ever got out of here . . .

Thoughts of home . . . of Carolyn. Was he ready to get married yet? He'd put that decision off and put it off, figuring it was too early to drop anchor and settle down yet. And the wife of a SEAL had no kind of life . . . her husband called away at any time of day or night, sent hopscotching across the globe to God knew where, and he wasn't even allowed to tell her about it so she could properly worry.

And his motorcycle. His was a beaut, a BMW K75. The feeling he had out on the road, feeling that thunder answer to the flick of a wrist . . . power. Freedom.

He'd always figured he would die young and spectacularly . . . either in a firefight somewhere, or a training accident—*those* happened regularly enough that every SEAL considered the possibility—or blazing down the highway pushing a hundred on his Beemer.

Not sitting in a freezing steel pipe as it slowly flooded, pounding out his last-gasp message with a ten-pound wrench.

Clang-clang . . . clang-clang . . . clang-clang . . .

Pittsburgh must have gone by now. It was almost midnight, and Captain Gordon wouldn't want to hang around these shallow, inshore waters longer than he had to. The Russian sailor's body bumped against his legs, and he absently shoved it aside. So why was he even still trying?

Clang . . . clang-clang . . . clang . . .

Hell, he should have tried to figure out how to run the damned submarine. He could have sailed it south through the Tatar Straits and come ashore in Japan, and wouldn't *that* have been a wild, ninety-day wonder?

Ahh, who was he kidding? She was flooding, and wouldn't have made it half a mile. He'd captured his very own submarine, and she was going down fast.

No . . . *he*. Russian ships were *he*. . . .

Clang-clang . . . clang-clang . . . clang-clang . . .

What the hell? That wasn't right. He stopped banging on the hull. Had he gotten so fuzzy-headed he'd started banging the wrong code?

Clang-clang-clang . . . clang-clang-clang . . . clang-clang-clang . . .

He stared at the spanner still gripped in his right hand. No, goddammit, he *hadn't* imagined that. Someone was outside, pounding on the hull!

The forward canopy was half-submerged. He couldn't tell if water was still coming in; it was possible that the pressures had equalized, trapping the boat's remaining air in a bubble in the upper half of the compartment. He couldn't see out, though . . . and didn't know if the unseen hammerers outside were Fitch and McCluskey, or Spetsnaz divers come to see what all the racket was about.

By God, if they were Russians they weren't going to take him alive. And he wasn't going to wait to die inside this cold, wet steel coffin, either. He touched the knife sheathed at his hip. He would go out and meet them in the sea. Hell, that was where a SEAL *ought* to die, in the open ocean, not locked away inside a box. . . .

He felt a momentary panic. The air tank and mask he'd found . . . he'd left them on the lower bunk, he thought, but it was underwater now and he couldn't see it. Desperately, he felt around on the mattress pad, which was trying to float but held down by something heavy . . . and then his hand closed on the cylinder.

He made his way aft. The airlock's inner door was still open. It was probably set up so that you couldn't open the outer door if the inner one was open; no wonder his guests hadn't come aboard. He stepped inside, ducking his head into the cold water to get through the low door opening. Dragging the watertight door shut and dogging it, he stood in the escape lock, head and shoulders only above water now.

Randall puzzled over the control valves for a minute. How did you flood an airlock already partly flooded? He opened the WRT flood valve, and the water began coming in faster.

He pressed the rubber mask against his face, almost panicked when he couldn't draw a breath . . . then remembered to crack the valve. As the water flooded up past his mouth, he could breathe.

Reaching up, he opened the blow valve, which ought to let the remaining air trapped in the airlock out . . . then drew his knife. Clumsily one-handed, because he needed to keep the air mask pressed in place, he began turning the wheel on the underside of the outer hatch . . . then felt someone turning it from the other side.

The hatch swung up and open, and the last of the escape-trunk air belched out, heading for the surface. Randall allowed himself to be carried with the rush, left hand holding his air tank, right holding his knife.

Wet-suited figures surrounded him . . . three . . . no four men. Not SEALs, then. There were only two SEALs aboard the *Pittsburgh*, so these guys had to be Russkis. He stabbed at the nearest with his knife, felt himself grabbed from behind, felt hands close on his arm and twist his weapon away.

He struggled, trying to break free. One of the men pressed his face close against Randall's face, the faceplate of his mask actually bumping Randall's nose. Randall could hardly see. There was almost no light at all, and the salt water was burning his eyes.

But the eyes he could see behind the faceplate were familiar.

Hell . . . that faceplate was a full-face rig. A *SEAL* rig. . . . McCluskey? . . .

The other man grasped his upper arm and gave a reassuring squeeze. They were SEALs. The two additional men . . . realization hit him. *Pittsburgh* carried her own complement of divers. They must have all come out to look for him.

He was having trouble with the emergency air mask. One of the *Pittsburgh* divers—they wore standard masks that covered the eyes and nose alone, leaving the mouthpiece free—passed him his mouthpiece and let him draw a deep, full breath of air at the right pressure and flow. Gratefully, he sucked it down, then handed the mouthpiece back.

Randall stopped them, though, as they cleared the Russian crawler sub, tugging at McCluskey's arm and pointing. Someone broke out a light, shining it into the murk as Randall pointed.

He might not be thinking clearly, but he was still a SEAL. Still buddy-breathing with one of the *Pittsburgh*'s divers, he led the group to the west side of the crawler, pointing to indicate where they should shine the light.

It took about ten minutes of searching—the mud was so thick here after the fight, and still hadn't been cleaned out by the current—but at last they found the bodies of three Russian Spets divers . . . and Tom Nelson.

SEALs never left their own behind, not even their dead.

Together, with Nelson in tow, the five men swam through darkness, leaving the flooded crawler sub behind.

Sick Bay, USS *Pittsburgh*
Sakhalinskiy Zaliv
0150 hours local time

Gordon crouched next to the rack. "How are you feeling?" he asked Randall.

The SEAL was lying in the bunk, an oxygen mask over his face. "Better now, sir." His voice was muffled by the mask. He winced, rubbing the inside of his elbow. "Some joint pain."

Chief Allison nodded. "A slight case of the bends. Too many jumps from two atmospheres to one, in too short a time."

"There wasn't exactly time to play it by the book," Randall said.

"Shit," Gordon said. "We're a long way from a decompression chamber."

"Shouldn't be a problem, Captain," Chief Pyter said. "If we can pop him back into the escape trunk for a few hours."

"Will that work, Doc?"

"Ought to. When you dive deep enough, and stay down long enough, the pressure forces nitrogen from your gas mix into your blood, where it stays in solution. Come up too fast, without giving the nitrogen time to be processed by your breathing, and the drop in pressure lets the nitrogen come out of solution . . . as bubbles that collect in your joints and a few other places like your brain, where they can cause some serious problems.

"It looks like our SEAL friend only picked up a mild case of decompression sickness. If we get him to the escape trunk, we can pressurize that back up to two atmospheres, then bring the pressure back down slowly."

"How long?" Randall and Gordon chorused together. They glanced at each other self-consciously, then laughed.

"Four or five hours should do it," Pyter said. "Just to be on the safe side."

"Four hours!" Randall exclaimed. "My God . . . you want me back inside that steel closet for another four *hours*? . . ."

"Well, it's that or crippling joint pain, and the chance of an embolism in your lungs or brain."

"Into the escape trunk with you," Gordon said. "That's an order."

"Aye aye, sir." But he didn't sound happy.

"I need to check some things with the COB," Pyter said. "Wait here, Mr. Randall. I'll be back for you in a minute."

"As if I have a choice." When the corpsman had left, he looked at Gordon. "Thanks for coming after me, sir."

"We couldn't very well leave you. I'm sorry about your buddy."

"Nelson. Tom Nelson" he said it as though it were important that Gordon remember the name. "That's the breaks of the game, I guess."

"Damned dangerous game." Gordon was fast becoming sick of the idea of this being a *game*.

"I'm just sorry I didn't get more intel on that Russian crawler while I had the chance. There were charts, circuit diagrams, even that fancy underwater pistol that nailed me. . . ."

"Well, you can hardly be blamed for not bringing that stuff out. You were pretty badly hurt."

"Wasn't that. I just wasn't thinking."

"Couldn't be helped. I'd say you did pretty damned well. Anyway, I imagine they'll debrief you when you get back to the world, and you'll be able to pass on a lot of what you saw in there."

"Maybe. But charts and a fancy rocket pistol would've been better. Damn, we could have learned a lot."

"Is that because you seriously think we need the intel? Or are you trying to justify a stunt as crazy as boarding and capturing a Russian minisub?"

Randall managed a weak smile. "I've been wondering that myself, sir. I . . . I guess it . . . I guess Tom's death would mean something if I'd been able to bring anything out except memories."

"He died doing what he believed in, what he thought was right. True?"

"Yes, sir."

"Then his death meant something."

"Maybe Fitch and McCluskey could go back across to the crawler. Those charts could be exactly what the Agency people were looking for when they set this recon up."

"That's a negative," Gordon said. "We were under way thirty seconds after the last of you locked aboard. We have some bad guys coming this way, and they're pissed."

"ASW forces? Do they have you spotted?"

"Hard to tell at this point. My guess is that they knew we were here . . . or knew we were *going* to be here, and are trying to flush us into the open."

"'*Knew* we were going to be here!' Christ, Captain! You mean the op was compromised?"

"That's exactly what I mean."

"Then . . . then our packages must have been captured. You think they talked?"

"I think it's worse than that. The Russians knew they, *and* we, were coming ahead of time, before we even entered the Sea of Okhotsk. That means the mission was compromised before we even left Mare Island."

"Shit!"

"The question is why."

"To capture the CIA people?"

"I think they want something bigger, something higher-stakes. I think they want the *Pittsburgh*."

"God in heaven . . ."

"Makes sense. The Russians are pissed because we've been penetrating areas like Okhotsk and the Barents and White Seas for some years now, waters they think of as their national territory. Whether the law is on their side or ours is immaterial. They think of these incursions as just that—incursions into their territory. They haven't been able to stop our operations, but maybe they can expose what we've been doing. And embarrass us for some good old-fashioned Cold War propaganda in the bargain.

"And maybe capturing and examining an American Los Angeles class submarine would be a feather in some Russian admiral's gold-braided cap. We've had a big advantage over them in submarine technology for a lot of years, despite the damage done by the Walkers and other spies. This would give them the opportunity to match us at last, and maybe even surpass us."

"That's a real scary picture you're painting there, sir. For one thing, it means a traitor pretty highly placed in either the Pentagon or the Agency."

"I know."

"Are you writing Johnson and his people off, sir?"

"I'm not writing anybody off. We're here to do a job, and we're going to do it."

"There may not be anybody to pick up tonight, Captain."

"I know."

Chief Pyter reentered sick bay. "Okay, Lieutenant, Captain. We're all set in the forward escape trunk." He gave a signal, and a pair of sailors appeared with a Stokes stretcher.

"I can walk, damn it."

"I don't want you doing *anything* but what you're told, sir. Get in the stretcher."

As Randall got into the stretcher, he turned again to Gordon. "I don't know if there's anything to this, sir ... but that crawler sub out there was parked and waiting, like it was in ambush. It was also packing a couple of small ASW torpedoes."

"Torpedoes?"

"Yes, sir: 406-mm jobs. Seventy kilos of explosive apiece. It would have taken at least two good hits to sink the *Pittsburgh*, but I'm thinking maybe the idea wasn't to sink her ... but to cripple her, force her to the surface."

"That would make sense, Lieutenant. Thank you."

"It's also possible, sir, that there are more than the one out there."

"What makes you think that?"

"Because visibility is so shitty ... and they wouldn't want to call attention to themselves by using active sonar. I think what makes sense is if they deployed, oh, half a dozen or so across the width of the Tatar Strait Channel. That way, no matter where the 'Burgh approached the pipeline to drop us off, there'd be a crawler sub within, oh, a mile or so. Maybe less. Close enough to hear us coming, maybe, and take a shot. A piece of fucking cake."

"I'll keep that in mind, Lieutenant. You have a nice stay in the escape trunk."

"Yeah. Right."

Gordon watched the SEAL being carried away. What Randall had said made deadly sense. The crawler subs, by their nature, would be hard to spot, lost in the ground clutter off the sea floor. The one Randall and Nelson had stumbled across had given away its location by leaving its engine on.

Had that been deliberate? Like bait? Or had they been counting on the fact that a crawler operating on its diesel engine
didn't sound like a threat? Or maybe they'd been getting into
position and simply hadn't shut down yet . . . not realizing
that the *Pittsburgh* was already less than a mile away.

It didn't matter. Right now, Gordon had to assume that
there were other crawlers out there, lost in silence, operating
on batteries . . . and each packing warheads that would force
Pittsburgh to the surface if they connected.

They were deep inside the Sakhalinskiy Zaliv, with Russian forces all around. Their single advantage was that the
Russians didn't know exactly where the *'Burgh* was. . . . but
that was an advantage that could evaporate at any moment,
as soon as they were touched by a Russian ship's active
sonar. All they had to do was make the rendezvous tonight,
and sneak back out of the bay again.

A piece of fucking cake.

Torpedo Room, USS *Pittsburgh*
Sakhalinskiy Zaliv
0235 hours local time

O'Brien stood next to one of the torpedo-room racks,
watching as McCluskey and Fitch stowed the last of their
diving gear after having carefully cleaned and checked all of
it. Benson and Chief Allison were there as well. "You mean
Mr. Randall killed a bunch of Russians out there? I mean . . .
he just *killed* them?"

McCluskey looked up at him with eyes that carried just a
touch of a haunted look, a dark expression that was hiding
far more than it gave away. "I doubt that it was as easy as
just killing them," the SEAL chief replied.

Getting the SEALs to say anything about what had happened outside was next to impossible. They were a closed-
mouth lot who didn't open easily to outsiders.

Yet there was enough of a shared bond already that Fitch and McCluskey had been willing to tell the submariners a little. They'd said that at least four Russians had been killed . . . and they'd said, too, that Tom Nelson was dead. That bit of news had already spread throughout the boat. Too many sailors had seen Nelson's body brought in through the airlock and stuffed into a body bag for transport to the sub's tiny morgue locker for it to be otherwise.

"I know," O'Brien said. "What I mean is . . . did they attack him? Or did he sneak up on them?"

"You'll have to ask him, kid," McCluskey said.

Fitch gave an evil grin. "Maybe he wants some company in the escape trunk, man. You two could swap sea stories."

"I think I'll pass on that," O'Brien said, rubbing a hand over his clean-shaven scalp. "He'd have me for breakfast."

"He's a good man," McCluskey said. "He'll make a fine Wheel."

"Wheel?" Benson asked.

"It's what we call the guy in charge of a SEAL platoon," McCluskey said. "Twelve men, two officers. The guys in charge are the Wheel and the 2IC. Mr. Randall's been 2IC, but he's in line to skipper a platoon when his promotion comes through."

"Cool," O'Brien said. For him, SEALs were a bit larger than life . . . real-life heroes combining the best of Rambo and James Bond who carried out exciting, deadly, impossible missions far behind enemy lines.

He wondered if he had what it took to become a SEAL. He was a submariner now, and he knew he wanted to stick it out until he got his dolphins, but after that he could apply for SEAL training, and if he made it . . .

"Those dead Russians," Benson said, sounding scared. "Does that mean there's going to be a war? A *shooting* war?"

"Not likely," McCluskey said. "The diplomats'll smooth it over."

"Right," Chief Allison added. "Y'know, a few hundred people have been killed in the Cold War already. I'm not talking about Vietnam or Korea or our people getting killed in the Mideast or even things like Flight 007 getting shot down by the Russians. There've been lots of missions like this one, and some of them haven't turned out so well, am I right, Chief?"

McCluskey shrugged. "Not really the sort of thing we can comment on."

"Yeah. I'll bet."

"In our line of work," Fitch pointed out, "if someone dies, or if word gets out that something went down, well, it means somebody fucked up."

"Your buddy was killed," Benson said. "And all those Russians. Does that mean *this* mission is fucked up?"

"That's one way to put it, kid," McCluskey said. "That is one way to put it."

"This op's been jinxed from the git-go," Fitch said. "Ol' Murphy's been working overtime."

"Murphy?" O'Brien asked.

"If something *can* go wrong, it will," McCluskey said. "Anybody who's been in combat knows Murphy's Law."

"I just wish I knew what was going to go wrong next," Allison said. "Way I hear it, half the Russian fleet is up there right now hunting for us."

McCluskey grunted. "Not surprised. From what Mr. Randall says, it sounds like this mission could've been compromised."

"You mean, someone knew we were coming?" O'Brien asked.

"That's exactly what I mean, kid."

"And a submarine's greatest strength is its invisibility," Allison said. "If the bad guys know where to look for you, you're dead."

O'Brien was used to the old hands on board the *Pittsburgh* painting gloomy pictures to bait the nubs, a reasonably harmless way of passing the time. Chief Allison, especially, liked to tell sea stories about some of his earlier boats, and some of *those* could stand your hair on end.

This, however, didn't sound like a sea story.

"There's a story going around the Fleet," Allison went on, "about an American submarine, a Sturgeon, I think, that got cornered by the Russians right here in the Sea of Oshkosh. She was spotted, boxed in, and depth charged until she was forced to surface. Of course what happened next was pretty well buried. They hushed it up completely."

"What did happen?" Benson wanted to know.

"I don't know," Allison said. "I told you they hushed it up!"

"Now you sound like Big C," O'Brien said. "A conspiracy of silence?"

Allison laughed. "Just because you're paranoid . . ."

"Doesn't mean they're not out to get you," the others chorused.

For O'Brien, it felt as though the laughter that followed rang just a bit hollow.

Control Room
Russian Attack Submarine *Krasnoyarskiy Komsomolets*
0245 hours

"It has begun, Felix Nikolaevich," Captain Vetrov told his executive officer. He jerked a thumb toward the speaker above the sonar console at the port-aft end of the control room. "You hear that? The wolves have scented the prey!"

The eerie, mournful ping of multiple sonars chirping and ringing through the ocean deeps punctuated the air in the compartment, each as sharp as shattering crystal. The initial chirp of each pulse was hard and clear; the returning echoes wavered and faded like dreams. The ASW surface vessels were roughly ten miles ahead, moving south, away from the *Krasnoyarskiy Komsomolets*.

The *starpom*'s eyes were on the waterfall displays at the Sonar Officer's station. "It doesn't appear the prey has been flushed yet," he said.

"No. No . . . but they will be! And when they are . . ." Vetrov's right fist smacked hard against his open left palm. "We will be there, torpedoes loaded and ready!"

"The orders are to force the American to the surface," the *starpom* reminded him.

He waved a hand. "Yes . . . yes, I know my orders. But I also know my duty. The Americans have entered our waters, attempting to play the old game on our back porch. This time, we will end it, once and for all. One way or the other, my friend, the American will *not* escape!"

Vetrov's smile broadened. He found he was eager for this confrontation.

Yes, he would show them.

He would show them *all*. . . .

Sunday, 26 July 1987

Control Room, USS *Pittsburgh*
Two Miles off Vlasjevo
Sakhalinskiy Zaliv
0130 hours

"I don't think we're going to work our way in any closer," Gordon said, face pressed up close against the Number 18 periscope's eye guard. "That place is way too lively for my blood."

He slowly panned the scope, studying the town. In infrared, the clapboard-and-shingle walls of the houses were plainly visible in shades of green and yellow. The heat signatures of people were brighter yellow, while the engine blocks of automobiles and several Zil trucks shone white.

Latham, Randall, and Master Chief Warren were watching the video feed from the periscope on one of the control-room monitors. "I like it better when you can get shots of girls sunbathing on the beach," Warren said.

"Not this time, COB," Gordon said. "We'll see what we can do back in California."

"Make it a nude beach, sir," Scobey said from the chart table, and several of the men in the control room chuckled.

"Request noted, Big C," Gordon said. "Fill out the forms and send them through channels."

"Those trucks," Randall said, breaking the mood, "they look military."

"Hard to tell with this resolution," Gordon said. "Those people on the beach might be soldiers, though."

"Who else is going to be running around on a beach at zero-dark-thirty?" Warren asked.

Gordon continued walking the scope. The town wasn't very large—a small huddle of ramshackle-looking houses and a few larger buildings, with a lot of clutter that gave the place a run-down and ill-kempt look. The waterfront consisted of a few tottering piers and pilings, with some decrepit fishing smacks and trawlers moored alongside. At least there were no military vessels—none that he could see, at any rate. Rodriguez had tracked several small ASW craft through this area two nights ago, but they appeared to have moved on.

There was no sign of the fishing craft code-named "Stenki." The craft moored at Vlasjevo's waterfront were all too small.

If the activity concentrated in the southern part of the Zaliv was indeed part of a tap aimed at the *Pittsburgh*, it was almost certain that Johnson and his confederates had been captured.

But Gordon didn't want to abandon them without at least an attempt to find out what had happened . . . or bring them back off the beach.

During the past fifteen hours, they'd worked the boat slowly up the coast, moving out into deeper water for the dangerous, daylight hours, then slipping in to the rendezvous point after dark. When Stenki failed to show at 2200 and again at 2300, Gordon had ordered maneuvering and helm to inch the submarine in toward the coast closer still, edging along a slowly shoaling bottom until they were just off the fishing village of Vlasjevo. In water so shallow that the top of *Pittsburgh*'s sail was just beneath the surface, Gordon brought the vessel to a silent hover and watched through the periscope, searching for some trace of the missing trawler.

With no trace of the boat to be seen in the village itself, he gave the necessary orders to set the *Pittsburgh* in motion, moving slowly west, parallel to the coast.

Two miles west of the town, he walked the scope around, centering at last on something glowing. "Mr. Randall? What do you make of that?"

Randall studied the object on the monitor closely. "Hard to say, sir. It *looks* like the Stenki . . . about the right size, anyway. But it looks like she was burned."

"That yellow glow on the screen means there are pieces that are still pretty hot," Gordon explained. "Up forward . . . that looks like a mast or a boom that fell across her deck, and most of the superstructure has been burned."

"Funny angle," Warren said. "Is she aground?"

"Looks like. I think there must be a sandbar or something there, and she was run aground . . . maybe deliberately."

"They *could* have gotten off," Latham said, but he didn't sound hopeful. "If a patrol boat or something was chasing them, set them afire, maybe, they might've run aground deliberately, jumped overboard, and made it to shore."

"A lot of maybes, there," Randall said. He looked at Gordon. "I'd still like to check it out, sir."

Gordon gave him a humorless smile. "Feeling responsible for the packages, Lieutenant?"

"Well, yes, sir. I am. It was my responsibility to get them to Stenki . . . and my responsibility to get the Americans back off again."

"I suggest you detail your two men. I can give them a couple of hours, no more. We're dangerously exposed here, and I want to be gone well before daylight."

"I'd like to go myself, sir."

"Negative. You've still got two broken ribs."

"Easy swim, sir. I've done worse."

"Not off of my boat, you won't. Or shall I call Doc Pyter up here?"

"That . . . won't be necessary." He obviously knew he would lose *that* encounter.

"Wise choice. Doc told me you might want to go swimming again, and threatened to have your hide off if you did. You need a full twenty-four hours out of decompression before you go in again."

"This is a shallow swim, sir. I wouldn't need decompress time. . . ."

"The answer is still negative. You want to call your people up here?"

"Aye aye. Sir."

Gordon returned to the periscope. It didn't look like there was any activity around the beached wreck of the trawler, but he wasn't going to bet money on the possibility of it being unguarded. "Down scope."

He met with McCluskey, Fitch, and Randall ten minutes later in front of the inner hatch for the forward escape trunk. "You both understand," Randall was telling them, "that the skipper can't hang around more than two hours. You get back before then, or you might need to hitchhike home."

"I'll hold the boat here as long as I can," Gordon added. "But there's a hell of a lot of ASW activity north and east of us, and we cannot afford to be in water this shallow when the sun comes up. Understood?"

"Yes, sir."

"Sure do, sir."

"Okay. Good luck."

"Thank you, sir," McCluskey said, opening the hatch. He grinned at Randall. "Don't you worry, sir. We'll be back in two shakes."

"You'd better be, Chief. I don't want you guys leaving me alone on this tub with all these submariners."

"They seem like a pretty decent group," McCluskey said. "I don't think you'll have a problem."

When the hatch clanged shut, and they could hear the hiss of the blow and flood valves filling the chamber, Gordon lightly touched Randall on the shoulder. "It's hard sending others out to do your bidding, isn't it?"

"Yes, sir. I didn't quite realize how hard."

"Been there," Gordon said simply. "Done that. And bought the damned T-shirt."

"At least you were able to look over my shoulder, sir," Randall replied. "When I was in Lebanon? It's hell just watching them go, and not knowing if you'll see them again."

"I know how you feel. C'mon. The coffee's on me."

SEAL Detachment
Three Miles West of Vlasjevo
Sakhalinskiy Zaliv
0218 hours

McCluskey swam the last hundred yards.

The two SEALs had locked out of the sub without incident, retrieving their rubber duck from a storage compartment atop the sail. With the IBS inflated, and an extra set of semi-closed-circuit SCUBA gear stowed aboard, they set off toward the coast, two miles distant.

With the outboard muffled, they were able to come in fairly close to the wreck without being heard, but McCluskey didn't want to give any sentries aboard a chance of seeing them, especially if they were equipped with low-light optics or IR. He left Fitch in the raft and rolled silently over the side, scarcely raising a ripple as he hit the water.

Swimming just beneath the surface, he kept kicking through the darkness, relying on his wrist compass to maintain his course. After covering an estimated sixty yards, he poked his head above the surface long enough to get his bearings. The night was clear, the waning moon not yet risen, but there was light enough from the sky and stars to dimly illuminate the wrecked trawler's silhouette. The off-shore current had swept him a bit to the east; he adjusted his heading and kept swimming.

When he surfaced next, the bottom was shoaling rapidly, and the wreck of the trawler lay just ahead, the hull heeled over at a twenty-degree angle, and most of the superstruc-ture charred and blasted. Carefully, he swam around the stern. His name, in Cyrillic lettering across the transom, was *Katarina*. It was Stenki, beyond a doubt.

It was also clear that he'd died fighting. Up close, his wooden freeboard was stitched with bullet holes and splin-tered gouges. It looked as though larger-caliber weapons had been used as well . . . 20mm cannon shells, or larger, had slammed into the deck housing and exploded.

Carefully, he pulled himself up out of the water and rolled over the gunwale.

The stink of smoke still clung to the wreck, and some of the blackened timbers forward were still smoldering, hot enough to light up the IR scope aboard the *Pittsburgh*. The afterdeck was completely trashed, a tangle of torn and partly burned netting, wreckage from a collapsed mast, smashed-open crates, and even some dead fish, adding considerably to the aroma of the wreck. He broke out a flashlight to give the deck a closer inspection . . . and to keep from stumbling over wreckage in the dark.

There was no sign of the occupants, save, possibly, one. All the way astern, just inboard of the transom, the sharply tilted deck was marred by two black stains the size of dinner plates. Under the light, the black residue turned rusty; it was almost certainly blood.

Johnson and Smith might be alive yet . . . but they would not be making their rendezvous. Switching off the light, Mc-Cluskey pulled his mask down and slipped once more into the cold, black water.

USS *Pittsburgh*
Eight Miles Northwest of Vlasjevo
Sakhalinskiy Zaliv
0350 hours

"We've done all we can do," Gordon said. "I'm declaring this op a wash and heading back for the barn."

Gordon, Randall, and Latham were in the control room, standing at one of the two chart tables aft of the periscopes. The current chart showed the bowl-shaped curve of the Sakhalinskiy Zaliv, and *Pittsburgh*'s current position.

The Hollywood image of a nuclear submarine's combat center/control room tended to stress electronics, computers, and high-tech gadgetry. Gordon had seen at least one recent movie which showed a submarine's computer-display chart table, complete with blinking lights marking the vessel's course.

The truth was a lot less dramatic, more practical, and less failure-prone. A standard navigational chart had been spread out and clipped down to the glass-topped light table, and the Quartermaster of the Watch had then spread a sheet of tracing paper over the chart and used grease pens of various colors to mark the current estimated plots for the sonar contacts, as well as *Pittsburgh*'s position and course. Decidedly low-tech . . . but it got the job done.

"It would be nice to know exactly what happened," Randall said, thoughtful.

"Nice, yes. But not nice enough to further jeopardize this vessel." He pointed to the blue, time-noted line curving west, then northwest along the Russian coast, leaving Vlasjevo to the southeast. "I intend to hug the coast until we're clear of this party down here at the mouth of the Tatar Strait. They don't know we've left, yet, but they're going to figure that out soon enough, and then they'll be baying at our heels. I want to get far enough away *quietly* that we can risk opening up on the throttle and making a bit of speed."

"That means creeping along at five knots or so for quite a while," Latham said.

"Exactly. I want quiet routine throughout the boat. The Russians probably have at least some seabed sonar pickups in this area, and there could also be submarines—maybe those tracked minisubs—just sitting and waiting for tourist season. I don't want any unnecessary noise to give us away."

"Yes, sir. The crew has been on quiet routine since we entered this area."

"I know. I just don't want anyone thinking that they can sneeze, now that we're moving again. We have a long way to go before we're out of the woods."

"Or the Sea of Okhotsk," Latham added. "I'll pass the word, sir."

"Good." He continued to study the chart and its overlay for several moments, trying to think ahead. He had to take the initiative, and be at least three jumps of the Russians at each step along the way. If he simply reacted to their actions, pretty soon they would have the *'Burgh* dancing around like a puppet, going exactly where *they* wanted her to go.

From the look of things, they still thought the *Pittsburgh* was in the bottom of the bowl, down near the opening to the Tatar Strait. The line of active-sonar craft were still moving south, now less than three miles north of the coastline and ten miles east of Vlasjevo.

Interesting. That was just about exactly where the *Pittsburgh* had been at this time *yesterday*, when Randall and Nelson had done their swim to check for seabed sonar arrays and the Sakhalin oil pipeline.

Was it possible, he wondered, that the Russian timetable was off? Suppose—just for the sake of argument—that a traitor had given away *Pittsburgh*'s timetable. Suppose he'd counted off the hours and days of the voyage . . . *and then forgotten to take into account the change in date, due to crossing the international date line from east to west?*

Damn, it almost made sense. Jules Verne had used the

Date Line to his heroes' advantage in *Around the World in Eighty Days*, allowing them to gain a day in their race when they crossed from west to east. This would be working the opposite way . . . but it might answer several questions . . . like why the Soviet ASW vessels had started scouring the southern part of the Zaliv just as *Pittsburgh* was getting ready to leave, and why the crawler sub had just been moving into position, and been idling on her diesels, breathing through a snorkel, instead of relying on quieter—and shorter-lived–batteries.

The suspected spy or CIA mole might have added up the days and told his KGB controller that *Pittsburgh* would be checking out that pipeline on Saturday, when in fact it had been Friday.

Wait . . . that was backwards. Had the spy simply gotten confused?

Well, the date line had confused more than one person in the past. And the fact that they'd caught the *Katarina* and the packages suggested that some members of the opposition, at least, knew what they were doing.

Whatever the cause, the Russians appeared to be just a little behind the *Pittsburgh*, closing their trap after the American sub had left the area. They were not stupid, however. They would figure out soon enough that one of their crawler subs had been compromised, and its crew killed. They might have the testimony of *Katarina*'s crew as well; any survivors would have been ruthlessly interrogated.

They knew the '*Burgh* was in this general area even if they were mistaken about her exact location, and they would have backup forces in place to stop, if possible, the vessel's escape through the net.

It was a case of blind man's bluff . . . but one where hunters and prey both were blindfolded, and able to locate one another only by sound.

The nearest sierras were a pair of Komar class patrol boats about two miles to the east, apparently searching the approaches to Vlasjevo. Most of the rest of the hunters were considerably farther off, concentrating their search just north of the Tatar Strait, perhaps ten to fifteen miles away. If there were any other hunters out there, they were . . .

"Conn, Sonar!"

It was ST3 Kellerman. "Sonar, Conn. Go ahead."

"Sir, we're getting noises almost on top of us. Sounds like a helicopter."

"Maneuvering, all stop!"

"Maneuvering, all stop, aye."

"Sonar, let us hear it."

"Aye aye, sir."

The sound coming over the 1MC speaker was muffled, muted almost to the point of inaudibility, but it was distinct, just behind the hissing rush of background noise . . . a faint, fluttering rhythm like the riffling of the pages of a book.

For the sound of the helicopter to be picked up by the *Pittsburgh*'s sonar, the aircraft had to be hovering just above the surface of the water. Why? What had it spotted? The sea was so shallow, and *Pittsburgh* was running so close to the surface that it was entirely possible that the periscopes or even the top of the sail had breached a little. Even at night, an aircraft might have spotted the wake and flown in to investigate . . . or the breach could have been picked up on radar. If they had seen something, the next step would be to lower a dipping sonar and try to detect the *'Burgh* directly. And after that . . .

For a long, long moment, as tension grew to unbearable levels in the control room, the *Pittsburgh* drifted silently just beneath the surface, slowing with the water's friction until she came to a dead stop. The helicopter hovering just overhead might be plying the surface with searchlight beams. Even fully submerged, something as large as a Los Angeles submarine could leave a telltale wake on the surface, a roiling of the water suggesting something large moving just beneath. By going motionless, the wake could be killed.

But had they been in time?

A submarine's deadliest enemy was another sub . . . but a close second was a helicopter outfitted for ASW search and warfare. A helicopter was fast and could cover an enormous search area. It could use dipping sonar to actively ping any suspected target, or to lay down a search pattern alone or as part of a larger effort.

And they could carry air-dropped 406mm torpedoes, the same kind Randall had seen mounted on the crawler, and they could put them down by parachute almost directly alongside the target sub. A torpedo fired by another submarine or by a surface warship was set to arm itself after it had traveled a safe distance from the launch tube . . . and the target boat had a chance to outmaneuver or even outrun a torpedo coming from some distance away.

But an ASW torpedo dropped from a helicopter could go hot and active as soon as it hit the water, and the target would have almost no time at all to maneuver clear.

Minutes passed . . . and more minutes. The thuttering sound was fainter now, almost swallowed by the vaster sounds of the ocean around them.

"Conn, Sonar. Air contact is moving off."

Gordon released the lungful of air he hadn't realized he'd been holding. "Very well, Sonar. Thank you."

The hunters had missed them, this time.

But the *Pittsburgh* might not be that lucky the next.

Torpedo Room, USS *Pittsburgh*
Sakhalinskiy Zaliv
0402 hours local time

Chief Allison laid his hand against the hull, and smiled. "Okay, gents. We're under way again. I'd guess about five knots."

O'Brien laid his own hand on the bulkhead, but couldn't convince himself that he felt anything other than cold, slightly damp, thickly painted metal.

"So . . . what was it, you think?" Benson asked. "Why did we stop?"

"Could be the skipper was checking to see if he'd forgotten anything back on the beach," Scobey said, grinning. "You know, car keys, wallet . . ."

The deck under their feet tipped slightly, angling down toward the bow. "Ah!" Allison added. "And we just went down-planes about five degrees. That means the water is getting deeper. Pretty soon, we'll be out of the amphibious Navy and back where we belong, in the Deep."

O'Brien by this time was beginning to get a feel for how his more experienced shipmates felt about such basic aspects of the universe as land and ocean. Submarines actually operated only within the uppermost skin of the ocean; a Los Angeles boat's operational depth of fifteen hundred feet— just a bit over four times her own length—was a tiny fraction of the typical depth of any ocean. The Okhotsk Deep east of northern Sakhalin reached a depth of over ten thousand feet, and Okhotsk was one of the shallower, more confining of the world's seas.

But submariners thought in terms of the freedom offered by the ocean's great depths. There was at least the illusion of three-dimensional movement through a three-dimensional world, and waters shallower than a couple of hundred feet were prisons, restricting the boat to a two-dimensional plane that made it far easier for the enemy to find and track her.

Everyone in the crew had seemed tense, ill at ease, while *Pittsburgh* had lurked within the shallows off the Russian east coast. Now, their mood was beginning to lighten as the submarine nosed her way north once more, and into deeper water. It was as though a palpable weight had been lifted from the shoulders of every man on board.

"So . . . do you think that's it?" O'Brien asked. "Are we going home?"

"Once we're in deep water, son, we *are* home."

"Amen to that," Randall said from his rack. "SEALs always think of the water as a friend. A place to hide, where the enemy can't find you."

"I've heard about drownproofing in SEAL training," Benson said. "That's where they tie your hands and feet and toss you into the deep end, right?"

"That's right, man," Fitch said. "You got to go all the way to the bottom—twenty feet, I think it is. Then push off and come to the surface again. Then let yourself sink. And they work you up to the fancy stuff, like finding a face mask on the bottom. You have to push your face into it, and clear it by blowing out through your nose while pressing it tight against your face, and all while your hands are tied behind your back! Yeah, by the time you're done with that, either you ain't afraid of the water anymore, or . . ."

"Or what?" O'Brien asked.

"Or else you're *dead*, man!"

"Kind of like sink or swim, is that it?" Allison said, laughing.

"That's the idea."

"So . . . how do I become a SEAL?" O'Brien asked.

"Why?" Randall asked. "You want to join the Teams?"

"I don't know. I'd like to explore the options, though."

"I thought you wanted to earn your dolphins, nub," Allison said. He sounded mock-hurt. "Not that goddamn piece of junk SEALs wear all the time."

"That's our Budweiser," McCluskey said. "'Cause it looks like the Bud logo. And I'll thank you not to call it a goddamn piece of junk."

"Don't join the SEALs, son," Allison said, grinning. "You wade around in the mud all day. You jump out of a perfectly good airplane, hike forty miles, sit around in one position all day so your legs hurt bad enough to keep you from falling asleep, then do your SEAL thing and hike forty miles back. Man, that's a drag!"

"Yeah?" Fitch said. "It's better'n what you guys do, sitting around all the time in a sewer pipe so small it makes a closet look like the great outdoors. Man, I wouldn't trade my mud for your sewer pipe for any money in the world!"

"To each his own," Randall said. "Go easy on them, Fitch. Remember, we *need* the truck drivers sometimes."

"I guess they're okay, sir," Fitch said, nodding. "But you *still* couldn't pay me to live in one of these things permanent, like . . ."

"Tell you what you do, son," Randall told O'Brien. "Soon as we get back to the world, you talk to your CO, and ask—"

"Fuck you, sir," Allison said. "The boy's a born submariner. And he goddamn is gonna finish his goddamn quals and win his dolphins before he thinks about crazy shit like being a SEAL!"

"Behold," Scobey said. "The battle of the marine mammals, SEALs versus dolphins!"

"Fuck you too," Allison said. "I have a half a mind to—"

"All hands! All hands!" snapped from the 1MC speaker on the bulkhead. "Torpedo in the water! Rig for collision!"

And then the deck tilted sharply to starboard.

Sunday, 26 July 1987

Control Room, USS *Pittsburgh*
Two Miles off Vlasjevo
Sakhalinskiy Zaliv
0405 hours

"Torpedo *is* arming itself!" Rodriguez's voice called over the intercom. "I repeat, torpedo *is* running hot! Range one-three-five-zero yards and closing!"

"Helm!" Gordon called. "Maintain turn to starboard!"

"Maintaining turn to starboard, aye, sir."

The kid at the helm control sounded as cool as the water outside *Pittsburgh*'s hull.

"Torpedo has gone active!" Rodriguez reported. "Active pinging." A pause. "Torpedo has acquired target. Bearing now two-three-five, almost directly astern!"

"Maneuvering!" Gordon snapped. "Ahead full! Let's race this thing!"

"Conn, Maneuvering. Ahead full, aye, sir."

"Depth beneath keel?"

"Eight-five feet beneath keel, Captain," Lieutenant Carver announced.

"Damn, this beach is barely damp," Gordon said, keeping his voice light. "Let's find us some open water, shall we?"

"Aye *aye*, sir!" Carver replied.

Faster . . . faster . . . Gordon bounced lightly on the balls of his feet, willing the huge boat to move faster.

The torpedo had suddenly appeared on the sonar screens, fired from about a mile away and almost dead abeam off the port side. Gordon had immediately ordered the sub into a hard turn to port, away from the torpedo. His guess was that it had been launched either from another helicopter or from one of Randall's crawler subs . . . most likely the latter. Had it been launched that close from another sub—a *real* sub, not one of those tracked toys—he might have tried turning into the torpedo to get inside its arming range, but this fish would have a short arming range, making that a dangerous tactic indeed. And he'd guessed right; the torpedo had armed itself long before *Pittsburgh* could have closed the range.

If it was a 406mm torpedo, it meant a battery-driven motor and a relatively short range. His only hope was to outrun the thing, and that meant *speed.* . . .

"Conn, Maneuvering. Now making turns for three-five knots."

"Give us all you can, Chief."

"Will do, sir." *Pittsburgh*'s stated top speed was thirty-plus knots submerged. In fact, she could manage thirty-five and, for short spurts only, could stretch that to something just shy of forty.

"Sonar, Conn! Give us a countdown on the torp."

"Aye, sir. Torpedo now at seven-zero-zero yards, and closing. Estimate speed at six-five knots!"

As a kid, Gordon had always hated word problems in math class, the sort of imbecilic nonsense that had trains leaving from different stations so many miles apart at different times and traveling at such and such a speed, and at what time would they pass one another? Several times, he'd rewritten the problem so that the trains wouldn't pass, but collide in a satisfactorily fiery explosion . . . which hadn't exactly endeared him to the teacher.

Here at long last was a practical application of those problems. The Russian torpedo was following the *Pittsburgh*, coming right up her ass. If the *'Burgh* was moving at thirty-five knots and the torpedo at sixty-five knots, the torpedo obviously was closing the range at thirty knots . . . about thirty-four and a half miles per hour.

Didn't seem like much . . . a slow cruise through town in a car. But at that speed it would cover seven hundred yards in a bit over . . .

"Forty seconds to impact," Rodriguez warned.

"Stand by the CM dispenser, COB."

"Ready to release countermeasures," Warren replied.

"Five hundred yards. Thirty seconds to impact."

Gordon closed his eyes, picturing the moving sub, the faster-moving torpedo homing now on active sonar. Countermeasures gave them a chance.

In World War II, the German U-boat skippers had perfected the use of bubble decoys. *Pillenwerfer*, they'd called it, the "pill-thrower," firing a capsule that released a dense cloud of bubbles that shielded the submarine from a surface ship's sonar or ASDIC.

Techniques and technologies were much improved nowadays. Torpedoes carried their own active sonar, allowing them to lock onto the target submarine and follow it.

Modern countermeasures were devices dropped from special launchers amidships and allowed to drift into a submarine's wake, generating a cloud of bubbles . . . and noise. That noise could mask the propeller noise of the sub, and confuse the people steering a wire-guided torpedo. And for an actively homing fish like this one, it could block and scatter the torpedo's homing pings, causing it to lose its target momentarily.

The key word was "momentarily." As soon as the torpedo punched through the bubbles, it would begin searching for a target once again, and was usually programmed to circle the area until it reacquired.

"Three-zero-zero yards! Seventeen seconds to impact!"

Eyes still closed, Gordon continued to visualize the encounter, the torpedo less than three boat lengths astern. If that seventy-kilogram warhead detonated on or near *Pittsburgh*'s cruciform tail, her screw would be destroyed, and her rudder and stern planes. She would *have* to blow ballast and surface, then wallow helplessly until Soviet surface vessels arrived to take her in tow. If she flooded and went down instead, she would end up resting in less than two hundred feet of water, an easy recovery operation for the Russians.

"Fifteen seconds to impact! Fourteen . . ."

"Release countermeasures!"

"Twelve . . ."

"Countermeasures away, sir!"

"Maneuvering! Give me *everything* you've got!"

He kept visualizing, counting silently to himself. He needed to allow time for *Pittsburgh*'s length to slide all the way through the bubbles now exploding up and out . . . a cloud hanging in place while the submarine continued to move forward at just over thirty-five knots.

"Ten! . . . Nine! . . ."

"Helm! Hard left rudder! Now!"

"Hard left rudder, aye, sir!"

"Seven! . . . Six! . . ."

The deck tilted sharply beneath Gordon's feet, and he reached out to cling to one of the periscope housings. This was as bad as angles and dangles; *Pittsburgh* was literally heeling far over onto her port side as she made the turn. There was a sharp clatter and crash as someone's coffee cup skittered off a surface and smashed on the deck. A deeper, hollow sound, a groan of stressed metal, echoed from above the control room.

"Conn, Maneuvering! We're at one hundred fifteen percent on the reactor! Making turns for three-eight knots!"

"Conn, aye. Helm! Maintain hard left rudder! All hands! Brace for collision!"

"Three! . . . Two! . . . One! . . ."

Gordon looked up toward the overhead, waiting.

"Plus one!" Rodriguez announced. "Plus two! Sir! He missed!"

"Keep on it, Sonar! Tell me which way it circles!"

"Sonar, aye! But it's getting hard to hear *anything* out there!"

The torpedo had punched through the cloud of bubbles, emerging to find the target looming just ahead of it . . . gone. Its computer brain would have a simple search pattern loaded aboard . . . a circle to either left or right, and possibly a change of depth as well, though in these shallow waters that probably wasn't necessary and could be ignored.

"COB. What are the stats on a Russian 406?"

Warren didn't even need to access the boat's warbook. "It'll be either an M1962 or an M1981."

"Assume the worst."

"M1981. Seventy-kilogram warhead. Maximum effective range six nautical miles. Top speed about thirty knots."

"That's what I thought." He'd been surprised by the torpedo's speed, but hadn't had time to think about it. Soviet 406mm ASW torpedoes were too small to mount the big and complex Stored Chemical Energy Propulsion System— SCEPS—of an American Mark 46, a pump-jet system that gave it a top speed of over fifty knots. They were powered by batteries, which made them slow and short-ranged for most ASW situations.

This fish was moving at better than twice an M1981's speed. The question was . . . what kind of propulsion system did it have, and had there been a trade-off in range? The older Soviet M1962s could travel three nautical miles before running out of juice, an M1981 about six.

That fish out there could burn through the water at twice the speed of earlier 406s, but you couldn't get something for nothing. There *had* to be a trade-off somehow . . . in speed, performance, or payload.

Which was it?

"Conn! Sonar! I think we have aspect change on target! Torpedo turning to starboard!"

Gordon allowed himself a small, inner sag of relief. The torpedo could have gone left or right, port or starboard, the tossing of a coin. Had it turned port, in the same direction as the *Pittsburgh*, its higher speed would have taken it in a much larger circle, bringing it back around on a new heading, directly toward the *'Burgh*'s bow. To counter, he would have had to turn inside the torpedo's turning radius, which would have put it on the *Pittsburgh*'s tail once again.

If it was turning to port, however, it would describe the same big circle, but clockwise instead of counterclockwise . . . and since *Pittsburgh* was already heading away from it at almost forty knots, by the time it reacquired—*if* it reacquired—the American sub would have a tremendous lead.

"Conn, Sonar! We're cavitating!"

"Understood, Sonar." *Pittsburgh* was traveling so swiftly that vacuum bubbles were momentarily forming on the surface of the rapidly spinning screw, then collapsing, creating a characteristic sound that could be easily heard by others. Even without the cavitation, *Pittsburgh* was putting out a lot of noise as she raced north through the water, so much noise, in fact, that her own sonar was almost deaf. Rodriguez had been able to track the torpedo, thank God, because it was close and loud, but he wouldn't be able to hear much of anything else.

But he wanted to put as much distance between *Pittsburgh* and that 406 as he possibly could.

Minutes passed, as the *Pittsburgh* continued to race toward the north.

"Conn, Sonar. Sorry, sir, but we're deaf as a post in here. I lost the torpedo."

"Not to worry, Sonar," Gordon replied. "Keep listening in case it gets close again."

"Aye aye, sir. But at this speed, and with it coming up our baffles, it'll be point-blank before we can pick it up."

"Understood. Stay on it."

"Aye aye, sir."

Latham caught his eye. "You like giving impossible orders, don't you, Captain?"

"Not impossible, Number One. Just improbable. And nothing *this* crew can't handle." He said it deliberately and loudly. By the beginning of the next watch, the enlisted personnel in the control room would have spread his words throughout the boat, a far more effective form of praise, in Gordon's opinion, than some sort of pat, "well-done-men" speech.

He checked the big clock on the forward bulkhead. The torpedo had been in the water six minutes now . . . long enough to have covered over six miles. Unless the Russians had developed some sort of super high-tech wonder-motor, chances were the 406's batteries were exhausted by now, and the fish was floating on the surface.

He ordered *Pittsburgh*'s speed brought back down to thirty knots, but held it there for another five minutes, just to be sure. By that time, they were well across the twelve-mile line and out into what were technically international waters.

Then he ordered the speed cut yet again, this time to a near-silent eight knots, and after a few minutes more, he ordered the *Pittsburgh* to be brought onto a new heading . . . of zero-one-five. That would take them past Mys Yelizavety, the northernmost cape of Sakhalin, fifty miles distant, and get them clear of this damned tight, shallow bowl.

At eight knots, it would take them just over six hours.

Control Room
Russian Attack Submarine *Krasnoyarskiy Komsomolets*
Sea of Okhotsk
0425 hours

Lieutenant Gennadi Lemzenko, *Krasnoyarskiy*'s Navigation Officer, placed the parallel rule on the chart and extended a green, grease pencil line across the paper. "At ten knots," he said, "five hours. If they slowed to eight knots to be certain of silence, more like six and a quarter."

Captain First Rank Anatoli Vetrov studied the tangle of straight lines, dots, and curves littering the chart of the Sakhalinskiy Zaliv. The American submarine had been fired upon *there* . . . probably by one of the Spetsnaz crawler subs the Fleet had deployed throughout the southern reaches of the Zaliv. The *Krasnoyarskiy Komsomolets*, now hovering virtually motionless 130 kilometers north of the action to allow his sonar the chance to listen carefully, had picked up the unmistakable sound fingerprint of the big Los Angeles when its captain had boosted its speed to over thirty-five knots and hurled it into a series of tight turns, attempting to outmaneuver the torpedo. For several minutes, the *Krasnoyarskiy* had listened to the deep Convergence Zone channel as the American vessel had sped north at high and noisy speed.

And then . . . the Los Angeles sub had simply dropped off the *Krasnoyarskiy*'s sonar screens, becoming, once again, invisible.

"That is his new course," Vetrov said with confidence. "Zero-one-five . . . or close to it." He brought a pair of calipers down on the grease line on the chart, just north of Mys Yelizavety. "We will catch him *here*."

Salekhov, his Exec, looked dubious. "That may be a bit too simple, Comrade Captain. The American could have kept moving north. We may have lost him as he left the convergence zone."

"No. His mission here is over, and the sooner he gets out of the Sea of Okhotsk, from his perspective, the better. Once he clears Sakhalin, he will have a straight run southeast to one of the northern Kuril channels." He used the calipers to walk out a course from Cape Yelizavety to the Chetvertyy Passage south of Paramusir. "That's nine hundred kilometers . . . or a bit more. That's four days at a quiet ten knots. Thirty hours at speed." He walked the dividers again, this time tracking south down the east coast of Sakhalin. "It is two hundred fifty to three hundred kilometers farther if he makes for La Perouse Strait or one of the southern Kuril passages. That's an extra five hours if he's running at full speed, fifteen hours at ten knots. In any case, it hardly matters." The calipers came down once again off Cape Yelizavety. "Here is where we will take the bastard! Before he must choose whether to go southeast, or south."

"I actually was concerned about him maintaining a northerly course," Salekhov said. "By running silent, he could follow the curve of the coastline up as far as Magadan, before cutting across the center of Okhotsk and making for the Kuril channels. It would be the smart move, avoiding any obvious way points where he might expect an ambush . . . such as the northern tip of Sakhalin, for example."

"*Nyet*. He must know that the entire Soviet Fleet in this region will be hunting for him, and he knows or has guessed that we have seabed sonar arrays everywhere. He runs too great a risk to remain in Okhotsk for even one extra day when he doesn't need to."

"You are right, of course, Comrade Captain."

"Good."

"There is also the possibility that our Fleet will find them first. The possibility of their passing close by Mys Yelizavety must have occurred to Admiral Andryanov and his staff as well."

"Bah. Fools! You notice how they botched the transit time for the American vessel from San Francisco to Okhotsk? I swear, I think they forgot about the Date Line! And this American captain is good. To have evaded our torpedo at close range, he must be good, and with a good crew.

"But we are better."

"*Da*, Comrade Captain."

"There will be elements of our fleet in the area, no doubt, but the American will be using them for cover. We will need to move in close and listen carefully to ferret him out. We may be able to pick him up when he makes a dash from cover."

"Yes, sir."

"Now. We are . . . one hundred thirty-five kilometers from Cape Yelizavety. To reach this point in five hours, we must increase speed to twenty-seven kilometers per hour. A snail's pace, Felix! They will never hear us coming!"

"No, sir."

"Helm! Come to one-seven-zero degrees! Maneuvering! Make turns for twenty-seven kph! We are going to catch ourselves a very big fish indeed!"

Silently, the Russian attack submarine accelerated, heading south now at a fifteen-knot crawl.

Control Room, USS *Pittsburgh*
Twenty Miles North of Cape Yelizavety
Sea of Okhotsk
0956 hours

"Which way out of this bottle, Captain?" Latham asked. They were leaning over the chart table, where the blue line marking *Pittsburgh*'s course ended just north of Sakhalin.

"Southeast is shortest," Gordon said. "At this speed, we could be through the Kurils in another ninety-six hours."

"Crawling all the way," his Exec pointed out.

"True. But I'd rather that than run the risk of triggering one of their seabed sensor arrays. Or getting tagged by one of their subs." His finger trailed south along the pearl-strand string of the Kuril Islands on the chart. "Here. We'll head for Proliv Bussol', south of Simushir. The channel is wide and deep. And it's not quite so obvious a way out as up here by Paramusir."

Latham nodded. "Last time out this way, we slipped out through the Proliv Yekateriny, down here between Iturup and Kunashir."

"Well, no need to repeat ourselves for the benefit of our friends."

"No, sir."

"Mr. Carver! Depth below keel, if you please."

"Depth below keel now eighty feet, sir." They were at a depth of 160 feet, and the bottom was dropping way rapidly. Soon they would be into the central deep of the Sea of Okhotsk, where depths plunged to ten thousand feet or more. Gordon could almost *sense* the yawning Deep ahead.

"Sonar, Conn. What are you tracking?"

"Currently three contacts, Captain. Sierra Three-three, Four-one, and Four-five. Range . . . about ten miles, bearing three-zero-zero."

Northwest, then, and well behind them. "Nothing ahead?"

"Not that we've been able to pick up, sir."

If I were the Russian admiral in charge of this operation, he thought, *where would I put my assets?* Part of the problem, of course, was that he wasn't sure exactly what the Soviet's local assets were. Simplest to assume they had virtually unlimited ships. Where would they concentrate them, though?

Along the Kurils, of course, with special emphasis on the passages between the islands leading into the Northern Pacific. And La Perouse Strait, between Japan and the southern tip of Sakhalin. That might not be as heavily protected, of course, because in that direction lay the major Russian Pacific port at Vladivostok, and yet another cramped, shallow, and narrow-straited sea, the Sea of Japan.

He was tempted to try that route simply because it *would* be unexpected . . . but the disadvantages outweighed the advantages. The western shoreline of the Sea of Japan was bordered by such unpleasant neighbors as the Soviet Union, all the way down to Vladivostok, and the People's Democratic Republic of Korea—no friends to the United States. There was the option of slipping into Japanese territorial waters if he needed to, or paying a quick visit to South Korea, but the northern reaches of that sea would be swarming with ASW craft out of Vladivostok and Nakhodka. If they were mad enough, they might try to mark *Pittsburgh* down, even when she was *clearly* in international waters.

No, the mid-Kurils was the best option.

"Helm! Come to course one-four-five."

"Helm to course one-four-five, aye aye, sir!"

"Make our speed ten knots."

"Make revolutions for ten knots, aye, sir!"

"Kind of an inglorious end to the operation, sir," Latham said. He sounded disappointed, as though the whole affair had wrapped itself up too quickly for him.

"What did you want, a blazing run home on the surface?"

"No, sir. I just man, well, this boat has never failed in its mission before."

"This boat hasn't yet. We delivered the people where they wanted to go. We made the rendezvous for pickup, even if they didn't. We conducted the seabed survey. And now we're going home. That's all the glory *I* care for, anyway."

"I guess you're right."

"In any case, I'm not going to breathe easy until—"

"Conn! Sonar!"

"Sonar, Conn. Go ahead."

"New contact, designated Sierra Five-zero, bearing one-one-zero, range estimated at ten thousand yards. I've got twin screws, a big sucker. Wait one . . . okay, the computer IDs her as a Kresta II. Probably the *Marshal Voroshilov*, sir."

"Do you have a heading on her?"

"Sounds like she's heading south, Captain, across our path. She's making turns for ten knots. Just loafing, sir. Not in a hurry at all."

"Thank you, Sonar. COB? What can you tell me about a Kresta II?"

"Big monger. Seventy-seven hundred tons' displacement fully loaded. Five hundred twenty-one feet long. Nineteen-foot, eight-inch draft. Top speed about thirty-four, thirty-five knots. Heavily armed. Ten 533mm torpedo tubes in two quintuple launchers. Two SS-N-3 Goblet launchers. Eight Silex ASW missiles in two quad launchers. RBU-6000 and RBU-2000 ASW rocket launchers. And various antiaircraft guns, 30mm and 4.57mm. She'll also have a helipad aft, with a Ka-25 Hormone helo for ASW work."

"Thank you, COB." He exchanged looks with Latham. "Coincidence? They're just passing through? Or are they tracking us?"

"No reason to think they've heard us, Captain. Chances are they're covering themselves by posting a few ships at each likely waypoint. Cape Yelizavety qualifies, if only because it's on the shortest route out of Sakhalin Bay."

"I concur. Maneuvering! Slow to five knots."

"Slowing to five knots, aye, sir."

"Well let him pass in front of us," he told Latham. "Helm, steady as you go."

"Helm, steady as you go, aye, sir."

"My only question . . ."

"Yes, sir?"

"A ship that big usually has escorts. Why is he traveling alone?"

"I imagine they're in a bit of disarray right now, after chasing all over after us."

"Hmm. Maybe. Don't care to gamble on it, though. The Russians are usually pretty methodical. Isn't like them to lose focus like that."

"You think it's a trap?"

"After what we've seen so far, Number One, it's definitely a possibility."

Control Room
Russian Attack Submarine *Ivan Rogov*
1006 hours

Captain First Rank Viktor Dubrynin held the headset to his ear, listening to the sonar signal. He could hear the deep, steady thrum of the *Marshal Voroshilov*'s twin screws, the hiss of his wake. And beneath that . . .

He thought for a moment he'd heard something, far out in the black and impenetrable depths of Okhotsk.

It might have been a submarine. Lieutenant Vladimir Krychkov had called him to the sonar console moments before, after thinking he'd heard the distinctive throb of a submarine power plant. The question . . . whose was it? The American was almost certainly in this area—Dubrynin was willing to stake his career on it—but so too were a large number of Russian submarines. An entire PLARB bastion had been designated in the waters southeast of here, almost straight ahead, and there would be ballistic-missile submarines hiding there. And there were the attack boats, some guarding the PLARBs, others hunting for the American.

No doubt Vetrov's *Krasnoyarskiy* was somewhere close by as well. The man wasn't that skillful, but he was lucky, and sometimes luck was more to be treasured than skill. Vetrov might have guessed the American would be passing this point as well.

What had Krychkov heard?

Ivan Rogov was running just ahead of the *Marshal Voroshilov*, probing the sea ahead with his sonar. Somewhere out there, the American sub was trying to sneak away.

And Dubrynin was going to find him. . . .

Sunday, 26 July 1987

Control Room, USS *Pittsburgh*
Twenty Miles North of Sakhalin
Sea of Okhotsk
1005 hours

"Captain? Sonar. Navigational request."

"Go ahead, Rodriguez. What do you have in mind?"

"Could you bring us forty degrees to port, please?"

"Very well. Helm! Come to one-eight-five."

"New course, one-eight-five, aye aye, sir."

"Mr. Latham? Take over here. I'm going up to the sonar shack."

"Very well, sir."

He ducked through the doorway into the long, narrow sonar room, where Rodriguez, Kellerman, and another rating were sitting at the consoles, headsets in place. "Well, Rodriguez? Where are you taking my boat?"

Rodriguez pointed to the waterfall on his monitor, green light cascading down the screen. "You see that, sir? That's the Kresta II."

"Okay. . . ."

"Now . . . this spike, right here? That is *not* a Kresta."

"All right, what is it?"

"Low-frequency noise . . . about fifty hertz. Sounds like a cyclic pump operating at three thousand revs per minute. Divide that by sixty cycles, and you get fifty hertz. The Soviets have pumps like that on some of their newer submarines, in the power-plant cooling assemblies."

"You think that's a Russian sub?"

"Yes, sir. A very *close* Russian sub, with most of its sound masked by the Kresta. It *could* be some sort of machinery operating on board the Kresta, of course. But . . ." He turned a pointer dial, changing the screen display. "Directional analysis puts that pump noise *ahead* of the Kresta. Not by much, but enough to make me think it's a sub. I figured if you could give me a look from the side arrays, I could sharpen up my DA."

"You got it."

Pittsburgh's main sonar was her big, BQQ-5A spherical array tucked into her bow, but she had lateral arrays as well. The bow sonar actually was omnidirectional, giving coverage across 150 degrees to either side of the bow, leaving only a sixty-degree wedge centered on dead astern to which it was deaf, and its coverage included all of the area to either side covered by the hull array.

However, the hull array could register much lower frequencies than the bow sonar, all the way down to fifty hertz, where the coverage for the bow sonar ranged from 750 hertz on up to two kilohertz.

And what was key to this tactical problem was the fact that the hull array was also stretched out across the length of the *Pittsburgh's* hull. Just as depth perception improved with eyes set farther apart, a sonar's resolution of the direction a sound was coming from improved with individual microphones strung along the vessel's 360-foot length, rather than from the equipment compacted into the spherical bow assembly. By turning broadside to the unknown source of sound, Rodriguez ought to be able to get a better look at it . . . and possibly distinguish it entirely from the Kresta II.

"Do you want to stream the towed array?" Gordon asked. Right now, Rodriguez was the most important man on the boat, and he didn't mind deferring to his expertise at all.

"Not necessary, sir. I think this is going to give us what we need."

Los Angeles class boats were also equipped with a BQR-15 towed array sonar, essentially a microphone which could be streamed aft at the end of a long cable . . . as far aft as five hundred feet. When fully deployed, the BQR-15 was also omnidirectional, providing coverage all the way around except for dead ahead, and to a greater range and a greater sensitivity than the boat's other arrays. It would have been perfect for providing the high-resolution scan Rodriguez needed.

Gordon had not deployed the towed array, however, for several reasons. It made a noise when streaming aft, and all noise was to be avoided right now if possible. More importantly, the *Pittsburgh* might have to accelerate and maneuver swiftly and without warning. It took time to reel in the TA, and a sudden sharp turn could lose it astern when the cable snapped.

There were other dangers as well. There was at least one case on record, just seven months ago, where a Russian PLARB, possibly a Typhoon, had become fouled on the towed array of a British submarine, the HMS *Splendid*, when the two got a little too close in the Barents Sea. The Typhoon, reportedly, had limped back to port with the *Splendid*'s TA still fouling one of her screws.

So Gordon had not deployed the TA, which might have given them a bit of a tactical edge in this encounter. But if Rodriguez thought he could hear what he needed to hear without it . . .

"Got it!" Rodriguez said, a grin spreading across his face. "It's our old friend, Sierra One!"

"What, the Sierra class boat we picked up off San Francisco?"

"The one and the same, yes, sir." He pointed to the screen, showing two clear sets of sound traces at slightly different bearings. "The Sierra II is running submerged, speed matched to the Kresta, and about a thousand yards ahead of her. A Sierra's sonar suite is a lot better than a Kresta's, especially her towed array. The sub may be hunting for the cruiser. The seeing-eye dog routine."

"Makes sense." He reached for the 1MC switch. "Conn, this is the captain."

"Conn, aye," Latham's voice replied.

"Bring us back to one-four-five degrees, ahead dead slow. I want to let these bad boys get past us before we get too close."

"Change course to one-four-five degrees, ahead dead slow, aye, sir."

Turning so her bow was again pointed at the other vessels would reduce *Pittsburgh*'s aspect, and possibly help hide her. Sound radiated from her hull in all directions, of course, but sound traveling up her length, from her screw and engineering compartment, might be absorbed by her length a bit as it was transmitted forward through the hull, reducing her signature slightly. Dropping her speed to a two- or three-knot crawl would help maintain her audio invisibility as well.

"Sierra Five-zero is slowing, sir. Range ten thousand . . . and almost directly ahead. Looks like she's just stopping dead in the water. Sierra One is pulling ahead of Sierra Five-zero, maintaining ten knots."

"Okay. I don't like the looks of this. I'm going back to the combat center. You keep an ear on both of them, and tell me the moment there's a change."

"Aye aye, sir."

Back in the control room, at the chart tables, he checked the transparent overlay, where the QM of the Watch had marked the new contacts in red.

"Conn, Sonar," sounded over the 1MC. "Aspect change on Sierra One. Looks like he might be pulling a Crazy Ivan."

Which made no sense if he was deliberately leading a

Kresta ASW cruiser. Crazy Ivan turns were performed to make sure they weren't being followed by Americans, not members of their own Fleet.

"Sonar, Conn. Which way is he turning?"

"Sierra One is turning to port, sir."

Turning toward the silently lurking *Pittsburgh*, rather than away. The range would be closing. Not good.

He looked up at Latham as the Exec joined him at the table. "Start thinking like a hole in the water, Number One."

"Hell, I'm not even here, Skipper."

"Good man."

"Conn, Sonar. Sierra One has changed course. New heading is two-seven-zero."

Gordon checked it on the chart. The Sierra II was now heading due west, and if he stayed on the new heading, would pass a mile or so south of *Pittsburgh*'s position.

"Maneuvering, ahead slow. Make turns for five knots."

"Ahead slow. Make turns for five knots, aye." He looked at Latham. We'll pass behind the cruiser's stern, quietly. That will put the Kresta between us and the Sierra, and give us a clear shot at slipping away and out through the Kuril passages."

Latham nodded. "Sounds like a plan, sir. We can't stay put, that's for damned sure."

Pittsburgh edged ahead, ever so gently. Gordon had complete confidence in her quieting; Los Angeles Flight II boats were almost embarrassingly silent. The Sierra was quiet as well—not as silent as an LA-class, but at least as good as a Sturgeon. The only reason *Pittsburgh* was able to track the Sierra at all was the level of her technology and, even more, the quality of her sonar crew. He doubted very much that the Sierra's sonar crew could track the *'Burgh*.

But that was no reason to get careless. At five knots, the *Pittsburgh* was effectively silent.

Minutes passed . . . and passed. After half an hour, *Pittsburgh* had closed the range to the Kresta to about five thousand yards. The Sierra II sub, meanwhile, had quietly slipped south of the 'Burgh, as predicted, and was now about two miles to the southwest, astern and behind the American boat. The other sub had also just slowed sharply, to about four knots.

"Conn, Sonar! I've got new sounds from Sierra One. Sounds like wake noises. I think they've raised their periscope."

Odd. They wouldn't be searching for the Pittsburgh on the surface, certainly.

But there might be another reason to raise something . . . like a radio mast.

"They may be communicating with the Kresta," Gordon said. "They might want to—"

A single sharp ping echoed through the American boat's hull, an initial chirp followed by a wavering, falling tone.

"Conn, Sonar! Sierra Five-zero has gone active! We're lit!"

"Shit!"

There was no way either the Kresta or the Sierra could fail to see the Pittsburgh now. That single sonar pulse had illuminated everything in the water for four nautical miles in every direction.

"It's roach on the plate time," Latham observed. A second ping echoed through the control room.

"Maneuvering! Ahead full!"

"Maneuvering, ahead full, aye, aye!"

"Conn, Sonar! Sierra One is turning to starboard. Looks like she's coming about to put herself on our tail."

"We've got a lead," Gordon said. "Let's use it. Diving Officer! Set depth to two-one-zero feet."

"Set depth to two-one-zero feet, aye, Captain," Carver replied.

The deck tilted sharply forward as Pittsburgh nosed downward.

"Conn, Maneuvering. Making turns for three-five knots."

"Leveling off at two-one-zero feet."

"Very good. Steady as she goes."

"Steady as she goes, aye, sir!"

At thirty-five knots, *Pittsburgh* closed the range to the Kresta class cruiser in a bit over three minutes. He could only imagine the consternation that must be spreading through her decks as her crews realized they were being *charged* by an American submarine.

The question was . . . would they open fire? How determined were they to nail themselves an LA-class sub?

"Conn, Sonar! I'm getting splashes on the surface! Repeat, multiple splashes!"

Gordon locked eyes with Latham, horrified. Splashes meant the Russians were dropping something on them . . . torpedoes, depth charges, RBU warheads, *something*.

"Hey! Those guys are *shooting* at us!" the QM of the Watch said, looking at the control room overhead with something like stunned amazement.

"And you find that surprising . . . how, Mr. Dandridge?" Latham asked.

"Sonar, Conn. Any follow-up sounds from those splashes?"

"Conn, Sonar. Negative. Whatever they are, they're not torpedoes."

Torpedoes would have fired up their engines as soon as they entered the water, and probably gone active with their search sonar as well. Silence meant that the weapons, whatever they were, must be unguided warheads, and that was about as good a break as the *Pittsburgh* could have hoped for.

"Helm! Come right five degrees!"

"Right five degrees, aye aye, sir."

Depth charges or RBU rockets would have been fired in a pattern based on *Pittsburgh*'s last-known course and speed. She could complicate things by changing her course slightly after the warheads had hit the water.

Explosions thundered outside, a jarring crash that sent the *Pittsburgh* lurching to starboard, then back to port. The detonations . . . at least twelve of them, occurred in a rippling cascade of thunderclaps well astern and to port of the boat. The control-room lights flickered, dimmed briefly, then came back to full brilliance.

"My *God*!" someone in the compartment cried.

"RBUs," Latham said. Gordon nodded.

"RBU" stood for *Raketnaya Bombometmaya Ustanovkal*, and it was a weapon little changed from the "hedgehog" launchers of World War II. The RBU-6000 was a twelve-barreled launcher arranged in a horseshoe shape on its mounting, firing 250mm projectiles, each with a 46-pound warhead. The RBU-1000 consisted of six tubes paired and stacked three high, firing 300mm projectiles with 198-pound warheads. Either type could be fused for depth, for contact, or for influence . . . passing through a submarine's magnetic signature, for instance. Since they were essentially free-fall weapons, they couldn't be foxed by countermeasures.

The barrage of twelve suggested that the attack had been carried out by the smaller RBU-6000, with depth-triggered warheads. The explosions had fallen well astern, however.

Moments later, *Pittsburgh* swept beneath the Kresta, untouched.

A third sonar ping illuminated the fleeing sub, but as soon as the pulse echoed back, Gordon ordered another change of course, coming around to a southerly heading paralleling the Kresta. A second barrage of RBU projectiles was fired, this time off the Kresta's port side . . . and again none of the warheads came close to her.

But Gordon was painfully aware that he couldn't keep this game up for long. . . .

Control Room
Russian Attack Submarine *Krasnoyarskiy Komsomolets*
Sea of Okhotsk
1042 hours

"Explosions, Comrade Captain!" *Starpom* Vasily Alesandjan, the *Krasnoyarskiy*'s sonar officer, cried out. "Multiple explosions, bearing one-five-nine, range forty thousand meters!"

"Damn it to hell!" Vetrov said. "Someone else has found them!"

"It does not sound as though the target was damaged," Alesandjan said. "I hear no breakup noises . . . no damage."

"Helm! Come to one-five-nine! Maneuvering! Give me all possible speed!"

"Sir," his Exec said, concerned. "Wouldn't it be better to move in carefully, to study the situation before charging in blindly?"

"You are a fool, Felix! Or a coward! Only the daring win!"

"I resent that, Captain!" Salekhov flared back. "You have no right—"

Vetrov waved him to silence. He had no time for this now. The American sub was there . . . and quite possibly on the verge of escaping.

"Maneuvering! I want full speed *now*! . . ."

Control Room, USS *Pittsburgh*
Twenty Miles North of Sakhalin
Sea of Okhotsk
1045 hours

"Captain! Sonar!"

"Go ahead, Rodriguez."

"Sierra One has the pedal to the metal, sir. They're coming after us hot. Sounds of outer torpedo doors opening."

"Very well."

"Splashes astern and to port, Captain."

"Very well. Helm! Come starboard ten degrees!"

"Helm to starboard, ten degrees, aye aye, sir."

For most of the men, Gordon thought, this was their first

time under fire. They appeared to be taking it well, calmly, deliberately, professionally. It spoke well of Mike Chase . . . and of the training these men had received at New London.

Explosions rocked the boat, tipping her nose down and rolling her to starboard.

"COB! Adjust trim!"

"On it, Skipper!"

"Release countermeasures!"

"Countermeasures away, aye, sir!"

CM bubbles wouldn't fool an incoming RBU projectile, but they just might mask the *Pittsburgh* from the next active sonar pulse which was due any—

Ping!

. . . moment now. "Helm, come left one-five degrees! What's our speed?"

"Helm coming left one-five degrees, aye."

"Conn, Maneuvering. Turns for three-eight knots."

The RBU-6000 had a range of six thousand meters . . . over three and a half miles. Somehow, the *Pittsburgh* had to get outside of that radius.

Unfortunately, a Kresta II was almost as fast as a Los Angeles boat, and with twin screws she could make tighter turns, was more maneuverable.

"Conn, Sonar. Sierra Five-zero is coming to new heading, two-zero-zero. Looks like he's firing up the boilers, too. Speed now fifteen knots."

"Sonar, Conn. Acknowledged."

He looked at the plot board, where the TMA watch was updating positions and headings. Gordon smiled. There was an opportunity here. . . .

"Helm! Hard left rudder! Come to new course zero-eight-zero! Make depth six-zero feet!"

"Come to new course zero-eight-zero, aye!"

"Make depth six-zero feet, aye!"

"Conn, Sonar! Splashes ahead and to port!"

Shit! "Helm! Belay left rudder! Right full rudder!"

He'd just unwittingly turned into the next barrage. . . .

Torpedo Room, USS *Pittsburgh*
Twenty Miles North of Sakhalin
Sea of Okhotsk
1048 hours

O'Brien stood with one hand on one of the bunk supports, with Chief Allison and Benson and the rest of his torpedo-room watch, all of them silently waiting for orders, all waiting for the next barrage. The three SEALs sat on two of the lower racks, staying out of the way.

Every eye was turned upward, toward the overhead, waiting. . . .

"Don't like this waiting, man," Fitch said.

"A little easier to dish it out than take it, huh?" McCluskey asked.

"They're *shooting* at us," O'Brien said. "They're actually *shooting* at us!"

"Yeah, well, shit happens, son," Randall said.

The deck tilted alarmingly toward the left, as it tipped high forward. "Skipper's bringing us hard to port," Chief Allison said. "And running us shallow. I wonder—"

And then the deck tilted back the other way, sharply enough that O'Brien had to cling hard to keep his feet under him.

"Uh-oh," Allison said. "Everybody grab hold! . . ."

"Why?" Benson asked. "What's—"

Three detonations boomed out close by, just beyond the *Pittsburgh*'s hull. The fourth explosion shattered fluorescent tubes in their overhead mountings, showering the deck with hot glass and plastic fragments. The hull shuddered, then groaned, as the shock wave slammed through the vessel from port to starboard.

O'Brien's grip was torn from the rack. He was knocked off his feet, slamming to the linoleum-tiled deck with a body-check thud and grunt. Benson landed on top of him, and the two men struggled in a tangle of thrashing arms and legs.

At the same instant, the torpedo room was plunged into absolute darkness, and with a shriek of ripping metal and hissing water, a thin, hard, cold spray blasted across the deck, drenching both men as they tried to rise.

O'Brien managed to get his feet under him. The deck was slippery, the air filled with spray and the shrill hiss and thunder of inflooding water. He was in complete darkness; damn it, the emergency lights *should* have kicked on!

He heard someone groaning, though it was hard to hear anything over the roar of the water. He heard Chief Allison screaming above the roar, *"Conn! Torpedo room! Flooding in the torpedo room! Flooding in the torpedo room! . . ."*

All O'Brien could think of were the training simulations at New London. Time after time he'd been through one variation or another of this exact scenario, locked in a cramped and tightly sealed compartment, plunged into darkness, drenched with icy water. Panic gibbered and bubbled just beneath the surface of his thoughts . . . but those thoughts were hard and determined. If that water was pouring in through a hole in the hull, he and the other men in the compartment were probably doomed. The watertight door out of the torpedo room was closed and dogged, the compartment flooding fast. They would drown, though the rest of the boat would probably stay dry.

Unless the flooding was so bad it dragged the *Pittsburgh*, crippled and helpless, to the bottom.

But . . . it was possible, even likely, that the flood was coming from one of the tangle of pipes forward or on the overhead. The torpedo tubes were wonderfully complex devices, each with a labyrinth of piping to fill, pressurize, and empty it, either with seawater or from onboard tanks. If one of those pipes had given way with the shock of the explosion, then they might be able to shut it off.

If they could find it.

He turned until he felt the spray blasting at his face, leaned into it, and started groping forward through the icy wet black. . . .

Control Room
Russian Attack Submarine *Ivan Rogov*
1048 hours

"Captain! Sonar! The American may be hit!"

"What do you have, Krychkov?"

"Sounds of flooding, sir. There was another barrage of explosions, but I'm picking up sounds of flooding!"

Dubrynin glanced at the plot board, then looked at his Exec. "We may have him. We need to get past the *Marshal Voroshilov*, however."

"We're close now."

The *Ivan Rogov* had completed his turn and been racing to close in tight with the suspected American sub just as the *Voroshilov* opened fire. The American had apparently slipped directly beneath the ASW cruiser, then turned south, weaving this way and that in an attempt to avoid the Kresta's RBU bombardment.

The American captain's last maneuver, however, had been a clever one, placing the Kresta directly between the American sub and the *Ivan Rogov*. At that angle, Dubrynin couldn't fire his torpedoes. They were wire-guided, and the *Voroshilov*'s wake might well break the controlling wires. If that happened, there was a chance that they would acquire a new target when they began circling and searching . . . the *Voroshilov*.

Dubrynin did not intend to fire, of course. The orders were to force the American to the surface and capture him. But the American couldn't know that.

Still, by putting the cruiser between the *Rogov* and himself, the American captain had confused the chase, and stopped the two hunters from triangulating his position. With all of the thunder in the water, it was difficult to hear anything, and the American was clever enough to use the noise and the confusion in order to slip away unharmed.

If he was damaged, though, that was the break the Russians were waiting for. If he was flooding, he might be forced to the surface in order to save his vessel. If the flooding were severe enough, the American submarine would sink.

But the Los Angeles class vessel would be raised. The water here was less than three hundred feet deep. Salvage would be difficult, but far from impossible.

There were rumors throughout the Soviet Navy that the American CIA had attempted some sort of recovery operation on a sunken Russian missile sub in the late 1960s. The stories were scarcely credible, almost certainly fictions, because they emphasized that the Russian submarine had gone down—victim of an explosion when she was recharging her batteries—in seventeen thousand feet of water.

Recovery from such depths was flatly impossible. The technology simply didn't exist.

But there would be no such problems lifting a Los Angeles class sub from a mere three hundred feet. The political coup would be impressive; the *intelligence* coup would be absolutely incalculable. . . .

"Captain! Sonar! Impacts on the water, directly ahead!"

"Eh?"

"Our own ship is firing on us!"

"Hard right! Hard right rudder!"

Damn the idiots! Either their own weapons-control people had become confused with two targets in the water, or they'd assumed that the *Rogov* was a second American submarine.

Explosions thundered directly ahead, rocking the *Rogov* back and forth violently. Several sailors on the bridge were hurled to the deck.

The *Rogov* had been heading almost directly toward the *Voroshilov*, intending to pass beneath her keel at a depth of 130 feet. By ordering a hard right rudder, *Rogov* was turning right, toward the south and parallel to the *Voroshilov* . . . but sluggishly, so sluggishly! . . .

"Surface!" Dubrynin shouted. "Blow all ballast! *Surface!*"

"Sir, we are close aboard the *Voroshilov!*"

"And unless those idiots see us, they will continue to assume that we are American! Get this vessel on the surface!"

"Yes, Comrade Captain! Blow all ballast!" With a bellowing, gurgling roar, pressurized air blasted the water out of the *Rogov*'s ballast tanks, and the Russian submarine began to rise. . . .

Torpedo Room, USS *Pittsburgh*
Twenty Miles North of Sakhalin
Sea of Okhotsk
1049 hours

O'Brien leaned into the icy spray, struggling against the blast. It became more than mere spray. The water pounding against his chest and belly and legs felt like it was hurtling from a fire hose. His legs went out from under him, and he hit the deck, but was able to struggle back to his hands and knees and drag himself forward, using pipes and conduits on the bulkhead at his left side as handholds.

The water, he was pretty sure now, was coming in from the Number One Flood Feed Line, one of the heavier pipes used to fill Torpedo Tube One with seawater before firing. A joint must have split.

But he remembered the location of a valve cutoff, a large red wheel high up on the pipe, just beneath where it vanished into the overhead just to the left of Tubes One and Three, where they angled into the port bulkhead.

He pulled himself forward, then lost his grip and was washed back. There was almost a foot of water on the deck already. He *had* to reach that valve. . . .

Sunday, 26 July 1987

Control Room, USS *Pittsburgh*
Twenty Miles North of Sakhalin
Sea of Okhotsk
1049 hours

"Damage-control parties lay forward to the torpedo room!" Latham bellowed over the intercom. "Flooding in torpedo compartment! That is, flooding in the torpedo compartment!" He turned and locked stares with Gordon. "It sounds bad, sir!"

"I'm having to adjust forward trim," Warren announced, working his board behind and to the left of the helmsman and planesman positions. "We're taking on a lot of water forward."

"Stay with it," Gordon said. "Helm! Bring us around to new heading . . . one-seven-zero. Maintain depth!" If they started to go down by the head, he wanted it to be a short trip to the surface if he had to blow ballast.

"Conn, Sonar!"

"Sonar! Go ahead!"

"Picking up sounds of a submarine blowing ballast, sir."

"What?"

"It's Sierra One. I think . . . I think Sierra Five-zero fired at him, and he's going up on the roof! But he's damned close to the Kresta, sir! Sounds like the cruiser is right on top of him! . . ."

This was fast becoming a comedy of errors . . . and would be funny if it wasn't so damned deadly serious. The Kresta must have confused the Sierra II with the *Pittsburgh*. That, or they thought the Sierra was a *second* American submarine.

But how was that possible? The Kresta and the Sierra had been working together. The ASW cruiser's skipper knew the Sierra was out there. So why . . .

"Conn, Sonar!"

"Yeah."

"Sir, picking up new contact, designated Sierra Five-one. Bearing three-zero-five, range ten thousand, speed . . . God, Skipper. Forty-five knots!" There was a pause. "Sierra Five-one identified. It's Mike Two, and he's coming in hell-bent for leather."

The Mike. Called in by the sounds of explosions, no doubt. Gordon could see the tactical layout, the unfolding of the situation in his mind's eye. The Kresta II's sonar people must have picked up the sounds of *three* submarines, where only one was known to be friendly. They had the Los Angeles to the southeast, a second target coming in from the west, and now a third underwater target coming from the northwest. They would have lost all of the sonar contacts each time the underwater explosions went off. And then, just when they'd hit the target to the southeast and were on the verge of driving it to the surface, they'd picked up one sub coming in at forty-five knots from the northwest, another coming almost directly toward them out of the west.

Someone had panicked, or simply made a bad call. The Kresta had fired an RBU-6000 spread at the second target. Apparently they hadn't hit it, but . . .

"Conn, Sonar! I have sounds of a collision! Sierra One just went afoul of Sierra Five-zero! . . ."

Control Room
Russian Attack Submarine *Ivan Rogov*
1048 hours

Dubrynin was hurled over the safety rail beside the periscope position, as thunder boomed from directly overhead. He slammed onto the deck, pain exploding through his back and side. The control-room lights dimmed, as lighting fixtures shattered behind their protective cages.

He could hear the throb of the *Voroshilov*'s screws . . . mingled with the hair-raising squeal of metal grating across metal. The *Ivan Rogov* heeled sharply to starboard as the grating shriek shrilled through the control room, as loud as the Trump of the Apocalypse.

Dubrynin had never considered himself religious, but his grandmother's teachings were flooding back now. They were all going to die, and he was not ready. . . .

There was another crash, even louder, and a violent shudder ran through the stricken vessel. Water began spraying down from around the rim of the closed but undogged hatch in the overhead leading up to the conning tower, until a seaman reached up and sealed the hatch. Several more bumping, grinding sounds echoed down from overhead, and then the control room was death-silent, save for the groans of several injured men.

Grabbing hold of a console, he levered himself to his feet, testing his back, wondering if he were badly injured. Miraculously, everything worked, though he hurt like hell, and a biting pain shot through his uselessly dangling left arm. It felt broken.

"Damage control to the bridge!" he called, and he heard

his order being relayed over the intercom. "Diving Officer! What is our status!"

"We are maintaining depth, sir, at one-three meters. Conning tower is awash. We have lost port-side trim and are listing to starboard by fifteen degrees. We may have flooding in the conning tower."

"But we're not sinking?"

"The situation is stable . . . for now, Captain."

He knew better than to check through the periscope. They'd just rammed the *Voroshilov* with the *Ivan Rogov*'s sail, and the delicate optics would have been smashed, the housings themselves twisted into uselessness.

"Sonar Officer! Where is the *Voroshilov*?"

"*Marshal Voroshilov* is off our port beam, sir," Krychkov replied. "Range . . . a few meters. We're close. Sir, I'm also picking up a new contact. It is the *Krasnoyarskiy Komsomolets*."

"Never mind that! Are we clear above? Are we clear to surface?"

"Clear to surface, Captain."

"Bring us all the way to the surface, Diving Officer." He did not add *if you can*.

His career, Dubrynin thought, was over, a casualty of this so-called Cold War. He should have checked before surfacing, but had thought they were clear. The Board of Inquiry would find him guilty of negligence. And they would be right. There were extenuating circumstances to be sure—the *Voroshilov* firing on his submarine, the clouding of the sonar picture by the RBU explosions all around. Perhaps they'd been fooled by the *Krasnoyarskiy*'s unexpected arrival out of the *Rogov*'s baffles.

None of that mattered. The Board of Inquiry would need a scapegoat for the collision. And he would be the easiest target.

Somehow, it didn't matter. Oh, it would matter later, of course, and he would fight the inevitable ruling.

But right now, he had to save his last command. . . .

Torpedo Room, USS *Pittsburgh*
Twenty Miles North of Sakhalin
Sea of Okhotsk
1054 hours

Randall clung to the steel frame of the rack, struggling against a most unSEALish surge of panic. It was as though he were back in the Russian sub again, trapped in a slender metal-walled pipe, plunged into darkness, with water thundering in.

This was, in fact, much worse than his time aboard the crawler sub; at least he'd had emergency lighting there, and the inflow had been a trickle compared to this.

But he felt the same catch at his throat as he contemplated a claustrophobic drowning, trapped aboard a flooding submarine in the icy depths of a sea most Americans had never heard of.

"I can't reach it!" he heard O'Brien's voice calling in the darkness to his left. "It's Flood Feed One! I can't reach it!"

He wasn't sure where the others in the compartment were. He'd heard Chief Allison announcing the flooding from the intercom, aft . . . and someone was groaning in the dark just in front of him. But it felt like he might be the closest to O'Brien, who evidently was trying to breast the force of the infalling water in order to shut it down.

"Drownproofing was never like this," he said aloud, and he released the bunk frame and started following the sound of O'Brien's voice. Then a new thought occurred to him, and he almost burst out laughing. "I wonder if water is *still* my friend? . . ."

Control Room, USS *Pittsburgh*
Twenty Miles North of Sakhalin
Sea of Okhotsk
1054 hours

"It sounds like the Russian boat is on the surface along-side the Kresta," Rodriguez informed him. "Both vessels at all stop. Can't hear Mike Two, though. He's on the far side, masked by the hull noises."

"What hull noises?"

"Sir, I don't know how bad it is over there, but it sounds like a mess. I'm hearing some minor flooding, and I'm hearing something . . . I think it's on the Kresta, that might be some hull plating partly torn open and banging on the hull."

Damage-control efforts would be under way on both of the Soviet vessels, as they were proceeding on board the *Pittsburgh*. Like him, their skippers would be concentrating on saving their ships.

But before long, they would be thinking about getting the damaged vessels back to port, and that gave Gordon an idea, *if* they could stop the *Pittsburgh*'s flooding. . . .

Torpedo Room, USS *Pittsburgh*
Twenty Miles North of Sakhalin
Sea of Okhotsk
1055 hours

O'Brien fell again. "I can't make it! The water's too strong!"

"Here, kid!" It was Randall, yelling above the roar from just behind him. He felt strong hands grab his boondocker work shoes, levering him forward on the slippery deck. "I've got you braced!"

Unsteadily, he pushed against the SEAL's hands, and moved forward, assisted by Randall's steady shove. Almost two feet of water covered the deck, and movement was more like swimming than crawling.

As water surged and pounded over his head, threatening with each breath to strangle him, he reached all the way forward and grasped the thick, cold vertical cylinder of Feed Line One. "I've got the pipe!" he shouted, gasping through the flood. "Help me push up on it!"

The pressure against the soles of his shoes increased, and he was able to work his way up, hauling himself erect against the pipe. Hand over hand, he pulled his way up the pipe. The split joint where the water was coming in was impossible even to approach; the water pressure was so high it was like trying to pierce a solid steel barrier, and the pounding stream threatened at any moment to break a bone or wrench him free of his handhold and slam him back across the pitch-black compartment.

"O'Brien!" Allison yelled. "Where are you?"

"I'm at Feed One! I've got it! I've got it!"

With Randall bracing his unsteady feet, he walked his hands up past the incoming stream, found by touch alone through numbed fingers the shape of the cutoff valve, grabbed the wheel, and started turning it.

And the water pressure died away, falling to a hard stream, then a fine mist . . . and then the water flow was stopped.

O'Brien clung there to the valve for a moment, gasping hard with each breath. He was also shivering, but that didn't matter. He'd managed to get to the valve.

"Great job, kid!" Randall's voice said.

Then there was a bang and clang from forward, and light spilled into the torpedo room as the main passageway hatch opened up. Scobey was there, leading a damage-control party armed with spanners, pry bars, and breathing gear. Water spilled out over the doorway's combing, but it was already starting to drain away.

"You're too late, big C!" O'Brien called.

"Looks like. Geeze, you guys made a mess of things!"

Reaching out, O'Brien leaned his hand against a bare patch

on the bulkhead, trying to hold himself up on shaking knees.

He felt the faint, far-off quiver of *Pittsburgh*'s engine, and her movement through the water.

He wondered where they were heading next.

Wednesday, 29 July 1987

Control Room, USS *Pittsburgh*
La Perouse Strait
North of the Japanese Coast
1725 hours

"We're almost home free, skipper," Latham said. His face was drawn, and blue rings emphasized the hollow, worn-out look to his eyes, but he was grinning.

"Thanks to our escort," Gordon said, jerking a thumb at the overhead. He looked at the chart. *Pittsburgh* was now about halfway through La Perouse Strait. Mys Kril'on, the southern-most tip of Sakhalin Island, lay fifteen miles to the north. The Japanese island of Hokkaido, the point at Soya Misaki and the port city of Wakkanai lay twenty-five miles to the south.

Overhead, the dull, monotonous throb of a surface ship's screw accompanied the *Pittsburgh* like a sheltering blanket, as it had for the past three days.

The tactical problem off Mys Yelizavety had been a serious one. The collision between the Sierra II and the Kresta would be bringing in Soviet ships from every quarter, and the second Russian submarine, the Mike, was only a few miles away and closing fast. *Pittsburgh* had been in no position to run. There'd been considerable damage to her torpedo room and the flood lines connected with it, and repairs would take a day or two at least . . . a day or two when they couldn't be moving more than a few knots.

With two damaged vessels to care for, the approaching Russian ASW vessels would be blanketing the entire area, banging away with their sonar, searching for the American sub . . . which might have gotten away, or which just possibly had sunk. They wouldn't know for sure, and they'd be damned certain to do their best to find out.

And so, Gordon had taken a chance . . . but it had given him a better hope of escaping from Okhotsk than simply turning and running, a move that would have had him cornered, caught, and pinned within a few hours. Carefully, quietly, he'd worked the *Pittsburgh* in close to the stricken Kresta II. While the Sierra II had ridden clumsily on the surface off the Kresta's starboard beam, the *Pittsburgh* had ridden just beneath the surface off her port. Before long, the Soviet Mike had entered the area, banging away with sonar, searching for the missing American.

And found nothing. From any one direction's vantage point, *Pittsburgh*'s sonar shadow would appear to blend with those of the Kresta and the Sierra, and those two vessels were making a hell of a lot of noise besides.

In another hour, the Soviet escort vessels had begun to arrive, and the Kresta had fired up her port shaft. Apparently, her starboard screw had been damaged in the collision, possibly by biting into the Sierra's sail, and was being left off-line. At a steady, sometimes faltering ten knots, the Kresta began steaming south.

Gordon had been gambling that the Kresta's port was Vladivostok, but it had been an educated gamble, and one that had paid off. The only ports inside the Sea of Okhotsk large enough to accommodate something as big as a Kresta class cruiser were Magadan—primarily a submarine base— and Nikolayevsk-na-Amure, at the northern end of the Tatar Strait. Vladivostok was the major Soviet Pacific port, headquarters of their Red Banner Pacific Fleet, with the largest and best-equipped anchorage and port facilities.

Vladivostok was almost certainly her home port. Even if not, the city was the best place around for the Kresta to receive repairs. From the sound of the water banging and clanking over loose hull plates and a badly gashed keel, she was going to need to be dry-docked for a long time to come.

And Vladivostok was on the Sea of Japan, on the *far* side of La Perouse Strait.

The trip had taken three days at a painful, ten-knot crawl, with several stops along the way. *Pittsburgh* had dogged the Kresta every step of the voyage. The ASW escort had ringed the two stricken vessels in and were pinging noisily, searching for any lurking American subs, but they simply could not see the *Pittsburgh* in her comfortable tucked-in hiding place beneath and behind the Kresta. The Kresta herself might have spotted the unwanted guest on that voyage, but either her sonar had been knocked out by the collision, or her captain was relying on the flotilla's screening escorts. She wasn't pinging, and if her sonar watch was listening, all they could hear were the sounds of their own damaged hull as it plowed slowly south through roughening seas.

"Mr. Latham," Gordon said, "let's say good-bye to our friends."

"Can't say I'll miss them, Captain."

"We'll cut our speed and drift deep. After their tail-end Charlie passes, we'll turn south."

"You're going into Japanese territorial waters?"

"That's the idea. We won't exactly be welcome, but we can put in at Otaru. They have decent facilities there. We can complete our repairs and report our situation."

Japan had a love-hate relationship with nuclear energy. While avid in their quest to become self-sufficient in energy production with nuclear reactors, they refused to allow vessels suspected of carrying nuclear weapons into their waters. *Pittsburgh* possessed no nuclear weapons—the Tomahawk cruise missiles in their VLS tubes forward all possessed conventional warheads on this voyage—but the fact that she could carry them made her suspect.

Still, the *'Burgh* had been damaged, and no nation could refuse her the right of a safe harbor while she completed her repairs.

"Maneuvering, Conn. Slow ahead. Make turns for three knots." That would keep her barely under way. "Mr. Carver, down planes fifteen degrees. Take us down to two-eight-zero feet." The water here in the strait ran around 360 feet.

"Conn, Maneuvering. Making turns for three knots."

"Down planes fifteen degrees. Make depth two-eight-zero feet, aye, sir."

Minutes passed, as the Los Angeles boat drifted deeper and still deeper into the eternally night-shrouded depths. Above, the last of the Russian convoy escorting the Kresta to a safe haven at Vladivostok chugged overhead, oblivious to the *Pittsburgh*'s presence. Except for infrequent spot checks, they'd given up on the active pinging two days before, when it was obvious that the American was either long gone . . . or sunk.

After fifteen minutes, drifting silently at 280 feet, Gordon gave his next orders. "Maneuvering, ahead one-half. Make turns for fifteen knots. Helm, bring us left to new course one-nine-five."

"Conn, Maneuvering. Increasing speed to one-five knots, aye."

"Coming left to new course one-nine-five, aye aye, sir."

For the first time in three days, the '*Burgh* was free of her blanket. She began gliding into a broad left turn, heading south once more. At fifteen knots, she began closing with the Japanese coast.

"Conn, Sonar! Torpedo in the water! Correction, two torpedoes in the water! Coming in hot from astern."

"Sonar, Conn! Confirm that!"

"Confirmed! Two torpedoes. Range five miles, speed fifty-five knots!"

"Maneuvering! Give me full power! All ahead! Give me all you've got!"

"Maneuvering, aye! All ahead!"

"Where the hell did *they* come from?" Latham asked.

"Sonar, Conn! Where did those torps come from?"

"Not sure, Captain. The torpedoes . . . wait a sec. Wait a sec. . . ." The silence dragged on for several moments. "Got him! Captain, it's Mike Two! He must have been trailing the convoy, just in case! He's popped two torpedoes into the water at long range, and he's starting to speed up. Bearing . . . zero-eight-five, range five miles. I can only hear him because he's cranked up to full speed. He's coming after us at forty knots!"

Gordon felt the tremble of speed and power through *Pittsburgh*'s control-room deck. "Quartermaster! How far to Japanese waters?"

Dandridge moved calipers across a chart. "Eight miles, sir."

At full speed . . . about thirteen minutes. The torpedoes would reach them first.

Besides, torpedoes were notorious in their inability to distinguish man-made niceties like national boundaries.

He wondered what the Russian captain was thinking, however. There could be no doubt that the *Pittsburgh* was in international waters. His firing those torpedoes constituted an act of war.

Well, these were the people who'd fired upon a civilian airliner, Flight 007, after she'd twice flown through Soviet airspace, but then emerged over international waters.

These same international waters, now that he thought about it.

The minutes dragged past.

"Mr. Carver! Depth under keel?"

"Depth below keel . . . eight-zero feet, sir."

"Mr. Latham, range and time to impact."

"Near torpedo now at two thousand yards, and closing. Time to impact . . ."

The oncoming torpedoes, chasing the *Pittsburgh*, which was moving at better than thirty-five knots, had a closure rate of about twenty knots. Two thousand yards . . . about one nautical mile . . . make it about . . .

"Three minutes, Captain."

"Thank you."

"Mr. Carver. Who do you have on the planes?"

"Archie Douglas, sir."

"Okay. Douglas, in a couple of minutes, I'm going to have you angle down on the bow planes ten degrees. You will hold them there until I tell you to bring them back up, and when I do, you'll have to move very sharply. If you're slow, we slam into the bottom. Do you understand me?"

"Yes, sir!" Douglas said.

"Okay. Stay alert."

The problem with what Gordon was about to try was that a 360-foot submarine with a 7,700-ton submerged displacement did *not* maneuver on the proverbial dime. A minute passed, then two.

"Nearest torpedo now three hundred yards, Captain," Latham reported. His voice was as cold as ice. "Impact in thirty seconds!"

"How far to the second torpedo?"

"Range four hundred yards."

"Okay, we'll hope for the best. Stand by, everybody. Mr. Latham, give me a countdown."

"Aye, sir! Impact in twenty seconds! Nineteen . . ."

"Mr. Douglas! Down planes ten degrees!"

"Down planes, ten degrees!"

The deck tipped precipitously.

"COB! Stand by the CM!"

"Ready, sir!"

"Impact in thirteen . . . twelve . . ."

"Release countermeasures!"

"Countermeasures away!"

"Up planes, Mr. Douglas! Take us up! Hard as you can!"

"COB! Blow stern tanks!"

"Blowing stern tanks, aye, sir!"

"Five . . . four . . ."

Pittsburgh's bow swung up, ponderously . . . but faster, then faster still. The deck sloped so steeply that Gordon and others grabbed for handholds, as BM1 Douglas hauled back on the wheel controlling the dive planes like a pilot pulling out of a dive . . . which was, in fact, precisely what he was doing.

There was a sudden, scraping shock aft as her tail brushed the seabed.

"Three . . . two . . ."

The explosion came a second early, and propelled the *Pittsburgh* forward and up like a vast, surging kick in her stern. Lights dimmed, then came back on. The deck rolled ominously, but then the helmsman corrected and the *Pittsburgh* continued her rise.

A second explosion detonated astern, but more distant this time. The rising submarine shuddered.

"My God!" Latham said. "You suckered those torps into the seabed!"

He nodded, too strained to trust himself to speak. The torpedoes fired from the Mike, close to the surface, had raced toward the *Pittsburgh* at a depth of around a hundred feet, guided by the Weapons Officer aboard the Russian vessel. When the torpedoes got close, the Soviet WO had nosed them over, homing on her propeller noise at the last moment.

Gordon had taken the *'Burgh* down so deep that she'd scraped bottom, released countermeasures, and swung back toward the surface. The torpedoes, traveling considerably faster than the sub, had simply not been able to react in time and had slammed, one after the other, into the sea floor.

But they weren't clear yet. . . .

Control Room
Russian Attack Submarine *Krasnoyarskiy Komsomolets*
Sea of Okhotsk
1727 hours

"Faster!" Vetrov shouted. "Filatev! I need more power if we're to catch this bastard!"

"Captain," the *Shtorman*, the navigator, said. "We are close to Japanese waters. We may already be across the line. . . ."

"I don't give a fuck about that. Follow orders!"

"Sir, it is my duty to—"

"Follow orders, *Shtorman*, or I will have you arrested on the spot!"

"Yes, Comrade Captain."

He turned, glaring at Lobanov, the boat's political officer. "Do you have any criticisms, Toad?"

"No, Captain."

"That American vessel was responsible for the crippling of two of the Pacific Fleet's vessels. He also invaded our sovereign waters and may have made off with secret information. I will *not* see him escape!"

"It would be best, Comrade Captain," Lobanov said, "to kill the American outside of Japanese waters."

"The line is blurred, Lobanov. We have him!" He shook a fist at the forward bulkhead. "*Vam kryska!*" the Russian proverb, literally "For you there is a lid," was the equivalent of the American "I've got you now!"

**Control Room, USS *Pittsburgh*
La Perouse Strait
North of the Japanese Coast
1735 hours**

"Quartermaster! How far are we from Japanese waters?"

"Sir, we're probably inside the twelve-mile line now. It's pretty hard to tell exactly, of course . . . but I think we've already crossed."

"TMA. Where's our friend?"

"If he's still coming hot and heavy, Captain, he'll be close," Carver said. "Range three thousand, bearing zero-five-zero. We could use another sonar fix."

But for that they would have to slow down. Even Rodriguez couldn't hear anything but rushing water when the *Pittsburgh* was hurtling along at thirty-five-plus knots.

Of course, the same was true for the Mike. Had he broken off the chase? Or followed the *Pittsburgh* across the line?

"Maneuvering! Slow to one-five knots. Helm! Come left two-five degrees!"

"Maneuvering, aye. Slowing to one-five knots."

"Helm, coming left two-five degrees, aye aye, sir."

"Sonar, Conn. As soon as you have your ears, tell me where he is."

"Sonar, aye." Seconds passed. "Sir! Contact still astern! Range three thousand yards, bearing zero-five-zero! Speed estimated at twenty knots."

"Bang on with your TMA," he told Latham. "Helm, come left to new course . . . zero-nine-zero. Weps? I need a solution, and fast."

"Working! . . ."

"Conn! Sonar! Torpedo in the water! He's launched!"

"Torpedo Room! Snapshot, three, two! . . ."

No time to wait for the target solution. If he could put his return shots in the water, Lieutenant Walberg could steer them in by sonar track . . . and it *might* make the other guy flinch. . . .

Torpedo Room, USS *Pittsburgh*
La Perouse Strait
North of the Japanese Coast
1736 hours

O'Brien heard the words over the intercom, words he'd hoped he would never hear: "Torpedo Room! Snapshot, three, two! . . ."

Chief Allison, standing on the other side of the compartment, nodded. "Fire three." O'Brien's hand came down on the big red button. With a loud hiss and rushing sound, and a lurch transmitted through the torpedo-room deck, the first fish slid out into the sea.

"Three fired!"

"Fire two!"

He hit the second button. "Two fired!"

"All hands, rig for collision!" the captain's voice called. The deck tilted to starboard; the *Pittsburgh* was in a hard turn.

He thought he could hear a new sound now, the shrill, high-pitched whine of an approaching torpedo. . . .

Wednesday, 29 July 1987

Control Room, USS *Pittsburgh*
La Perouse Strait
North of the Japanese Coast
1736 hours

"Time to impact, ten seconds," Latham announced.
"Nine . . . eight . . ."

"Mr. Walberg! This is no time to polish the cannonball!"

"TMA complete!" Walberg yelled from the weapons
board. "Solution fed to torpedoes three and two!"

"Seven . . . six . . ."

"Cut the fish loose!"

"Cutting wires!"

"Countermeasures, COB! Now!"

"Countermeasures away."

"Hard left rudder! Down planes! Take us deep!"

"Two . . . one . . ."

Every eye went to the control room's overhead as a faint,
throbbing whine shrilled in from forward, passed overhead,
and dwindled astern.

"Maneuvering! Ahead full! Helm! Come right two-five degrees!" The torpedo had missed, but it would begin to circle, seeking a target. "Weapons Officer! What's the status on our fish?"

"Closing with target, Captain! Running time . . . now twenty seconds."

Control Room
Russian Attack Submarine _Krasnoyarskiy Komsomolets_
La Perouse Strait
1737 hours

"Enemy torpedoes, dead ahead! Torpedoes in the water!"
Vetrov's eyes widened. "No! . . ."
"Torpedos approaching at fifty-five knots, range five hundred . . ."
"Hard left rudder! All ahead full!"
"Hard left rudder! Ahead full!"
The deck tipped precariously as the helmsman pulled the steering yoke hard to the left, forcing Vetrov to grab hold.
"Enemy torpedoes turning to compensate."
Shit! There would be no more promotions . . . no new commands. . . .
He could hear the rising hum of the incoming enemy Mark 48s.

Control Room, USS _Pittsburgh_
La Perouse Strait
North of the Japanese Coast
1737 hours

"Five seconds to target . . . three . . . two . . . one . . ."
The detonation thundered through the sea, a deep,

swelling rumble like incoming surf. A few seconds later, a second detonation sounded, rumbling, blending with the first, sending a rippling shudder through the American boat.

"Conn, Sonar. Two direct hits. I've got breakup noises."

"We *got* him," Latham added.

But his voice was solemn . . . and there were no cheers, no smiles in the control room. Every man there knew what had just happened.

Another submarine, and over a hundred submariners, had just died.

"Sonar, Conn. Where's the Russian torpedo?"

"Bearing three-two-zero. Executing turn to starboard."

"Helm! Come left five-zero degrees! Maneuvering, ahead full! Give her every damned bit that you've got!"

"Helm left five-zero degrees, aye."

"Maneuvering. Reactor is at one hundred fifteen percent. Making turns for three-eight knots."

Again the deck canted sharply underfoot. It was like angles and dangles all over again . . . but with a death-serious twist. The Russian sub had been destroyed, but it was still possible that it could reach out from its watery grave and kill the *Pittsburgh*, with a weapon already loosed.

"What's our depth?"

"Depth one hundred ten feet, Captain. One hundred thirty feet beneath our keel."

"Thank you, Mr. Carver."

"Now on new heading, two-zero-five, Captain."

"Thank you. Sonar! Conn. Where's our friend?"

"I've lost him astern, Captain. We're going too fast. Last-known position would put it three thousand yards astern."

"If it completed the turn as advertised," Walberg said, looking at his TMA board, "it's now twenty-five hundred yards astern, closing at twelve knots. Time to impact, six minutes, ten seconds."

"COB. What's the running time on a Soviet Type C?" That was the standard 533mm wire-guided torpedo in general use in the Soviet Navy.

"Well," Master Chief Warren said, "eight nautical miles at fifty knots . . . make it nine minutes thirty."

Gordon checked the big clock forward. The enemy torpedo had been in the water a little less than two minutes out of a total run time of nine and a half minutes. It *would* catch up to them . . . but if they could dodge it that one time, the torpedo wouldn't have the fuel for a second pass.

"Depth beneath keel."

"Deepening, Captain. Depth beneath keel now one-eight-five feet."

"Diving Officer. Take us down to two-zero-zero feet."

"Make depth two-zero-zero feet, aye, sir."

"Let's see if it chases down after us."

Torpedo Room, USS *Pittsburgh*
La Perouse Strait
North of the Japanese Coast
1738 hours

"So . . . this is how you spend your spare time?" Randall asked.

The deck was tilting sharply forward. They were diving again, and from the faint, trembling shudder in the bulkhead, they were moving full ahead, tearing a hole through the water. They'd all heard the double detonation of *Pittsburgh*'s torpedoes striking home. They must be running now to escape a final Soviet salvo.

"You know what they say, sir," Chief Allison said. "Submarine duty is ninety-nine percent boredom, sitting around on your ass wishing something would fucking happen. It's that last one percent that keeps life interesting."

"It's pretty much the same in the Teams," Fitch said. "You're bored most of the time, except when you're scared shitless."

"You people have a favorite watering hole ashore?" Randall asked. The sailors in the torpedo room didn't exactly seem nervous, but the air was tense. The question was meant to vent some of the pressure.

"Huh?" Boyce said. "Sure, coupla places. The Ram and Ewe was our favorite, until the bike gang took it over."

"Bike gang?"

Several of the torpedo-room crew started telling him about their last liberty ashore at the Tup 'n' Baa.

Minutes passed. . . .

Control Room, USS *Pittsburgh*
La Perouse Strait
North of the Japanese Coast
1742 hours

"Time to impact, forty seconds," Walberg announced.

That was if the torpedo were racing up their ass. *Pittsburgh* was still moving too fast to detect the noise of its approach. Gordon was doing this all by the numbers, placing a hell of a lot of faith in the probability that the enemy torp was where he thought it was.

"Stand by CM."

"Ready with the countermeasures, Captain."

"Time to impact, thirty seconds."

Gordon waited out the seconds in a control room gone utterly silent, though as he listened, it seemed that the air was crackling with suppressed tension.

"Time to impact, twenty seconds."

He picked up the microphone for the boat's 1MC circuit. "All hands, this is the captain! Grab hold, everybody. This is going to be rough!" He released the transmit key and found the Diving Officer, at his station behind the helm and planesman. "Mr. Carver! Blow ballast, full up planes! Put us on the roof!"

"Full up planes, aye aye, sir! Blow ballast!"

"Release countermeasures!"

"Countermeasures away!"

The *Pittsburgh* shuddered, then gave a mighty belch as water was forced from her ballast tanks by blasts of compressed air. Bow nosing high, she started to rise.

Faster now, and faster still. "Depth now one hundred feet!" Carver called. "Eighty feet! Sixty . . . fifty . . ."

They could all hear the high-pitched whine coming from astern, now, as the torpedo tried its simple-brained best to mark them down.

"Thirty feet! Broaching! . . ."

The deck was slanted now at a sixty-degree angle, forcing everyone to cling to the nearest stanchion, table or console just to keep from being flung against an after bulkhead. For a moment, the *Pittsburgh* seemed to hang suspended there, halfway between sea and sky, trying, incongruously, to fly . . . before her bow began to descend in a fearsome blast of spray and shuddering, wrenching white noise.

Gordon felt the *Pittsburgh*'s nose come down, felt the shock as her forward keel struck the water.

"Helm! Bring us to starboard! Hard over! Sonar! Can you track that torpedo?"

"Negative track, Captain!"

"We're at plus five by the TMA," Walberg said. "Plus eight . . . plus nine . . ."

"The torpedo missed, Captain," Rodriguez announced. "I have its screws, bearing two-zero-five, directly ahead of us, and opening the range. Damned thing passed right underneath us as we grabbed for daylight."

A few more seconds passed, as Gordon tried to find his stomach.

"Conn, Sonar. Torpedo has just gone inactive, sir. I've lost it."

Gordon nodded. "Very well. Maneuvering, ahead slow. Helm, bring us to new course two-zero-zero." He exchanged a long look with Latham and Warren and the other men at their stations. "I'm tired of this *game*, gentlemen. Let's go home."

Tuesday, 4 August 1987

Golden Wok Restaurant
Alexandria, Virginia
1235 hours local time

"So," the thug said. "Have you heard?"

John Wesley Cabot frowned. The man sitting opposite him, seedy, a bit oily, reminded him of a thug, a heavy from an old movie, with his drooping mustache and shifty dark eyes.

"If you mean, have I heard the *Pittsburgh* is returning to port today, yes. Of course."

"What are we going to do about it?"

"My dear Grigor, what *can* we do about it? Your people had their chance. I gave you the information they needed. If they can't be more efficient in their operation—"

"Damn you. We lost one of our newest submarines! The captain was related to one of our most prestigious naval commanders!"

"I'm sorry for you, Grigor. I really am. But I did *my* part. It was up to your people to do theirs."

He looked away from the Russian—ostensibly a junior clerk at the Russian embassy, but in fact an agent for the GRU, Russia's military intelligence agency. Outside, the sun was shining brightly, as people—shoppers, mothers, businessmen, lawyers—went about their daily routine. He'd used this Chinese restaurant, trendy and upscale, several times before to transact business with this man and others over the past year or so.

"What happened . . . was very bad, Mr. Cabot. *Very* bad."

"Indeed, yes! A Soviet submarine, firing on one of our submarines, inside Japanese territorial waters? Yes. What will the world press have to say about that?"

"The incident is being, as you people say, hushed up. The story appeared in several Japanese papers, but we have taken steps to ensure that it goes no further. The Japanese government is not particularly stable just now. If word came out that a nuclear submarine had exploded and sunk within a few miles of their coastline, their environmentalist factions would go wild. It is in their best interests that they cooperate with us in our salvage and cleanup efforts."

"Of course." Cabot smiled. The Russians must know that, by now, U.S. Navy SEAL divers had been all over the wreckage of the sunken Mike, submerged in just two hundred miles of water ten miles off the north Hokkaido coast. He wondered what intelligence coups they'd turned up already.

"We want your assurances, Mr. Cabot, that our property be respected. We want no CIA recovery attempts . . . like your theft of our Delta submarine in the 1970s."

"I can make no promises."

"This incident could hurt you personally, Mr. Cabot. You, a senior CIA officer? Betraying his country? You are already in far too deep to back out of our agreement."

Cabot sighed. "You can't threaten me, Grigor. I am not one of your agents to be ordered about like a clerk. I have my own connections. And my own security. If I was to name you and several of your . . . associates as the men who'd approached me, tried to get me to sell you secrets, who do you think they would believe? You? Or me?"

Grigor folded his hands. "Why did you turn traitor, Mr. Cabot? You seem to be a wealthy man. Respected. Secure. The money we are paying you . . ."

"Is a pittance, yes."

"Then . . . why?"

"Let's simply call it ideological reasons, Grigor."

Grigor would never understand, because he did not see his own country as did Cabot, who'd spent ten years as a high-level Agency analyst of the Soviet economy. The Soviet Union was very nearly bankrupt, and it was their military, as much as the rampant corruption and inefficiency of their bureaucracy-managed industry, that was running their treasury face first into the ground. They were spending hundreds of billions in an attempt to keep up with the United States in ballistic-missile defense, in space- and electronic-warfare systems, in ICBMs, and in submarine technology. The efforts of the Walker family and other traitors had helped them leapfrog their submarine technology almost on a par with that of the U.S., but they were not going to be able to hold that parity for long. It was simply too expensive.

If, however, they could capture and copy one of America's latest SSNs, they could not only achieve tactical parity, but they could *anticipate* coming technologies, and keep up with the United States, or even surpass her, for the next several decades. And they would save tens of billions of dollars in the effort.

And why did Russian tactical parity interest Cabot and a few of his highly placed, well-manicured friends? Simple, really. If the Soviet Union went bankrupt, the government could fall. Outright anarchy and civil war were possibilities, as was a military coup. In any case, the Soviet Union would be forced to drop out of the Cold War, no longer able to play the superpower game.

And if that happened, certain defense contractors and military-technology industries—including the Electric Boat Division, which built America's nuclear submarines, and several West Coast aircraft companies—might well suffer catastrophic losses as they stopped receiving government contracts for new weapons systems. Projects like the new Seawolf submarine project, or the almost magical Aurora hypersonic reconnaissance plane, might be canceled by a cost-conscious and myopic Congress.

And that would cost Cabot and his friends millions in secret investments, and potentially billions in future profits and dividends.

Ideology indeed. Cabot was a devout capitalist.

It would have been perfect, he mused. The loss of the *Pittsburgh* would have helped the Soviets in their race to catch up with American submarine technology, and would also have been a blow to American defense assets. The playing field would have been leveled.

The game would have gone on.

"I do not understand you, Mr. Cabot."

Cabot smiled. "It's not important that you do, Grigor. Cheer up! We lost our chance this time. But there will be another! I promise you!"

Yes, the game would certainly continue. . . .

Wednesday, 5 August 1987

Macy's Ram and Ewe
Vallejo, California
1725 hours local time

O'Brien stood beside Benson, Scobey, Boyce, Jablonski, and Douglas, watching as the bikers swaggered toward them.

"It's *you* pukes again, is it?" the leader sneered. "Didn't learn your lesson last time? Maybe you faggots want some special instruction!"

"We just came here for a drink, gents," Scobey said. "We don't want any trouble."

"You *got* trouble, sailor boy! We don't want your kind hanging around here, ain't that right, guys?"

The other bikers chorused their assents. There were twelve of them, all of them big and heavily built, most tending toward paunches and overweight, but all powerfully muscled. Twelve bike gangers and six sailors squared off against one another in the parking lot next to Macy's Ram and Ewe. The back of the lot overlooked the Mare Island Channel, with a view across to the southern half of Mare Island. The *Pittsburgh* was visible from there, tied to her moorings at Pier 2. A dozen motorcycles were parked en masse, up against the low guardrail that separated the parking lot from the twenty-foot drop to the channel.

"Maybe you guys don't understand," Douglas said. "This is a public bar, not your personal, private hangout. So, if you boys have a problem with us having a drink here, maybe *you're* the ones in need of an education."

"C'mon, Dutch," one of the bikers said. "I'm sick of this. Let's redecorate the pavement with these pansies."

"Yeah," said another. "Let's do 'em."

O'Brien touched the needle mike he wore, a loaner Motorola borrowed from the SEALs. "Rattlesnake, this is Sewer Pipe. We have positive target acquisition."

"Roger that," a voice said in his ear. "Stand by."

"Huh?" one of the gangers said. "What's that all about?"

"Reinforcements," O'Brien said. And then the motorcycle thundered around the bend, cornering off the street and tooling across the parking lot.

Randall pulled to a halt a few feet away, dropped the kickstand, swung out of the saddle, and tilted back the visor of his helmet. He was wearing civvies—leather, mostly, but with a Grateful Dead T-shirt underneath. The crazy idiot had flown down to San Diego on a military hop as soon as *Pittsburgh* had docked and he'd been debriefed . . . then caught another transport all the way back to Mare Island. He'd claimed he wanted to make an impression, and that his bike was the way to do it.

A battered Chevy followed him in and parked. Fitch and McCluskey got out, banging the doors behind them.

"Nice bikes," Randall said, eyeing the herd. He picked out the leader with a glance. "Which one's yours?"

"The chromed panhead," the biker said. He spat, hands flexing. "What's it to you, shithead?"

"I just heard you weren't extending proper hospitality to out-of-town visitors. Thought maybe you needed a lesson in manners." He jerked a thumb at one of the machines. Fitch and McCluskey walked over, picked up the 450-pound machine between them, and slung it in one smooth heave over the guardrail and into the channel.

"Hey!" The biker took a staggering step forward, eyes bugging from his head. "You . . . you . . ." He sputtered a string of acid epithets, then shrieked and charged, hands outstretched.

Randall took two steps forward, caught the front of the

biker's leathers, and tugged him forward, off-balance as he ran. The man yelped . . . then dropped gasping as Randall rammed his windpipe with fingers sharply folded at the middle joints.

"What the fuck?" a big ganger screamed. He reached into a pocket and produced a switchblade, which flicked open with a click, the blade shining in the sun.

Randall rolled aside as the ganger lunged. One hand slashed down, grabbing the knife hand and turning it inward. The knife spun from nerveless fingers . . . and then that biker joined his leader on the pavement.

"Anyone else?" Randall demanded. A second bike, chosen at random, sailed over the safety rail and hit the water with an oily splash.

The fight that followed was mercifully brief. O'Brien had expected that the submariners would get to join in . . . but ten seconds after the third biker crashed to the parking-lot pavement, five more were on the ground with them, unconscious or groaning, and the remaining four were in full flight down the street.

"Well," Scobey said, slapping a high five with Randall, "buy you guys a drink?"

"Absolutely, Big C," Randall replied. "After you?"

Laughing, the seven sailors entered the Ram and Ewe.

"It's the *'Burgh*ers!" the waitress cried.

"Hello, Carol."

"*Roger!*" She embraced him. "You're all right? I was so afraid when those animals walked out of here. . . ."

"Never better. Let me introduce my friends. . . ."

Scobey and Douglas walked up to Macy, who was at the bar. "What do we owe you?" Douglas asked.

"Wha—huh?"

"We're the ones who were in here last month, and the place got kind of dinged up. We want to pay for the damages." Master Chief Warren had let them tap the enlisted man's fund aboard the *Pittsburgh*; it was important to maintain good relations with the civilian element ashore.

Macy licked his lips, looked tempted, then shook his head. "Doesn't matter. Insurance took care of it all, y'know?" Flashing lights pulsed outside the front windows. The police had shown up a few minutes after the sailors had gone inside, along with an ambulance. They were picking up the garbage left on the pavement outside, and not asking too many questions. COB, it turned out, had some friends with the Vallejo Police Department after all.

"I . . . ah . . . I gather the gangbangers aren't coming back?" Macy added.

"If they do, it'll be a mistake they won't forget," Scobey said. "Y'know, this used to be a pretty nice liberty hole," he added, looking around. "I think we can guarantee you a good weekend business. If you don't mind '*our* kind' hanging around."

"Why should I mind? I *love* Navy guys! Hey! Carol! First round of drinks is on the house!"

The others cheered. "We'll even help you decorate if you like," Scobey told the owner.

Later, they sat at a table, hoisting filled glasses. Carol sat on Benson's lap, listening to the stories, and adding a few of her own. She seemed like a good sort, O'Brien thought. She and Benson made a great couple.

He was glad that Ben had decided to stick with the Silent Service.

"Here's to the *Pittsburgh*!" Scobey cried.

"*Pittsburgh!*"

"And to shipmates," Randall added, "old and new!"

"To shipmates."

SEALs and submariners.

It seemed an unbeatable combination.

EPILOGUE

Gordon Residence
Alexandria, Virginia
2000 hours

She was gone.

Gordon had finally stopped roaming the empty house, finally accepted the fact that she was really gone. He'd returned to the living room, poured himself a drink, and sat now, trying to sort out his life. The hell of it was, Becca had left two days after *Pittsburgh* had sailed from Vallejo, taken the kids to Admiral Goldman's house, dropped them off, and left. The divorce papers were waiting when he returned.

Out of the blue. Out of the fucking *blue*. . . .

She'd left word at the base, but *Pittsburgh* had been incommunicado at the time. It didn't matter. Even if she'd been able to send a Familygram, the base authorities might have censored it. They did that, in the case of bad news like a death in the family, so that a man's performance at sea wasn't adversely affected.

Admiral Goldman had been as shocked, as stunned as

Gordon was now. He was clearly torn between a desire to support his daughter, and his support for Gordon. What did you say at a time like this? What *could* you say?

He hadn't realized she'd hated Navy life so much. It was kind of obvious now. She'd been in the Navy, in a sense, all her life, growing up with Goldman as her father. Maybe she'd just reached a snapping point, been unable to face any more.

God, he was worried about her.

Had he been that bad a husband?

There weren't any answers, no easy ones, anyway. He'd known she'd been depressed, known how she hated his tours at sea. She'd needed him, and he'd let her down.

Was he willing to trade his command of a Los Angeles boat for her happiness?

What about *his* happiness?

Again, no easy answers. Married life was supposed to be a constant compromise, with each partner giving a hundred fifteen percent. But military service placed special demands on both partners.

Was it any wonder that so many military marriages ended in divorce?

Was it worth it? The duty . . . the sacrifice . . . all of it?

He'd taken an oath when he'd donned this uniform, to protect and uphold the Constitution of the United States. Duty . . . honor . . . and a fair measure of responsibility.

He'd brought all of the people in his charge home again . . . including young Tom Nelson's body. That was something.

Was it worth his marriage?

Well . . . maybe there was no point in making comparisons. He did know that for the past six weeks, there'd been two women in his life. One of them had left.

But he still had the *Pittsburgh*. . . .